THE DISPENSARY

THE DISPENSARY

JERE G. MICHELSON

Michelson Publishing
Printed in the United States of America

First Edition: Summer 2021

www.michelsonpublishing.com
The publisher is not responsible for websites (or their content) not owned by publisher.

Library of Congress Cataloging-in-Publication Data
TX 8-976-271
Michelson, Jere G.
The Dispensary / Jere G. Michelson – First Edition

ISBN 978-0-9980282-3-1 (hardcover)
ISBN 978-0-9980282-4-8 (softcover)
ISBN 978-0-9980282-5-5 (e-book)

Men must learn now with pity to dispense,
For policy sits above conscience

- William Shakespeare

1

Inside the mind of a criminal. If you asked me to describe what I thought that looked like a year ago, I would have given you a wholly different response than today. I was of the mind a criminal possesses stereotypical socio- or psychopathic tendencies and likely lacks a conscience; and while those may be rational assumptions, I've learned first-hand there can be so much more there. Lorenzo Garibaldi, or Enzo as we call him, changed how I view the world and who I have become.

Man … the degree to which I cared about Enzo – and my mom for that matter – couldn't have possibly been any lower prior to our reunion a little over a year ago. I would rather have shit in my hands and clapped than to have reconnected with either of them over the dozen-plus years following my parents' divorce; that is, until they came thundering back into my life. And boy did they come thundering. After Mom walked out on my father just as I entered junior high school, I thought she and Enzo simply disappeared. What I didn't know, but subsequently discovered, was they were both a big part of my life behind the scenes helping to support me through my Uncle Danny after Dad died. Now Danny and Mom are gone, too. God, I miss them all.

Sure, Enzo's a criminal, make no mistake, but he likewise harbors an inexplicable level of humanity within him. He cares deeply for those he loves, conducting himself with grace and a captivating gentleness. I bore witness to a level of patience and pure unadulterated love he exhibited for my mother that one couldn't help but respect.

So, after a year or so of what Enzo describes as 'forced healing' and self-reflection, he came back to pay us a visit. Alison and I met up with him tonight at Asbury's for dinner. She was pretty pumped up when I called her this afternoon from work to let her know he's in town. The three of us sit at a high-top table with our drinks, waiting for our server to come over and take our order. I'm content to watch Enzo and Alison chat about nothing, really. He wears a white and black Fila track suit, a gold necklace with a pendant I can't quite make out, and a matching gold bracelet. Vintage Enzo. I take a slug from my Pabst Blue Ribbon while he carries on with her effortlessly, seemingly without a care in the world. I know better, though. Even now, he positions himself with his back to the nearby wall – a prime vantage point to see everyone within the room. I'd bet a week's pay he parked his vehicle as close to the front door as possible for ease of visibility and exit. Old habits die hard. Old gangster habits die harder and more painfully.

"How long are you staying?" Alison asks him, breaking me out of my mini-daydream.

"I'm not sure, but I'll be around here and there. I have business from back home and throughout New England all the way up here to southern Maine."

'Back home,' I've learned, is Providence, Rhode Island. Enzo grew up in the hard-knock seventies in the Federal Hill block back when organized crime ruled the streets. At that time, Providence's colorful and oftentimes corrupt mayor, Buddy Cianci, hadn't yet begun the city's remarkable resurgence.

"What kind of business?" I'm almost afraid to ask.

Enzo instantly detects my apprehension. "I'm glad you asked. I could use your help. And let me answer your question before you ask it

– no, I'm not doing anything illegal," He pauses, then lowers his voice considerably while alternating his gaze between us. "Anymore, but I … well … we have some dirty money to clean."

I glance toward Alison. She's looking at me with her beautiful almond eyes and I notice her bottom lip quiver slightly – an irrepressible manifestation of hers, indicative of fear or duress. I can usually talk her down fairly successfully and put her at ease, and this time is no different. I enjoy a starring role in the Jon Williams and Alison Brigham action-adventure romance, and I couldn't be more thankful for it.

"Alison, Enzo and I talked briefly about this back at the office. We can take care of this through the firm like we've always planned and be done with it and not look back."

"Ya, I understand." She responds softly. "It's just … we've had a really good run this past year getting the firm up and running and bringing some normalcy back to our lives. I don't want to screw it up."

She's right on that. J.K. Williams, P.A., has only been operational for a few months and I don't want to screw it up, either.

"I don't have many clients, Enzo. It'll be hard for me to push much cash through the business."

We put our conversation on hold when the server returns. I order a burger, and while our waiter moves on to Alison and Enzo, I take a moment to look around the room. A's is reasonably packed this Friday evening. We're on the cusp of summer tourist season, so it's not much of a surprise. Alison dressed herself to kill tonight, as she usually does, and like any twenty-seven-year-old smoking hot young woman should. Tight jeans show off her fine bottom and a custom-cut t-shirt leaves just enough midriff exposed to tantalize the mind and body.

"I understand and agree. I don't want the hassle anymore, either. I'm too old for that game." He says to Alison after the waiter leaves. "This is a completely legit business I'm in. I don't need to push the cash through your accounting firm, but I do need you both, and you need to clean your money as well."

"So … where do we fit in then?" I ask.

Enzo pauses for a moment, appearing to choose his words carefully. "I want you to bid on and perform a credit union audit for me … well, for the credit union I use."

"What? Why?" I reply skeptically. Alison appears equally unsure.

"Because I push my business cash through this credit union. I'm working with a high-level employee inside to facilitate a traceless process. They need an audit performed to satisfy the federal and state regulators."

"Why us?" Alison interjects. "If this business is legitimate, why not use anyone?"

Fair question.

Enzo exhales deeply. "It is a legitimate business, but until I'm able to feather our old money in with the new, I've got to be very careful how I proceed with traditional business banking."

"No one's going to hire us. I'm brand new and I have no banking experience." I wave my hand, dismissing the idea.

"Yes, they will." Enzo counters. "You simply have to bid on it. I've made sure your bid will be accepted."

"Still, it doesn't address my complete lack of experience with bank auditing." I look to Alison for help.

"Well, maybe we don't have the experience, Jon," She begins. "But think about it, we had a robust financial services division at Harding-Williams before the collapse. I bet we could get Hannah or Kelly to come over and take the lead on it. Even without knowing your actual business," Alison directs to Enzo. "I like the idea of using an unrelated source to make this work. I'd much rather clean our money outside of our own accounting firm than through it."

"It wouldn't be outside of the firm, though. We'd have to bring them on as employees – the audit opinion needs to be issued by a licensed firm." I remind her.

"Ugh. You're right. Of course, it does."

Enzo watches our exchange but says nothing. I don't know what to make of this. Introducing others into the fold doesn't seem like a good idea on its face. Why put someone else at risk, and more importantly, how can you trust anyone else? Hannah Morgan was a good friend of Alison's back at HW. I didn't know her very well, except I thought she was a colossal asshole. I never had a particular beef with her I could point to; she's just one of those women sporting perpetual 'resting bitch face.' She always looked irritated. Kelly Cookson, on the other hand, is pretty damn cool. He's a little redneck-y, but he drives a sweet late-model Corvette Z06, sporting a 'ROCKOUT' vanity license plate he rolls into work with during the summer. The T-tops are always off and either Skynyrd or something along the lines of Kid Rock cranks through the sound system. Not exactly your stereotypical auditor, but who am I to judge?

"I don't know about Hannah. I don't think she likes me. I'm not sure why I think that, but I kind of get that vibe from her. It's probably all in my head."

"No, you're totally right." Alison replies matter-of-factly. "She doesn't like you. She thinks you're a young, snotty know-it-all. But she doesn't really know you."

That stung more than I anticipated.

Alison continues on, blissfully unaware of the shade she's just thrown on me. "Kelly's a real smart guy, though. And he's got more than a little rebel in him."

Enzo quietly calculates the back-and-forth between Alison and me, but still he doesn't interject.

We spend the next few minutes drinking and debating the capabilities, pros, and cons of Hannah and Kelly. I'm scratching my head on this one, though Alison seems solidly on board.

"Yeah, well, let's take some time to think about this." I say. "I'd like to learn more about what kind of business you're talking about."

Enzo re-engages in the conversation. "Absolutely. I think you'll be intrigued."

2

Our waiter arrives with a hurried drop-off of our food and another round of drinks. He promptly departs with a group of servers to deliver an average dessert with a crooked candle hastily jammed into it, attempting to walk and light it at the same time. Shortly thereafter, we're subjected to a low-energy *a cappella* rendition of 'Happy Birthday' resonating somewhere on the other side of the restaurant.

His brief appearance set off a welcomed break to our conversation. It was beginning to weigh heavily on me. When I first started J.K. Williams, P.A., I convinced Alison we could slowly filter money through operations until our million-and-a-half-plus nest egg was fully recycled and no longer dirty. Now that we're here tonight with Enzo and it's become real, it has me somewhat spooked. No matter, Alison and I both knew this day was coming; we ought to face it head on and get it over with. Thankfully, Enzo is content to put the business discussion on hold until after we finish our meal. Conversation consists of current events, mindless banter, and reminiscing on happy moments we've shared together.

"You've been doing a lot more than getting J.K. Williams up and running." Enzo says, and before I ask what he means, he finishes his thought. "You've been hitting the gym. I can easily see it."

Well, that jacks up my ego.

Alison laughs and beats me to a response. "He's *swole* alright. He's got some guns now. Show 'em off, baby."

"For Christ's sake, stop." I try my best to appear embarrassed, but I love it, and she knows it. She's squeezing my right biceps trying to get me to flex, and I pull my upper body away from her slightly, only for the effect. She counters by reaching under the table with her other hand, casually but firmly latching onto my tool like a bull rider gripping the flank rope while straddling a Texas Longhorn. Thankfully, this goes unnoticed by Enzo. I, on the other hand, merrily skip down a path to a raging hard on.

"Yeah, I'm working on it. I spend most of my free time pretty much living in the gym. I had a challenging recovery and rehab from the bullet at Bernie's; hey, that could actually be a cool movie name – *Bullet at Bernie's.* Uh … anyway, I did a lot of weight work to regain full use of my arm and now I'm hooked on lifting."

"Nice. There's a lot worse you could be hooked on. Stay with it, man, it'll come in handy."

That boosts my self-confidence, but also gives me a pit in my stomach at the same time, like, what do you mean, *it'll come in handy?*

"So, what have you been up to, my dear?" Enzo directs to Alison.

She removes her hand from my penis and repositions herself in her bar seat. "Well, I've been working with Jon to get the firm up and running, as you know, and really just going to the gym with him. Pretty low key."

"Sounds awesome if you ask me." Enzo chuckles.

"Ya. It kind of is. So how do you like the firm name?" Alison asks, knowing full well he loves it.

"Whew. I couldn't describe the feeling that came over me when I saw it. Thank you both for keeping a piece of Sabrina alive with you."

"I miss her." Alison blurts. "I miss her and for what we'll never have."

Enzo's eyes begin to well up. He fights back tears which causes us to well up, too. I try to push through the heartache, with only marginal success.

"And to think I couldn't stand it when she called me 'J.K.' " I say half-laughing, but with no joy. "What I wouldn't do now to hear her say it again."

Enzo reaches down into a fairly large leather satchel resting on the floor. Surprisingly, I hadn't noticed it when we arrived, but he was seated at the table when Alison and I walked in. In all likelihood, he was standing in front of it when we greeted him.

"I made a promise to Sabrina and also to you." Enzo says softly while removing an ornate box from the satchel and delicately positioning it on the open place setting next to him.

He need not say a word. Mom's ashes. I run my finger alongside the oak exterior, pausing at her engraved initials, SMG – Sabrina Marie Garibaldi. Alison openly weeps, albeit silently. I feel emotionless, and yet, overwhelmed.

"How did you do it?" I ask solemnly. "How did you get them?"

Enzo struggles to maintain his composure. "I called in one last favor. Ultimately, she was traced back to the evidence vault in Portland. Truthfully, I was relieved she was there. Once I found her, it wasn't difficult to make her disappear."

Looking at the box causes me to re-live the mayhem Enzo and I experienced together. I want so badly to talk about it with him – but not in front of Alison. For as much as she's seen, like Bob Roberts' bloated body dangling from his bedroom ceiling; much of it she hasn't, and I'd like to keep it that way. The scenes play out in my head – Detective Bond propped up lifeless in his Crown Victoria … the confrontation at the mall with Brown and subsequent discovery of Reyes and Uncle Danny … the ambush from Brown at the crematorium and Bernie's tragic outcome … disposing of bodies at the waterfront. It goes on and on.

"Tell us what you've been up to lately. Where have you been?" Alison asks, trying to change the subject and bring an end to our painful conversation.

Enzo breathes out a cleansing breath as though washing away all the negative karma that's gripped us over the past year. "That's a good segue into discussing the business I'm into now. I went back home to Providence, like I told you earlier. I felt the call to get back to my roots and rediscover myself. I don't know … it's all so different now, but I think it helped." He continues. "I met up with some old friends; most of them are gone now, either dead, in jail, or moved away. But I've always kept in contact with one guy – one of my junior high buddies. He makes a modest living operating private ATMs; you know, those small-scale, no-name ATMs you find around strip malls and convenience stores?"

He doesn't pause for a response. "There isn't a ton of money in it, but with enough of them in the right locations, the fees generated per transaction add up. I quickly thought of how I could parlay the business into *our benefit*."

He places a distinct vocal emphasis on 'our benefit.'

"I did all the research into how this works legitimately. I'm not looking to generate any more dirty money. I simply want to wash the old money and then provide a good, clean stream of revenue going forward."

"I like the sound of that." I say, in part to head off any pushback from Alison. She understandably wants nothing to do with Enzo's life of crime, and I can't blame her. I don't either.

It's getting decidedly busier at A's, and as a consequence, louder around our table. Enzo pauses whenever our server appears as well as when surrounding tables turn over. It becomes clear to us this conversation should continue outside of A's, and fortunately, Enzo suggests we call it a night and continue our conversation tomorrow. That's fine with me. We didn't spend a lot of time discussing how Alison and I fit into the picture and I'm sure she'll have some impressions when we get home. I suspect Enzo will suggest we push the money we have through the ATMs and have it come back to us in audit fees and other client services quickly and be done with it.

"Where are you staying?" Alison asks Enzo.

"The Fairfield by the mall."

"Really?" I'm completely stunned. A jolt of numbness surges through my body as I re-live the image of the Cougar exploding in the hotel parking lot, Mom trapped inside. Oh God, the sound … that burnt smell … the oily feel of the heavy smoke in the air …

"Enzo, you can't stay there! You have to stay with us!" Alison protests.

He places his hand over the oak box, caressing its length with slow deliberateness. "Thanks, but I'm better off there. I'm closer to her."

Enzo raises his glass in a toast, and we follow suit.

"To Sabrina …"

"To Mom …"

3

It's a speedy ride across the city from Asbury's to our apartment. The streets are quiet, and the cool but comfortable May evening teases us with a breath of the wonderful summer weather on its way. I'm a tad bit self-conscious with the level of noise we're producing from Danny's Jeep (well, mine now) as we approach the apartment complex. We don't exactly arrive discreetly in the oversized Green Machine. I feel as though a part of Uncle Danny rides with me when I'm driving it. Its loud, growling engine fit his brash and unapologetic personality perfectly, as did its fun-loving utility and purpose. He left it to me after he passed away along with most everything he owned – his beach property; now nothing more than a vacant parcel, his impressive firearms collection, and probably the most valuable possession to me – a family photo album.

Neither Alison nor I said much along the way home, though I'm sure she's processing how the evening unfolded as much as I am. We've agreed to meet Enzo at the apartment in the morning to go over the details and map this whole ATM and audit thing out.

"Hey." Alison abruptly snaps, breaking the silence and causing me to flinch in my seat. "Oh, I'm sorry, baby, I didn't mean to jump you." She places a comforting hand on my thigh. "So, Enzo asks us to bid on an audit for the credit union, right?"

"Yeah. That's how I heard it. Why?"

"Follow me on this. You said when he surprised you at the office this morning, he appeared genuinely intrigued with the idea we had started a firm. He said something tongue-in-cheek about doing his cleaning, or dirty laundry, or whatever …"

She offers this as a hanging statement without any trace of asking a question. I listen attentively while keeping my eyes focused on the tight opening of the garage doorway as we enter the underneath-building parking of our apartment complex. Likewise, I keep my mouth shut.

"Are you certain he didn't know we started a new firm?"

I pull into one of our two reserved spots directly next to Alison's white Fiat, shift the Jeep into park, and shut the engine down.

"I hadn't thought of it. How could he have known we started a firm?" We both open our doors and get out, pausing to look at each other over the hood. "What does it matter, anyway?"

As I say this, it hits me right between the eyes where she's going with this.

"Jon, if he didn't know we had an accounting firm, how would he have known to already arrange an automatic bid acceptance between the credit union he uses and our firm?"

§

We think better of continuing the discussion outside and make the four-floor hike using the stairs. I flick the light switches on as soon as the apartment door swings open, and I rapidly scan the area. I'm the first to enter – always, out of habit and history. Following a cursory walk-through, I come back to the kitchen, pop a cold PBR, and consider Alison's observation and question. Dang, she's dead right. I can't imagine a scenario by which Enzo discovers we opened an accounting firm in the morning, processes a plan of action in the afternoon, and has a slam dunk deal worked out for us to complete a financial audit by dinner. It's undeniably too coincidental.

"I think you're right on Enzo." I say, taking a chug of beer and sitting down on the couch. "He had to have known about us and the firm for some period of time."

Alison stands in the kitchen and nods her head but doesn't respond.

"So, the next obvious questions are, how did he know about the firm and why is he pretending he just learned about it?"

Alison pours a glass of wine and joins me. "Well, I'm less concerned about him *pretending* he just learned about it. That may be benign so as not to take away from our happy reunion. What I'm more concerned with is *how* he found out about it."

We sit in silence for a short time while the television produces buzzing background noise. I wrap my arm around her, and she promptly settles into my chest in our natural snuggle position. I trace a few fingers lightly through her hair; I know she loves this, and it usually relaxes her quickly. I thought she might fall asleep like this, but I discover she has another idea. A much better one, in fact. She slowly rises from the couch while unbuttoning her jeans and proceeds to shimmy out of them enough so that only one pant leg remains on the crown of her foot. She exaggeratedly draws her leg back and flings them across the room, logging an impressive distance. As she slides her t-shirt over her head, I'm tempted to remove a few bills from my wallet and try and entice her into a full-on stripper fantasy show. I decide it won't work – she isn't wearing any underwear. I'll have no place to stuff them. No matter, she's doing very well on her own with no monetary incentive.

By some strange happenstance, an *America's Got Talent* musical act booms from the television, providing her with some reasonably fitting background music to move to.

"You know, when we were at A's, that really turned me on with our under-the-table encounter." She purrs, reaching behind her back.

She abandons her bra, concealing her breasts with her hands and continuing to dance for me, never breaking eye contact. Goddamn, she does this way too proficiently for this to be her first time. Not a chance I'm going to ask her, though.

"Do you like what you see?" She asks in a sultry voice, removing her hands and exposing her extraordinary boobs.

I bob my head stupidly. She continues moving in a way that has me straining in my jeans and she enjoys every moment of it. I quickly pull my shirt off and slide out of my pants, pushing them aside.

"Oh, the guns are out again?" She smiles while kneeling down in front of me, enveloping my rock hardness between her breasts. "Now, where was I?"

4

"Run, Jonny, run! Go son!! Run!" Dad smiles from ear to ear. His arm motions wildly for me to round third base and head for home plate. I see Mom in the background; she's working the concession stand but watches me enthusiastically as I stretch for the home run. After crossing home plate, my nine-year-old self triumphantly launches my batting helmet from my head, and I turn and race down the third base line back toward Dad. Behind him in the parking lot, I spot Mom waving to me as she stands in front of the old burnt-orange Cougar. I transform into twenty-four-year-old Jon again and wave back, passing by Dad as I jog over to her.

"Can I ride with you?" I ask.

Mom's eyes light up. "I would absolutely love that!"

We both get in – Mom behind the wheel and I'm in the passenger seat. She looks so beautiful wearing an athletic outfit, her long blonde hair pulled back into a ponytail.

A coldness filters through me. "Wait! Don't start the car! Something isn't right!" Mom doesn't seem to hear me. She reaches for the key in the ignition and turns. I'm paralyzed. "Noooooo!"

§

"C'mon baby, wake up. Hey, I'm right here."

"Wha … huh …?" I groggily open my eyes to find Alison hovering over me. She rubs my back soothingly.

"You were having that dream again."

That damn dream. A perverse hybrid of two recurring dreams, one of which I've had since I was about nine and my dad coached my little league baseball team. The other one, less than a year ago from when Mom and I reconnected. Now they've morphed into one wretched version of *This Is Your Life*.

"Oh … uh … thanks. Yeah, I was."

"We should probably get up. Enzo will be here in an hour or so."

Alison slips into her Dalmatian pajamas and heads out to the kitchen. I roll back over with the intention of sleeping a little longer, but within minutes the smell of coffee glides into the room, sweeping me out of bed magic carpet-style and into the kitchen.

"Man, I am so ready for a mainline coffee I.V. I'm totally drag-assing this morning."

"Understandable. You rarely sleep well when you dream like that."

Alison hands me a steaming cupful. She didn't make any for herself; she's drinking Diet Coke – not unusual for her.

"Thank you. After we get through with Enzo today, I want to hit the gym. Clear the cobwebs out."

"Great. I'm in. What do you want for breakfast?"

Before I can answer, I hear a text chime ding from my phone:

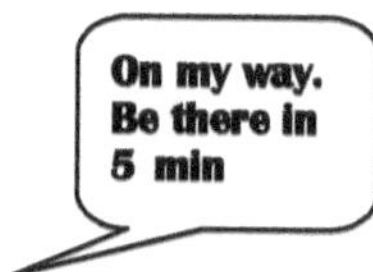

"Speak of the devil. It's Enzo. He's five minutes out."

"Shoot. I need to get dressed."

Alison cruises out of the kitchen and heads for the bathroom. Meanwhile, I send a message back:

I'm not doing anything to get ready. Sweats and a t-shirt work for me. I turn the television on SportsCenter to catch last night's Red Sox highlights and plop down onto the couch.

Within minutes, I hear a soft knock at the door and experience a flashback of when Alison and I were quarantined at the hotel with Mom while Enzo went out for takeout. He always lightly knocked on the door whenever he came back home to my mother then, too. I'm off the couch and over to the door quick-time, greeted by the sight of Enzo holding a dozen doughnuts from Holy Donut.

"Goddamn, LoZo, if you didn't just read my mind!"

"I had a feeling."

Alison breezes out of the bathroom looking pretty damned good for the minimal time she took getting ready.

"Hey, Enzo. Come on in." She says, giving him a hug.

"Thanks. I brought doughnuts."

"Looks like you made Jon's Christmas card list. Again."

Alison shoots me a sideways glance, feigning disapproval for stuffing my gullet without delay. I beam a powdered doughnut-infused smile and keep right on eating. She's feisty this morning, but in a good way. She gives me an eyewink and then redirects her attention back to Enzo.

"Alright, let's get down to business. Tell me what all this ATM stuff's about."

"Perfect. Yeah, let's do it." He sits down on a kitchen bar stool, joining Alison and me at the counter. "Well, the long and the short of it is I own a few dozen ATM kiosks from Rhode Island up to Maine, all of them around the I-95 corridor. I'm what's referred to by state licensing agencies as a 'servicer.' I travel around filling up my own ATMs, but I also regularly supply money to independent contractors to replenish my distant ATM locations to keep them full. Most of the time I can't get to them all, so I need other people to help me out."

Enzo pauses briefly, opening the door for us to ask questions. I do have a thought – what exactly does an 'independent contractor' mean to Enzo. I suspect his version differs from the conventional employment definition. I think the better of asking, though. Instead, I reach for another doughnut.

"My state licenses allow me to establish and maintain a relationship with a 'processor.' Processors are federally-approved and state-licensed companies that record the ATM transactions and reconcile the funds with the servicer's bank."

Again, he gives us an opportunity to ask a question or at least to let his description of the business sink in.

Alison's impatience bubbles up some. "Go ahead and get it all out. We'll wait to ask questions."

"Fair enough." He pauses for a moment to gather his thoughts. "Okay. I'm a servicer who owns a bunch of ATMs. I have a bank and a credit union I use as funding sources, both of them in Rhode Island, each with main offices in Providence. I use the bank only for legitimate business purposes – I borrow money from the bank, stock my ATMs with the cash, customers come in and withdraw money from the ATM, and the money withdrawn from their account gets credited back into my bank credit line through the processor which acts as the collector and remitter of funds. I walk away with the transaction fee income minus some bank interest and a processor cut. Easy, right?"

"Yeah, sounds slick." I say.

"I charge three dollars and fifty cents per transaction – not too bad. But if someone wants to make a living, they need to own a lot of ATMs in high-traffic areas. The capital outlay to buy these machines can become pretty steep."

"So where does the credit union fit in?" Alison asks, ignoring her own directive to hold off on questions.

"I'm getting to that. See, sometimes people simply own ATMs and go a different direction. They don't want to go through the hassle of securing and maintaining state licenses or establishing relationships with the processors, so they connect with other ATM owners. They pay guys like me a fee to stock their ATMs with cash and run it through my processor. They own the kiosks and collect the transaction fee and pay me a percent for essentially managing their asset."

"You use the dirty money for the people who contract with you on their ATMs." I posit.

"Exactly. Like I said, with my own ATMs and the bank business, I borrow bank money through a line of credit, stock the ATMs, and then routinely pay down the LOC back to zero when the processor reconciles the withdrawals from the ATM users' accounts and then credits my bank account."

"You mean when the processor sends the money back to your bank, and the *bank* credits your account." Alison interjects.

"Right. You definitely know that side of it better than I do."

I repeat Alison's earlier question. "So how does the credit union fit into all of this?"

"I use the credit union for all of the people I deal with who own their own ATMs and pay me a fee for servicing them. I don't borrow any money from the credit union. I stock those ATMs with dirty money. An ATM user withdraws the money, my processor facilitates the withdrawal from their bank account, then puts it into my account at the credit union. I get a small percent of the transaction fee; the ATM owner gets the rest and becomes an unwitting conduit for cleaning the money."

Alison looks for clarification. "Then why the credit union? Why not use the bank for everything?"

"Two reasons." Enzo replies. "One, credit unions aren't subject to the same stringent federal and state regulations as banks, though we still need to be careful. It isn't as though they operate without regulatory supervision. And two, I have someone on the inside at the credit union helping to facilitate a smooth flow of funds."

"And that brings you to us for the credit union audit." I surmise.

"Bingo. My inside person covers the trail, and you corroborate it."

We take a collective moment to process what we've discussed.

"Well, that does sound like a plan." Alison says while walking to the kitchen for another Diet Coke. I can't readily get a read on what she means by that. She sounds neutral.

Enzo adds, "And we can feather your cash through in the same way. Either personally or through the business. Your choice."

"And how many ATMs did you say you own?" I ask.

"I have about three dozen, give or take. And I have a few people who contract with me to process their ATMs, including my oldest friend, Jimmy; the guy I told you about earlier. Those are the credit union people."

"Sounds like a Steven King horror movie. 'CUPs.' "

Enzo and Alison look at me like I have three heads.

"CUPs." I repeat. "Credit Union People. Acronym, you know?"

"Good grief." Enzo snorts.

"Dork." Alison adds, smiling.

"I know, I can't help it. So, can we meet with your inside person? Who is it and what do they do?"

"That's a great idea. She's the BSA-AML officer, which is short for Bank Secrecy Act and Anti-Money Laundering, if I remember right. She's responsible for ongoing monitoring of accounts and reporting suspicious activity. She can control the information that gets reported up the chain of command. I also want to introduce you to Jimmy. He's the real reason how I came up with this. We can go down anytime you like."

"Let's go tomorrow. I'm going to hit the gym hard today. Work off the doughnuts and get my head on straight."

"I'm with you on that." Alison says.

"Perfect. I've got stuff to do here today, anyway. You guys can follow me back tomorrow."

5

We leave Enzo and the apartment around eleven or so, cruising out in Danny's Jeep. It's automatic we take the Jeep when we head to the gym. Alison teases it's because I like to act tough and drive up in an aggressive, brash ride – and she's right – but equally it's because I one hundred percent feel like a pussy rolling up in her white Fiat.

As we pull in, we see the gym's packed this morning. There are hardly any open parking spots in the lot. It's not uncommon, though; late Saturday mornings are almost always this busy. We go inside to check in and stash our stuff in lockers, then meet out on the floor to warm up.

Although it's active in here, there aren't a lot of women around. It's mostly made up of men with a smattering of what Alison and I cattily speculate as local exotic dancers sneaking in a pre-striptease workout in preparation for their evening shift.

"The Hardos are out in full force today." Alison observes.

'Hardos,' as Alison calls them, represent a significant segment of today's clientele. She's referring to the exceedingly jacked bodybuilders with so much bulk, they most likely have difficulty reaching around and wiping their own asses.

"Maybe someday I could be a Hardo." I reply.

"Baby, you already are. I love your Hardo." She says in a soft voice, smiling. "And your muscles are catching up, too."

"Damn girl, you know how to get me going. Alright, let's get started. I can't wait to crush it."

"Working on the pipes today?" Alison good-naturedly inquires while flexing her right biceps.

"Well … you know … when the sun's out …"

"… guns out!" She finishes.

"Right on. Actually, today's chest and abs day for me. What's your game plan?"

"I'll do some chest with you, then I'll do cardio."

"I'd like to do your chest."

"Pig," She winks at me then pauses. "But maybe later if you're good."

We claim an unoccupied bench press and alternate warming up with very light weight to stretch out and get the blood flowing. We engage in mindless conversation consisting of where we're going for lunch later and what we're going to do tonight, temporarily avoiding a discussion of this morning's conversation with Enzo and how we'll approach the trip to Providence tomorrow.

Alison sticks with light weight, while I work through my progressions until I'm fully ready for heavy lifting. I'm respectable, but middle of the road when compared to the Hardos; however, I can still move some serious poundage. Typically, I can get two-seventy-five for two or three reps, and today is no different. Then, I move up to three hundred.

Goddamned three hundred. I have a love/hate relationship with bench pressing three hundred pounds. I was super pumped the first time I got it. I had been getting really close, and in anticipation, some of my friends in the gym helped me celebrate by having a t-shirt ready for me that said *Benchin' Three Hundo* when I finally got it. Since then though, I fail on three hundred more often than I can successfully perform the press, and Alison knows this.

As I psyche myself up to move the weight, Alison stands over me in a position to offer a safety spot. She won't need to give much help if I can't press it, just enough to help me pass the stick point and then I can do the rest. As I set up under the bar, pinning my shoulders back onto the bench, she leans down close to whisper to me.

"If you can get three hundred, when we get home I'll give you the best blowjob you've ever had." She breathes, sliding her super sexy tongue along her front teeth.

I steel my arms and press the weight out of the cradle. I release down to my chest, then very slowly but steadily, I move the bar through the stick point, extend to lock out, and rack the weight. Whew, heavy as hell, but the smoothest I've ever gotten it.

"Nice job, baby! You got that easily!"

"Not easily, but thanks. That was a solid lift for me."

"Amazing what a blowjob bribe can do for you, right?!"

"You have no idea."

We spend another thirty minutes or so together before Alison breaks off and starts her cardio routine. I move to the dumbbell racks to continue my lifting, attempting to put the vision of my forthcoming oral session temporarily out of mind and concentrate on finishing. I'm only marginally successful.

Later on, I peep over to Alison – she's on a StairClimber looking chiseled in her Gymshark outfit showing off her curves and working up a serious sweat. She's a natural Hardo magnet, but they're typically respectful and attempt to check her out without being too obvious. Oh well, it comes with the territory. When you date a hottie, you've got to expect it. She's chatting away with a decent looking woman exercising on the machine next to her when she spots me. She excitedly waves me over, and I willingly oblige.

When I get there, they step off their machines.

"Hey babe, meet Darcy. Darcy, this is Jon." Alison says while wiping off forehead sweat with a hand towel. "We went to high school together and we haven't seen each other in what … ten years?" She looks to Darcy.

"Ya. Almost ten years. Crazy we connected in here. Pleased to meet you, Jon."

"Same here. That's kind of cool you ran into each other."

Alison agrees. "Right? I told Darcy all about you and that we're heading for lunch soon and invited her to join us. Is that okay?"

I can't help but wonder what 'all about you' entails.

"Of course, it is." I reply. How the hell could I say no with her putting me on the spot, not that I have any issue with her coming.

"Great! Let's clean up and head out!" Alison's visibly excited.

I guess my workout's finished, I contemplate as I wander back to the men's locker room.

§

We agree on Bulldog Brewing for lunch. Alison and I have been back many times since our impromptu kidnapping by Enzo's people, so we don't have any reservations or residual PTSD when eating there.

Our drive to the brewery and ensuing parking lot activity differs substantially this time around than when we made the trip that crazy day, though. And that's good by me. Alison's happy, so I'm happy. Turns out, Darcy and Alison were pretty solid friends before they went their separate ways to college following high school.

"I'm so excited to see you, Darcy! Tell me everything you've been up to!" Alison gushes from across the table.

"Well, I've been back in Maine for about a month, and I'm just getting out and about. My last name went from Allen to Abelman, and six months ago went back to Allen."

"Oh, I'm sorry." Alison offers.

I only observe the exchange.

"God, don't be." Darcy replies. "I'm so happy to be out of that marriage and the fuck out of South Florida."

My positive impression of Darcy just multiplied tenfold. I like a woman who can cuss. She's a skinny girl and decent looking, with an easy way about her. She wears a Red Sox baseball hat with a dirty-blonde ponytail pulled through the back. I like that, too. She has a loose, billowy t-shirt on, so her body is still a mystery; however, I can see she has spindly legs protruding from her ratty gym shorts. Although she appears a bit raggedy, she actually has an attractive face that I'm certain looks even better when she's cleaned up.

She continues. "I got married right out of college. Big mistake. *Big mistake.*" She emphasizes. "What a toxic relationship."

"I've had my share of those." Alison replies and kicks me under the table.

Isn't that easily the understatement of the day.

Darcy graduated from college with a degree in pharmacy and came back to Portland after years of working in a Miami shopping mall drug store. The dissolution of her marriage coupled with the constant fear and threat from addicts gripped by the opioid epidemic made for an easy decision to move back home.

Alison handles the majority of the conversational exchange, and I'm content to watch. She educates Darcy about Harding-Williams, its subsequent demise, and our new venture in J.K. Williams, P.A.

Darcy can hardly contain herself. "I heard about that! First my mom told me about it, and then I heard it on TV! I can't believe you guys were a part of that!"

Neither can I. If she only knew how much a part of it we were. To some degree, we still are. The conversation's direction causes me to think about our trip to Providence tomorrow. I attempt to ease myself into the conversation mainly to change the subject.

"Speaking of our new firm, we're traveling to Rhode Island tomorrow to meet up with a client. Well … a client of a client." I amend.

"Are you going, too?" Darcy asks Alison. "I'm getting a mani-pedi tomorrow, and on a longshot, I was going to ask if you wanted to come."

Darcy has no idea the nerve she just struck. Alison's gorgeous doe eyes swivel over to me in record time. No words needed. I simply say, "Oh, wouldn't you rather do that, babe?"

"You wouldn't mind?" She asks.

Hell, no. I'd much rather go alone with Enzo until I get a lay of the land down there, anyway.

"Not at all. You should go." I think back to her last spa day with my mom. They had such an enjoyable time; it will do her some good to hang out with a girlfriend for an afternoon.

"Perfect!" Alison says to me, then turns to Darcy. "It's a date!"

Darcy reacts positively. "Great! It's good to have someone to hang out with again. It's been a while for me."

We spend the remainder of the lunch discussing more mundane topics, mostly their old high school experiences – boyfriends, parents, and such. I get the sense Darcy was on the more 'adventurous' side of dating and boys than one would normally expect from a teenager.

When the topic of Alison's parents comes up, it appears Darcy is well aware of the issues they faced, despite the actual divorce occurring when Alison went off to college.

"How's your mom been?" Darcy asks.

"She's Mom. Still as crazy as always." Alison replies.

"Ya." Darcy says contemplatively. "And what about your dad? What's he been up to?"

"Honestly, I'm not entirely sure. He lives in Connecticut and I think he's semi-retired, but I don't really see him anymore."

"That's too bad. I always liked him. He really was a nice guy."

"Ya, well, I did, too."

There's a lingering sadness in her voice that hangs over the table one can't help but empathize with. I can sense she's traveling down a rather forgettable Memory Lane.

Alison suddenly sits up straight as if to shake off the negative energy of the conversation. "Well, tomorrow's another day. One with a mani-pedi, in fact. I can't wait."

6

"So, you're really okay with me skipping the trip tomorrow?" Alison asks.

I'm doing a walk-through of the apartment as she follows me inside. "Absolutely. I'll report back to you everything I find out."

"Jon Williams, you are so damn good to me. I don't know what I'd do without you." Her speech pattern morphs from grateful to sensual, very quickly capturing my attention. "Now … let me make good on my promise."

Wow. I only got as far as the kitchen bar. She didn't waste any time. She strides over to the couch with a purpose, snatches a throw pillow, then brings it over to me, placing it at my feet.

Alison neatly slips her t-shirt and sports bra over her head, and I take the opportunity to massage her breasts while she lifts up my shirt and kisses my chest. Eventually, she works her way across my stomach, descending below my reach until her knees are situated on the pillow and her head is directly in front of my steely erection.

While slowly lowering my shorts and underwear, she begins by licking the shaft at the base, taking her sweet time and working her way along its full length. This is driving me batshit crazy. She pauses at the top, swirling her tongue around the head of my penis, all the while delicately squeezing my balls. She has just the right grip on me, giving me a smooth handjob as she takes me into her mouth.

Ahhh … sweet Jesus that feels so good.

Her lips glide tightly around me, sucking passionately and enthusiastically, and occasionally she locks eyes with me with a confidence that seems to say, *look what I can do!*

I grasp tufts of her hair in each hand, squeezing gently, moving my hips back and forth, faster and faster. She responds in rhythm, speeding up and taking as much of me into her mouth as she can.

My body begins to shudder as I approach orgasm. She can feel it, and in response, she pauses and whispers to me while continuing to steadily increase the pace of her stroke.

"Where do you want to cum, baby?"

"Don't stop," I groan. "Ahhh, don't stop."

Alison buries my cock deep in her throat just as I let loose the first of several mind-numbing jets, my body convulsing with every release.

After I'm completely drained, she slows considerably; careful not to overstimulate, until she feels my body relax and sees my contorted face return to normal.

"Well, there. You must feel better." She laughs while standing up, still topless, and bringing the pillow back to the couch.

"Oh, man. Do I ever." She leaves me standing at the threshold of the kitchen bar with my underwear and shorts perched at my ankles and a half-hard dick poking straight out like a three-meter springboard in an Olympic diving competition. Not exactly a sight to behold I imagine, but in my outstanding post-orgasmic funk, I'd do well simply to remember my own name.

"You should probably pull your shorts up, baby." Alison casually suggests as she goes to the bedroom to change, and as if she hadn't just had her perfect lips wrapped snugly around my rock-hard rod.

§

"This could be the best beer I've ever had." I'm sitting on the couch having a post-workout, post-spectacular-oral-sex beer when Alison exits the bedroom.

"Really … a marginally cold PBR tallboy? Somehow, in your twenty-five years, I find that hard to believe." She replies. "I suspect it has something to do with your stellar morning. Everything tastes better after an orgasm."

"Truth. Hey, I meant to ask you this on the way home. I got the sense Darcy was a player back in high school."

"I didn't hear a question there. What exactly are you asking?"

"You know. Was she easy?"

"You mean a slut?"

"Yeah, right. Slutty."

"Ya … pretty much, I guess. Darcy got around, but no more so than the rest of us." She says indifferently.

Damn. I wasn't expecting that enlightening a response. I should probably quit while I'm ahead.

Alison continues. "I don't know how she was after high school. We were great friends in middle school and up to about halfway through senior year. We didn't spend much time together as we got close to graduation, and nothing afterwards. I hadn't seen her at all again until now."

"What happened? Did she steal your boyfriend … or you steal hers?"

Alison looks at me but says nothing. I can't get a solid read on her face, but if I had to guess, it looks more irritated than anything. After a pause, she finally speaks. "Something like that."

I'm waiting for her to elaborate.

She can see she's not getting out of an explanation, and so begins with a drawn-out sigh. "Back when we were in high school, Darcy and I had a group of girlfriends that all hung out. We were both closer to one of the girls in the group than the rest, and the three of us had sleepovers at each other's houses all the time. When we were over to Megan's house one weekend," She hesitates. "Her name was Megan; Darcy had disappeared for a long time … she said she got her period and had been in the bathroom cleaning herself."

"Yeah." I respond with anticipation.

"There was speculation she may have done some stuff with Megan's dad instead. And had been doing stuff for a while."

"Like, stuff-stuff?" I gesticulate a humping motion while proposing the question.

"Yes, Jon. Stuff-stuff." She counters irascibly, clearly not impressed with my sex-act simulation, nor does she try to mask her disdain for it. "My parents were friends with this girl's parents, and they all spent time together, too. That's initially how I learned about it. My mom told me there was a rumor floating around."

"And you're okay reconnecting with her now?"

"Ya. It was a long time ago. It bugged me, but it was never actually proven. I'm not sure I believe it, anyway. It was a big thing back then, but I honestly don't care anymore." She considers this, then adds, "Besides, I really could use a girlfriend."

Alison's statement hangs heavy in the air. Her last 'girlfriend' was my mom, and coincidently, they had just gotten their nails done, too, prior to Mom's horrific death.

"Jesus, did you talk about it at the gym?"

"No. And I don't plan on bringing it up, either. What good could come from it?"

"None, I guess."

"Right. I'm over it."

I'm not. I want to ask Darcy about it next time I see her, but no way in hell would I ever. I can only hope it pops up organically and I'm within earshot.

7

"This is your ride?" I ask as we approach a cream-colored Cadillac sedan parked curbside in front of the apartment complex. My hand sets against my forehead in a pathetic military-type salute, attempting to emulate a sun visor. I've been squinting since I came out from the elevator to combat the bright morning sunlight.

Enzo responds without pause as he draws near the driver's side door. "Yeah, I know, it's a grandpa car."

I want to ask him what happened to his Mercedes SUV, but I suspect I know the answer. Too many painful memories of Mom inextricably linked to it.

Sunday's weather is proving to be an awesome extension of Saturday's quintessential day, and a perfect one for a road trip. Enzo arrived at seven-thirty, without doughnuts I note, and now we're out and at his car ready to go by eight o'clock.

Enzo seems to be in business mode this morning. He's not much for small talk generally, and I don't feel as though I should lead the conversation. This is his show, so I'm content to sit back and let him guide the discussion on his own terms. I recline my seat back some and take my phone out to text Santa. We've been exchanging messages over the past few days, attempting to plan out a trip for him and Merri to visit Maine. It's hard to believe they've been in Nebraska for over a year now.

I fire off the opening salvo message of the day. In the meantime, I scroll through our text history from the previous few days, to reread the timeline. We're almost certain Merri and Santa are coming up for a week in the middle of June. Alison and I can't wait – especially me. Then, we reciprocate at the end of July and travel to Nebraska for their wedding, where I'm the best man.

A text chime sounds and my phone auto-scrolls to Santa's response:

"Ah, man. Cool. I'm psyched."

Enzo looks over. "What's cool?"

"You remember my buddy, Santa? The guy whose wedding I'm in?"

"Yeah. There aren't many Santa's out there."

"Right. Well, he's coming up with his girlfriend to visit in June. Kind of a last tour before their wedding in July. Alison and I are heading to it in Nebraska. We're planning out their visit now."

"Keep in mind you need to get an audit done."

"I got it." I momentarily pause. "So, can we talk about that? I have a few questions Alison and I were mulling over last night. The usual stuff, like when is it due, who will we be dealing with. Stuff like that."

"I can't answer the technical stuff. You'll need to connect with the credit union lady on that."

"How do you know her?"

Enzo looks at me stone-faced. "Jimmy connected me with her."

"Damn, man. Easy. Just asking." Christ, he woke up foul today. "When are we meeting Jimmy?"

Enzo attempts to lighten his demeanor. "Eleven or so. Doesn't matter much if we run late. Jimmy always hangs out at the same place. He'll be there."

"Where is 'there'?"

"Foxy Lady."

"Um. Is that a strip club?"

"Yeah."

"On a Sunday morning. Nice." I remark a touch sarcastically.

I discover there really isn't much for Enzo and me to talk about on the ride down. We need to meet with Jimmy and the credit union lady to keep the ball rolling. It's just as well. Enzo's grumpy and I'm not much interested in dealing with it. Time to fully recline my seat, pop in my air pods, and crank the music.

§

A series of tight turns jostles me from my sleep. I awaken as we decelerate to a stop at an intersection with a panorama of rundown, probably vacant old mill buildings standing in front of us. Windows are broken and there's graffiti on the exterior façade, but not too severely; only a couple of street tags here and there. We've exited the highway and now make our way through back streets.

"Where are we?" I ask.

"Rhode Island. Providence to be exact. We'll be there in about five minutes. Maybe less."

I look around. This is definitely inner city. It reminds me of a bigger version of Portland, but smaller than Boston. As Enzo approaches another intersection, I see from his turn signal he's planning on taking a left onto Douglas Street. Not long after he makes that left, he bangs another left into a long entrance leading to a tucked-away parking lot.

As Enzo kills the motor, I exit the Cadillac and begin to size up the establishment. It's not as big as I expected, though I'm not sure why I thought it would be bigger. The building presents a unique main entrance with carnival-esque lights out front reminding me of a cross between a drive-in movie snack bar and a 1960's-era wooden amusement park carousel ride. Surprisingly, there appears to be a lot of activity going on.

"On a Sunday? Before noon?" I muse, looking at the collection of vehicles.

Enzo points up to a large sign posted near the entrance. It reads: *Legs and Eggs*.

"Breakfast buffet." He responds.

"All you can eat, I'm sure." I speculate.

"Goddamn it, I knew you were going to say that."

He shakes his head slightly, though I can tell he's not mad. He's feigning exasperation, but he's cool.

"Never want to disappoint you, LoZo." I clap him on the back, then pass ahead of him to the front entrance.

"Twenty cover and minimum twenty in change." The front desk attendant barks to me firmly as I walk in. She notices Enzo entering immediately after me. "Go ahead, you're good." She amends.

Her demeanor softens considerably when she sees Enzo, generating a pit in my stomach. He's clearly known here, and I can't help but feel on edge. Enzo says nothing but lays two twenty-dollar bills on the counter then peels off two additional one hundred-dollar bills. She responds by collecting the cover, then hands him a stack of bills in return, which he in turn, hands to me. They're all two-dollar bills. One hundred very crisp, very clean, very new two-dollar bills.

Enzo slips ahead of me to face a darkly-tinted, closed interior access door obstructing any view of the action inside. We hear muffled thumping of a driving beat seep into the front vestibule. Black felt wall coverings act as a billboard showcasing the strippers working inside and promoting national acts visiting the club, as well as provide soundproofing for exterior noise control.

He pauses at the door until he hears a 'click' indicating the attendant has disengaged the auto-lock, then swings the door wide open. The muffled beat sharpens into a driving, pulsating bassline. Rotating stage lighting crisscrosses the walls and ceiling, occasionally passing by us and illuminating the interior entranceway.

We enter to see a main stage located directly in front of us with two attractive topless women slithering over one another under a working mobile stage shower. Mötley Crüe rocks *Girls, Girls, Girls* in the background, espousing the virtues of the many strip clubs they've visited across the United States. The two performers display their affections for each another while intermittent jets of water spray over them like a rogue phallus. It triggers both to react in exaggerated ecstasy with every blast, and jacks up the half-dozen or so men gathered around the stage.

Enzo bypasses the main stage for a smaller, more intimate stage on the opposite end of the building. Two men sit with their backs to us facing one extremely attractive young lady performing exclusively for them.

"Jimmy," Enzo says, sitting down next to the guy on the right. "This is Jon; Sabrina's boy."

I sit on Enzo's opposite side, so he's situated between Jimmy and me. The guy on the far side of Jimmy gets up and leaves immediately with no interaction among us.

"Hey, Jon. Good to meet ya. I heard a lot about ya."

Now, where Enzo has lost or suppressed his Rhode Island accent, Jimmy more than makes up for it. He's a little guy, wearing jeans and a tucked in royal-blue flannel shirt. He's tidy, with clean cut brown hair streaked with a few lines of gray.

Enzo continues his introductions. "Jon, this is Jimmy O'Brien. My old friend I told you about."

"Hey, Jimmy."

Jimmy has a stack of bills in front of him, occasionally tossing them into the stage pit absentmindedly. The performer smoothly sweeps them up without breaking stride in her routine. I planned to follow his lead, but she has another idea. She plops down on the elevated stage, so her high-heeled chunk boots rest on my thighs and her boobs are at my eye level.

"Hi!" She chirps energetically. "I haven't seen you here. What's your name?"

I look at Enzo. He's distracted with Jimmy and seemingly unaware of my new friend. What the hell. I'll go along with it for a while.

"Jon. What's yours?"

She extends her hand. "Meridian. Nice to meet you, Jon."

"Meridian … unusual name."

"I know, right?" She rolls her eyes, acknowledging the silliness of her stage name. Her self-deprecation is somewhat endearing.

She leans in, squeezing her boobs together in the universal stripper signal to place money between them. I procure a few bills and dutifully comply.

"Thank you." She smiles and sweeps the bills out and onto the stage pit.

Meridian resumes dancing and I resume contributing funds until the song ends. She promptly glides over to me and reclaims her sitting spot. Enzo's still busy with Jimmy.

"My name's Pamela. I go by Pammy." She offers unsolicited.

"Pammy. That's nice. Why did you tell me?"

"I don't know. You seem nice and you don't usually come to strip clubs. I can tell."

"Yup. You're right. So, what do you do when you're not stri … uh, when you're not here?"

"It's okay." She smiles. "I know what I do. And I make a boatload of money at it. Most of it tax free."

Me too. I think to myself.

She soldiers on. "Anyway, I'm a student at Providence College, believe it or not."

"I don't doubt you." I reply, though I don't really care, either.

"Well, this is the last song on my shift."

I respond by pinching off several more bills from the diminishing stack which she boob-squeezes from me and then stands up.

"Bye, Jon. Nice to meet you."

"Same here."

§

"Meridian's fuckin' hot, right?" Jimmy blurts after she exits the stage, and I laugh a little at his pronunciation. When he curses, it sounds more like 'fah-kin.' "She's my personal entertainer when she's here."

"Cool." I reply, half-wondering what he means by 'personal entertainer.' I wouldn't have to wait long to find out.

"Whenever she's here, she always dances at my stage. Nobody else's." He says proudly.

Enzo cuts in. "Jimmy and I have been talking. There isn't much more for us to discuss here. We need to go to the credit union and connect with the bank security officer."

"Good by me." I respond.

"First, we need to spend down the rest of those bills." He says, eyeballing the remaining cash. "Doesn't look like many left."

Pammy's replacement drifts onto the stage to the smooth sound of Kendrick Lamar warning us about being a sinner in *Bitch, Don't Kill My Vibe*. The song's title fits her personality. She's mechanical and detached, the antithesis of stripper protocol, and dreadfully disappointing.

She moves in, rapidly vacuuming up a number of bills, causing me to slow her roll. I shift the bills into my lap, spurring her to get down on her knees in front of me for the customary boob bill-squeeze. I decide to make her work marginally harder for it. Placing a bill against her chest, I lazily sweep back and forth as if holding a dust mop to clean cobwebs from a ceiling corner. After a few revolutions around her boobs, I release the two-dollar bill. Unfortunately, an edge of this crisp, stiff bill catches the top of her nipple and slices a half-centimeter long paper cut along its length.

"Ow, you fuckin' asshole!" She squeals, quickly standing and pressing the palm of her hand against her breast.

Enzo and Jimmy look at me like, *what the fuck?*

"I think she just got a paper cut." I surmise.

"Jesus Christ." Enzo responds.

After a minute or two, behind me I hear, "Excuse me, sir."

I turn to face a three hundred-pound Hardo bouncer.

Jimmy cuts in. "We got it covered, Glen. We're leavin'."

8

I didn't exactly get kicked out of the strip club, but it wasn't an entirely voluntary exit, either. Whatever. I don't care. I didn't want to be there, anyway. I just want to meet the credit union lady, get the information, and head back to Maine.

"A paper cut on her nipple?!" Enzo squawks in disbelief. "How in the hell does that happen?"

"I don't know. It's not like I meant for it to happen. I was basically sliding her the cash and I caught an edge, I guess." I respond sheepishly.

Enzo waves a dismissive hand. "Screw it. Forget about it. Don't be concerned."

I pretty much have forgotten about it, and I'm not concerned in the least. We follow closely behind Jimmy in Enzo's Cadillac heading to the credit union. Jimmy's driving a black Ford F-150 truck. It looks like he's customized it a little; it sits up higher than normal and has chromed rims, but nothing too extreme.

"What's the name of the credit union, anyway?" I ask.

"Equinox. Equinox Federal Credit Union, I think."

"Why is Jimmy leading us? What does Equinox have to do with him?"

"The credit union lady is his wife, Lorraine. They're married. That's how I met her, though I don't know her very well. Jimmy likes to keep his personal life private and separate from his work life."

"His wife? Were you planning on telling me at some point?"

"I just did." He replies gruffly.

"Hold up a second." I stop for a moment to gather my thoughts. "Does Jimmy know you're doing anything illegal? Is Jimmy doing anything illegal?"

"No. Jimmy knows my past; he has a similar one, but now we're straight. He knows I only need to get through this old money."

I stare at Enzo but say nothing.

He looks at me forthrightly. "Jimmy isn't doing anything illegal that I know of, and he's doing me a favor in helping to clean the cash. That's it."

He punctuates 'that's it' with a pronounced head bob to indicate it's the end of the discussion for him. It's just as well; we arrive at the credit union operations center entrance and pull into the parking lot. If this goes anything like our morning, we ought to be in for an interesting afternoon.

§

We enter through a side door after Jimmy successfully scans a key fob over a security pad. Lorraine must have provided the device to him, though I can't imagine that's an accepted credit union practice. The door leads to an employee kitchen and breakroom complete with soda and snack vending machines. Tables and chairs fill the interior and tall, heavy cardboard recycle bins lined with clear plastic trash bags set flush against the far wall; one marked 'trash,' the other 'cans and bottles.' It's somewhat reminiscent of a high school cafeteria.

Jimmy walks toward a very large woman seated alone at a center table. There's no one else in the room. On a Sunday, there's likely no one else in the building. As he draws near, she stands up and they proceed to embrace. I can't help but watch the logistics of the hug – he cannot reach his arms around her girth in any meaningful manner, nor can she reciprocate. They're roughly the same height, but polar opposites in body type.

"Jon, this is my wife, Lorraine. She's the credit union's secrecy and security officer. Lorraine, you remember Enzo, my old buddy from the neighborhood. Jon's his boy."

I opt not to correct him on his inaccurate lineage reference.

"Nice to see you again." Enzo says, extending his hand to greet her. I follow suit, greeting her as well.

"Hi guys. It's good to see ya. Let's get outta here and go to a conference room." She brashly directs, wasting no time.

As we exit the breakroom with Lorraine and Jimmy leading the way, I whisper to Enzo. "You really don't know her well, huh? I thought you were exaggerating."

He doesn't acknowledge my question or statement, and I understand his unspoken message of waiting until later to discuss.

We enter a small, windowless conference room where Lorraine takes charge. She's clearly the boss of the two. "Alright, this is what I know. You have some cash you want to blow through Jimmy's ATMs." She addresses Enzo as she begins to speak, then looks to Jimmy to confirm. He nods back in agreement.

"You," She turns to me. "You're gonna oversee our next audit engagement in case my cover-up don't work and I need auditors to look the other way." She pauses. "Now, tell me what I don't know."

Enzo speaks first. "I think you got it. Not much more to it than that."

"How 'bout you?" She snaps, scrutinizing me.

"Nothing from me. I have a question, though."

She waits for me to ask it.

"How does this all work?"

"What do you mean?" At this moment, Lorraine isn't a happy woman.

"Your role. How do you fit in to all of this?"

She glares at Enzo, then to Jimmy, and then back to me. "You ain't never done a credit union audit?" She blusters.

"Nope. First one."

Enzo cuts in. "Don't worry about it. He's got guys that can handle it."

Lorraine fidgets while wedged into her unforgiving, too-narrow conference chair and sighs audibly. "For fuck's sake. Pay attention. This is how it works. When banks and credit unions deal with businesses that handle a lotta cash, we got software that analyzes people's behavior and what they do with the cash. I try to catch people doin' illegal stuff and I gotta report 'em. Sometimes the software has me report 'em, and sometimes I do it on my own."

She continues. "We gotta file SARs, or suspicious activity reports on people who we think may be trying to launder money. It goes to police and FBI and wherever else. We don't worry about it after we file it. It's out of our hands. I'm gonna make sure any time your guys's name pops up, the SARs disappear."

Aside from her butchering the King's English, I like the sound of that.

"So, you don't have interaction with the external auditors? My people? It sounds like as long as you intercept or prevent a SAR from generating, everything in the audit should go smoothly."

"Yeah, exactly. I shouldn't hafta deal with outside auditors unless they find fraud in the audit. You're the insurance policy on anything that slips through me. You're gonna deal with our CFO and a supervisory committee. You report to them. I'll be around, but you and me? We don't talk, really."

Thank God for that. "Alright, so I prepare an engagement letter to conduct an audit and give it to who? You? The CFO?"

"You get the letter done and over to me. I'll get it to the CFO and signed. Meantime, get ready to do an audit."

"What are you getting out of this?" I ask her.

"Don't matter to you. Ask your dad."

9

"Fucking weird-ass people. Why do they have to be so damn creepy?" I wonder out loud as Enzo and I thankfully maneuver our way out of Rhode Island and head back to Maine.

"What are you talking about? These guys are helping us out."

"What am I talking about? One guy's in a strip club on a Sunday morning and has his own private dancer. Hello … strip club much? And his double-trouble plumpkin wife runs a credit union scam. Don't tell me she's not covering up for something Jimmy's doing, either. She's not doing this out of the kindness of her overworked heart."

"No, she's not. She's doing it for ten thousand cash every month until we don't need them anymore."

"Well, there you go. Now that makes some sense." It also made sense to Bob when he started pocketing a monthly stipend from Enzo as well. Look where that got him.

Enzo appeals to my sensible side. "Besides, what do you care? It sounds like you can bring somebody on to do your audit completely legit and pocket some easy cash, and without any risk of interaction or overlap with Lorraine."

I consider this for a moment. "True. It's a low-risk proposition for me and I don't see anybody getting hurt on this. We're not stealing anything from anyone."

"Nope. Only cleaning cash."

§

When Enzo and I stop for lunch on our way back, I text Alison some general points from today, but nothing specific. Enzo sits across the table from me within snooping distance and I don't want to risk him trying to color my impressions of how the day went. I mention the strip club, but leave out details of my new friend, Pammy, nor do I mention my unintentional nipple assault. I finish with a description of the 'Lorraine Experience' and that I'm comfortable we play a minor role in helping Enzo clean his money. Ours too, I suppose.

"You're eating a salad." I comment while stashing my phone.

"Yeah. You got a problem with that?" He good-naturedly challenges.

"Heck, no. Lots of women like salads." I tease.

"You dick." He laughs. "Not all women, though. We met one today who hasn't seen a salad in a long time."

"No doubt. Hey, that reminds me. You really hadn't seen much of Lorraine before today. I figured you were yanking my chain."

"Nope. I can count on one hand the number of times I've run into her."

I'm starving, so I opt not to press the matter further, and dig into my lunch. I ordered buffalo chicken wings, and the hot sauce instantaneously causes my nose to run. "I'd like to hear some more about Jimmy." I ask while wiping my sauced-up hands on a napkin.

"What do you want to know?"

"Your timeline. How long have you known him? Where'd you guys meet?"

"Man. I've known Jimmy since seventh grade." He reminisces. "We went to different elementary schools in the city, but they all dumped into the same junior high school in seventh grade. Like everybody else, they grouped us in a lot of the same classes."

I let him continue uninterrupted.

"We had the same background, you know, a tough upbringing. I used to hang out at Jimmy's house all the time. I liked his old man. He was hard, but he protected his own. He was into bookmaking, loansharking, stuff like that; but he was a small-time player. Nothing too big, and Jimmy and I got to ride with him sometimes."

Enzo briefly pauses his story. He stares intently at the table, reliving a past experience. Eventually, he starts up again. "When we were in eleventh grade, his old man was found in his doughnut shop murdered a day after Superbowl Sunday. Shot in the head execution-style. No robbery. Nothing. Nobody really knew why, but we knew it had to do with squelching on a bet or something like that."

I know I need to tread lightly here, but I have to ask the question. "Is that how you got into … into the stuff you used to do?"

"Yeah. Sort of." His eyes penetrate into me. "It was a training ground, for sure – but not right away. I kicked around with Jimmy until we were about twenty, then I felt like I had to get my act together. I went to community college and did okay, then worked some low-pay, odd jobs over the next couple of years. I lost touch with Jimmy during that time. I thought I needed to leave the old life behind for a fresh start, but I was wrong. So, I went back and reconnected with Jimmy, and by then, he had gotten married to Lorraine. I never saw her much; only a few times. She worked a lot and didn't like anybody Jimmy hung out with."

The mood in the room takes an icy turn, and I'm not comfortable pressing him any further on it. I focus on finishing my lunch.

When my plate resembles a massive boneyard, Enzo asks, "You ready to get out of here?"

"Yeah, but I need to wash the buffalo sauce off my hands first. I'll be right out."

I head to the men's room to pee and wash up. After I finish my business, and just as I exit, I spot Enzo wrapping up a call and disconnecting his cellphone.

"Who you talking to?" I ask as I get back.

Enzo gets up from the table. "One of my guys who helps me out with the ATMs. I need to begin a restock through my network. That's where I'm headed after I drop you off."

"Got it. Alright, let's hit the road."

The ride's easygoing and low key, getting us back to the apartment in decent time. We split up around six o'clock with Enzo heading south and with an understanding to connect in a few days after I get my engagement paperwork done for the audit and he deals with his ATMs.

I climb the stairs to the fourth-floor landing, making noise unlocking and cracking open the apartment door so as not to startle Alison. I had sent a text a few minutes prior to arriving, giving her a heads-up.

The safety doorstop allows for a two-inch gap, and I hear Alison hustling over to release it.

"Hey, babe!" I greet her eagerly as the door swings open.

"You're back!" She wraps her arms around me for a hug. "I've been waiting here all day for the expanded report!"

"Yeah, I didn't want to get into a full-on texting conversation with Enzo looking over my shoulder."

She's thoroughly excited. "I get it. So now fill me in!"

"Well, here's the low down. If we can get the right audit staff, we should be outside any association with Enzo's operation."

I explain to her our audit responsibilities (of which she is familiar with), Lorraine's involvement, and Jimmy's connection to the credit union.

Alison cuts in. "We need Kelly. He knows this stuff, and as long as Lorraine is good at what she does and he doesn't detect any fraud, I agree we'll be good to go."

"Right, we need him. But I don't think we should fill him in on Enzo."

"Totally agree. He shouldn't even run into him. How Enzo was able to score state licenses to operate ATMs, I'll never figure out." She digresses.

"I know, right? He most likely uses his real name on the licenses for the first time in his life. I bet his felonies are under assumed names." I laugh.

Alison giggles along with me as I go over next steps with the audit engagement letter, fee quotes, timing, and the like. Also, I tell her I'll contact Kelly to see where his head's at from a work standpoint.

"Sounds like a plan." She says, then changes the subject. "Now, let me tell you about my day with Darcy."

I don't respond, but instead walk to the fridge for a beer, leaving the door open for her to begin her story.

"She did." Alison says plainly.

"She did … what?" I ask as I pop the top on a cold PBR, and then I quickly understand. "No way! She told you?"

"She absolutely did! A few times, actually … slept with him, that is, not told me a few times."

"Damn, that's cold. Does she feel bad about it?"

"Um … no … she didn't so much feel bad about sleeping with a friend's dad, but she did feel bad about messing up the family."

"Well, that's good, I guess. Did you have to ask her?"

"Ultimately yes, but we were dancing around the topic, so I felt like it was okay for me to ask."

"That's crazy. How do you feel about it?"

"Fine. It was a long time ago. We're all different people now."

"That's for sure." I take a slug from my beer. "Hey, I'm getting hungry. Head over to A's?"

"Exactly what I was thinking. Why don't you call Kelly and see if he wants to meet us there? We can try to get him on board sooner rather than later. I think I have his number from our old office group text."

"Great idea."

10

I did finally get in touch with Kelly. It was good to reconnect, if only by text. I hadn't seen nor heard from him in a long time. We were in the same draft class at Harding-Williams, but he went directly into the financial services audit track and I went into corporate, so our paths didn't cross very often in a work capacity.

Alison and I sit at a high-top table at A's having drinks while we wait for him to arrive. I'm situated strategically as Enzo would – back to the wall with my eyes on the door so as not to miss him when he arrives. We got here fairly late, so the place is mostly cleaned out on a Sunday night. I'm actually relieved. I've had enough unanticipated stimulation for one day.

"What time did you say he was coming?" Alison asks.

"Eight-thirty. He had something going on earlier."

"It's after eight-thirty now."

She's eyeballing me as if to convey, *do something*, but I'm not taking the bait. Instead, I opt to take a slow pull from my beer and let the moment pass. Thankfully, the tension doesn't last long; Kelly appears in the front atrium and barrels through the inside door.

He's still rail thin, that hasn't changed, but he's adopted a new hair style. He's swapped out a grungy shoulder-length cut; flat with fine strands that often appeared greasy, for an awesomely messy, faux-hawk-inspired look. Undercut and edged on the sides and back, it has a stylish flow on top giving the appearance his hair was tossed around by waves from the sea. It's a compelling look – one I wasn't expecting.

Nor did Alison, evidently. "Oh, wow! Kelly Cookson, look at you!" Her voice rises considerably as we get up from our table to greet him. "You look fantastic! I love your hair!"

"Seriously dude, solid effort." I add, giving him a bro hug after Alison steps back.

"Thanks. I appreciate that. How you guys doing? Man, it's been a while."

"We're great!" Alison responds, then swirls her arm in a circular motion to draw attention back to his ensemble. "And I love that jacket. You've done a whole makeover thing. Here, sit down."

She gestures to the chair next to me and Kelly obliges. Quickly our server is over and asking what he would like to drink.

"What are you having?" He asks, pointing to my beer.

"PBR draft."

"Perfect. I'll roll with that, thanks. A tall one." He clarifies.

Our server leaves and Kelly refocuses on us.

"Yeah, I needed a change from the Kid Rock look. I figured this would work."

"You figured right! I love it!" Alison gushes.

I may need to re-evaluate my own pedestrian haircut. I feel a stab of jealousy beholding Alison's over the top adulation. Kelly seems unfazed with the compliments, though. I respect that.

"So, what have you guys been up to? I heard you were a couple now and you started your own practice. Crazy how things work out." He repositions in his seat.

"Yes, and we have Sharon!" I blurt out. I'm not sure why that's so exciting to me, but it is. Sharon was a stalwart executive administrator for Harding-Williams. "She could work anywhere, but she chose us!"

"That's pretty cool. Tell her I said 'Hi.' "

Alison responds first. "Definitely, we will. Tell us what you're up to these days? Where are you working?"

"Well, that's part of my reasoning for the new 'do and clothes. I was just with a potential client. I'm running my own small bookkeeping and software training business."

"Really?" I reply.

"Yeah. There wasn't much out there for me after Harding-Williams went down. Too many out of work auditors and tax people floating around to compete with. I didn't press too hard, anyway. I figured I'd do my own thing."

"We have a similar story." Alison says.

Hardly. I can't imagine Kelly was dodging homegrown terrorist arms dealers, fighting for his life, and dumping bodies in the bay since the firm shut down, but whatever.

She continues. "We decided to start a small practice, as you already know, to work for ourselves. We're liking it much better."

Yes. To work for ourselves laundering money. Don't forget that detail. Christ … I need to squash my inner sarcasm before it develops into something perceptible to others around me.

"Are you super busy?" Alison asks Kelly, breaking me out of my funk.

"With work? Eh, not really. Enough to pay the bills I guess, but I've only just started."

Alison looks at me, and I understand she wants me to pick up where she has left off.

"Good move working for yourself. It's a lot of upfront effort, but it's worth it."

"No doubt. Maybe we could connect on some client referrals. I can pass along bookkeeping clients for tax and audit work, and maybe you could send some clients needing bookkeeping and software training my way."

"Absolutely." I respond while the server brings Kelly his beer, and Alison and I reorder. "We asked you to come by tonight because we want to see if you have any availability to help us with an audit client … to work an engagement with us."

Kelly looks to me then Alison. "As an employee?"

"Yeah." I reply. "I think that's how it would have to be. You'd need to operate under our firm's state license." Alison nods her head in agreement. "But it wouldn't stop you from doing your gig." I add.

"Right. Sure. I understand. Uh, tell me more about what you'd want me to do."

We spend the better part of two hours first discussing the credit union client, being very careful to only touch on matters relevant to the engagement. Then we backtrack in time to when we began J. K. Williams through to the present day. He seems engaged and energized by the direction of the conversation. Honestly, with Kelly not knowing the true backdrop of the audit engagement, it doesn't take long to go through the deal. It's pretty straightforward. What proves tricky is explaining to him how we came about the client referral and won the bid with absolutely no one in the firm experienced in bank auditing.

"How'd you score a credit union client, in Rhode Island no less, as a new firm with no banking experience?" Kelly asks.

I'm ready for him. "I know, right? I have a relative who works there." I lie. "She's a second cousin or maybe a cousin twice-removed on my mom's side, I don't know, I could never figure that out. She said there wouldn't be a problem with it. The regulators for the credit unions aren't as stringent as the FDIC according to her."

"Credit unions like to think so. I haven't met one yet that didn't think the National Credit Union Association was weaker than the FDIC." Kelly argues.

This sends a chill down my back. And not in a good way. Much of this hinges upon no in-depth, outside scrutiny.

"In my experience, they're just different. Not any less effective necessarily. They're still under Congressional oversight."

We have a few more beers while talking about 'what if' scenarios: time commitments, audit duration, engagement fees, and scheduling. Much of it I couldn't answer. I'm winging this to a much higher degree than he's aware of.

"What are you quoting for the fee?" Kelly asks, bringing the conversation down to a more personal level.

"One fifty."

His eyes widen considerably. "What? Really? The most our old firm ever charged for a credit union audit was under a hundred thousand, and that was for a lot more work than what's needed on this."

I avoid answering his pointed question by redirecting the conversation. We'll see if he's as rebel as I think he is.

"I'm willing to pay you half of the fee."

He glances at Alison, who slightly nods her head in a *go for it!* gesture, then looks back at me where a resultant wide smile breaks out on his face.

"So, does this mean you're in?" I ask.

"I'm in." He says. "I'm really in."

Yes, Kelly. Yes, you are.

§

"That was a huge win!" Alison bubbles as we drive back to the apartment.

"Yes, it was. I'm pretty psyched we reeled him in. I'll have to let Enzo know straight away. You know how he gets when he's impatient for a resolution."

"Sure do. Connect with him tomorrow. It can be a good start to your Monday Fun Day!"

"Ha, right. It'll be pretty cool with Kelly, Sharon, you, and me all together in the same office again. It's like we're building a mini-Harding-Williams."

"I could take that two ways. I prefer the pre-Enzo HW best."

"I agree."

11

Monday morning arrives promptly, and I'm up and fueled to go. Kelly's coming in to get the ball rolling on the audit planning process and I'm preparing to call Enzo to fill him in on my progress and recruitment of Kelly.

I reached the office early, not long after seven, to connect with Sharon who routinely beats me into work. I wasn't disappointed with her reaction to my news of Kelly's arrival. She's super excited and it sets her up for a very pleasant morning as we wait for him to come in. Alison and Darcy plan to meet up for lunch; Alison set it up, and I think she has in mind to invite Kelly along with us to connect the two.

I complete a few other minor tasks, and now it's time to scratch Enzo off my to-do list. I pull out my cellphone and call him. He answers before the first ring finishes.

"Enzo. It's Jon. We're ready to go." I crow proudly.

"You got your guy?"

"Sure do. He's starting this morning. He's coming in to get the pre-planning work underway."

"That's great news, Jon. What's his understanding of the project?"

I appreciate the underlying subtext of the question – he'd like to know how much I've told him about what's going on with our side business.

"Strictly the audit engagement. Completely straightforward."

I try to answer Enzo as I imagine he would answer me. Succinct, to the point, and offering nothing more than necessary. He seems to be satisfied.

"Excellent. What's the timing on your end looking like?"

"For the whole audit? Tough to say, but we'll start with today's planning process. Then we'll need to connect with Lorraine and begin the information dump. We'll see her in person sooner rather than later for introductions to the team – well, Kelly anyway, and then conduct the engagement interview. I don't know how long the process will take."

"I'm not worried how long it will take as long as we have the ball rolling."

"Roger that. Hey, where are you, anyway?"

"Massachusetts. I'm on the road and headed over to the Lowell area."

"Cool. I'll contact Lorraine today and suggest we come down tomorrow. You around?"

"Yeah, actually. I'll get back to Providence tonight. Let's connect when you make it down."

"Perfect." I disconnect the call without waiting for a response from him. No disrespect meant – it's standard issue between us that we cut the call when we're finished with no ceremony or fanfare.

It's not long before Kelly arrives, and I can't help but smile as I watch him reconnect with Sharon. As expected, she can't hold back from shedding tears. I never told her about his radical style makeover, so it's funny to see her reaction as he strides through the door. She didn't recognize him at first and her look of astonishment as she figured it out amuses both of us.

We spend the next half hour chatting about our former firm and what we've all been up to. This is old news for Kelly and me as we re-hashed it all last night, but allows for Sharon to reconcile her past experience with how events unfolded following the bombing of Harding-Williams.

"It's so good to see you, Kelly!" Sharon bubbles, giving him a last meaningful hug before he and I head over to his new office.

"Thank you, Sharon. I'm glad to be here."

It's a cute scene; Sharon hugs Kelly, and he stands still with his arms straight to his side because Sharon never gives him the opportunity to hug back. She wraps her arms around him, entrapping his arms like a mother hugging her child before sending him off on the bus ride to elementary school.

As we break away and go to Kelly's office, he looks at me and we exchange smiles to communicate, *well, that just happened!*

"Sharon hasn't changed a bit." He laughs.

"Nope. Not one bit."

Kelly's anxious to dive right in as soon as we get to his space. "Alright. Let's get started. What's the plan?"

"It's probably going to be a little like hurry up and wait. There isn't a whole lot to do today. As I said at A's, tomorrow we'll head down to Providence and meet up with Lorraine, the credit union's secrecy and security officer. She's the one who's a distant relative of mine; though to be clear, we really don't acknowledge being related. Could be seen as a conflict of interest."

"I get it."

"You won't need to spend any meaningful time with Lorraine after that. We'll meet with their internal audit liaison and hopefully some members of the audit committee. Then we'll jump right into testing and start compiling workpapers."

"Sounds good. But I am going to want to meet with Lorraine as well, to discuss required audit inquiries and such relative to fraud prevention and control."

"I understand. I can take on that role with Lorraine. I'll be down there with you to help on the engagement." I need to curtail Kelly's involvement with Lorraine as much as possible.

"Sounds good."

"In the meantime, there's not much to do for audit prep. Alison's meeting me for lunch and bringing her friend Darcy, too. They went to high school together. I just met her, but she seems nice and she's cute. You in?"

"Is she single?"

"Yeah, she's freshly divorced. She moved back here from Miami a month or so ago."

"Definitely in."

§

"What do you do for work?" Kelly casually asks Darcy.

We're sitting in a booth, boys on one side and girls on the other, in a semi-deserted pub down on the waterfront. We could pass for high schoolers out on a double date, or at least that's how I feel.

"I'm a pharmacist." Darcy answers.

Kelly tries to be funny. "You're a drug dealer. Sweet."

"Never heard that one before." She says dryly, but with a smile on her face.

Damn, Darcy looks solid when she's made up. She's ditched the baseball hat and her long, dirty blond hair gives her a somewhat untamed look. Kelly's clearly into her, and I don't blame him. She's wearing jeans and a tight-knit black top fused to her body.

"Ya, I deal drugs … but only the legal kind." She teases. "Not that off the street garbage you're used to."

I catch the wink Darcy throws out at him. I think they're going to get along just fine.

"Fair enough." He counters. "I'll be in touch when I'm in need."

Kelly's double meaning wasn't lost on her and their risqué exchange slowly develops into a one-on-one conversation between the two of them.

Alison provides us both a temporary reprieve from our voyeuristic watch party by initiating a conversation with me; not that Darcy or Kelly are paying any attention to us, anyway. "Jon, come with me to the bathroom."

"I prepped her for Kelly. That's why she's dressed up." Alison whispers to me when we're out of earshot.

"She looks great." I reply. "They're clearly into each other."

"I know, right? Hey, I asked you over here because I have an idea. I want to go with you and Kelly to Providence tomorrow, and can we invite Darcy? I think she's into him."

I think about this for a moment, walking through the timeline of our day at the credit union in my mind. "I don't see why not. We do need to get some work done, but we should have some rec-time in the afternoon and evening. It's up to them. It's all good by me."

She claps her hands together excitedly. "Yay! That's awesome! Okay, wait here for me to go pee."

As I wait, I can't help but stare out the window toward Enzo's building some two hundred yards away. I can't actually see it; it's tucked around a bend, but it's very close to us. Come to think of it, I don't really know if it's his. I've been operating under that presumption simply because he's the only person I'm aware of associated with it. It causes me to think about all of the blue barrels sunk in the harbor. No doubt there are many more resting on the seabed than those I'm aware of – just Reyes and Osterman.

"Hey! Oh, I'm sorry baby, I didn't mean to jump you."

She jumped me alright. Her loud 'Hey' jolted me from my daytime nightmare and off the carpet an inch or so.

"Are you okay?"

"Yeah … yeah," I trail off. "I was thinking about our happenings in and around Enzo's building. It's right there, out past the gas station." I point through a dirty window guarded by a stack of children's booster seats piled high to its dusty sill.

She draws a deep breath. "Right. It hadn't crossed my mind until you mentioned it."

"Sorry."

"No worries." She says as she starts back to our booth. "Forget about it. Let's go see if Darcy's in for the Providence trip."

Easier said than done. Alison wasn't an active participant. She rode out the storm mostly in Enzo's back office.

"Hey guys," Alison broadcasts as we approach the booth. "We have a great idea if you're interested."

I smile a little at Alison's inclusion of me into her matchmaker plot. Both Darcy and Kelly look to Alison, then me, then back to her.

"I'm planning on going to Rhode Island with Jon and Kelly to-morrow." She directs to Darcy. "What do you think about coming with us? We're going to stay the night."

Kelly's eyebrows rise up on his forehead, but he doesn't otherwise react.

Darcy turns to Kelly. "Is that alright with you?"

"Fine by me." He responds, attempting to dampen down his enthusiasm.

Darcy turns back to Alison. "Sure, why not? I can take a couple of personal days. Lord knows I have enough of them available."

"Awesome!" Alison giggles. "We can figure out hotel room logistics and such when we get there. The boys can shack up together and we can have a 'girls only' room." She says it like a middle schooler teasing the boys at summer camp, and we all laugh at the impression.

What a productive day for Kelly. Generating big bank with J.K. Williams and scoring a hook-up with Darcy. Not a bad way to kick off a work week.

12

"We're on the road. We have about two hours; maybe a little less until we're in town." I say to Enzo through my cell-phone sitting in a cradle mounted to the dash of Danny's Jeep. "Where you at … um … or where you going to be?"

"I'm around. Finishing up some restocks. Call me when you get into the city. I'll meet you."

"Perfect." I stretch my arm out to disconnect the call, and in one continuous smooth motion, crank the radio volume back up. I'm rolling with a Classic Rock genre for Kelly's (and my) benefit, and it does not disappoint. Lynyrd Skynyrd seduces us with timeless, sage advice of being a *Simple Man*. We both sing obnoxiously:

> *Oh, take your time, don't live too fast*
>
> *Troubles will come, and they will pass*
>
> *You'll find a woman, and you'll find love*
>
> *And don't forget, son, there is a someone up above*

The significance of the song lyrics isn't lost on me.

"Will you turn that down?" Alison whines. "Better still, switch the station."

Kelly and I eyeball each other. Probably a good call to change it. I nod and he laughs a little while reaching for the tuner.

"Pop music? Country? What's your preference?" He asks.

"I don't care, just not that." Alison responds.

Kelly changes over to a Top-Ten Hits format to satisfy them but leaves the volume on low. He turns to face the girls and fires off a question to Darcy. "So where exactly do you work?"

She pauses from looking at her phone. "Remedy Rx. It's a boutique pharmacy on the Eastern Prom. We're a small shop. I've done my thing with the big-box chain stores."

"They're okay with you taking off for two days?" I interject.

"Ya. There's not a lot of walk-in foot traffic. They make their money from online sales and wholesale, mostly. You know, mail order and direct delivery stuff. Makes being there in person less important."

"Cool. Sounds like a good gig." Kelly replies.

"It's not too bad. I'm earning my way into a minority ownership position. I'm thankful for that."

"Let us know if you need some accounting and finance advice." Alison chuckles. "There's enough of us in the car to help out."

The rest of us laugh along with her. After a pause, Darcy reacts. "I'm going to take you up on that, and it may be sooner rather than later with today's quickly changing world of cannabis and CBD-related stuff. Our senior leadership team is handcuffed by discrepancies between regulators and lawmakers. We don't know what we can and can't do."

"Welcome to the world of legal weed. Well, legal for state, but not federally. That's mostly the problem." Kelly opines. "Then you have issues with banks on financing, handling cash, state versus federal law enforcement agencies, and everything else that goes with it. Not to mention the physical security measures you need to take."

Damn, Kelly knows a lot about the marijuana business.

Darcy nods her head. "I get the concerns over security, for sure. Our dispensary is exceptionally safeguarded with the types of drugs we have in stock."

"It won't be like this for much longer. Cannabis is headed the way alcohol did with Prohibition. It's only a matter of time. And frankly, it's long overdue in my view."

Looks like Kelly laid his cards bare on the table. This could be a good thing – he seems game to bend or break rules.

§

We make small talk the rest of the ride by discussing what we're going to do tonight. I suggest checking out an event Enzo told me about.

"Tonight's the seasonal opening night for WaterFire. It's some sort of fire sculpture art show downtown. I guess it floats on the surfaces of rivers throughout Providence. Supposed to have food, music, performers, and stuff like that. I think it's a walking tour."

"That sounds awesome to me." Alison replies.

"Me, too." Darcy agrees.

"Cool." Kelly says. "Let's do it."

"Great. Let me call Enzo and let him know we're close. We'll get lunch, then drop the girls off at the hotel to check in, and we'll head over to Equinox."

I dial him up on speaker, and predictably, he answers on the first ring.

"Yes, sir."

"Yo LoZo, we're close. Five minutes out. What's the plan?"

"Meet me at Ladder 133 … the old fire station converted to a restaurant. It's on the corner of Douglas Street next to the entrance road to the Foxy Lady. I should be there right around then. There's an ATM on my list outside the building." He explains.

I stiffen at his reference to the club. "Got it. See you there."

"Um. What's the Foxy Lady?" Alison presses after I disconnect.

"It's a strip club. I told you about it in the text I sent you when we were on our way back. Enzo's guy hangs out there and when I came down last week, I had to go there with him." I avoid looking at her in my rearview mirror.

"Mhmm." She murmurs disapprovingly.

"I'd like to go some time." Surprisingly, the appeal comes from Darcy.

"Come again?" Kelly stammers, his head swiveling to the back seat.

"Ya. I would." She directs this more to Alison than anyone. "I want to see what the big fascination is."

"Really none." I shrug. "It's kind of sad, actually."

Alison snorts. "Quit while you're ahead, cowboy… and I'm in. I want to see what the big deal about it is, too."

Kelly and I exchange glances. What in the upside-down world of exotic pole dancing is going on here?

"Okay. Let's do it." I mildly taunt, expecting to call their bluff.

"Fine." Alison counters.

Before I can test her resolve any further, I catch sight of Enzo's Cadillac. He's parked about a block from the restaurant, and as we get closer, I spot him kneeling on the sidewalk tending to someone splayed out beneath him.

I quickly park the Jeep behind his Cadillac and beeline it toward him.

"What's going on?" I ask quietly after lightly tapping his shoulder. "Is this guy dead?"

"I'm not entirely sure, but we may have an issue. I think I feel a pulse on him, but I'm no doctor."

"What? C'mon. You know this guy?"

"Let's get out of here. We can talk inside the restaurant."

In the meantime, everyone else makes it over to Enzo and me. Collectively, we stare at the guy collapsed on the ground. He's a sizeable dude with long, stringy brown hair; probably twenty-five to thirty years old. Actually, he looks a lot like a fat version of Kelly prior to his recent miracle makeover. His eyes present pinpoint pupils and unnaturally protrude from the sockets.

"Ugh. Is that throw up?" Alison asks.

"Ya. I think it is … or he's foaming at the mouth. Christ, his lips are blue." Darcy adds.

Alison runs her hands through her hair in exasperation. "What do we do?"

"I've already called rescue. Nothing else for us to do. Let's get out of here. Jon," Enzo directs, while reaching for the dude's shirtsleeve. "Grab his leg and let's turn him on his side so he doesn't choke out."

What the fuck. I do as instructed, then throw an impatient hand up to signal to everyone to follow us into the restaurant. After we enter, I aggressively break away from Enzo to hit the men's room. I go slowly to wait for the rest of the group to catch up and we walk to the bathrooms together.

"What's going on?" Alison shudders, clearly shaken up.

"I don't know, but I think it has something to do with Enzo. He said he would talk to us inside."

She breathes a deep sigh. "Nothing's ever easy with him."

Kelly and I finish our business and wait for the girls to exit the ladies' room. The four of us walk into the main dining room together and spot Enzo at a high top, his back to the wall facing the front window. We take seats and hurriedly grab menus, more so to hide behind them and muffle our conversation than to read.

"So, what's going on out there?" I ask, straining to look through the etched-glass front window and gain an unobstructed view. A crowd has assembled, and emergency vehicles have arrived on scene.

"That guy out there," Enzo gestures. "I think he overdosed. He was finishing with the ATM."

We pause to order drinks, then wait for our server to leave.

"Who is it?" I ask.

"I don't know. I think he's one of Jimmy's guys. We must have gotten our signals crossed. He was getting ready to leave when I got here so I was talking to him one minute about who was supposed to restock this ATM – Jimmy's ATM. He started looking funny and collapsed."

"How do you know he OD'd?" Alison interjects.

"Before he dropped, he complained about feeling dizzy and he said he may have mishandled some drugs … fentanyl, I think he said, and that he didn't feel well."

I process Enzo's narrative for a moment. "He said he 'mishandled' some drugs? He didn't say he took the drugs, like, with a needle or snorting?"

"Yeah, and I saw an open package of what looked like dope on the sidewalk. Before he collapsed, he asked me to pick it up and hide it. No way was I touching it. It's underneath him. He passed out on top of it."

"I've seen this before. It's not a 'mishandling.' " Darcy scoffs. "He had to have ingested the drugs."

We collectively stare at her, waiting for her to go on.

"Especially if it's fentanyl. Fentanyl is an incredibly powerful opioid; much higher concentration than heroin and is used as a cut additive to heroin and cocaine. Some people argue you can overdose simply by contact if the concentration is high enough. I've heard of cops contending this happened to them on drug busts."

"Who are you?" Enzo snaps impatiently.

"Darcy." She replies timidly.

I interrupt. "Enzo, this is Darcy, a friend of ours who rode down with us. She's a pharmacist and it sounds like she knows her business."

This placates Enzo momentarily. Enough so that Darcy can continue.

"He didn't get sick from touching it, I'll guarantee that. You got a guy out there who probably snorted some fentanyl or heroin, or more likely, both. People say they inadvertently got high from casual contact to avoid getting in trouble. It doesn't work. The science doesn't work."

We're interrupted from our discussion by an ambulance leaving the scene with sirens blaring. A smattering of curious observers disburses from the area to carry on with their daily routine, likely ambivalent and uncaring to the unknown man's condition.

Enzo appears resigned to his next move. "I need to call Jimmy. Tell him what happened."

13

Kelly and I dropped the girls off at the hotel for check-in and now we're heading to Equinox FCU. I can't wait to hear Kelly's impression of Lorraine. We have a meeting this afternoon with senior management to go over the audit plan … well … Kelly will go over the audit plan. I'll watch and contribute occasionally to give the impression I know what I'm doing. It'll be an easy afternoon at the outset. We can establish contact, gather information, then be out the door in a reasonable amount of time – and I'll pick up a check for fifty percent of my fee. I'll keep half and give Kelly half. Thirty-seven thousand five hundred dollars will brighten his and my afternoon considerably.

We arrive for our two o'clock meeting right on time and ready to work. The sun shines brilliantly, glinting off cars as we turn into the parking lot, triggering us to adjust our sun visors in sync. I shut the Jeep down and step out while Kelly fishes around in the back seat for his work materials. I take a deep breath of warm, afternoon air to clear my head and steel myself for our meeting.

"You ready, buddy?" I ask.

"Ready. Let's do this."

§

Lorraine doesn't meet us in the lobby, which is a smart move in my view. The finance department meets with us, we exchange pleasantries, and then they lead us to a conference room where Lorraine waits. Kelly gets right into the audit plan with the internal audit liaison, and I leave with Lorraine.

We enter her office, and she heads straight to her desk. "Catch the door." She instructs as she sits down.

She motions for me to take a seat and wastes no time with small talk. "So, what does your guy know about any of this?"

"Nothing. This is a legitimate engagement to him … and it is a legit engagement. We plan on performing a top-level audit."

"How did you explain getting the job?"

"Oh, yeah. By the way, you're a distant cousin of mine. You got me the gig."

"Fair enough. I got it." She lowers her voice considerably, leaning in to minimize the distance between us. "What the hell happened at the ATM today?"

This takes me by surprise. I had momentarily spaced out on the fact Jimmy and Lorraine are married. Enzo must have connected with Jimmy after lunch, and Jimmy updated Lorraine.

"I don't know." I reply truthfully. "I came on the scene as it was happening."

I convey the rest of the details as best I can remember, and she takes a moment to process. "His name's Mike. We call him Fat Mikey. He's one of our guys. He didn't say anything about the ATM?"

Fat Mikey? If he's Fat Mikey, I wonder what they call her. "No. Like I said, he was already passed out when I got there."

"What about Enzo? Mikey didn't say anything about the ATM to Enzo?"

Man, this lady's crazy. Her frizzy, reddish-brown hair undulates slightly in the gentle air flow of her office. She reminds me of the Heat Miser from *The Year Without a Santa Claus* Christmas special.

"Enzo said something about the guy, uh, Mikey feeling like he got sick from touching drugs."

"Did you see any drugs?" Her tone softens noticeably, but she's clearly on edge.

"No, but Enzo did. He said the guy fell on a package."

"Jimmy told me he didn't pick it up." She says this so quietly I barely catch it.

"What's that?"

"Nothing. Forget it."

"How's your guy doing?"

"I don't know yet. Jimmy's checking in on him now."

We spend the remainder of our time actually discussing audit matters. I eventually excuse myself and find Kelly poring over papers in the conference room.

"You're right." He says, looking up from the table.

"About …?"

"Lorraine. A real stunner."

"Oh, right. Personality to match. You almost done here for the day?"

"I'm getting organized right now. We can shoot out in about five minutes. Hey, any chance we can turn this into a three-day trip? I could use another day here."

"It's fine with Alison and me. Only need to check with Darcy. We can see about it at the hotel before we head out to dinner."

§

Alison booked adjoining rooms at the Omni and she and Darcy decided to pre-game our evening with a wine party. The door separating the rooms is swung wide open. My and Kelly's gear sets on each queen bed in one room, and they have their stuff in the other.

"Hello boys," Alison greets us. "Your bags are in one room and ours are in the other. Don't think this is summer camp and you're going to paddle across the lake to our cabin late at night, either." She smiles at me.

Darcy comes into the room holding a glass of wine. "If you're lucky, maybe we'll come over."

I'm sure Kelly would like that.

Darcy continues. "And we got you provisions. What do you say to a twelve-pack of PBR Tall Boys?"

"We go together like cocaine and waffles." I drawl in my best Ricky Bobby voice from *Talladega Nights*. "Hey, any chance we could stay an extra day? It would really help us out." I direct to Darcy.

"Absolutely! I already took an extra day off."

"Cool." I crack a beer and proceed to fill them in on my earlier conversation with Lorraine.

Alison keys in right away on the strangeness of the conversation. "The drug thing bothers me. Her questions seem connected to it."

"That's what I thought, too. I'll check with Enzo to see what he told Jimmy."

"Okay!" Darcy announces, changing the subject. "So … strip club or WaterFire tonight?"

14

We opt for WaterFire tonight and maybe we'll hit the strip club tomorrow. A wave of relief flooded through Alison when she learned we decided on WaterFire. This is a cool setup downtown. Street vendors sell food of all ethnicities while people mill about chatting contentedly. We walk the riverfront, mesmerized by seemingly endless platforms of burning wood floating just above the surfaces of the rivers flowing through Providence. Shadows of the people tending to the fires dance in the flickering light while music from across the globe complements the experience. It's such a good scene – it radiates with a communal, almost spiritual vibe.

Alison reaches for my hand, and I willingly surrender it. "This is so beautiful." She scans the riverfront hypnotically. "I love it."

Kelly and Darcy walk together behind us far enough away such that we can't make out their conversation. They appear to be connecting, much to Alison's delight.

"What do you think they're talking about?" Alison wonders excitedly, sounding like a parent chaperoning a child on a first date.

"No idea. Probably something about the fires, I'm guessing. I doubt it's anything too salacious."

"You don't know Darcy."

I laugh at her response then pause and turn to face them, giving them a minute to catch up. "Where does everyone want to eat? I'm craving me some Jamaican jerk chicken at the truck over there." I propose, pointing to a nearby food truck.

Kelly goes Mediterranean. "I'm feeling a gyro from the Greek truck."

Darcy aligns with me. "I'll go Jamaican."

Alison evens out the choices. "Then I'll go Greek with Kelly."

Good luck, Kelly. Alison's likely to grill you on your interest in Darcy.

As we split up, a text chime chirps on my phone. It's a message from Enzo:

I text back while walking with Darcy:

Shit. I hope Alison's down with it, I already played my hand.

"Wish me luck." I say to Darcy.

"Why? Who was that?"

"Enzo. He's here. He wants to meet up."

We arrive at the truck and take our place in line. This food truck is super popular; the line fills in behind us rapidly. Fortunately, it moves equally as fast, and we advance to the order window before we know it.

I order first. "One jerk chicken wrap with lemon rice, please."

"Make it two, please." Darcy requests.

I pay the bill and we drift to a cluster of nearby picnic tables to sit.

"Wow. This is really good." Darcy mumbles with a mouthful of food.

I see Alison and Kelly looking for us as they approach, so I give them a wave. "Hey babe. Enzo's here. He's going to stop by in a minute."

"Oh, okay."

Hmm. She let me off easy. I expected her to sling some sort of negative comment.

"I think I see him." Kelly motions to a group of nearby people. "Is that him?"

I spot him right away. "Yup. That's him."

Enzo comes into view wearing his typical white Fila track suit, replete with dangling gold chains.

"LoZo," I call out. "Yo. Over here."

He sees us and waves, slightly course correcting his route. "Hey everyone."

Alison gives him a big hug. "Enzo! This is really awesome!"

"Yeah, WaterFire's pretty cool. I thought you'd like it."

"What are you up to?" I ask him.

"Nothing much. I was around and thought I'd drop by."

"Did you connect with Jimmy? After lunch today? I saw Lorraine earlier at the credit union. She was grilling me on what happened."

"What did you tell her?"

Classic annoying Enzo. Answers my question with a question.

"Pretty much exactly what happened. We came onto a guy, who she called Fat Mikey by the way, and he passed out on the sidewalk after complaining about touching drugs."

"How did she react to that?"

"I don't know ... concerned. She said Jimmy was out looking for him. Did they find him?"

"Not yet, last I heard. I talked to Jimmy after lunch and told him what happened. He was worried about it."

The conversation morphs into a one-on-one between Enzo and me. The others lose interest and drift into their own conversation. Probably better this way; I'm losing interest, too.

"Well, it's not our problem." I say matter-of-factly.

"Nope. It's not. It's strange, though."

Enzo's contention 'it's strange' is meaningful, but his body language suggests it's not overly concerning to him. That's good enough for me not to press further.

The five of us spend the rest of the evening wandering the waterfront, admiring the magnificent fire sculptures lining our walking tour and enjoying each other's company.

§

"I missed sleeping with you last night." I kiss Alison's forehead as we leave our hotel rooms and walk to the breakfast buffet.

"Aww, me too. I was so tired. I crashed hard when we got back."

"We didn't stay up, either. It's good though, Kelly and I need to get a lot done at Equinox today."

"We have a busy day, too … at the spa!" She flashes a thousand-watt smile.

I softly spank her bottom. "Tough day. Meanwhile, we'll slave away working all day." I give her my best hang-dog look.

We enter the buffet excitedly, looking like the lead characters from the *Wizard of Oz* arriving in Emerald City. "Oh please," She argues. "You're not doing jackshit today."

I can't disagree with her. "You're right." I smile and begin constructing my first plate.

After we sit, we have a short roundtable on timing for the day. "We'll be done by what, one o'clock, Kelly?"

"Sounds about right, give or take."

"Perfect. We should be done by then, too." Alison replies.

"Cool, we can meet up for lunch!" I propose with a mouthful of food.

Alison doesn't let it slide. "Jon, we've talked about this. Chew first, please."

"Got it." I say, swallowing hard. "And after lunch? Maybe we'll all take a nice rest and get ready for tonight!"

§

Back-office employees escort us to the conference room where Kelly picks up where he left off. I spend my time looking at sports scores on my phone and avoiding Lorraine. After a while, Kelly comes up for air from his pile of papers.

"Do you know what SARs are?"

I feel an instant tightening in my chest. "I've heard of them – suspicious actions, or something like that?" I respond, intentionally off on my accuracy.

"Right. Suspicious activity reports. Generated by software analyzing human behaviors and transactions. It catches money laundering, check kiting ... stuff like that. Not foolproof, but a strong tool."

"What about it? Are you looking at some?"

"Yeah. Check this one out. It says, 'Suspicious source of funds; marijuana or marijuana-related business.' What a joke these still come through."

I feel a wave of relief filter through me. "I agree. There's bigger fish to fry out there." Lord knows, I may be one of them.

"Oh, that reminds me. I need to ask Lorraine the standard fraud question next time I see her. Don't let me forget."

Well, there goes my plan of avoiding Lorraine.

§

After a couple of hours playing around on my phone, I run out of things to do. I'm ready to beat feet out of here and get some lunch.

"How much more time do you need?" I ask.

"Not much. Stage one of fieldwork's virtually complete. I can pack up soon and take this all back to Portland to work on. Only need to have a conversation with Lorraine."

"Right. Fraud question." I change the topic. "So, what do you think about the strip club tonight? Should we really push it?"

Kelly smiles while gathering up his papers and shutting down his laptop. "Yeah, why not? If they chicken out, they chicken out. Nothing's lost."

"Good point. I'll send Alison a text to make sure they're still in."

Before we finish up at the conference room table, Lorraine bustles through the door, saving us a trip.

"Just the person we need to see." Kelly whispers a touch louder than he meant to.

"Yeah? How's that?" Lorraine responds irritably.

"I need to ask you the standard audit fraud question for the record."

Lorraine's eyes rapidly dart to me then back to Kelly.

He continues in a monotone intonation. "Are you aware of any fraud, defalcations, and/or acts of impropriety; or has anyone made you aware of any fraud, defalcations, and/or acts of impropriety?"

She wastes no time in her response. "Nope."

Kelly tucks his audit binder under his arm. "Thank you. I think we're done here for today."

I clap my hands together signaling the end to our visit. "Okay. I think we're good here. We're going to head out."

Lorraine stands in the doorway wearing a serious look of concern, her girth obstructing our path. "Hold on. Jimmy still ain't found Fat Mikey."

"What do you want me to say?" I try to get the point across it's not my issue.

She doesn't respond. Ultimately, she stands aside to let us pass. We exit the building without stopping to talk to anyone else, and when we get to the parking lot, Kelly breaks the silence. "She's pretty fucking high strung, huh? Is she on your mom's side or dad's?"

"Mom's. Definitely my mom's." I lie, then look at my phone. "Holy Jeez. The girls are in for tonight."

Kelly looks at me with a stupid grin. "Hot damn, we're going to the Foxy Lady!"

15

The parking lot's as jam packed on this Wednesday night as it was on the late Sunday morning when I was here last – maybe more so. I suspect it might be busier on weeknights than Fridays and Saturdays, when all the middle-aged 'family' men are home with their wives and kids. As we hike the length of the lot, I casually check out the surrounding vehicles ranging from junky, old beaters to top-end rides. Evidently, the attraction of naked women dancing for money spans the socio-economic spectrum. As we come up to the building, the front façade paints a much different picture at night than daytime. The exterior lighting makes it appear less a carnival ride and more an energetic night club.

We climb the short stairs leading to an access landing where a couple of Hardo bouncers flank either side of the entry door. They stand with arms folded menacingly, glaring at us without an ounce of welcoming hospitality. As we pass between them, Alison becomes tentative, then puts her head down and pushes on. Goddamn, she's going through with this.

We enter the building through the front vestibule and any white clothing we wear instantly radiates under the black lighting. I experience a short-lived flashback to Uncle Danny's house and the presence of blood spatter revealed under Enzo's portable black light. I physically shake my head to dispel the thought and redirect my focus over to the exceedingly hot hostess collecting cover charges. It's the same young woman at the raised booth I saw with Enzo, but tonight she's dressed entirely in black. Her Goth face makeup and piercings complement her outfit, fashioning an erotic vampiress look. She doesn't remember me, and yet, she's not gruff like she was before. In fact, she's very welcoming.

"Hey, come on in!" She bubbles. "Ladies, always great to see you! Never a cover at the Foxy Lady for my homegirls." She thoroughly inspects Alison and Darcy, approvingly. For Kelly and me, not so much. "Gentlemen, twenty dollar cover, please."

I chuckle to myself. I wonder how she would react if I dropped Enzo's name. I opt to remain anonymous and hand over forty dollars to cover Kelly and me, and a hundred to change out for tipping money.

As Kelly steps up to change bills as well, the blacked-out door to the main floor swings open, releasing a wall of bass-pumping music into us. A loud group of mostly men squeeze past us to go outside and do whatever people do when they leave a strip club. The girls charge ahead and I'm stuck waiting for Kelly to complete his transaction. When he and I finally enter, we've lost sight of them.

It's sensory overload walking into the club. We face the main stage with two dancers flanking either side working a throng of patrons. Strobe effects flash and colored lights dance in unpredictable patterns to the driving beat of the music. Kelly spots Alison and Darcy and lightly backhands me on my upper arm to draw my attention. He nods in their direction and I see them waving to us from a table roughly twenty feet away.

I'm relieved the hostess sat them near the main stage, though not within arm's reach. We spend some awkward time looking around, feeling each other out until a roving drink girl arrives with test tubes of assorted, colorful alcohol slotted in a sectioned box container hung from a strap around her neck. It reminds me of a concessionaire walking up and down stadium aisles selling beers at a baseball game. *Get your ice-cold beer here!* But much better.

"Hi! Ten dollars for a shot!" She announces. Although it's difficult to hear her, she easily gets her message across. Kelly puts up four fingers and hands her some cash. The server collects the money then positions herself in front of Alison. She bends over and raises the container for Alison to select her choice, revealing her perfect bare breasts.

"Oh my!" Alison squeaks. "Um … pick one?"

"Yes! And you can do the shot from between my boobs!"

"Uh. I think I'll just drink it, but thanks!" She replies, amusingly apologetic.

Darcy, however, steps up in a big way. When the server gets to her and goes through the same motion, she excitedly nods as her indication she'd like to go for it. The server removes the box from her neck and reaches for a miniature airhorn strapped to her waistband and sounds it loudly.

The DJ sitting in the control booth quickly turns the music down a few levels to draw everyone's attention.

"Alright, alright, we have a Shooter!! Everyone, put your hands together now and encourage the beautiful young lady with Esmerelda! On three, now. Ready?" He counts off. "One … Two … Three!"

When he finishes his count, the club patrons chant in unison. *No hands! No hands! No hands!*

Alison looks at me, eyes big as tennis balls and her mouth slung open in a frozen laugh. Esmerelda situates a test tube shooter between her boobs, then straightens up invitingly. Darcy dives in, no hands as instructed, and emerges from Esmerelda's heavenly delight with the test tube engulfed snugly between her lips. She exaggeratedly tosses her head back and swallows the alcohol.

"WOOOOOO!" Darcy howls to the crowd's delight, raising the empty test tube high over her head like an NHL champion hoisting the Stanley Cup. Esmerelda gives her a departing congratulatory hug, then straps into her contraption and merrily moves on.

"That was awesome!" Alison squeals, giving Darcy a high-five.

Kelly's super stoked, adding his appreciation. "Seriously! That was crazy hot!"

Before Darcy sits down, she responds to Kelly's compliment by leaning in and kissing him. Kissing doesn't quite describe her technique – it borders more on devouring him.

"Whoa … hey … right on." Kelly splutters barely intelligibly, clearly not knowing what to do with his hands.

§

As entertaining as this is, I wonder if Jimmy's here tonight. I'd like to find out how the drugged-up guy at the ATM made out. I wonder if Pammy's here, too.

"Hey," I call out over the music to Alison. "I'm going to hit the head. I'll be right back."

"Okay, bye." She shoots back, mostly uninterested.

Man, I'm psyched she's having such a good time. Truly a crazy world we live in. Thankfully, Darcy provides her with a partner in crime tonight. I get up from the table and walk around the back side of the main stage toward the area with a side stage where Enzo and I last met Jimmy. It's much less crowded over here, and as I expected, it looks to be filled with regulars, including Jimmy. He's surrounded by a bunch of younger guys and he's holding court, clearly in charge.

He sees me approaching and begins talking to me before I reach him. "Hey. You're just the guy I'm looking for. You know that guy at the ATM that you guys said you seen? The guy that passed out?"

Alarmingly, Jimmy reminds me a lot like Joe Pesci's character, Tommy, in *Goodfellas* right now. "Yeah. Fat Mike, or whatever it is you call him."

"Yeah. Fat Mikey. There ain't no record of him makin' it to any hospital around here. Or in Massachusetts. I checked everywhere."

"Really? That's strange." He looks at me funny, like I'm hiding something. It's making me moderately uncomfortable.

"And I can't get ahold of him, neither. You sure you got ya story straight? An ambulance took him away?"

I try to redirect his line of questioning and deflect responsibility to Enzo. "Definitely. I saw it. You call Enzo?"

"He didn't answer my call. That ain't normal, neither."

"Check in with him again. I barely saw your guy … Fat Mikey … before the ambulance got there."

Jimmy takes a deep breath. "Alright, but hey, gimme your cell. I wanna call you if I can't get Enzo."

Halfheartedly, I give him my number more to extricate myself from the conversation than anything. As I take a step back to slip out, I detect someone coming up from my periphery. I swing around, on guard, and come face to face with a dancer. It's Pammy. Or Meridian tonight. She's dressed in an Egyptian theme; sexy as hell with red-glitter smokey eyes drawn out and filled in like a Siamese cat. She wears shiny, liquid-gold metallic genie-in-the-bottle pants and a fake gold Queen of the Nile necklace adorned with a plastic jewel resting between her topless boobs.

"Hey, Jon." She purrs. "It's nice to see you back." She trails her fingers around the back of my neck, to my chest, and down to my stomach. "Are you by yourself?"

"Uh, no." I stammer. "I'm actually here with my girlfriend and a couple of friends."

"Ooooh. Can I meet her?" She asks seductively.

"Probably not."

She throws out a quick laugh, dropping the temptress persona. "I'm just messing with you. Where are you guys sitting? I'll come over in a few minutes."

Truthfully, I'm relieved she came over to interrupt Jimmy and me. "Okay. We're over by the main stage; on the other side. Jimmy," I turn back to him. "I'll let Enzo know I saw you."

"Yeah. Okay."

Jimmy's visibly pissed off with 'his Meridian' showing attention to someone other than him. I slowly back away then make it back to my table in time to come across Alison commentating on the show unfolding before us on the main stage.

"Look at her. I could do that, you know. It's not that difficult." She contends, observing a bleached-blonde girl squeezing her fake boobs while impressively spiraling from the top of a stripper pole down to the stage floor using only her legs.

I'm half-inclined to say, 'prove it,' but one – she's getting pretty buzzed, and secondly – there's a solid chance she may hop up there and try. Her mini-rant promptly subsides though, when two young ladies appear at our table and begin to whisper in her ear. Alison nods her head, then looks over and throws me an eye wink. They guide her out of her seat and to a roped-off VIP area designated for clients who want one-on-one attention but aren't worried about or interested in complete privacy. Those of us nearby can watch and cheer her on. They seat her on a plush sofa and begin a choreographed routine of alternating attention between each other for Alison's visual enjoyment and focusing solely on her.

The two dancers get downright naughty, attempting to persuade Alison into removing her shirt much to the desire and delight of everyone else watching. I squirm in my seat, knowing if this progresses too far, I'll have to take a walk over and interrupt, which is not what I want to do. However, Alison does a decent job of playing into their routine without going overboard.

"Is that your girlfriend? She's beautiful. And she seems really fun."

I look up from my seat to find Pammy standing over me watching Alison as well. "How about a lap dance for you?" She feathers her fingernails into my hair, massaging my scalp and sending tingles shooting down my back. "What's good for her is good for you too, no?"

I'd like to get a visual gut check from Kelly if I should accept the offer, but Darcy's busy giving him a lap dance of her own.

"What the hell. Why not?"

Pammy shifts into gear, hovering behind me and massaging my chest and shoulders. We both face Alison as she finishes with her tandem dance team and returns to the table. I momentarily become uneasy, but the warm smile on her face indicates she's supportive, which calms me down.

Alison adjusts in her seat, intently watching with a mischievous smile on her face. I maintain eye contact with her throughout the duration of the dance. I don't touch Pammy at all. She seductively slides her body over my chest and lap, grinding into me, all the while watching Alison. I quickly realize Pammy uses me as a tool to seduce Alison and the dance is really between them. I've never been so happy to be used as a prop. I don't feel cheapened at all. Not one single bit.

The erotic exchange between Pammy and Alison lasts throughout the dance. When the song ends, I compensate Pammy generously. She whispers into my ear, "Thank you. You are so hot ... and so is she."

I smile and say nothing. Alison rises from her seat, approaches us, and places a stack of bills in Pammy's gold belt strap while kissing her on her cheek.

"Thank you so much." Pammy breathes softly, acknowledging the substantial tip.

Alison's equally as appreciative. "You are so welcome."

After Pammy leaves, Alison bends over to whisper into my ear, her hand firmly massaging my rock hardness. "I'm so fucking horny." she growls, bewitching evil dripping from her voice.

I look to Darcy and Kelly. They're already up and out of their seats waiting for us to head out.

16

It's nice to be back at Asbury's. Providence is fun, but I'd much rather be on my home turf. We dropped off Darcy and Kelly; both of them at Kelly's apartment, notably. We cruised into Maine just past five o'clock, and after our drop off, our order of operations entails a straight shot to A's for an early dinner. There's something about a cold PBR draft at A's that grounds me. Probably because it's the first real hangout I've had since being an 'adult,' or more likely, because it's a big part of where Alison and I first connected the night after Harding-Williams went down. From our vantage point, I can see the table where we sat that crazy evening.

"… a one-time thing or if they're going to be together? Hey … Jon … are you listening to me?" Alison snaps.

"Huh? Yeah, right. I don't know, we'll see."

"What did I just say?" She challenges.

"Um, you're talking about Darcy and Kelly." I'm purposefully vague in my response because I was completely spacing out on our conversation, but I have no doubt she was gossiping about them.

She perks up. "Yes. So, what do you think? Are they going to hook up full time?" She clasps her hands together in anticipation of my response.

"I have no idea."

"I'll find out." She maintains resolutely. "I'll get Darcy to spill it."

I'm sure you will. The bar isn't busy tonight; only a smattering of people sprinkled about. Baseball news dominates most of the televisions as the night games get close to first pitch.

Alison's voice breaks through my second zone out. "I bet they slept together."

"Of course, they did. You could hear them as well as I could. Why else would they have kicked me out of the room? I don't buy that Darcy was being nice to let me sleep in your room. Did you see her at the club all over him?"

"Ya. Good for them."

"I agree. When I got my gear out of the room in the morning, one of the queen beds was fully made up. It hadn't been slept in."

Alison thankfully changes the subject. "So, what's next? With the audit? Are we done with Rhode Island?"

"For now. We'll let Kelly do his thing. We'll go back for clean-up stuff and the exit interview process, but we can do the majority of the work from up here."

"Sounds right to me." Although she changed the subject, Alison reverts back to one event from last night. "It was such a turn on to see you with that dancer. I wouldn't have thought so, but it was." She looks at me with seductive eyes and brushes her leg against mine under the table. I decide it's best she not know about Pammy or my previous meeting with her. That would likely change her disposition.

"You know that dance was between you and her, right? I was merely a prop."

She tilts her head slightly to one side as she contemplates my assertion. "I think you might be right. That must be why it's so hot. On some level, I guess I knew that."

I feel my phone vibrate in my pocket. I look and find a message from Santa:

"Sweet! It's from Santa. He and Merri will be in next Wednesday."

"I know! I just got a text from Merri! Only one week!"

We switch over to a group text conversation and spend the next half hour discussing the logistics of their arrival.

"We can introduce them to Darcy and Kelly!" Alison bubbles.

"Yes we can, but remember, Santa already knows Kelly."

"Duh. Of course." She bonks herself on the forehead. "I forget about HW. It seems like a lifetime ago."

"I know. It feels the same for me."

She leans closer to me. "Tell me how it's going with Enzo. Actually, with Kelly, too. I haven't heard how he is to work with."

Fair questions. "Enzo's great. He hasn't engaged with us at all on the audit. Totally hands off. He's keeping his distance and letting us do our thing – *so far*." I stress. "Who knows if that could change. As far as Kelly goes; he's solid. Guy knows his shit."

"You're only there to look pretty?" She teases.

I waste no time in responding. "And to put on the gun show." I proceed to flex both arms in my tight t-shirt.

"Ooooh, I love it!" She reaches over to grab onto my arm.

"Someone's gotta do it."

We both laugh and take a breather from the conversation as our food arrives. I remember this server. When Harding-Williams was still up and running, she burned me hard one night when I was out with some friends. I ordered tequila shots with lime and salt, and she said, 'Oh, you want it with training wheels?' She lit me up solidly, but how could I be mad? Her response was pure gold. I've used that line a couple of times myself since then.

Alison poses a sensitive question after our server leaves. "Have you said anything to Kelly about what we're doing?"

"No. I haven't had to. As near as I can tell, he's performing a regular audit like he always has."

"It's good Enzo isn't around then. That would be weird and hard to explain."

"Right. Enzo's been solid so far."

"Well, good. Maybe we'll get Kelly through this without an issue and move on."

I can't help but think, *right, because that's what always happens for us ... nice and smooth with no problems.*

We switch to more mundane topics as we eat dinner. It really is good to be back home. After a few more PBRs and two additional bathroom trips for me to pee, we recline in our seats, stuffed like Thanksgiving turkeys.

"Can I bring you anything else? Dessert or coffee?" Our server asks while clearing plates.

I look at Alison and she subtly shakes her head, 'no.'

"I think we're good." I reply.

"Excellent. I'll bring your check over … unless maybe you'd like tequila shots?" She offers, winking at me as she walks away.

17

I stare up at the bedroom ceiling, attempting to will myself into fully waking up. My arms and legs feel weighted down like lead anchors sunken into my bed. I manage to roll onto my side, where I see Mom calmly seated, with legs crossed, on a kiddie-cornered lounge chair; her strawberry-blonde hair framing her beautiful face. She wears her usual white running suit, augmenting her young appearance and enhancing her athletic frame.

"I'm sure I don't have to tell you this, but you know to be careful, right?" She speaks softly. "With Enzo. You've seen by now he truly means well, but he has a knack for going down the rabbit hole."

I laugh a little. "Yes, I've noticed. And on more than one occasion. I'm not certain he's heard either of the phrases, 'cut your losses' or 'quit while you're ahead,' or any other one like it for that matter."

Mom smiles along with me. "I know what you're thinking. We used to sing it all the time when you were in grade school. Ready?"

"Ready!" I chuckle, and in unison we begin to sing:

You got to know when to hold 'em
Know when to fold 'em
Know when to walk away
And know when to run

"What?" Alison mumbles sleepily, poking a gentle elbow into me.

"Wha … huh?" I grunt.

After a moment to gather my senses, I drag myself out of bed and into the bathroom for a world record pee, then shuffle off to the living room to catch last night's sports scores. Coffee's brewing and the overwhelmingly aromatic smell expedites a full return to normalcy for me.

What a spectacular sunrise this Saturday morning. The weather app on my phone shows a bright, sunny day climbing to a high of sixty-eight degrees. I relax on the couch where the sun blazes through the living room double window, warming up the apartment nicely. If we owned a pet, I imagine it stretching out and basking where the sunbeam washes over a swath of the carpet.

Unlike me, Alison breezes into the living room with awesomely messy hair tied back in a ponytail, carrying a Diet Coke. "Good morning, sexy."

She kisses my forehead and sits down next to me on the couch, instinctively resting her head on my chest.

"Good morning, angel. How'd you sleep?" I reciprocate with a robust head scratch and scalp massage. She loves this.

"Great, I think. I feel good. Hey, were you singing … in bed?"

"Me? No. You must've been dreaming."

"Huh." She pulls back a little to get a good look at me. "I'm so excited about Merri and Ben! Let's plan out everything we're going to do!"

"Sure."

I lower the television volume. "Well, they come in on Wednesday and we'll pick them up later in the day like we talked about last night. Probably have a low-key night; dinner at A's or something. Really, it's the weekend we need to plan."

"What do you think about including Darcy and Kelly?"

"I don't know. It wouldn't bother me any, but I don't know what Santa and Merri expect."

Alison wriggles her body, burrowing deeper into my makeshift cocoon. "I kind of want Merri to meet Darcy."

"That's fine. We can go out a time or two, but we don't need to invite them every night. Darcy and Kelly might not want to hang out with us all the time, who knows? They haven't figured each other out yet."

"True."

Alison emerges from her cocoon to bring an empty Diet Coke can to the kitchen. I hear her rummaging through cabinets and the refrigerator. After a moment, she calls out, "Do you want me to cook breakfast or go out to eat?"

"Anything good to make?"

"Not really."

"Let's go out."

§

That was a great call. We're heading to Eggscellent Choice, our go-to breakfast place, with the top off Uncle Danny's Jeep and the warm, spring air blowing through our hair.

While Alison scrolls through her phone, my mind drifts to Uncle Danny, Mom, and Dad. I feel a pang of grief roll through my stomach, ultimately replaced with loving memories; some older and some not so much.

Alison watches me with an amused look on her face. "What are you smiling about?"

"Me? Oh, just thinking about Danny. Mom and Dad, too. The happy stuff. I didn't realize I was smiling."

"Ya. That's cute." She looks at me lovingly for a moment as we enter the parking lot. "It was funny watching you. Your lips were moving like you were talking to someone." She reaches for my leg and gives a comforting squeeze. She always knows when I'm hurting.

A few minutes pass and we find ourselves in the restaurant. As expected, it's super busy but that's okay by me for two reasons. One, as a people watcher, I'm always preoccupied with everyone around me; and two, Alison called ahead to reserve a place in line. Pro tip – always use call-ahead service. Alison's picked up my habit of people profiling, so we're entertained throughout our tolerable wait.

"These things are so disgusting. Fecal germ factories." I grouse while eyeballing the octagonal gadget sitting on the bench between us that lights up when your table's ready. "I hate touching them."

Alison nudges me with her elbow and nods across from us toward a roughly nine-month-old baby boy sitting on his mother's lap. He happily squirms in his onesie while using their gadget as a teething ring.

"Ugh. You gotta be kidding me." I mutter softly. Luckily, Alison's pre-planning pays off and our device activates indicating we have a table waiting. Perfect timing. We're whisked out of the entrance vestibule and onto the floor to the dismay of everyone sitting here before us who didn't avail themselves of call-ahead service.

"Alright, back to planning for Merri and Ben?" Alison suggests after we're seated.

I pick up a menu as though I may order something different than every other time I come in here. "A's for sure. Multiple times, probably.

Then we'll take them to see Sharon at some point." I put the menu down. "Merri's family's here, too; she'll want to see them. Also, lots of outside stuff to do now that it's getting warmer."

"Great ideas. I wish we could show them WaterFire."

I wait to respond until after we order. "Hmm. Let me think about your WaterFire suggestion. Might be a fun weekend trip."

"Yes! It would!" She enthusiastically agrees. "That's when we should bring Darcy and Kelly into the fold. We could all go down."

"I could check in with Enzo and Kelly could touch base on any loose ends with the audit. Might be good from multiple angles."

She bounces excitedly in her chair. "Okay! Let's see if they're down for it!"

After our food arrives, we become silent as we eat like it's our last meal. As is customary, I finish way before her and stand by to tackle anything she doesn't eat. When she's done, she slides her plate over to me for clean-up duty and asks what we're doing today.

I was waiting for this question. "Gymmmmm. It's Leg Day."

"Perfect. I'm down with that. Do you want to invite Darcy and Kelly?"

"If you want to. Not sure Kelly's ever seen a gym, though."

She laughs. "I think you might be right. I'll message Darcy, you message Kelly."

18

Darcy accepts our invitation to come to the gym, but Kelly opts out. We meet her in the parking lot – she's waiting for us – and when we walk in, she and Alison break away right off and bee-line it to the cardio section.

I'm working on legs today; the male species' least focused-upon body part. Leg Day always starts off with barbell squats, so I head over to the squat racks, taking in the scene as I go. I love this gym. It accommodates every type of exercise enthusiast – fitness fanatics, powerlifters, bodybuilders, cross-fitters, and cardio-hitters. It offers an unrivalled palette of people to profile – even better than Eggscellent Choice. It's a psycho-analytical paradise.

We have plenty of Hardos lifting today; some are powerlifters, some bodybuilders. A Hardo can fall into multiple categories of gym attendee. A couple of them here are Grunters. They're the ones who believe people are impressed with their sheer, raw strength and ability to fight through pain if they yell loudly enough with each repetition. More likely than not, they're using very light weights. Most people laugh at them.

Then we have my least favorite group. The Creepers. Creepers are guys who don't blatantly stare at the women, but rather stalk them by positioning themselves at discreet angles produced by the placement of wall-mounted mirrors so as not to draw any attention. Geometry exploitation at its finest. Every gym has a Creeper – you just may not know it.

I purposefully keep my distance from the gym's resident Coach. Now, don't get me wrong, I respect trainers and other educated fitness professionals very much. I'm talking about the guy who feels it necessary to give you unsolicited tips and pointers relative to your program whether the advice is correct or not. We've all had an uninvited and unwelcomed Coach in our lives.

Weight Monitor hangs out here as well. He'll chase you down if you replace a dumbbell in the wrong spot or if you don't properly re-rack your weights. Weight Monitor typically doubles as Cart Monitor at the grocery store. Fare thee well to anyone who doesn't bring a cart back to the corral in the presence of Cart Monitor. In fairness, if one wanted to categorize me, I'd more than likely identify as a quasi-Hardo with a Weight Monitor tendency. I wouldn't go to the length of calling someone out for not re-racking weight, but I would definitely give them a mental beatdown.

The women here are not immune to my analytics. Oh, no. We have several Makeup Mirror Workout female members. They don't actually exercise. They dress in tight clothes and strut the floor – makeup and hair perfect – searching for the elusive, perfect Instagram selfie. Typically, they're the focus of the Creeper.

I have a soft spot for the painfully thin women who work incessantly and vigorously on the cardio machines. I don't have a 'gym name' for them, in fact, I worry about them. I worry there's an eating disorder and body image insecurity lurking behind the workout.

Rounding out my profiling, I spot the Talker. He carries on a one-sided, self-initiated conversation with you despite your best efforts at not reciprocating, even if you're wearing headphones. The Gear Carrier wears a weight belt, holds a shaker bottle in one hand, lifting chalk in the other, with a bulging gym bag slung over his shoulder containing all manner of straps and supports. One hundred percent of the time, the Gear Carrier sports a hoodie sweatshirt positioned such that no portion of his face is visible. He's also known as the Faceless Warrior.

And finally, the Couple. I also fall into this category. The Couple arrives together and intermittently meets up throughout their workout for a quick kiss or other public display of affection much to the disgust and resentment of everyone else. Get a life. Wait until you get home. I can't say I blame anyone for that response, but too bad. They don't have a woman like mine. A variant on the Couple – the Hardcore Couple – possess all the qualities of the Couple, plus they work out together. That's definitely not us. Among these standard gym patrons, intermingle new fitness enthusiasts through experienced, grizzled veterans. Definite social strata exist here.

After a quick warm up and stretch, I drop my phone and protein drink to the floor and begin loading weight onto the bar. My usual routine consists of: I do a set, look at my phone, do another set, look at my phone again, and so on. I slap my headphones on my head, crank up the volume with some AC⚡DC for motivation and to block out the Talkers, then rip off my first set. Ahhh, this gets the blood flowing.

I steadily increase poundage, working through my progressions until I'm ready to go heavy. After a few sets, it dawns on me the guy in the squat rack one space over from mine continually moves at the same pace as me. He starts his set when I start and finishes when I finish. Wait a minute … I think I may have inadvertently discovered a new category of gym patron. Is this guy a … a One Upper?! I test my theory by increasing the weight on my bar by twenty pounds, then casually stand by to see his reaction. Sure enough, after a few moments, he increases his weight by twenty pounds. This sequence repeats a few more times – resulting in his bar always five pounds heavier than mine! Alright, it's on, now. I keep pushing the intensity, steadily increasing the weight and lifting with more fervor even though I know it's getting unsafe. He doesn't flinch, continuing to match me repetition for repetition. We look like the two race car drivers from *Days of Thunder* who try to pathetically out-race each other in the hospital while strapped into wheelchairs. Appropriately, their injuries resulted from having recently wrecked on the race-track by taking each other out in a heated exchange.

This guy's a total asshole. Create an unspoken, uninvited competition out of our lift? I opt to pull back and lighten my weight to finish out my squatting, effectively terminating the match. After I re-rack the weight, with only one set remaining, the One Upper approaches me, motioning for me to remove my headphones. I'm giving him my best *what the fuck do you want* face, when he extends his hand to me, offering to shake.

"Hey, just wanted to thank you for the motivation today. I pick up tips by watching people and incorporating the best routines and stuff into my workouts. You've got a seriously solid squat. Best one I've seen. Thanks again."

"Oh, uh, thanks. You gave me some motivation, too. I enjoyed that."

"Cool. See you around." One Upper says, then walks to another area of the gym.

I feel like an idiot for about a minute as I prepare for my final squat set, though it disappears roughly at the same time I finish. As I re-rack the weight, I catch sight of my phone lighting up. Enzo's calling me.

"LoZo, what's up?"

"Jimmy's dead."

19

"He's dead." Enzo repeats, his voice cracking in anguish.

"What? Really?" I reply in mild shock and disbelief. "What the hell happened?"

"Heart attack, near as we can tell. I just got off a call with Lorraine. She's a wreck."

"I bet. Where was he? Where'd it happen?"

"In his bed. Lorraine found him this morning."

"How does she know it was a heart attack?"

"I don't know. It's what she said." I feel the sadness in his voice.

I take a long pause before responding. "Damn, that's a shame. I'm sorry, man. I know you guys were close. You okay?"

He breaks down as he tries to speak. "Eh, I'm okay."

"I'm going to come down. When's the service?"

"You don't need to do that."

"No. I want to. He was a decent guy, and your friend. I want to support you."

"Thanks, I appreciate it. I'm not sure, but more than likely this coming weekend. I'll let you know."

Interestingly, Enzo doesn't immediately hang up after our business concludes like he normally would. He lingers on the line for a moment.

"Hey … you good?" I press him.

"Yeah. Yeah, I'm good. I'll talk with you soon." The line goes dead.

Man, that's tough. Enzo has a dark cloud hanging over his head, for sure. I guess to some degree, we all do.

I clean up my squat rack and walk over to the cardio machines where Alison has worked herself into a sheen of glistening sweat on a StairClimber. She could see me talking on my phone from her angle and wouldn't think anything of it but for the fact I came over to interrupt her workout.

She hits pause on her machine and steps off. "What's up?" She asks, uncertain of the situation. Darcy's mostly uninterested and continues her cardio routine.

"I just hung up with Enzo. You remember Jimmy? His friend? He passed away this morning. Heart attack, I guess."

Her face transforms from lighthearted to pained. "Oh, no! Poor Enzo! Is he okay?"

"Tough to say. He says he's okay, but I can hear the pain in his voice."

"That's too bad. Do you want to leave?"

I contemplate her offer. "Nah … I'm good. I'm going to finish my workout."

"Sounds good." She kisses my cheek. "See you in a bit."

She turns to remount her machine and I walk back to the weight-lifting area, where I resume my workout. I've lost my mojo somewhat, but I'm able to push the news aside and get back into a solid groove.

I take up position in front of the dumbbell rack for a lunge routine. The walls behind the rack are lined with floor-length mirrors, ostensibly so we can watch our form and insure we're using good technique to avoid injury. Let's be real. In reality, we want to admire ourselves in the mirror. I'm as guilty as the rest and I don't care. I've worked for it – I want to enjoy it. Like most everyone here – and the one common denominator of us all – I'm as insecure as the next guy.

§

I ponder how Jimmy's passing will affect our upcoming week. Not only from a funeral service standpoint, but from a 'dealing with Lorraine' perspective. To complicate matters further, Merri and Santa arrive Wednesday and Alison has some grandiose plans. Maybe it makes matters easier. We discussed coming to Rhode Island for the weekend, anyway. This would clinch it. We could all come down, then I would break away for the service and burial and reconnect with them later. And back on Lorraine, she's rough to deal with on a good day. Will she lose interest in helping us? Tough to say. We didn't do anything negative to her and presumably Enzo will continue her payoff. Who will take over Jimmy's machines? Lorraine? A flood of questions and an even greater flood of potential outcomes wash over me the more I think about it. A best-case scenario for me would be to finish the audit and let Enzo extricate himself from Lorraine. As I reason this out though, I breathe a deep, unsettled sigh. Who am I kidding? Enzo won't extricate himself until he's done cleaning his money. He'll find a way to keep Jimmy's ATMs going and Lorraine supporting him, and life will go on somewhat normally.

Until it doesn't.

I move over to the raised-calf machine to finish my leg routine. I notice a sign cautioning me of the dangers inherent in using this equipment. It reads: *Warning – intentional misuse can result in serious injury and/or death.* An accompanying image depicts a rudimentary stick figure hunched over with ex'd-out eyes and a hand bent in half, fingers crushed, with lightning bolts jolting into it. I'm not certain what prompted me to ruminate over it, but I did. You simply cannot escape the fact there's risk in everything we do. Even the mundane … even the beneficial. We don't let it paralyze us. We can't. Sometimes it's best to embrace it and use it as motivation to push us harder. With that thought pinballing around in my head, I jack the weight stack up crazy high and rip off a brutal final set.

My legs are completely smoked – they tremble as I walk to the locker room to wash up. They'll be super sore later tonight through tomorrow, but in a satisfying I-worked-my-ass-off kind of way. One Upper passes me by on his way out and nods in acknowledgement of our earlier competition.

I grab my gear and head out of the locker room, where Alison and Darcy wait for me. "Hey guys, all set?" I ask.

Darcy replies first. "Yup. All set."

"Want to get lunch?" Alison proposes.

"Oh, yeah. I'm totally down with that." Sweet. We're going to get lunch. I've got the Treacherous Triple on my mind.

20

B ulldog Brewing never tasted so good. I stopped worrying about ordering the Treacherous Triple burger in front of Alison long ago; it's not a composition to take lightly. Cold beers on a warm Saturday afternoon don't taste any better than after an intense workout – unless they're cold PBR drafts. I chow down contentedly while Alison broaches the subject of Merri and Ben's impending arrival with Darcy, including coming with us on a weekend Rhode Island trip.

"Jon and I want to see what you and Kelly are up to this week and also on the weekend."

"I'm working during the week. I assume Kelly is too, but you'd know better than I." She directs this last part to me. I don't respond.

"Right." Alison confirms, drawing the attention back to herself. "Kelly's working all week in town." She momentarily diverts the trajectory of the conversation. "By the way, what's up with you two? Are you officially a 'thing'?"

Alison's demeanor shifts from casual to gossipy on a dime. It's slightly unnerving.

"Well, we've screwed every night this week." She replies unabashedly. "Not sure if we're officially a 'thing,' but we're definitely officially *not* 'not a thing.' "

I swallow hard. I think I follow that.

Alison smiles at her response. "I'd say that constitutes a 'thing.' So, listen, we have some friends coming in on Wednesday we want you to meet. They're good friends of ours who moved to Nebraska last summer. Jon and I used to work with one of them. Kelly too, actually. We used to hang out with both of them. A lot."

As Alison goes into greater detail explaining our relationship with Santa and Merri to Darcy, I think back to some of the good times we've had. Now everything and everyone's changed – maybe Santa the most, at least physically. He's always been a big man, but with his college football career falling further and further into the rearview mirror, he's packed on some pounds. I haven't seen him in person in almost a year, but he posts photos regularly on social media. He's gotten *really* big. Merri, on the other hand, trimmed down significantly. She's always been beautiful, albeit on the chunky side, but that is no more. She's gone the opposite of Santa in preparation for their wedding day this summer.

"… I think he'll jump at it." Darcy says, breaking me out of my funk. I know without having heard the exchange between them she's referring to Kelly's interest level in a Rhode Island weekend trip. What I didn't catch is their status with hanging out with us during the week.

Darcy continues. "I'll check with him, but I'm sure he'll go. He wouldn't want me going without him. I wouldn't if the roles were reversed."

Good point. Who would?

"Cool. As we get closer to Wednesday, we can firm up plans." I take a chance I'm right on Darcy and Kelly hanging out with us before the weekend.

We engage in low-key conversation for the balance of the time we're here. After lunch, we split off from Darcy – she brought her own car – and make plans to meet up later at A's with Kelly joining us.

§

I washed away the sweat and stank of the day in an awesomely hot shower where Alison surprised me with much-needed shower sex. After I got dressed, I popped a couple more beers and now I'm sporting a decent buzz-on. It may be an Uber night tonight, we'll see. I wonder if Homerunners still exists or if Uber and Lyft effectively wiped them out. Homerunners probably went the way of the dinosaur.

I watch SportsCenter while waiting for Alison to finish getting herself ready. There's a basketball documentary airing detailing the life of Kobe Bryant. What an absolute heartbreak. I want to watch it, but the setting sun blazes through the window casting a bright light over the television screen, disrupting its clarity. I walk over to the window to close the blinds, and my eyes are drawn to a white van in the parking lot. It's a classic Econoline van, one typically associated with pedophiles you see frequently on investigative news magazines on national television. The rear coffin doors are propped wide open where the ends of two large rolls of carpet protrude. Someone must have moved out. I can tell someone's in the van, but I can't make them out. I've grown overly suspicious of cars, people, and anything out of place. It's not so much this vehicle captures my attention; I only notice it because it doesn't belong here.

"You ready, Freddy?" Alison comes out of the bedroom dressed to kill.

"Damn. You are so hot."

"Oh, yeah?" She poses with hands on hips, feigning a challenging stare down before breaking into laughter. "C'mon, tough guy, let's get out of here. I'm driving."

Excellent. I grab another beer for the ride, and we take the stairs to the underground parking. As we exit the garage, I see the white van pulling out of the parking lot ahead of us. I can't help but think about the penguin box truck Agent Brown and Reyes chased us around in. Now, along with Reyes, the truck rests on the ocean floor.

"You look like you have a decent buzz going. Smell like it, too." Alison says good-naturedly.

"Yup. As a matter of fact, I feel great. My legs are sore as hell, but the beers have taken the edge off. I'll have to pee every ten minutes as soon as we get there, but I'm okay with that."

"What's new."

The cross-town trip passes quickly, and we pull into A's right behind Darcy and Kelly. They wait for us to exit Alison's Fiat and we all walk up to the building together.

"It must be country night." Darcy speculates. "Look at all the cowboy hats."

She's right. I look around at others walking toward the building and see varying styles of cowboy hats worn by both girls and guys. Some wear a traditional Johnny Cash design while others opt for a more rock 'n roller, trashy, Bret-Michaels-with-an-awesome-bandanna look. And then there's every style in between.

A's rocks tonight. An Asbury's hostess wearing overalls with a tight white t-shirt collects names and cell numbers at an outdoor podium set up to queue new arrivals. Thankfully, they're using a texting system to notify patrons when tables are ready versus the octagonal, fecal teething ring we endured earlier at breakfast.

I approach the interior waiting section and take a look around. Music's pumping and taps are flowing. People gather waiting for tables while servers busily hustle the floor.

"Ho-Lee-Shit!" I broadcast loudly, capturing the attention of everyone within earshot. "I see the reason why people are wearing cowboy hats. Hot damn, they brought in a mechanical bull!"

"No way!" Alison pushes me aside to look, then turns back to us. "Oh my God, they did!"

While Darcy and Kelly step up to the waiting area to catch a glimpse, I notice the sign out front. It reads:

Come Ride Teddy The Mechanical Bull!

Funny, I missed that on our way in. Within ten minutes, Alison gets a text indicating our high top is ready. We push our way in where another friendly hostess greets us and leads the way to our table.

Alison taps me on my shoulder. "Hey, Darcy and I are going to the bathroom."

"Alright, do you want us to wait for you to order drinks?"

"No, go ahead. Order for us, too."

"What do you want?"

"Surprise us." She calls out over her shoulder as they head off to the ladies' room, leaving Kelly and me hanging back to wait.

"Dude, this is funny as hell." Kelly says to me while the country duo Big & Rich plays on the sound system. We watch a newly-minted, twenty-one-year-old kid attempt to straddle Teddy as *Save a Horse (Ride a Cowboy)* resounds in the background. The song fits perfectly. Or almost perfectly. It should only be allowed when females ride. He does a solid job until the bull unpredictably reverses course and bucks him off and into the padded-cushion riding pit.

After a few minutes, Alison and Darcy rejoin us at the table.

"You up for it?" Kelly asks Darcy, nodding toward the bull.

"Hell yeah, I'm doing it! I'm going to need some liquid courage first, though."

Alison looks to me. "Did you order drinks for us, yet?"

"No. Not yet. No one's been over."

"Oh, good. I was second guessing myself when I asked you to order for us."

We all spend a few minutes observing people testing their luck and skill with Teddy as we wait. Eventually, a server makes it over to us. "Sorry this took so long," She apologizes, out of breath. "It's crazy busy in here right now."

"No worries." Alison responds. "We're in no hurry. It's pretty cool in here tonight."

The server nods while poised with a pen and notepad to write down our order. "For sure. What can I bring you?"

I'm glad I didn't order for the women. They both asked for completely different drinks than I ever would have thought of. Kelly and I get beers. I'm on psycho-analytical profiling overload with tonight's patrons and I have to force myself to be present and engage in conversation at the table. This is super entertaining. Most people riding the bull manage well as the operator starts off, but last only a few seconds when it speeds up. We continue to order drinks and work up the courage to ride Teddy while picking up tips from previous riders.

Eventually, the girls are ready. "Okay, I'm going to sign us up!" Darcy informs Alison and disappears from the table without waiting for a response, thus not allowing Alison to back out. Yet.

Darcy's back in no time, a giddy look on her face. "I'm the third song from now, and you're the fourth!" She advises Alison.

Alison cringes. "Oh God, I need more alcohol!"

We all laugh and catch the server for another timely round.

"I picked Man! I Feel Like a Woman! for my song and I signed you up for Save a Horse Ride a Cowboy." Darcy forewarns Alison.

Lovely. It's my female who's going to ride to that song.

"Okay." Alison responds apprehensively.

I lean over to her. "You don't have to do this, you know."

"I know. I want to, though. I need to be more adventurous."

Really? We haven't had enough adventure? I think we've had enough for a lifetime. We soak in the atmosphere, watching and waiting for Darcy's turn with anticipation. When the volume drops on the song before hers, signaling she's next up, Darcy takes a quick gulp from her drink, scoots her seat back, and silently leaves the table, clearly steeling her nerves.

She talks to the operator for a couple of seconds before climbing into the cushioned pit and awkwardly mounting Teddy. Moments later, Shania Twain's synth-country intro jumps to life followed by the opening line 'Let's go, girls!', triggering Teddy to begin a slow, taunting circle. Darcy unnecessarily raises her right arm into the air as though she's digging right in and riding hard like a professional bull rider. She follows with a loud *yee haw!*, getting the audience's energy level jacked up.

Kelly leans over to me and laughs. "That looks familiar."

I spit out a mouthful of beer.

The operator cranks up the speed of the circling, and Darcy does an admirable job of rolling with it, until Teddy unexpectedly reverses course and spills her into the riding pit. She stands up and bows to her audience as they clap for her effort.

"That. Was. Awesome!" She gushes when she returns to the table. "Your turn!" She says to Alison.

Alison's off and on her way over to the operator for her check-in, quickly following the same procedure as Darcy. She enters the pit and gawkily climbs onto Teddy, clearly more intimidated than her more outgoing friend. She sits and waits patiently for the operator to cue up the music; however, it seems he's having some trouble, leaving Alison with no alternative but to continue waiting. God, she is so beautiful. She wears a black, short-sleeve crop top and ripped jeans, accentuating every luscious curve. She drips with sexuality.

Eventually, the operator solves his issue and cues up the music. The driving beat of the song triggers Teddy's start and the bull begins its program. The operator leaves the difficulty level very low, presumably because he wants Alison to stay on Teddy until the chorus kicks in, proclaiming loudly, 'save a horse … ride a cowboy!'

When the chorus hits, everyone sings the line boisterously and the whole place goes wild. After a moment or two longer, Alison endures her inevitable toss from Teddy into the riding pit and emerges to appreciative clapping from everyone.

A particularly effusive group of guys seated across from us on the other side of the mechanical bull stage catches my attention. I noticed them earlier but thought nothing of them until now. One of them pats his lap and calls out, "Hey baby, why don't you come over here and ride this cowboy?"

Alison hears it, turns to him, and extends her middle finger before turning again and walking back to our table.

"Bitch." He calls out.

Nope. No way. Not happening. I quickly survey their table as I rise from my seat, everything and everyone in my periphery blocked out. Three guys. Offender roughly my size, far end of the table.

"You looking for trouble?" He snarls at me as I reach the table.

"Apologize." I growl. "Now."

"Go fuck yourself."

I move toward him and it quickly escalates. He shuffles backward in his chair, just out of my reach, and I feel a sharp pain in the back of my head, driving me to the floor. I manage to roll out before I'm hit again and locate the asshole who insulted Alison. I hook him by his elbow, sliding him out of his seat and into an armbar and quickly dislocate his shoulder. He yells out in pain and 'taps out' in an indication he submits, like we're in an MMA fight and I'm obligated to let him go. I respond by lowering my arm and twisting further as he screams from what I think may be his newly-broken elbow.

Kelly dives to the floor, barking in my ear, encouraging me up. "Jon, we gotta go! Now!"

I disengage with this podunk asshole and stand up, surveying the scene. Everyone in A's is dead silent and staring at me. Lights have been turned up and the music's off. The entire establishment has come to a screeching halt. I see Alison and Darcy crying. The two other guys both lay in a bloody heap on the floor aside the overturned table.

As my sensibilities return, I realize we need to get the hell out of here. Quickly. As I head to the front door with the others closely in tow, I ask Kelly about the two other guys. "What the hell happened to them? Was that you?"

"Hell no," He breathes heavily, his voice teeming with excitement. "When you lunged after that guy, one of them hit you on the head with a chair."

Ah, so that's what happened. I wait for him to go on.

"This dude shot out from nowhere. Big guy, big ass beard. He thrashed the holy hell out of both of them. Then he jumped over to help you, saw you were okay with that guy, and disappeared. He just disappeared." Kelly guides us out the front door, his voice incredulous.

Damn, this unfolded so quickly and finished just as rapidly. The night came to an unsatisfying early end and on top of everything, I have to pee. We hastily say goodbye to Darcy and Kelly, promise to connect to go over in greater detail what the hell happened, and hop into our cars. As Alison careens out of the parking lot and onto the street, I see a white Econoline van up ahead of us, but I don't see any carpets sticking out of the back. I absentmindedly wonder if it's the same van I saw at our apartment complex earlier this evening. Maybe it's not real. Maybe it's only a figment of my imagination caused by the pop to the back of my head.

That one's going to leave a mark, for sure. What I am certain of is seeing the blue flicker of lights and hearing sirens blaring when police arrive at A's as we bail out. I look at Alison. She stares back, eyes wide, but says nothing.

We approach a traffic intersection not far from the parking lot exit, stopping at a red light directly behind the white van. Well, I'm not imagining it, anyway. The traffic light promptly turns green, and as the van pulls away, I'm surprised at what I see.

It has Rhode Island license plates.

21

Damn, my head hurts this morning. And it's not from a hangover, unfortunately. I have a golf ball-sized lump on the back of my head courtesy of an Asbury's high-top stool wielded by a Grade-A asshole. I still can't believe I was in a bar fight. I've been involved in a few in the past, but more in the role Kelly played last night – helping somebody more heavily embroiled extricate themselves from the scene before we all get in trouble. He did a respectable job; we haven't heard anything from anyone about it.

"Hey baby, how are you feeling?" Alison winces while asking as though she could feel the throbbing herself. She's come into the bedroom with a fresh ice pack to help with the swelling.

"I'm fine. No worries." I smile at her so she can attempt to relax. She's feeling super guilty her middle finger set off a powder keg at A's. I try to reassure her the other guy needed a smackdown for his overture and she ought not feel bad about it one bit. I don't.

"I'm good on the ice pack, though. I've had enough; I think my scalp is frozen now."

She smiles and slides into bed with me, cuddling up and lightly tracing her fingers on my chest. It's enormously relaxing.

"You were amazing, you know." She peers up at me. "You always make me feel so safe."

I smile but don't respond. I'm thinking about the big dude who helped us out last night. He's got to be related to the white van I saw after we left A's, and more than likely back at the apartment. It couldn't have been Enzo. The description from Kelly doesn't match. Besides, I know he's in Rhode Island. Or at least I think he is … maybe he's not. In any case, the description definitely doesn't fit. I have too many questions and not enough brain power to work with right now. I need to connect with Kelly to gain a clearer picture; we didn't have time to talk last night, nor did I have the capacity to.

Alison stops tracing on my chest and burrows further into me. "It's probably good Enzo wasn't at A's with us."

"For sure. Could be a few more blue barrels resting on the channel floor this morning."

"Oh, don't say that." She shivers. "I only meant we can't afford to get into trouble when Enzo's with us."

"No doubt." I pause for a moment. "I can't wait to talk to Kelly about the guy who helped us out last night. You get a good look at him?"

"Not really. He was an enormous man and it happened so fast. I was totally focused on you and then he was gone."

I decide not to tell her about the white van and my suspicions linking our mystery hero to it. No sense opening that Pandora's Box for now. Eventually, we let the conversation wane, content to lay in bed in silence and relax in each other's warmth.

§

Sometime around noon we shift ourselves into gear. In addition to my reaching out to Kelly, Alison and I have some planning to do for the upcoming week. Merri and Santa come in late Wednesday afternoon and we offered to pick them up at the jetport. I should also connect with Enzo at some point on the logistics of Jimmy's funeral service. Finally, we'll need to firm up plans with Darcy and Kelly for Wednesday and the approaching weekend in Providence.

Alison disappears into the bathroom to shower, leaving me with a good opening to call Kelly. I dial his number and hit speaker on the audio – my uncomfortable, low-grade headache precludes me from holding the phone up to my ear. Unlike Enzo, Kelly doesn't answer his calls until they're on the verge of going into voicemail.

"Yo."

"Kelly. It's Jon."

"Hey. I was going to call you. What a night. How's your head?"

"Hurts like a bitch, but I'll survive."

I barely make out someone in the background asking, 'Who is it?', with Kelly responding, 'Jon.'

"Sorry," He offers. "Darcy wanted to know who you were."

"Oh. She's over at your place?"

"No. I'm at hers. First time. She's got a good setup."

"Nice." A fleeting image of Darcy riding the mechanical bull with Kelly's observation, *'that looks familiar'* passes through my mind. "So, tell me how it shook out from your vantage point last night."

"Dude, it was nuts. I didn't hear anybody say anything to Alison." He explains. "I only saw her flip someone off at that table. By the time I put it together something was about to go down, you were already halfway over there. I didn't find out what was said to her until Darcy told me on our way home."

"What about the dude who backed me up? Where did he come from?"

"I don't know. Somewhere behind me." Kelly's voice escalates in pitch as he recounts the progression. "I got up from our table and went to follow you. I didn't get two feet forward before I felt a huge paw on my shoulder stiffly holding me back. He said, 'I got this' as he cruised past me."

I don't have to encourage him to go on. His recollection of the incident comes flooding out. "He nearly reached that prick who hit you with the chair before he swung it at your head."

"Too bad he didn't. I'm lucky I didn't get knocked out."

"Seriously. Man, I thought you were laid out cold. So like I said last night, the big dude calmly thrashed the holy hell out of that guy and crushed the other one with a flurry of punches. I don't know how else to describe it. He pounded both of them to the floor and then left. Crazy."

"Wow. I wish I could have thanked him. No idea who he is?"

"Nope. He reminded me of Hagrid from *Harry Potter*, but with shorter hair."

"You're right. That is nuts."

"Yeah. By the way, I'm equally impressed with how you handled yourself. You fucking busted that guy's arm without thinking twice. You've changed a lot since we were all at HW."

You have no idea. I slightly shake my head while reprocessing the incident, letting his statement go unanswered.

"You remember Santa, uh, Ben and his girlfriend Merri fly in on Wednesday, right?" I ask, digressing from the conversation. "Alison and I are picking them up, sometime late afternoon. We wanted you to hang out with us. Should be fun."

"Definitely. Darcy mentioned that. I haven't seen Ben in forever. And he would be a good dude to have around if we get into another fight." He laughs.

"Right. Hey and also, we're going to take them down to Providence this weekend. I need to go down for Jimmy's funeral service on Saturday. We plan to show them WaterFire if you want to come. Darcy's supposed to talk to you about that, too."

"She did, and she told me about Jimmy, too. Sounds good to me. I'll confirm with her after we're off the phone, but plan on it."

"Sweet. We'll make it happen."

Kelly pauses. "Man, I can't believe Lorraine's old man gave up the ghost. I wonder how that's going to frig up the audit."

"I thought about that as well."

I was mulling over more than just that, though. Mainly, if this will throw a monkey wrench into our money laundering efforts.

Alison exits the bathroom sporting only a towel turban crowning her head. "Who's that?"

"It's Kelly."

"Hi, Kelly!" She calls out animatedly, then disappears into the bedroom.

He hears her greeting. "Tell her I said, 'Hey.' "

"Kelly says, 'Hey.' " I relay loudly before wrapping up my conversation with him. "Alright, let me know if anything changes after you talk with Darcy, otherwise I'll catch up with you in the office tomorrow."

"Perfect. Later on."

I disconnect my call with Kelly and follow Alison into the bedroom. She faces her floor-length dressing mirror wearing only thong underwear as she combs out her freshly washed hair. I utterly lack the self-control to not walk up from behind and squeeze her boobs in a friendly reach-around.

"Well, hello there." She purrs, enjoying my impromptu body-work. "Can I help you?"

"Mhmm." I whisper to her as I kiss her neck. "But first, let me tell you about Kelly. We're all set for them hanging out on Wednesday and coming down with us on the weekend."

"Awesome! We're going to have so much fun!" She giggles as I sweep her up and bring her over to the bed.

"I agree. And speaking of having so much fun ..."

22

I have a fondness for the Portland Jetport. When I was a young boy, some of my first memories were of my father bringing me here so we could spend time together watching the planes take off and land. He thought air travel was one of man's greatest modern miracles and I wholeheartedly agree. To this day, I'm still mesmerized by the sight of enormous tubes of metal seemingly floating on the horizon as they approach a runway. Then it all disappeared when I was roughly six years old. September 11th arrived, and a mass of cowardly, vile terrorists destroyed a part of our nation and collective sense of security. It's mind-bending to think two of those sick bastards flew out of Portland to Boston's Logan airport that devastating morning. In fact, they slept at a hotel the night prior within a stone's throw from where I now sit.

I'm waiting in the cellphone parking lot with Alison as we bide our time until Merri and Santa arrive on a blustery, early May evening. Darcy and Kelly plan to meet us at A's after we make a stop at the hotel to drop off luggage.

"I can't wait for them to get in!" Alison bubbles.

"Same here. Shouldn't be too much longer. FlightTracker has them twenty or so miles out." I say while examining the air travel app on my phone. "Maybe fifteen minutes. Twenty tops."

I continue fidgeting with the app as Alison idly scrolls through her phone. We suspend our conversation as a woman walking her miniature dachshund passes by, pausing for the dog to suspiciously sniff a weed pushing through a crack in the pavement. I can't help but to watch; I'm intrigued as to what the dog could possibly perceive as a threat. Evidently, the dog reaches the same conclusion. Not long thereafter, it becomes bored, urinates on the weed, then happily trots on.

"Sorry!" Its owner calls back to us as the wiener dog leads her onward to greater adventures.

"I should try that." I contemplate.

"What's that?" Alison responds uninterestedly, not looking up from her phone.

"Peeing on something I worry over or find threatening and then subsequently investigate."

Alison looks up from her phone. "What?" Her pained face suggests she finds my comment asinine.

"Not literally." I quickly add. "The dog that went by, it saw the weed in that crack over there." I point to the pee spot. "After a thorough inspection and determining the weed was not a threat, it happily peed on it and went on with its day without a second thought. I need to start doing that."

Alison rolls her eyes.

"No, hear me out. Whenever I'm dealing with a problem or setback, whether it's with Enzo, or the douchebags at A's the other night, or even my mother before our reconciliation, I always endlessly perseverate over it. It causes me constant anxiety and stress. It's not healthy. I need to face my issues head on and reconcile them, then put them in the rearview mirror and move on. Like that dog did. No unresolved conflicts and no looking back."

She considers my explanation. "Fair point. But if we ever have a significant conflict, don't try and pee on me."

Her response catches me off guard, and I let out a chuckle. "You got it."

Alison smiles and goes back to her phone. Within a few minutes a passenger jet comes into view – FlightTracker confirms it's Santa and Merri's. Its deceivingly slow approach commandeers my attention, and I can't help but to think of my father.

Within fifteen minutes of landing, Santa and Merri exit the circle-slide automatic doors from baggage claim, waving as they approach. Merri leads the way carrying a large Louis Vuitton shoulder strap duffel with Santa trailing closely behind her lugging two hard shell roller suitcases. He struggles somewhat with the uneven, bumpy sidewalk leading to the cellphone lot.

Alison and I hustle over to help with luggage, reaching them at virtually the same time.

"Hi, honey!" Alison gushes to Merri, drawing out the words extraordinarily long while wrapping her arms around her.

Merri responds equally as effusive. "Alison, oh my God, it's so good to finally see you!" She looks at me while still embracing Alison. "Hi, Jon!"

"Hey, Merri! Dang, you look fantastic!" I call out, then turn my attention to Santa. "Hey, big man. Damn, it's good to see you."

Santa releases his grip on the roller suitcases to give me a solid bro hug, but the suitcases immediately begin to roll backward on the uneven surface.

"Hey, buddy … oh, shit." He laughs and lunges for the handles before they travel out of arm's reach. "Almost got away from me!" He drags them back and situates them such that his foot backstops a wheel, holding them steady.

"How was the flight?" I ask while reaching for a suitcase to lend a hand.

"Bumpy as a toad's ass, but fast." He smiles.

"Ya. We had an awesome tailwind." Merri adds.

"I know." I say. "We were watching you on the flight app and saw you were cruising!"

Merri gives me a once-over, head to toe. "Damn Jon, you got big."

I'm only wearing a t-shirt, admittedly to show off my arms. I'm freezing, but I don't care. Her acknowledgement feels great.

"Yeah, you did!" Santa adds and then pats his belly. "Me too!"

We all laugh, standing in a circle next to Danny's Jeep, chatting away and feeling the love. After a short while, I pose a very easy question. "Alright, who wants to get out of here? We got some drinking to do!"

§

Santa quickly unloaded their gear in the hotel room while Merri freshened up, and we're out and on our way to A's in no time. They're psyched to go, but honestly, I'm nervous I'll be recognized from Saturday night's melee. When we roll up, I notice the sign announcing Teddy the Bull's tour stop no longer appears on the road signage.

As we walk into the front vestibule and up to the check-in stanchion, Alison throws me a quick sideways glance as though to convey, *here we go, cross your fingers.*

"Hi, four tonight?" The host cheerily inquires.

I hang back while Alison and Merri stand up front, leading the way. "We have six; two more are joining us." Alison responds.

"Very good. This way, please." He removes a stack of menus from an unseen receptacle, then turns toward the high-top table section.

After we're seated, I whisper to Alison, "Well, that went over okay."

"What went over okay?" Merri asks.

Alison interrupts before I can respond. "Oh nothing, really. Jon got into a little scuffle here on Saturday. He was defending my honor." She says this last part in a pretty decent British accent reminding me of Princess Buttercup's appreciation of Westley's chivalry in *The Princess Bride*.

"Moving on, m'lady ..." I say, trying to divert the conversation. "So, tell us everything you've been up to, as if we didn't already know!"

"Yes! The wedding!" Alison chortles.

We spend the next half hour enjoying cocktails and beers, chatting animatedly over the soon-to-be Crindle couple's wedding plans as we wait for Darcy and Kelly to show up.

Santa surveys the room. "A's hasn't changed at all."

"You should've seen it on Saturday." I respond. "They brought in a mechanical bull."

"Really? Did you try it?" Merri asks me.

Alison interjects. "I did! It was fun!"

It was fun until she finished her ride. "Nah. It wasn't really my scene."

Before I proceed into further detail, Darcy and Kelly appear at the host station and spot us before the host has an opportunity to greet them. They gesture toward us, presumably in an indication they're with our party, and head over to us unaccompanied.

Kelly instantly connects with Santa. "Ben … what's up, buddy? How you been?!"

"Man, I've been great! How are you? You look totally different. I like it!"

"Yeah, I changed it up once I left Harding. You know, so I could get hired somewhere." He laughs. "Now I'm working with Jon!"

"Keep the look!" I quickly react, generating a chorus of laughs.

We take another moment exchanging 'hellos' and introductions for Darcy to the group before settling back into our seats. We spend the next hour or so reconnecting before the conversation expectedly turns to Harding-Williams.

"You guys ever see anyone from the firm?" Santa asks.

"Well," I begin. "You know Sharon works for me, uh, for us at J.K. Williams."

"Oh, right. I'd like to see her before we go back."

"That's an awesome idea. She'll be so excited to see you!" Alison bubbles.

"What about the partners? What are they all doing now that it's shut down? Do you ever connect with Harding or Osterman?"

Alison and I hastily glance at one another before I answer. "No. No idea where any of those guys are." That's not exactly true. I have no idea about Calvin Harding, but I know exactly where Harold Osterman spends his days – dirt napping in a blue barrel resting on the bottom of North Bay.

Kelly jumps in. "I've seen a few of them around town, including Harding, but I haven't seen Osterman."

This is such a strange conversation. Santa witnessed Bob Roberts dangling lifelessly from his bedroom ceiling fan and someone subsequently torching his house, but he's unaware Osterman staged the fire attempting to kill us. He has no clue what ultimately happened to Oster-man. Kelly doesn't know anything about the true story behind Harding-Williams' demise, let alone Osterman's role in it. Yet, he's unknowingly involved and active in our current situation with Enzo, of which Santa has no knowledge. And Alison and I know everything. It's proving to be a delicate dance jockeying the conversation among the six of us and not revealing anything to those not otherwise informed.

Fortunately, after a few more drinks and a couple of bathroom breaks for me, we move on to more enjoyable topics such as what we'll do in our upcoming weekend in Providence. We agree that following my commitment at Jimmy's funeral, we'll show Santa and Merri WaterFire and then go out afterward. As the evening rolls on, Asbury's starts crank-ing up with patrons and energy. We have an awesome time with no men-tion of last Saturday night's incident, and as luck would have it, no one from A's recognizing our part in it.

23

We spent the rest of the week keeping it relatively low key. We were hungover most of Thursday and opted to chill on Friday in anticipation of a 'raise the roof' weekend. We cruised out early Saturday morning for the drive to Rhode Island taking two cars – guys in one and girls in the other. We needed two vehicles to fit all of us and our gear, plus Kelly and I aren't heading back until Monday night. We're going to spend an extra day at Equinox to hopefully clean up loose ends with the audit. The boys ride in Uncle Danny's Jeep – I would have rather ridden in Kelly's Corvette, but we needed the room. The drive time to Providence isn't long; a little less than three hours, and after arriving at the hotel for an early check-in, I put on my suit and break away from the group to meet Enzo for the service. He arrives at the hotel right on time in his cream-colored Cadillac and we make the short drive to the funeral home mostly in silence. Alison would have come if I wanted her to, but I didn't feel the need to expose her to Jimmy's cast of characters and his Rhode Island crime family.

There're quite a few people here – many more than I expected – maybe a hundred, maybe more. Jimmy can pack a house. Although the receiving line begins outside wrapped around the corner of the funeral home, Enzo and I enter the building through a side door where the men huddle outside to smoke. This is decidedly an Irish experience – gentlemen donning kilts scatter about in full authentic Irish regalia. I appreciate the look and the pride.

After we're inside, I take a second to locate Lorraine, so I'm not blindsided and steamrolled when she sees me. It also crosses my mind maybe Pammy's here. After all, Jimmy maintained she was his 'personal entertainer.'

It doesn't take much effort to find Lorraine. From afar she appears surprisingly composed, but as I draw near, I can see the weary hurt and stress she carries in her sunken eyes.

"Lorraine, I'm so sorry." I offer.

"Thanks for coming." She burbles. "I never knew he was sick. No idea."

I don't know how to respond to her. While Enzo steps in to hug Lorraine, I approach the casket and peer inside. It's Jimmy, alright. Aside from some pancake makeup applied to his face, he looks like he could be sleeping. I kneel at the casket, perform the sign of the cross, then step aside, making room for the next mourner. I scan everyone congregating among the three adjoining living rooms. No Pammy in sight.

As with many wakes, the attendees, particularly the older men, regard this as an occasion for celebration. Celebrating the life of Jimmy O'Brien. I'd wager that a fair amount of them are drunk by now, though we're only an hour past noon.

I attempt to perform my psycho-analytical guessing game, but quickly lose interest. Too many like-minded people here and not enough diversity.

"You're Enzo's boy." I turn and come face to face with a man appearing to be in his mid-thirties. I don't have the energy to correct him.

"Yeah. I'm Jon." He's a big man with hands like bear paws that dwarf my own when he shakes my hand. "Nice to meet you. You know Enz … uh, my dad?"

"Yeah. He's a friend of mine." When he speaks, his brown lumberjack beard bobs with every word. He has medium length brown hair to match, but he's used gel to slick it back, making it appear darker. With his mediocre black suit and tie, he looks like he could sell snake oil out of a covered wagon in an 1880's western town.

"Really? He's a friend of yours? How did you meet him?"

He tugs on his beard, forming it into a point. "I do some occasional work for him."

"Oh? On the car lot?" I lie.

"No, not a car lot. I didn't know he owned one. With his ATMs. Jimmy's, too." His response sets me at ease somewhat and I let my guard down.

"I'm Tommy. Tommy Bungheimer. People call me Bung." He introduces himself as sincerely as one could possibly do.

"Bung?"

"Yeah, Bung." He says cheerfully.

"Well, Bung, nice to meet you."

Enzo walks up and joins our conversation. "Hey, guys. I'm glad you've met."

"Yep. Bung here, was telling me he does some work for you." I slightly widen my eyes when saying 'Bung.'

Enzo reacts with a barely perceptible shoulder shrug and fleeting smile at my reference to his nickname. "Good. I meant to connect you two at some point."

"Yeah, Jon, it was good to meet you. Catch you around." Bung excuses himself and continues working the room.

"He goes by 'Bung'?" I pose to Enzo. "Does he get that? I can't believe he doesn't get that."

"Heh, I know. I think he got the name as a kid and it stuck. He doesn't seem to mind."

"Right. He may enjoy it. Who would make fun of him, anyway? He's a frigging beast. Reminds me of an oversized Uncle Danny."

"Exactly."

"So, what's the plan? I'm ready to go."

"We're going to head out in about a half hour. The funeral starts at three. It'll give us plenty of time to get to the cemetery."

That's disappointing. I was kind of hoping to see Pammy at the wake, though I'm not surprised she didn't show up.

§

Thankfully, it's tolerable weather outside; not too chilly and the wind died down. The sun isn't terribly bright, yet nearly everyone wears sunglasses. No big surprise. Those closest to Jimmy stand in a tight circle around the casket as it straddles the open grave, resting on a coffin-lowering contraption. I'm set back outside of the ring, though not far from the action. Enzo stands back-to with his arms draped around people positioned on either side of him, neither of whom I know. Lorraine does the same. I presume she's flanked by Jimmy's relatives on one side and possibly her own on the other. A couple of kilted men round out the rest of the group. In unison, they each place a single red rose on the coffin. The two Irishmen open alcohol bottles and pour the contents over it as well.

As they chatter among themselves, I begin to look around at the greater assemblage. One faction swiftly catches my attention. Along the roadway, roughly fifty yards away from us, sit three large black SUVs. Lined up in front of them stand seven or eight sharply dressed men. Most are middle aged, but a couple of them are elderly. It's not hard to figure out who they are – Rhode Island Royalty. Enzo told me about them. The guys who made Federal Hill. They may have run on the wrong side of the law, but they took care of their own. They were Good Fellas, and also good guys.

The crowd around Jimmy breaks up and filters into the outdoor seating and we do the same. Everyone except for Lorraine. She walks up to a podium to address the attendees.

"Thanks for coming, everybody. It means a lot. Jimmy woulda been proud. He was really proud of you all. He told me just a couple days ago, he says, 'Rainy' – he used to call me Rainy – he says, 'Rainy, I got the best friends. I'm so proud of 'em.' "

This is no MLK – *I Have a Dream* speech, that's for certain. My mind wanders, as do my eyes. I turn to look back at the Old Guard behind us, but they've left. Those are some quick hitters. Get in and get out (and don't get caught.)

Lorraine finishes her speech and approaches the coffin. Tears stream down her cheeks, and in a very touching moment, she bends over to place a final rose on the coffin and give Jimmy a final kiss.

She steps away and watches as a cemetery worker operating a remote-control unit initiates the process of lowering the casket. A bag-piper corps begins a very emotional rendition of *Going Home*, moving nearly everyone to tears.

24

“Tell me about the guys standing out back by the SUVs. Do you know them?”

Enzo slowly drives out of the cemetery parking lot. He seems distracted and only half-listening to me. Following an extended silence, he responds. “Most of them. The older guys I know better. The younger ones, not so much.”

“You okay? You seem preoccupied.”

He turns his head to face me. “Yeah. Yeah, I’m good. Just thinking about Jimmy. What else do you want to know about them?” He asks solemnly.

“Why were they at Jimmy’s funeral?”

“Those were guys paying respects Jimmy knew when he was a kid. They were involved with Jimmy’s dad, mostly.”

“I figured as much. The old guys who ran Federal Hill.” I say as a statement and not a question.

Enzo doesn't immediately react, but eventually nods his head thoughtfully. "They didn't just run it. They made it." He knows the question coming next, so he preempts it with an advance response.

"The old guy with the cane. He was hunched over in the middle of the group. Did you see him?" He doesn't wait for my acknowledgement. "That's Francesco Antonetti. He's called Frankie Humps. He was really close to Jimmy's dad." He looks long and hard at me. "I told you a while back I used to be second in command in my region … he's the Boss. The Big Boss."

I'm staring back at him. "You worked with these guys, too?" I look away. "Shit."

We ride the remainder of the trip mostly in silence, but as we get nearer to the hotel, I have a couple of lingering questions. "You once told me you were a marked man because of protecting me and as a result, you 'turned.' How did you get out of it? Did you get out of it?"

"Yeah, I got out of it. First, you've got to understand the Rhode Island mafia isn't what it once was. In the seventies and eighties, I would never have been able to show my face around here again without getting whacked. Today, it's less organized. There are a lot of crews still around, but they're detached. All the respected and feared leaders who brought everybody together are long gone; either dead or locked up in the ACI. Today, the crews don't get into the big stuff like they used to – loansharking, racketeering, bookmaking, extortion. It's mostly pushing drugs now. Don't get me wrong, they can still be dangerous."

I can't help but notice he continually squeezes and releases his grip on the steering wheel, giving the impression of a nervous twitch.

"Are you still working with them?" I try not to be antagonistic.

"I told you, no. I'm done with it. Everything I do is legit."

"Fine."

Enzo flicks his turn signal on, and we pull into the roundabout drop-off entrance at the hotel. I exit the car and before turning and walking away, I lean into the open window to ask him a final question. "Why Frankie Humps?"

"He doesn't use a cane for support because he's old. He's got a deformity on his back since he was a kid. It's a hump, like a miniature hunchback of Notre Dame, pressing on his spine."

§

It feels good walking around the city with friends, particularly after a depressing morning with Enzo. The sky glitters with a never-ending fabric of stars framing the waterpark basin where a collection of braziers burns brightly. It's warm tonight; much warmer than in Portland, offering us a sneak peek into the much-anticipated summer to come. Alison doesn't realize it yet, but I've booked a private gondola ride for two along the fires of the Waterplace Park installation, one of a few locations hosting fire sculpture tours on the water.

While everyone chats contentedly, I lead the group toward the launch point for our excursion. Upon arrival at the ticket booth, I stop, generating a halt to our walk and our conversations.

"Hey, babe. We're stopping here?" Alison wonders.

"Yes. I thought we could take gondola rides down the river for a closer view. More private, too. They each fit two to a boat."

Darcy's all in. "Excellent! Great call. Let's do it!"

Fortunately, everyone else is on board as well, so to speak.

"Cool. We buy tickets here and launch down on the shoreline." I point to a collection of boats moored nearby. "Each boat has an operator. We're only along for the ride."

After squaring up with the operators, they guide us down to the launch area, hastily give us some safety instructions, then board the six of us into three separate boats. We begin our ride at the basin, and as we float off, Alison and I are immediately greeted by a man whose expertise entails gargling with a flammable liquid then spewing a remarkable volume of fire from his mouth. Further down, a woman spins ignited wheels of circular flame in either hand.

"Absolutely mesmerizing." Alison softly murmurs as she takes in the sights.

When I look at her, I'm drawn to the reflection of the surrounding flames dancing in her eyes, presenting the perfect visual representation of her vitality, spirit, and mischievousness. At this moment, I don't think I could love her any greater.

"If you could have anything in the world, what would it be?" I ask.

She continues to watch silhouetted shadows soundlessly stoking fires along the channel. "Is this a trick question?"

"No. Not really. Just asking."

She plays along with me. "Well … for us to be happy, I guess. That's a loaded proposition, right?"

I didn't anticipate the ambiguous ending to her response. "How so?"

"A lot goes into making us happy, considering our history. First off, I want to be safe." She ruminates for a moment. "I'd like our situation to normalize, too, or at least be as normal as it can be. And I'd like the same for you."

"To be happy …" I contemplate. "Me, too."

I steel my nerves and swallow hard. I've gone over this countless times in my mind, but no matter how ready I try to convince myself that I am, I know I'm really not. I reach into my coat pocket while carefully bending down on one knee, mindful of not upsetting the boat. My hand trembles uncontrollably as I open a small box containing the ring I hope with my entire being Alison will accept and allow me to place on her finger.

She watches me, unsure of what I'm doing. "What … are you …?"

"Alison," I gently interrupt while taking her hand. "I've loved you ever since the first day I met you."

She quickly realizes what's happening. Her eyes instantly well up and she begins to softly shudder.

"With each passing day, I love you more than yesterday and I don't want to go another without you as my wife. You are truly the peanut butter to my jelly." I smile.

Alison expels a phlegmy laugh as tears stream down her cheeks.

"Will you do me the tremendous honor of being my wife? Will you marry me?"

She places her hand on my cheek. I close my eyes and tilt my head, leaning into her love and warmth, accepting and absorbing as much of it as I can.

She nods unreservedly. "Yes. Yes, I will marry you!"

I slip the ring on her finger deliberately, attempting to savor the moment and set it indelibly into my memory. Alison extends her hand, admiring her engagement ring before throwing her arms around me. We embrace, tears flowing irrepressibly from both of us.

"Congratulations! That's a first for me." Our boat operator injects lightheartedly.

"Me, too!" I add.

"Me, three!" Alison finishes.

The remainder of the ride for us is simply a blur. Alison and I focus completely on ourselves as though nothing else in the world exists.

For me, in large part, nothing else does. We arrive at the gondola launch before the others, scarcely able to contain our excitement until they arrive.

"I can't believe this!" Alison gushes. "How long have you had this planned?"

I laugh. "Since I met you!"

"Oh, come on!" She slaps my forearm good-naturedly, striking a nerve that hasn't properly healed from my gunshot repair surgery. It sends a jolt of pain through my elbow and sizzles up to my shoulder. I do a reasonably decent job of covering it up, but she notices me wincing. "Oh, I'm sorry, baby. Are you okay?"

"Yeah. I'm fine." I smile. It's a stark reminder back to the crematorium and the earlier events of that day leading up to our confrontation with Agent Brown. Ultimately, it concluded with Uncle Danny's cremation. "I wish we could tell Uncle Danny we're getting married."

"Sabrina, too. And your dad." Alison muses sadly.

She's right. "Seriously, though, I've been planning this for the last couple of months. This was perfect!"

"Yes, it was! Look, they're all at the shoreline."

The two gondola operators tie up on the dock and we see the group climbing the footbridge to where we wait.

"Hey!" Alison squeals as they approach us, holding up her left hand. Merri processes it before anyone else.

"Holy! No way! Ahhh!" She shrieks, and everyone quickly figures out what just happened. "Yay! Congratulations!"

Santa bounces in place, throwing me a high-five. "Dude, that's awesome!"

Kelly claps me on the back. "Congrats!"

"Thanks! We're so pumped!"

We spend some time talking about how it all went down – thinking up the proposal, buying the ring, Alison's surprise, and so on. Eventually, we realize we're starving and need to eat before the food trucks close down for the night. As we walk from the docks, we continue with our separate conversations, bantering about wedding planning, how cool WaterFire is, and what type of food we want.

Kelly abruptly interrupts the dialogue, curbing the upbeat vibe. "Jon. Look at that guy right there." He directs my attention ahead of us and off in the distance.

"Which way?" I strain to focus in the darkness through the glare of portable lighting illuminating the outdoor eating area.

"Right there." He points to a man rising from a picnic table and turning to face us. "That looks a lot like the guy from …"

He doesn't have an opportunity to finish his thought before my head jolts forward from a punch from behind followed by my knee buckling from another blow, driving me hard to the ground.

"Ah, what the fuck?" I curse, rubbing the back of my head as I stare up at a guy I've definitely never seen before standing over me, his firearm exceedingly visible and accessible in his waistband. He appears well-built in a white t-shirt and jeans, though it's tough to tell while he looms over me. Another man stands just to his right a few feet back.

Santa steps up quickly, but immediately retreats when he gets a visual of his gun as well.

"Back away, asshole." He directs to Santa while lightly tapping the pistol's grip. "This don't concern you."

As Santa takes another step back, my assailant returns his attention to me. "Williams, right?" I can tell he knows full well who I am. His eyes form into thin slits and he looms above me in a dramatic aggressive stance. "Make sure your old man falls into line."

"I don't know what you're talking about." I respond, my voice strained.

Before we have any further exchange, the guy from the picnic table Kelly spotted moments ago reaches us. Goddamn … it's Bung. I spot a firearm clenched in his hand as he protectively steps over me without saying a word. He simply stares him down.

"Not a smart move, Tommy. Turn around and walk away." The white t-shirt prick warns, trying to sound tough, but clearly threatened.

Bung still doesn't say anything. He stands his ground in a stare-down with him. Following what feels like forever, white t-shirt guy eventually drifts back a few steps and returns his attention to me. "Make sure Enzo falls into line," His voice intensifies as he backs further away. "You better, too!"

After the mystery assailant disappears, along with the impending threat, Bung finally lets his guard down. He holsters his pistol, then offers his hand to help me up.

"Thanks." I grunt, accepting his assistance. "What the hell just happened?"

Kelly butts in before Bung can respond. "You know this guy?" He asks wide-eyed, referring to Bung. "He's the dude who helped you at A's, then disappeared!"

I look at Bung and he nods. "Yeah. It was me. We gotta talk but first I need to call Enzo."

25

"Who the fuck was that?" I croak. "What did he want? Why did he tell me and Enzo to fall in line?" I prattle on rapid-fire, peppering Bung and not pausing for answers.

"Jon, we *can't* do this again!" Alison's bent over, hands on her knees and lower lip trembling, imploring me as though I have any control over, or knowledge of the situation.

Bung doesn't seem overly excited. "Doesn't matter. Hang on a second, I'm calling Enzo." He dials his phone and after the call connects, he puts it on speaker so we can all hear. I scan the group, registering the concern and uncertainty on their faces.

Enzo answers. "Hey, what's up?"

"Yeah, we got a problem." Bung informs. "They made contact. We're at WaterFire and you're on speaker with Jon."

"Shit. Hey, Jon. You okay?"

"Been better. What the hell's going on?" I've managed to compose myself and clear my thinking somewhat.

"Ah … well, we may have a situation here. I learned Jimmy has some stuff going down on the side. Bung, can you follow them back to the hotel? Make sure they get in alright? I'm gonna be tied up for a little while."

I don't give Bung an opportunity to respond. "What's it got to do with me … and with you?"

"Eh, I'm not sure yet. That's what I'm finding out. I'm thinking it's a big mistake or misunderstanding."

"Sure as hell didn't feel like it." I say while patting the back of my head.

"Damn. What happened?"

"I got cuffed upside the head from behind. More of an assault on my pride than anything."

"Sorry, man." He consoles. "Bung, did you catch me on following them back to the hotel?"

"Yeah. No problem."

"Good. Jon, I'll connect with you in the morning when I know more."

"We're leaving early." I warn. Well, everyone except for Kelly and me, anyway. He and I are staying an extra day to work on the credit union audit, but I think the better of disclosing that to him. I'm perceiving the need to implement a key tenet of Enzo's *Unofficial Handbook of Mafia Guiding Principles* – disclose or disseminate information on a need-to-know basis only.

"Got it." He says, then disconnects the call.

Bung catches me gawking at him as he puts his cellphone away. He preempts a question from me by offering his meager understanding of events. "I don't know much. Enzo wanted me to keep an eye on you guys tonight. That's really all I know."

"Then why did you say to Enzo, 'they made contact' as soon as he answered the phone?" I challenge.

He doesn't skip a beat. "Because he said the reason he wanted me to keep an eye on you was because he was worried somebody might be pissed off about some stuff you two were working on."

I'm not exactly certain why, but I believe him. More than likely, Enzo has him on a need-to-know basis only as well.

"So, when you told me at the funeral you did occasional work for Enzo, this is what you meant?" I surmise.

"Yeah. Pretty much."

I exhale a deep sigh.

§

As we head back to our cars parked a few blocks away, I manage to allay Alison's angst somewhat, but her understanding and patience understandably wears thin. I split off from her mid-way and fall in alongside Bung for the remainder of the walk – I want to ask him a few more questions before we separate. "Who was the guy who suckered me? The one you confronted?"

Bung tugs on his beard, fashioning it into a human hair arrowhead. I suspect it may be a nervous habit of his. "Yeah, I was surprised to see who it was. I went to high school with him. Pete O'Shea. He's a douchebag who always caused trouble growing up. We used to call him Piece O'Shit because his name sounds like it, plus his initials are P-O-S."

"Ha. That's fitting. Who's he working for? Jimmy?" I ask.

"I'm not sure. I know he hung around with Jimmy, and Jimmy was a guy he looked up to. He probably did work for him, and now works for whoever Jimmy was connected to."

"You don't know who that is?"

Bung looks at me apprehensively while responding earnestly. "Yeah. You need to talk to Enzo about that stuff."

I opt not to press him any further on Enzo's business, but nevertheless I want to know about the night at A's and how our coming together unfolded. "What happened at the bar in Portland? Why didn't you tell us who you were then?"

Bung shakes his head almost imperceptibly. "I needed to get out before police got there. That wouldn't have been good if I was stopped by anybody."

I can appreciate that. We needed to hustle our asses out for the same reason. "I get it. We got out just as fast."

"Yeah. I saw you as I was leaving the parking lot. Nice work in there, by the way."

His compliment strokes my ego, but I don't noticeably let on. "Thanks. You, too. Adrenaline takes over, I guess. Did you know any of the guys at the table?"

"Yeah, no. They had nothing to do with Rhode Island. It was a coincidence. They were random punks who got in a bad spot."

"I'd say so. Why didn't you say anything to me at Jimmy's funeral?"

"I'd been meaning to talk to you when I got the chance, but it wasn't really the place. I wasn't supposed to be a secret. At least I don't think I was."

The more interaction I have with Bung, the more I kind of like him. He's a soft-spoken guy, but without a doubt dangerous. Much in the mold of Enzo, which is probably why Enzo uses him.

When we arrive at our cars, Bung talks directly to me, but loud enough for everyone to hear. "Yeah, I'll talk to you sometime later. My van's around the corner. Give me a couple of minutes and I'll follow you back to the hotel and peel off after you're inside."

§

We drove to WaterFire with the girls in one car and boys in the other. Now Alison, Santa, and Merri ride with me, while Kelly and Darcy ride separately. In my rearview mirror, Bung's headlights from his Econoline van shine brightly, almost blindingly, illuminating our interior. No one says anything at the outset of the trip, I suspect to process what transpired. I spend my time worrying about Alison, though. Not even an hour ago, her one desire for anything in the world was for us to be happy. As a prime component of that, she wanted us to be safe and our life normal. I couldn't even make it last a single hour.

I don't think Alison will want to talk about anything on the ride back to the hotel; she'll wait to discuss it with me privately, but as expected, Santa has questions.

"What's going on, dude?" He asks uneasily. "That wasn't a random thing. This feels like a black cloud hanging over us again."

He couldn't be more right. "It's not random, but I'm not exactly sure what it was about. Like you heard, I need to connect with Enzo."

"Did this have anything to do with when you were with Enzo and got shot?"

"Nope." I answer truthfully. That resulted from a confrontation between Agent Brown, Enzo, and me. He waits for me to elaborate. "I'm doing some work with him, though. He's helping us with the money Bob left for Alison. Somehow this is related."

I never got in depth with Santa as to what happened after Bob's house burned down. He knows Bob left Alison money after his 'suicide,' but beyond that I was as generic as possible with him for his own safety. On top of that, he has no idea Mom and Enzo gave us a boatload of cash.

"You're laundering money?"

I decide to be upfront with him. "Yup. Enzo is, anyway. Otherwise, we can't use it." I feel Alison stiffen next to me.

"Oh. Okay."

Santa seems satisfied with my answer with no need to explain further, and I appreciate that. We arrive at the hotel, lose our escort, and head up to our rooms without incident.

"Goodnight, guys." I say to everyone before heading into the room. "I'll see you all in the morning before you head back to Maine."

Alison stays behind to talk with Merri in the hallway for a few minutes before coming in. She's surprisingly calm after the door closes behind her. "You really don't know what that was about?"

"No. I really don't. It must be something to do with Jimmy and Enzo, but beyond that, I have no idea. You heard him on the phone. No doubt he knows more than he's telling us, but he needs to figure it out, too."

Alison sighs resignedly. After a brief pause, she decides to call it a night. "I'm tired. I'm going to bed."

"I'm right behind you. I need to text Enzo first, though. I don't really want to connect with him tonight or tomorrow. I'll tell him I'll call Monday when Kelly and I are at the credit union."

I also need time to calm down. I can't deal with another sweat-soaked recurring dream tonight.

26

Kelly and I grab a hurried breakfast Monday morning after checking out of the hotel and head directly to Equinox. We have little need, and less desire, to hang around Equinox or Providence any longer than necessary. The prime objective this morning – wrap up fieldwork, then hit the road.

Lorraine is nowhere to be found, nor did we expect to see her. Thank the Lord for small blessings. Kelly works diligently most of the morning while I review his work product. It feels like we're on a regular audit. Almost.

Late in the morning and closing in on lunch, Kelly peers up at me amidst a stack of workpapers and miscellaneous binders. "I thought a lot about what happened Saturday night." He begins apprehensively. "I hesitate to bring this up, but what a crazy situation. From a wedding proposal to a street fight. About as far apart as you can get. I'm not sure what you're tangled up in, but I'm wondering if you're okay."

Kelly's a perceptive guy. He knows something's up.

"I know what you mean. I'm alright. I think it was a big misunderstanding." I hope so, anyway.

He seems to be placated by my response, though I'm not certain I'm fully placated by my response. Nonetheless, he switches up the conversation entirely. "Hey, did you notice every time Bung says something, he starts it off with 'yeah'?"

"Yeah." I say, and both of us chuckle at the joke.

"I still can't believe the guy from A's was Bung. You said Enzo sent him to Maine to look after you?"

"That's what he claims. I have no reason not to believe him."

Kelly lets it go, but his unspoken thought comes through loud and clear. Why the hell would Enzo have this guy traveling all over New England if something wasn't wrong?

As the clock approaches noon, I hear a text chime ding from my phone I left in a jacket pocket. I pull it out and check the screen. It's not what I'm expecting. I have an incoming message from an unknown caller using a blocked number. After opening the message, I'm instantly taken aback by the directive:

I have no idea who this is, but they undoubtedly know me. A number to call from a blocked phone, no less. I have a flashback to the answering machine message Enzo played at Danny's house from Agent Brown that terrible night directing me to call a number. I can still hear his filthy, distorted voice in my mind.

I experience a visceral reaction in my gut generating a massive adrenaline flow as I dial the number while walking out of the room. I put the phone to my ear just as it first rings.

A woman answers on the other end, quickly executing a standard greeting. "Good afternoon. Providence College, Office of Residential Life, how may I help you?"

"Uh. Hello. My name is Jon Williams. I'm calling because –"

"Jon! It's Pammy … Meridian from the Foxy Lady. Do you remember me? You need to come and see me!" She's almost breathless as her thoughts rapidly bubble up. "I overheard a meeting with your dad at the club and you need to know about it."

I'm totally confused. "Of course, I remember you." How could I forget. "He's not my dad, though." I clarify.

"Listen to me carefully. While you're here in Providence, I need you to come and see me now! It's very important!"

"What's going on?" I ask with an uneasiness in my voice matching her alarming tone, wondering how she got my cell number and knew I was local.

"I can't talk. It's not safe on this phone line or in this office. You need to come see me now!" She repeats. "I'm at the Slavin Center at PC where the bookstore is. Meet me in the lower level near McPhail's. Can you get here within an hour?"

"Yes. I'll be there."

"Okay. I'll see you here."

After I hang up the phone, I head back to the conference room where Kelly sifts through his workpapers.

"Hey dude, I'm going to head out and get us some lunch. What do you want me to bring you back?"

"Ah, sweet. Turkey sandwich and chips or something like that."

"You got it. I'll be back soon."

I hope I'll be back soon. Pammy's got me right up on edge and that's not a place I want to be.

§

Providence College boasts an impressive little campus, and interestingly, it sits very close to the Foxy Lady. I drove past the strip club's entrance road to arrive at the school in under five minutes. The welcoming security attendant at the gatehouse graciously directed me through the rotary access toward the Slavin Center. I opt to continue beyond the parking garage, replete with tennis courts resourcefully positioned on its rooftop, and park directly in front of the college's fitness center in a reserved spot for the Athletic Director.

It doesn't prove difficult to find my way through the building's access doors, snake down to the lower level, and ferret out the bookstore. We're getting close to graduation, so there's a substantial amount of activity and a large number of students milling about getting ready for life after the safe cocoon of college. Enjoy it while you still can kiddos, it's a tough battle out here.

McPhail's, the college's on-campus pub, comes into my view. Pammy sees me as I see her, then stands up and waves me over to her dimly lit corner. As I approach, I get a better look at the real Pammy. She looks young – really young, with light brown hair bordering on a blonde shade, and I can't help but to wonder what the impetus was for her becoming a stripper.

"Hey," I say hesitantly. "What's wrong?"

"Here. Come sit down." She instructs, her face flush.

I casually scan the room as I take a seat on a dingy, well-worn couch. It doesn't appear as though anyone takes note of us.

"Listen to me." She begins softly but firmly while grasping my hand. "I overheard some guys at the club having a pretty heated discussion about what happened to Jimmy."

"What about Jimmy? He had a heart condition."

"No," She shakes her head. "I don't think he did. It was a set-up. Someone did this to him and made it look like a natural death. I heard it."

"What are you talking about? Enzo … the guy you thought was my dad … told me what happened. He had a bad heart."

"No! That's why I'm reaching out to you! It wasn't an accident. Your dad … I mean … he was part of it! I think he might have done it!"

I feel an instant flare up of anger and frustration.

"Look, I'm sorry, I don't think you have your story straight." But as the words exit my mouth, I fully grasp and appreciate Enzo's capabilities and history.

Pammy regards me with a simultaneous mishmash look of concern, sadness, and fright.

"Slow down." I say. "First, let's start from the beginning. How did you get my number? How did you know I was here in Providence?"

She pauses a moment, presumably to collect herself. "Okay." She takes a deep breath and exhales. "I was dancing at the club Saturday night. I overheard Enzo talking to the guys that he …"

"Wait. Enzo's one of the guys you overheard?"

"Yes. He was there!"

That catches my attention. Enzo was at the strip club during our phone call – her timeline matches up. I wait for her to go on.

"That's how I got your number. He had your contact info open on his phone and I was close enough on the stage to see your name and number upside down and I remembered it. I thought about it all day yesterday if I should call you or not." She fidgets with her fingers, and I can't help but to be distracted by it.

I interrupt. "Let's say this is true. What's this have to do with me?" I don't really care about Jimmy, but I'm more than a little curious as to her story involving Enzo and why he was connecting with me from there.

"Before Enzo came in, every now and then I heard these guys I'd never seen before say your name. I didn't think anything of it; Jon's a common name, but when I saw Enzo, I got worried. He sat with them." Her speech pattern undulates akin to a young girl's fervor at meeting a teen idol. "I started really listening, and I could hear him talking about it! Enzo was a part of it, and I think he may have actually done it!"

My face contorts in disbelief. "What?! There's no way. No fucking way." I think back to Enzo utterly distraught at Jimmy's funeral.

Sensing I'm getting ready to leave, Pammy grasps my wrist. "I could hear them grilling Enzo to see if he covered his tracks with Jimmy. If it was all set and nobody knew."

Pammy breathes a deep breath and collects herself. She's given me all of her intel and now appears spent. "Look, my break's almost over. I need to get back to work. I only warned you because I'm worried you might not be safe."

That sends chills down my spine. "Why?"

Her face becomes pained. "Why did I warn you? I don't know. I like you."

I was more wondering why she thinks I'm not safe, but before I react or respond, Pammy rises from the couch, leans into me, places her hand on my shoulder, then disappears around the corner.

27

"**H**ey. What do you say?" Enzo buzzes cheerfully, answering my call on the first ring.

"Tell me what happened to Jimmy." I bark from behind the wheel of Danny's Jeep. I can't hide the burn in my voice as I leave the campus.

A fleeting moment of dead air ensues followed by a gauged response deflecting my demand. "Jimmy? I told you what happened. He had heart issues."

"Don't bullshit me. I know he didn't have a heart attack."

Enzo predictably goes into defensive mode. "What are you talking about? What did you hear?"

"Goddamn it! Enough with answering my questions with more questions! Just fucking be straight with me!"

His voice drops low … calculating. "Listen to me carefully. Not on the phone. Let's meet up tonight."

I calm down in turn. "Okay. Where?"

"I'll get a message to you. You're at the Omni?"

"I checked out."

"I'll have a message waiting for you at the concierge desk, then. Later this afternoon." He disconnects before I answer, leaving me hanging on a dead line.

Shit. We're in it, now. Nothing's felt right since we've been in Rhode Island, and now it's coming to a head. I can feel it. Kelly can feel it. Everyone else can feel it, too.

As I approach a traffic intersection on my way back to Equinox, it hits me I need to bring lunch back for Kelly and me. I hastily put my directional on indicating I want to change from my far right lane over to the left lane and then enter a nearby sandwich shop parking lot. Before I can make a move, a black SUV pulls alongside me, filling in the space and blocking me before I can shift lanes. I slow to let him pass, expecting to drop in behind to make my turn, but he slows as well. It forces us both to stop side by side as the traffic light turns red.

I annoyingly gawk at the passenger side of a heavily-tinted window on a late-model black Ford Expedition. The window abruptly glides open revealing two middle-aged guys, both of whom are looking directly at me. I can't really make out the driver well; he's African American and mostly out of view, but I can see the passenger. He sports black hair tied back into a ponytail protruding from beneath a navy-blue mesh trucker baseball hat, with oversized aviator sunglasses dominating his otherwise pale, thin face. He slides them down to the tip of his streamlined, pointy nose, revealing two beady eyes, and cocks his head forward in a deliberate demonstration he's checking me out. Without taking my hands off the steering wheel, I lift the fingers of my left hand in an acknowledgement I saw them and would not have changed lanes and knowingly cut them off. He doesn't acknowledge my wave. He readjusts his glasses, closes his window, and the Expedition moves through the still-red light. After a moment of reflection, I reach for my glove box, open it, and feel a slight modicum of relief confirming the presence of my loaded pistol.

§

When I make it back to Equinox, Kelly is more than happy to see me with our food.

"Thank Christ. I'm starving. What took you so long?"

He's not expecting an answer, but I'm going to give him one. One that will catch his interest, and more than likely alter his world view a touch. I look at him calmly, but concernedly. He picks up on my affect pretty quickly.

"Dude. What's up?"

This is my final opportunity to redirect the conversation, but I don't want to anymore. I need to get this off my chest and come clean with him. The audit's essentially complete. If Kelly decides he wants out, well, then he gets out. His payment from me buys his silence, and if that isn't sufficient … I don't even want to go there.

"I talked with Enzo while I was out." I elect not to disclose my visit with Pammy or the odd encounter with the black SUV.

He stares at me. "And?"

"I haven't been completely honest with you." I shake my head and look up from the floor. "You've noticed some weird shit going down beyond what happened Saturday night – attitudes and such with Lorraine even before Jimmy died."

He nods knowingly.

"I'm not related to Lorraine." I blurt.

He doesn't seem surprised. "I got that. There's no way. I can tell by how you two relate. So, here's my question to you – what the heck is going on here? Really."

Kelly threw the door wide open for me. "I'm not related to Lorraine." I repeat. "She was connected to me by Enzo. He got us this gig through Jimmy."

Today is not the day to tell him about my, Alison's, and Enzo's connection to the spectacular fall of Harding-Williams. It's not relevant to what we're doing here, and I'm not sure he could handle it, anyway. Baby steps.

"Enzo needed me to do this audit for him because he's working with Jimmy … uh … was working with Jimmy."

"What does Equinox have to do with Jimmy beyond his wife working there?" He predictably asks as his first question.

"Enzo and Jimmy grew up together. They were friends … close friends." I take a deep breath, then just spit it out. "Jimmy was helping him move money through his ATMs. Lorraine and Jimmy were getting a fee; she may still be, for pushing the cash through."

"What for? Dirty money?"

I nod.

"For real? You knew about this? Are you in on this?"

"A little." I reply somewhat skittishly.

He grimaces. "A little? What the hell does that mean?"

"Enzo helps me out with stuff." I'm trying to disclose the least amount of information as possible.

"A lot of this makes sense now." Kelly realizes. "The fat audit fee. You paying me half." He locks eyes with me. "Lorraine balking at me testing internal controls around the SARs process. Is she intercepting SARs related to Enzo?"

I nod again. He nails it dead, and I'm not surprised he got there so quickly.

"That's some serious federal lawbreaking shit right there, man. We should go." He says, lowering his voice considerably. "We need to finish this conversation outside of here."

"Right … let's bail. And by the way, I have to see Enzo tonight on a problem I need cleared up. I don't want to involve you any deeper than you already are, but this would probably be good for you to hear." I leave the quasi-invitation hanging out there for his consideration.

"You kidding?" He smiles at me. "I think I already dove head-first into the deep end. Luckily, I'm a damn good swimmer."

§

We haul ass out of Equinox and head back toward the hotel. I feel as though a huge weight has been lifted off my chest and I've received a pardon of sorts as I let Kelly in on the arrangement. I'm speaking freely now, though still mindful of not disclosing anything I deem irrelevant to what we're doing here.

Kelly breaks down the operation. "So, to summarize, Enzo filters dirty money through Jimmy's ATMs."

I nod periodically while driving when I detect Kelly pausing for confirmation.

"He banks through the credit union with Lorraine managing the SARs process and concealing his activity. Your participation provides cover allowing Lorraine to conduct her affairs without interference from a third-party external auditor." He pauses and looks at me. "What am I missing?"

"Nothing, really. You've pretty much nailed it." I prefer truthfully responding to his questions rather than offering information unsolicited. Damn, I've learned a lot from Enzo.

"You have money flowing through the ATMs, too?"

"Yes. Enzo's given me some cash over the years." I agree to his conclusion of me using ATMs as conduits to avoid implicating J.K. Williams, P.A. in any money laundering role.

He looks at me like I'm stupid. "Why don't you push it through the firm? Easy enough to do."

I laugh at his observation but don't acknowledge the idea.

"How did Enzo make his cash?"

"I have no idea, and I don't want to know." That's mostly true. I know how he made the General Defense money, but not the rest of it. And it's one hundred percent true I don't want to know.

"Earlier, you said Enzo wanted to meet up tonight. Will he be okay with me there? I'm putting this all together – Enzo isn't someone to mess with."

"No, he's not – someone to mess with, that is." I confirm. "He'll be fine with you there. I'll take care of it and give him a heads up."

"Dude. I'm a little afraid of you now." Kelly confesses jokingly, but with a grain of underlying truth. I kind of like that.

I lean toward him and crack open the glove box, exposing my Glock nine-millimeter, pause for a moment to allow him to register its contents, then close it again. "Just in case."

Kelly's eyes open wide, and he nods appreciatively. "When are we meeting him?"

"Not sure. We'll see. He said a message would be waiting for me in the hotel lobby."

We enter the self-park section of the parking garage connected to the Omni where Kelly asks his final two questions. "What does Alison know about Enzo? About this?"

I shut the engine down, let my hands drop to my side, and stare into my lap while thinking back to our brief time together with Mom and Enzo.

"Everything."

28

The concierge hands my driver's license back to me coupled with a handwritten note. "Thank you, Mr. Williams. Have a nice evening."

"Yes, thank you as well. I appreciate you asking me for identification." I say, acknowledging his conscientiousness while replacing my wallet in my pocket. He smiles in appreciation and continues on with his duties.

Kelly looks on interestedly as I open the note and read it aloud. "Old fire house. At four." I turn to him. "I'm not sure what this means."

"That's where he wants us to meet him."

"No shit. What fire house, though." I hesitate and check myself. "Sorry, man. Didn't mean to be a dick."

"It's all good. I think it's the restaurant where we ate when that guy was carted off out front. Ladder 130-something, right? The old fire station?"

Of course, Ladder 133. He's dead on. "Exactly. Nice call. Let's head over there now; we'll be a little early, but that's not a bad thing."

§

My eyes are drawn to the *Foxy Lady* signage visible next door within a stone's throw of the restaurant entrance. As we get closer, I see Enzo through the etched-glass front window seated at a high-top table, paging through a newspaper. Apparently, he had the same idea to arrive early. The heavy front door slams behind us with a loud crack, catching his attention, and he raises his hand to signal us over.

"Hey, guys. Take a seat." He offers while rolling up the newspaper and placing it atop a bag set next to his feet. He launches into his explanation without waiting for any reaction or acknowledgement from us. "Alright, this is what I know. I thought Jimmy might be doing something similar to me – pushing dirty cash through his ATMs. I found out he was into other stuff." He focuses his attention directly on me. "Jimmy ran drugs for the guys you saw at his funeral."

"Okay, so what's that have to do with us?" I ask uneasily.

"It's convoluted." Enzo expels a deep breath, brushing his hair back on his forehead. "I got pulled into a situation, and you did too, by happenstance."

"What situation?"

"Do you remember the guy who passed out in front of the ATM outside? Fat Mikey?"

"Yeah." How could I forget. Both Jimmy and Lorraine grilled me on what happened to him. "What about him?"

"I figured out why he had a drug overdose there."

"Because he did drugs?" I throw out cynically.

Enzo looks at me stone-faced.

"Sorry." I offer sheepishly. "I'm trying to piece together where you're going with this."

"Hang on, it'll make sense in a minute." His face softens and he resumes. "The drugs the guy used came from inside the ATM. He was there to make a pickup, but the dumbass decided he needed to use right there, and he OD'd." Enzo pauses for us to absorb his narrative and ask questions.

"Jimmy stored drugs in his ATMs?" Unexpectedly, this comes from Kelly. Up until now, he's been silent as a church mouse.

"Yes." Enzo replies while alternately looking at Kelly and me. "Fat Mikey was working for Jimmy to pick up drugs from the ATM."

"So, where is Fat Mikey? Lorraine asked me at the credit union if I knew where he was. Jimmy asked me the same thing at the club."

"You saw Jimmy at the club? The Foxy Lady?"

"Yeah, it was a few weeks back. Kelly and I went with Alison and Darcy, but that's a whole different story. He wanted to know where Fat Mikey was because he never made it to a hospital. He said he checked everywhere and that he couldn't get in touch with you, either."

"Okay, I got it now. That makes sense. He was asking me about him, too." He pauses to process. "I think Fat Mikey never made it to a hospital."

"Then where is he?" I press.

"That brings me to my next part. I told you I found out Jimmy was working for the guys, or the guy, at his funeral – Frankie Humps." Enzo stares with a pained expression at his clasped hands resting on the table. "Frankie did something to Jimmy as punishment and to hide tracks from Fat Mikey's mess up at the ATM out front here."

He struggles to get the last of his sentence out without breaking down, and I give him a moment to compose himself before I respond.

"Okay, two things. First, I understand what you're saying, but I still don't understand what it has to do with us. And second, now I get why you were surprised when we were on the phone earlier and I asked you what really happened to Jimmy and that I didn't think he had a heart attack."

Enzo's face dawns with realization. "Right ... why did you ask me that? How'd you know?"

I explain to him my interaction with Pammy at the club the night I went with Alison, Kelly, and Darcy, followed by my meeting with her today. He didn't know who I was talking about until I referenced the girl who typically danced for Jimmy.

"Holy shit. We had no idea she was listening in. Damn, she better hope no one else figures that out."

"Listening in on what?" I can't hide the frustration in my voice.

"That goes back to your opening question of what this has to do with us. Frankie knows I'm running cash through Jimmy's ATMs. He also thinks I owe him for some other stuff I used to be into."

Enzo stares hard at me. I understand exactly what he means. He was a marked man for saving Alison and me following the Harding-Williams attack. I'm thankful he didn't go into detail in front of Kelly.

He resumes his explanation. "He wants me to run the ATM drug business on his behalf ... basically take over Jimmy's operation. I think he feels like I owe him and this will wipe the slate clean, but it's bullshit. I don't owe him anything."

"This is why you had Bung tailing me." I realize. "He told you on the phone, 'they made contact.' I get it now."

"That surprised me. I only had Bung on you as a precaution."

"You have no idea what really happened to Jimmy?" I ask.

"I know what happened, but I'm not completely certain how. It wasn't a heart attack. At least not a natural one."

"Which would explain why Lorraine wouldn't know the difference." I reason. "Pammy said she heard someone ask you if you 'covered your tracks.' What does that mean?"

Enzo looks up to the ceiling, presumably to recall the conversation. "Frankie was asking me if I covered my tracks with Jimmy on the cash I was pushing through his machines. He wanted to make certain he wasn't trading one headache for another."

It's a rational explanation. "What happens if you decide to tell him no?"

"I've been wrestling with that question for a couple days now." His eyes peer up at me while his head droops toward the table. "I think I need to go with it for a little while for all of our safety until I figure out how to extract myself."

I shake my head. "No way. You're on your own, then. I'm not a part of this and I'm not finishing the audit. This is way beyond what I signed up for. Does Lorraine know what Jimmy was into?" I'm totally amped up.

"I didn't ask her, but Jimmy told me she's clueless as to what he does except for with me. Listen Jon," He implores. "You have to do the audit. You can't back out now. We need to see this through."

Enzo's affect worries me. He's nervous and he's not trying to hide it. I haven't seen this side of him before. Normally, interactions with Enzo embody calmness and composure.

His face appears pained. "Listen, Frankie knows who you are from Jimmy, and he knows what you're hired for. You need to go with it, at least for now."

I look to Kelly for his input. "We can buy some time." He maintains coolly. "I can fabricate some reasonable fieldwork roadblocks without creating suspicion."

It's at this exact moment Kelly generates an enormous amount of respect from Enzo.

"Good. That would be very good." Enzo states matter-of-factly, his mood improving significantly. "Carry on business as usual. I need to process all of this and figure out where to go from here."

"I assume you mean extricating us, right?"

"Absolutely."

We spend another half hour or so combing through the events that led us to our present situation. I'm relieved Kelly's here to gain an understanding firsthand from Enzo, but uneasy because he's neck deep in it. He doesn't seem to be too worried about it, though.

I'm more than ready to make tracks and get out of here, but we need to eat first before we head back to Maine. "One last question – why hasn't a single server come to see if we want anything?"

"I told them not to come to the table until I signal we're ready."

29

We arrived back at the apartment around eight o'clock. Thankfully, Santa and Merri went to her parent's house for dinner, so only Alison and Darcy were here when we showed up. For the past hour or so, Kelly and I downloaded our afternoon with Enzo to them.

"Okay, let me see if I understand this correctly. The ATMs store drugs that Jimmy would pick up and distribute for coverage in different areas of the city?" Alison queries. She sounds more sad than angry we're going through another rough patch with Enzo. "How do the drugs get to the ATMs?"

I address her first question which will answer her second question. "Not exactly. Jimmy, or somebody Jimmy trusted, would load the ATMs with bulk drugs ... heroin, cocaine, and fentanyl, mainly. Then a street leader, or soldier as Enzo calls them, picks it up. Fat Mikey is – or was – a soldier. After the pickup, the soldiers break the bulk dope down into smaller units and deliver to runners for sale on the street. Every drug-filled ATM has a service area, and they act as drop boxes in the logistics pipeline of drug distribution."

Darcy poses a question, and it's an exceptional one. "You said Enzo services some of Jimmy's ATMs. Why didn't he find drugs when he was stocking them?"

"I asked him a similar question. He said he learned there're false compartments in specific ATMs concealing the drugs. You can identify which machines store dope by a thick red stripe painted around the exterior perimeter. He said Jimmy never had him service any of them."

"Thank heavens for small favors." Alison grumbles.

"The guy we saw passed out on the sidewalk … nobody knows where he's at." Kelly adds.

Alison and Darcy look to me for confirmation. "Enzo said the guys Jimmy worked for got rid of Fat Mikey for being careless and stupid. He was using the drugs from the ATM and OD'd right in front of us. He may have survived in the ambulance if they administered Narcan in time to reverse the overdose, but somebody intercepted him and made him disappear."

"How could that happen?" Alison scoffs. "You can't just make someone disappear from an ambulance."

I shrug my shoulders. "Maybe if you're these guys, you can."

We fall silent, collectively processing the discussion and connecting it to what happened this weekend in Providence. Although Kelly heard everything at the restaurant today, I'm hesitant to bring up Enzo's short-term plan of playing along with Frankie's demand in front of him or Darcy, nor do I want to mention the truth about Jimmy's death. I'd rather talk with Alison alone so she can be brutally open and honest with me.

"They really made that guy disappear?" Darcy wonders.

"It looks that way." I say. "You were right, though; that wasn't a contact drug situation. Fat Mikey definitely ingested dope."

Darcy blinks rapidly, eyeballing each of us in the room. "Those red-striped ATMs … they function as more than purely a money dispensary – they double as a drug dispensary."

Leave it to a pharmacist to put it in those terms.

§

Darcy and Kelly head out around nine, leaving Alison and me to discuss where we go from here. I expand upon my account of Jimmy's funeral and relate Enzo's oral history of the mob guys who showed up at the burial. It leads us to a discussion of Frankie Humps and his objective to rein Enzo back into an active role by essentially having him step into Jimmy's shoes. I also share with her Enzo's intent to ride out the short term with Frankie until he comes up with an alternate solution, and my reticence in continuing with the audit. Finally, I discuss Kelly's belief he can delay its completion until we figure out a reasonable resolution.

Alison goes to the kitchen to pour a glass of wine. "So, the a-hole who confronted you at WaterFire works for this Frankie guy?" She calls out, returning with a beer for me, which I gladly accept.

"Yeah. Pete O'Shea. Bung said he went to school with him, and O'Shea was an asshole back then and still is now. He hung around with Jimmy, and Bung thinks he probably works for Frankie."

I spend some time explaining to Alison the relationship among Jimmy, Jimmy's dad, Enzo, and Frankie Humps. The account lasts for about two beers and brings me to how Jimmy died.

"He didn't have a heart attack. That much is certain." I choose not to disclose my encounter with Pammy where she contended Enzo played a role in Jimmy's death. I'm confident he wasn't involved, and it only muddies the waters further. On top of it, I don't want to risk facing Alison's wrath at discovering I met up with her privately.

"Enzo believes Frankie took out Jimmy somehow and made it look like a heart attack as punishment for sloppy management over his business, maybe for a lack of trust in him, maybe to cover tracks, or more likely, for all of it."

"If you told me all of this before I met Enzo, I wouldn't believe a word of it." She softly shakes her head. "So, what about his wife?"

"Enzo says she doesn't know anything about what Jimmy was doing on the side; only about him cleaning money for us. Enzo will find a way to preserve it. Besides, she'll have to keep it going; Jimmy's gone and any one of us could implicate her if she balks."

"Why can't we walk away from the audit? Enzo's not saying he wants you to get involved with the ATMs and the drugs. Why are we stuck?"

"Because Enzo says Frankie knows about us. Jimmy was also cleaning the dirty drug money from his business for Frankie in the same way Enzo is."

She nods her head in understanding before I finish my thought, then expands upon my explanation. "Which is why Jimmy was so quick to set up Enzo with his own business. He's already using his wife's bank position to clean his own money. Why not add Enzo's, too?"

"Exactly. And Enzo paid them a fat monthly fee on top." I add. "And another reason not to walk away, maybe more importantly, is if we go along with this, at least for now, we can hide in plain sight and not have to do what we did when Enzo and Mom snatched us. I don't want to have to disappear and stay in an out of the way hotel again. Besides, we can separate ourselves from Enzo's responsibilities. We only have the audit to contend with."

She doesn't respond, and not because she disagrees. Quite the opposite. It's a begrudging indication she understands it's the best course of action for the short term.

Alison exhales a deep sigh of resignation while rising from the couch and walking to the kitchen. "I have no idea how Sabrina managed all those years with the constant crap storm Enzo faces." She calls back while placing her wine glass in the sink.

I'm not sure, either. The reality is, in the end she couldn't survive the storm. I think about her so much. I think about what could have been … but won't. I become absorbed in thought only to be pulled back to the present by Alison returning to the living room without a stitch of clothing on her body. She extends an arm, encouraging me to take her hand and follow her. "Come to bed with me, baby. I need to be close to my fiancé."

30

Well, isn't this a sight to behold. I'm not certain I'm seeing this correctly. "Would you mind telling me what this is about?" I politely request, grinning at the two of them.

"What?" Mom giggles. "You didn't expect us here together?"

She's as beautiful as ever, sporting her white track suit and hair pulled back into a high ponytail. "Can't say that I did. I definitely didn't see this one coming."

I look at Dad seated next to Mom, smiling at our exchange. He appears healthy; in fact, better than I've seen in more than a decade. His color's decent and he's put on weight. Strangely, we're seated in plastic Adirondack chairs on the fifty-yard line of the football field in my old high school sports complex.

"What do you say, Dad?"

"Not much, my boy." He continues smiling.

"Why are you both here?"

Mom answers first. "You tell us. It's your dream."

"Right. I'm dreaming. This is the first time I've been conscious of it as it unfolds."

Dad turns more serious minded. "You know why we're here." He surveys the surrounding area. "Maybe not physically here at the high school field; that's peculiar, but the reason we're meeting. You're struggling and want guidance from us."

Mom nods her head in agreement.

"I feel like I'm running on a hamster wheel and I can't get off or make it stop." I confess.

Dad takes a deep breath and audibly exhales. "Jon, you've always been levelheaded, if not downright cerebral. Think about what you need to do. Remember what I always told you. Analyze the situation and break it down into manageable buckets, then address each bucket individually. Don't become overwhelmed with the totality of all the buckets. Take them in order, one at a time, and knock 'em down. What's your first bucket?"

I consider his question. "My first bucket? Alison's well-being. No doubt. And mine."

"Good first bucket." Mom concurs.

Dad considers this. "Okay, how do you accomplish that?"

"Over the short term, I stay close to her – making certain she's always physically protected. Over the long term, I extricate myself from Enzo and his operation."

"I agree with you. The extrication piece, in my view, becomes bucket number two." He recommends.

Mom expands upon my safety approach. "You ought to keep in mind, Enzo's main goal will be to keep those close to him safe, as well. As you formulate a plan, stay close to him so you know what he's doing and it doesn't conflict with your plan."

"I hear you, but staying close to him may jeopardize our safety."

"Have you ever heard the expression, 'Keep your friends close and your enemies closer'?" Dad asks.

"Of course." I reply.

"Well, I can't tell you Enzo's your friend or an enemy. Maybe he's both, like a frenemy, but either way, it's better to be vigilant about his actions and stay alert as to what he does."

I consider his assertion. "Good advice. Better to dance with the devil you know."

He claps his hands together producing a loud crack. "Exactly."

"So, where do we go from here?" I inquire.

"You go back to living your life and handling your buckets." Mom recommends. "We'll be here if you need us."

"Always." Dad adds.

I stand up to hug them in an awkward three-way embrace. After a moment, they drift off together toward the school parking lot where in the distance I see a perfectly preserved, burnt-orange Mercury Cougar.

I walk across the turf field to the starting line of the quarter-mile school track and begin to jog. Lap after lap I run, reflecting on my buckets. How do I keep Alison safe? How do I keep myself safe? And Kelly? Darcy? I continue running, a hamster on a spinning wheel unable to get off, faster and faster until I feel my heart bursting through my chest. The sky turns an angry black as storm clouds move in, intensifying in size as they roll through the surrounding area … hunting me. I'm so tired. I need to stop … just a minute or two of rest. As I approach the brink of collapse, a booming voice washes over me:

GET OFF THE WHEEL!

My eyes pop open and I spring awake in bed, sucking in air as though I'd broken through the water's surface after swimming an underwater lap the entire length of a pool. My matted hair feels almost as wet as if I had. I take a second to establish my bearings and realize Alison's already up and out of the bedroom.

"Hey! I'm up!" I call out to her.

"Good morning, baby!" She calls back.

As I remove my sweat-soaked t-shirt and toss it onto the floor, Alison comes breezing into the room. "Ooh. Look at you … getting naked for me?" She plops down onto the side of the bed and massages my scalp, gently scratching with her fingernails. "Hmm. Your hair's damp. You okay?"

"Peachy." I reply wryly before redirecting the conversation and brightening up. "How are you this fine morning?"

"Great! I'm sorry I fell asleep on you last night. I don't know why I crashed so quickly."

"Because you were tired. You needed it."

"Ya, I guess. But I'm not tired anymore … and I have an idea."

Ah, yes. Alison has her naughty look going. A dominant hunger radiates from her sensual, almond-shaped eyes. She fixates on me visually, removing a hair tie encircling her wrist and pulling her hair into a ponytail. I lay in bed with my arms submissively at my side in anticipation – like a kid on Christmas morning waiting eagerly, yet patiently, for presents to be distributed.

"Let's get you out of these." She purrs, grasping my underwear on either side of the waistband and sliding them down to reveal my ready rock hardness.

I raise my hips to accommodate, causing my engorged penis to come tantalizingly close to her lips as she leans over me. She responds by licking the shaft from base to glorious tip during the progression of separating me from my Calvin Kleins.

She tosses them aside and settles in between my open legs, allowing me an unobstructed view of her promise of paradise. Oh man, it feels so good. I rock my hips in rhythm, enjoying every second of every sensation … but … Dad wants to know how I'm going to accomplish my first bucket.

Wait. Stop. Why on earth are you thinking of that? Pay attention to Alison, dummy. There. That's better. Worry about that mess later. I reach out and caress her head, stroking her loosely pulled-back hair. Ahh, I can feel my orgasm building. It's going to feel so good; I can't wait … still, what's the plan for the second bucket … how do we safely extract ourselves?

Damn it. What in the holy hell is wrong with me? My insanely hot fiancée is giving me a first-class blowjob and I'm thinking of strategies for dealing with Enzo? Get ahold of yourself, man. Focus! Alright, alright, I'm good now. I'm almost there. Now we're rolling.

Alison kicks it up a notch, moving increasingly faster until I'm virtually levitating off the bed and can't hold back any longer. "Ah, yes! Ahhhhh!"

After my orgasm, she continues to hold me firmly in her mouth, waiting for my body to relax, then proceeds to lightly rub my cock over her cheek and lips. "Did you enjoy that?" She breathes.

"God, yes. You're amazing. Have I told you you're amazing?"

Alison removes her hair tie and shakes her hair out, combing her fingers through her wild mane. "Well," She says while rising from the bed. "It ain't much, but it's honest work."

I burst out an unanticipated laugh. "What the …? Did you just say that?"

"I sure did." She chirps proudly, tilting her head as though to good-naturedly convey, *got something to say about it?* When she hears no argument from me, she bobs her head in approval, smooths out her shirt, then turns and disappears from the room.

God, I love her.

31

My first bucket – keeping Alison and me safe. Provided I conduct business as usual and finish the credit union audit timely, we should stay out of harm's way. At least for now. The thing is, I have no intention of issuing an audit report; at least not one with my name on it. I'll carry on as normal, or make it appear so, until I can figure a way out of this.

Next up on the docket today, I need to connect with Kelly and find out where we are with the 'roadblocks' he feels would extend the audit timeline and buy us some time. After that, I'll call Enzo and reassure him. I won't tell him about my stall tactics on the audit, though. And then … let me see … what's next?

Before I can finish mapping out my morning, Alison breezes in unannounced, startling me. "Will you hurry up? I need to use … oh, dear God, that's horrible!" She chokes, stopping dead in her tracks and drawing her shirt collar up and over her nose. "Jon, what the hell makes you smell this bad? Ugh. That's so nasty!"

"I'm sorry. Maybe you could give me another minute?" I lightly protest as she does an about-face and retreats from the bathroom.

"C'mon, get a move on! I need to go pee!" She whines from the hallway.

"Okay … okay. Sheesh." I grumble under my breath. "Can I get five minutes of privacy to take a dump?"

I swiftly conclude my transaction and depress the toilet's handle, catching sight of the swirling water circling the bowl and disappearing down the drain. It may well be illustrative of my future.

"Don't come out without spraying first." She instructs.

"Wouldn't dream of it."

I reach for the air freshener situated on the tank cover and spray liberally throughout the room. As I put the can back, I find myself examining the toilet bowl. It could use a second flush.

After I finish washing up, Alison passes by me while pinching her nose as I dry my hands on a small bath towel.

"Is it safe to go in?" She asks nasally.

"Walk in the park."

§

Kelly answers my call after the first ring. "Yo, Jon. What's up?"

"Hey, bud. Where are you? Home?"

"Yeah. I figured I'd stay away from the office until I connected with you and found out what's what."

"Good call. Hey listen, when we were with Enzo yesterday, you said we could throw up some roadblocks to keep the audit going without anyone getting suspicious. How do we do that? We need to make it happen."

He pauses. "First off, the easiest thing we can do is request information that's either time consuming or hard to get … like telling them we need to contact certain business customers with official requests for information to support the audit process. Loan balance confirmations or deposit balance info. That's totally legit. I've already done some of that work; enough for the audit, but they don't know that. On top of it, can't we tell them we need to figure out the second partner review? We only have one partner at J.K. Williams."

"Officially, we have two. Alison's an equal partner in the firm."

"Oh. Good to know. Well, we can still use that strategy to delay."

"I agree. I like those ideas. Let's go with both."

"I'm on it."

"Hold up a minute. I'd like to be with you when you call Lorraine and then you can go ahead and touch base with the finance department. First though, I want to call Enzo."

"No problem. I can come by if you want, and we can do the call from there."

"Perfect."

§

No sooner am I off the phone with Kelly, that I'm following up with Enzo.

"Hello?"

"LoZo. What's shakin'?"

"Hey, Jon. Not much going on with me. How about you? I'm actually in the car headed up your way as we speak."

"Really? Everything okay?"

"After a fashion."

"Huh? What does that mean?"

"It means to some extent. I'm getting out of Rhode Island for a few days. Sabrina and I have a special spot we go to up there in Camp Ellis on the breakwater. I need to be close to her right now."

It's interesting to me he says they *have* a special spot up here and not *had*. "I get it. Hey, just wanted to let you know we're moving along fine with the audit. No complications. I'm calling Lorraine today to check in and see how she's doing and let her know everything is good from my end."

"Excellent. I appreciate you sticking with this."

"No problem. Now, tell me why you're really getting out of R.I. for a couple days." I hear a faint puffing noise and I can sense he subtly laughed at my request.

"I had a meeting with Frankie's guys. I confirmed with them I would fill in for Jimmy until they found a suitable replacement. I didn't really have a choice, but we played the game like I did."

"Why don't you bail out? Just take off and disappear."

"There would be a domino effect that jeopardizes your safety. I need to see it through to a satisfactory outcome for everyone."

"So, you're valuable to Frankie as long as you cooperate? I'm okay as long as I keep on with the audit? What about police? You have to deal with drugs in ATMs for Christ's sake."

"Only in Providence and Frankie owns anybody who matters. I'm not worried about it."

"Sounds like you have everything covered." I reply cynically. What could possibly go wrong. "Listen," I say, changing the conversation. "We're having a dinner tonight for Santa and Merri. They're heading back to Nebraska tomorrow. Come meet us."

Enzo pays no attention to my sarcastic reply. "Sounds good, actually. Where?"

"It's at DiMillo's. You know, the floating ship restaurant a few blocks down from your ... waterfront business ... whatever. Meet at six o'clock."

"Yeah. I got it." He replies dryly. "See you then."

§

Alison joins Kelly and me at the kitchen table. She appears to have successfully recovered from her earlier bathroom trauma and now readily awaits our call to Lorraine. Kelly dialed Lorraine's direct line and set his phone centered among the three of us on its speaker function so we can all participate.

"This is Lorraine." She answers.

"Hi, Lorraine. This is Jon Williams. I'm calling you from Kelly Cookson's phone."

"Jon, I'm glad you called. You gotta get moving on this audit. I gotta close out these SARs and get rid of them. I can't have them hanging around anymore."

I guess we're dispensing with pleasantries. "I fully understand. That's the purpose of this call. I'd like to apprise you of the status of the engagement. Currently ..."

"Cut it with the 'business voice' bullshit." She barks. "Jimmy's gone. I don't need you and Enzo's aggravation no more on whatever it is you got going on. Get it done quick and get it done right. Got it?"

"I got it. Loud and clear."

"Good."

Lorraine disconnects the call, leaving the three of us looking at one another.

"That didn't go well." I suppose.

Kelly disagrees. "It might not be all that bad. She's all bluster and no bite."

"Angry bitch." Alison hisses. "You told me she doesn't know about her husband's business." She directs to me. "Enzo told you that. She thinks she's doing us and Enzo a favor."

"For ten grand a month." I clarify.

Alison nods. "Right, but we still have her cornered. We can turn her in if she forces our hand. She can't say anything."

"You might be right on that. Let's run this past Enzo. He's on his way into town, and earlier on the phone I invited him to the send-off dinner for Santa and Merri at DiMillo's tonight."

Alison's mood swings from irritable to melancholy faster than beans through a cowboy. "I wish they didn't have to go back."

"I know. Same here." I agree, then swiftly switch topics before either of us gets too sentimental. "Kelly … my man … we're heading to the gym today. You interested?"

"Rather eat a turd dipped in diarrhea."

Alison's face sours. "Ew."

32

The gym isn't notably busy today. Vehicles occupy less than half of the parking spaces, and that's fine with me. I wouldn't expect a large crowd on a Tuesday afternoon anyway; at least not until the business workers let out after five o'clock.

I collect my phone, wallet, and keys from the dash console and open the Jeep door. Before I get out, I turn to Alison. "Alright. Let's get at …"

She's already stepped out of the car. "Yup. Keep up if you can."

I kick it into high gear to catch up, happy to participate in her good-natured competition.

"Excuse me! Sir! Excuse me! Can I have a word with you?"

We pause to locate the source of the outwardly insistent request. A large, well-built black man in tan khakis and a navy-blue blazer strides determinedly toward us from roughly thirty yards away. He's followed closely by someone; a white dude I think I recognize.

"Are you talking to us?" I ask, looking around.

He closes the gap swiftly, reaching into his jacket pocket. "Yes. My name is Clyde 'C.J.' Calhoun, Special Agent with the United States Drug Enforcement Administration. This is my partner, Agent Ron Harmon. Do you mind if we have a word with you?"

He positions a slim, black leather billfold containing his photo identification on the left side and his 'Special Agent' eagle shield on the other, in front of me for my inspection. I stiffen at the visual. Christ, these guys are DEA. Agent Harmon also presents his billfold, indicating a rank of 'Agent.' I can't help but wonder what makes Clyde 'C.J.' Calhoun so special.

"What can I do for you, Special Agent Calhoun?"

"Please. Call me C.J."

I don't respond. I'm lost in thought trying to recall how I know Agent Harmon. Then it hits me. His thin, pointy nose – he was the passenger in the black SUV that pulled up alongside me at the red light back when I met with Pammy at Providence College. Calhoun must've been the driver. I was unable to get a good look at him because Agent Harmon obstructed my view.

"Mr. Williams, we'd like to speak with you regarding someone you know who we have reason to believe may be connected to a drug distribution operation in Rhode Island."

He knows my name. This can't be good. "I remember you guys. At the intersection in Providence."

"That's right." Agent Calhoun confirms.

"You ran the red light." I childishly point out.

He shrugs dismissively. "Anyway … we'd like to speak to you about Lorenzo Garibaldi."

"Hang on a minute." I interrupt. "Baby, go ahead inside. I'll be in soon. It's okay." I quietly reassure Alison.

She doesn't protest, slowly withdrawing from the group before spinning and briskly walking toward the entrance. I revert my attention back to the agents. "Please," I encourage with a sweeping arm gesture. "Continue."

"You appear to have a high degree of confidence swirling about you right now, Mr. Williams." Agent Harmon squeaks reproachfully. Up until now, he's been silent. His shrill voice matches seamlessly with his ponytailed, pin-straight, oily black hair and pale, angular face. "I'm not so sure that's wise."

Special Agent Calhoun intercedes, countering Agent Harmon's prickly interjection. I suspect it's somewhat scripted roleplay with Calhoun 'on my side' and Harmon playing bad cop. "Listen, here's the situation. You've probably already spoken to Garibaldi about us, and our contact with you here today isn't entirely a surprise …"

Shit, I'm seriously screwed. Calhoun launches into his monologue, explaining the 'who's' and 'what's' of their concerns, but I'm unable to concentrate on his message. Harmon accuses me of being overly confident? Hell, no. I'm pissing in my pants. Calhoun thinks Enzo told me about the DEA making contact with him? Negative. That's a big, fat 'no.'

"Hey. Something wrong?" Calhoun snaps his fingers, breaking me from my zone out. "You with me?"

"Yeah. I hear you loud and clear."

He nods approvingly. "Look, the bottom line is, we know Francesco Antonetti oversees the drug trade in Providence. O'Brien paid the ultimate price for that, and Garibaldi will too, unless he chooses to work with us. We want Antonetti, not Garibaldi, and we know you're close to him. You can help us guide him into making the right choice – the obvious choice. Or …" He simply shrugs, leaving his statement unfinished.

"Gentlemen," I direct to both. "I don't know anything whatsoever about this. I don't get involved in Enzo's matters. We're not very close. He married my mother, but I don't have a meaningful relationship with him."

Agent Harmon counters my assertion with a well-placed challenge. "Then why were you in Rhode Island?"

"Fieldwork on an audit engagement. I own an accounting firm."

"J.K. Williams, P.A., correct?" Calhoun presumes. "A newly-established Maine entity?"

I shouldn't be overly surprised the DEA delved into my background prior to contacting me, nevertheless, I'm rattled. I need to bring this conversation to a close – it's morphing into an interrogation and I'm at a huge disadvantage. "Correct. Well, good chatting with you. Gotta run. I have an upcoming appointment."

Special Agent Calhoun reaches into his jacket pocket. "Thanks for your time, Jon. We'll definitely be in touch at some point. Or, if you'd like to reach out, here are our business cards."

§

Alison nervously waits for me on a couch in the sitting area just beyond the front vestibule. Her positioning conveys to me she's super anxious. Barely perched on the edge of a cushion, she hunches over with knees pressed together and arms tucked into her body as though suffering through an upset stomach. Maybe she is.

"Hey, I'm back."

She jumps up from the couch. "What's going on?"

"Oh man, it's a shit show. You heard those guys are DEA. They know all about Jimmy and what he was doing. They know Enzo's been recruited to take over, but they don't want to bust him. They want Enzo to be an informant so they can take down the whole operation. Frankie Humps is the main target."

"So, what did they want with you?"

"They said Enzo blew them off, but I don't know how it went down. They assumed I had probably spoken with him and that he warned me DEA would be seeking me out. I didn't let them know one way or the other if Enzo connected with me."

"Enzo didn't tell you anything, did he."

I roll my eyes. "No. You know him … only discloses what he feels he needs to. No doubt he didn't expect DEA to reach out to us."

"Right." She waits for me to continue.

"They're not explicit about what they want. They basically say they know I'm close to Enzo and they want me to 'help him make the right choice,' whatever that means."

"It means to convince him to work for the DEA."

"Yeah, I know." I concede. "But I think there's something more to it."

Alison watches me with quiet unease.

"They asked me what I was doing in Rhode Island. When I said I was conducting an audit, they blurted out our firm's name and knew it was a new company. They've been investigating us, Alison, and I have no idea to what extent."

She shakes her head. "Holy. Maybe we should forget about the gym today. We need to figure out what we're going to do."

"Can we stay?" I appeal. "I have my best focus and clear thinking when I'm lifting."

"Ya. Of course. I didn't think you would want to work out after that, but I'll stay, for sure."

"Thanks. I appreciate it. I'll catch up with you in a few." I give her a kiss on the cheek and head to the stretching area for a warm up and to process what just went down.

I place a blue foam exercise mat on the artificial turf and sit on it cross-legged, stretching out my hips and groin. Okay, relax and take a deep breath. Figure this out. It's all part of your second bucket. Clearly, step one, I need to talk to Enzo and find out what happened in his meeting with the DEA. Second – eliminate myself as a bargaining chip for them to influence Enzo. Could we walk away? Enzo says 'no;' Frankie's operation won't let us. Maybe Calhoun could protect Alison and me. This option has to be on the table.

I rotate onto my stomach and press myself up to stretch out my lower back. No doubt DEA's trying to figure out why a new practice like mine has a Rhode Island credit union client. Can they trace the connection? Do they know Jimmy's wife works there?

I finish up stretching with more questions popping into my head that I have zero answers for. Hopefully, Enzo can sort out some of them. In the interim – time to hit the weights and work off some of this aggression and frustration. I'm working chest today, so I walk over to a bench press, place my phone on the floor, and pick up a forty-five-pound plate. As I raise the plate in preparation for placement on the bar, I freeze. I see him. He looks like a mirror image of me … and also poised to place a forty-five-pound plate onto a bar at a bench press setting next to mine. He locks eyes with me. It's the One Upper.

33

Alison and I spent our post-gym afternoon mulling over our im-promptu parking lot meeting with Agents Calhoun and Harmon and attempting to sketch out next steps. We've determined we need to talk with Enzo before we can formulate any reasonable or viable plan. It may be a tricky proposition to discuss it tonight at dinner though, while still preserving a lighthearted going-away celebration for Santa and Merri. Unfortunately, it can't wait; we need to take care of this now.

Everyone arrives on time, just a little before six o'clock. Santa and Merri ride with Alison and me, Darcy and Kelly arrive together in Kelly's sweet 'Vette, and Enzo comes alone. DiMillo's Floating Restaurant, a long-standing, awe-inspiring landmark of Portland, floats in North Bay at Long Wharf in the heart of the Old Port. It's quite large, boasting three decks and hundreds of seats surrounded by a yacht marina and residential condos stretching out over the Atlantic. An elaborate gangplank bridging the parking lot to the ship funnels us on board, and a cheery host shows us to our reserved table for seven in the main dining room. It's not especially busy tonight; the summer swell of vacationers and day trippers hasn't come into full swing, so we're looking at a relatively uncrowded evening ahead of us.

Enzo chooses his seat and I pick out the one next to him, wasting no time in opening a discreet dialogue.

"Guess who I ran into today?"

He looks at me quizzically, waiting for details.

"Only your friendly, neighborhood DEA agents, C.J. Calhoun and Ron Harmon!" I say this like an animated pitchman hawking product on seldom-watched late night cable channels. *But wait ... there's more! Operators are standing by!* It has the desired effect.

"What happened?" He breathes heavily.

At this moment, we both realize everyone else watches our exchange. I don't care. This needs to be done. "They told Alison and me they're taking down the drug trade in Providence. They want me to convince you to work with them – Calhoun said you turned them down."

"Do you really want to discuss this here?" Enzo asks, slightly exasperated.

I scan the table. "Might as well. Everyone here knows the deal."

"Fine. Just keep your voice low, please."

Our server arrives at the table for our drink order, effectively pausing the conversation. When I look at her amid the outline of a window framing the ocean in the backdrop, I perceive a slight motion produced by the restaurant's subtle rocking on the water. It's an odd feeling. Speaking to someone seated close to you doesn't generate the same sensation. After she finishes taking the order, Enzo and I resume hammering out our conversation. Thankfully, Alison distracts the others by initiating a wedding dialogue with Merri.

"Why didn't you tell me about them?" I barely whisper.

Enzo shrugs. "It didn't matter. They don't matter. Look, I haven't figured it all out yet, but I'm not going informant for the DEA. And

I'm not going to work for Frankie, either. Like I told you a while ago, it's only for long enough until I figure a way to get us out of this."

His calm rationalization provides a modicum of relief for me. "Enzo," I pause and lock eyes with him for effect. "You need to share stuff like this with me. I get it – you feel like I'm safer if I know less, and I agree with you if I'm not directly involved, but these guys are on to me. You need to keep me in the loop now so I'm not caught off guard."

He nods appreciatively, understanding our circumstances have evolved such that it's a liability and a dangerous disadvantage for me to be less informed. His acknowledgement coupled with our much-needed drinks arriving, provides a good breakpoint to close out our discussion and rejoin the group. It's also a perfect opportunity to give our soon to be married friends a heartfelt tribute. I stand up and raise my glass. "To Ben and Merri, two friends I love dearly and wish for nothing but love and happiness for the rest of their days."

As I deliver the toast, I glance at each person at our table, beginning with Alison. With her wine glass poised, I feel the warmth in her eyes and her love for me radiating from within. Darcy and Kelly sit close to one another, signifying the deepening relationship emerging between them. Santa and Merri overflow with excitement and anticipation of their upcoming nuptials; their broad smiles divulging all. And finally, like me, Enzo watches everyone with a warm admiration, and perhaps a touch of melancholy.

After concluding the toast and putting our dinners orders in, I head off to the men's room to pee. That doesn't bode well, having to go so early, as I plan on downing at least four more beers throughout dinner. When I get back to the table, Merri turns her attention to me.

"So, Jon," She begins. "Have you written your best man speech, yet? We're getting close to the wedding day!" She warns in mock caution.

"I know, right? I only have a month left! I'm thinking of writing a raunchy, tell-all roast. The truth is, I've started it, but I'm struggling to keep it rated R."

Everyone laughs, including Santa. "Dude, be nice. I don't want my marriage to end before it starts." He jokes.

"Don't worry, I won't do anything to get you in trouble on your wedding day. Now, your bachelor's party … that's a different story. No promises." I tease.

"You better not!" Merri chastises jokingly, feigning anger. She tosses a dinner roll at me for emphasis and the table erupts in laughter.

"And you'll have to deal with me!" Alison forewarns.

"Fair point. I'll behave."

We spend the rest of the evening eating, drinking, and enjoying each other's company until we're all pleasantly full. The conversation wanes, as it naturally will, as we approach the end of the evening. Nature calls for me again, but before I can get up to pee, Alison addresses the group.

"Guys, we love you." She directs to Merri and Santa. "We can't wait for the wedding. And I really hope this next month goes by quickly so we can come do it again in Nebraska."

Her comment is a perfect segue to the end of the evening and a timely opening for me to hit the head. As I stand up, I nearly bump into our server approaching from behind while carrying an oval tray chock-full of refreshed drinks.

She sets them on a tray stand. "Alright. I have another round for the group."

"We didn't order this." Alison puzzlingly responds. "We're actually ready for the bill."

"Certainly. I'll bring the bill right over. And the round was compliments of those two gentlemen. Right there." She points to the bar.

We swing around to find Agents Calhoun and Harmon perched on bar stools facing us. Calhoun raises his hand in an unnecessary, half-hearted gesture to draw our attention. In response, Enzo rejects the offer. "No thanks. We're good. We'd like to send these back."

I immediately look to Enzo for guidance.

"Do not acknowledge or respond to them." He firmly instructs after she leaves. "They want to intimidate us. We'll go about our business, pay the bill, and leave." He scans the table, looking for silent affirmation from each of us. Although only Enzo, Alison, and I know who they are right away, the others figure it out quickly.

Enzo clears the check and ushers everyone out ahead of him, acting as a buffer between the group and the DEA should they decide to follow us out. Although I have to pee badly, I'm not going here. No way. I'll find a spot outside.

34

Alison deposits another used tissue into her purse and thrusts her hands onto her thighs with a frustrated finality. "Enough of this blubbering, already. Why am I so emotional right now? We'll see them in a month for crying out loud."

I try to soothe her. "Cut yourself a break. It's totally understandable. Emotions run high when you have the type of shared experiences we have."

She sniffles in response. We've just dropped Santa and Merri off at the jetport and they fly out in roughly an hour. Now we're heading to Eggscellent Choice for a late-morning breakfast. Personally, for me, I'm relieved they're traveling back home. I don't like exposing others to my dysfunction.

I cruise into the parking lot probably a little too fast, coming in hot in Danny's Jeep. It doesn't take us long to get here, the restaurant's located close to the jetport. We breeze inside, and although there's no wait in the front atrium, it's reasonably busy for a Wednesday morning. We see mostly full tables as we're led to our booth.

"I know I wasn't into talking about this stuff last night or this morning with Ben and Merri still here, but what's your plan for dealing with Enzo?" Alison asks after we sit down.

I open my menu and peek over the top edge. "I'm not so much thinking about doing anything about Enzo. It's the DEA on our tail I'm worried about. I'll pull back from pushing our cash through his ATMs, to start. Really, the only thing I think we need to manage is whether we complete the audit. I'd like to walk away, and I will if I can, but for now we ought to tread lightly. Enzo needs some time to figure out his next move with Frankie."

Alison puts her menu down and sighs with resignation. "Okay. I guess that sounds good. You always keep me safe."

Aw. That hits me right in the feels. I close my menu as well – I don't know why I bother to open it at all, honestly. I get the same breakfast every time we're here.

I reach out to the jelly holder. "You ready?"

"Yup!"

Alison loves strawberry jelly, so we have a tradition now whenever we eat here. She forms a goalpost with her fingers, and I attempt to flick a single-serve container to her through the uprights for a field goal. She'll even play along, color commentating the play:

> *He sets ... he flicks ... oh, off the crossbar! He barely had enough, but he knocked it through! Man, that's a big kick ... I mean ... flick for Jon Williams!*

As we celebrate my successful field goal, my phone vibrates in my pocket and I pull it out to see who it is.

Signed off as 'P'? Maybe Pammy? It must be, and it's from an unblocked number.

An instantaneous pit forms in my stomach. Not solely for whatever message Pammy has for me, but also, I don't feel comfortable with her reaching out to me again and keeping it from Alison.

"Who is it?" She asks.

"Enzo. Letting me know he plans on heading back tonight. He wasn't sure if he was staying another day." I hate the lie, but I don't want to layer more worry onto her shoulders. She's already super emotional.

"Good deal. Hopefully, he takes the DEA guys with him, too."

I spew out a nervous laugh. Alison likely assumes it's because the DEA agents have me spooked. Truthfully, I'm more afraid of what Pammy may have overheard at the Foxy Lady. For now, I set my apprehension aside and enjoy a delicious breakfast and Alison's company. As usual, I finish before she does, and also as usual, I wait patiently to clean up what's left behind.

"Hey, after we've finished do you think we could go over to the mall? I need to get some girl stuff at the girl store."

"I don't even want to know." I chuckle. "And yes, of course we can."

She laughs along with me. "Goofball. I'm talking about makeup and hair stuff."

"Right on."

Excellent. While she's inside, I'll have an opportunity to connect with Pammy, and if needed, Enzo. "Okay. I'll hang back in the Jeep and wait. I want to call into the office and see how Sharon's doing."

I will connect with Sharon, that's not a lie, but purely for a cursory check in. Pammy has my real focus.

"Sounds perfect. It won't take me long. Promise!"

§

Whenever we go to the mall now, I intentionally avoid the area where my confrontation with Brown and Reyes occurred. Assholes. I'm glad they're dead. Even so, simply the act of parking nearby triggers me to think about Uncle Danny and re-live our horrifying discovery of his bloated, battered body in the scummy penguin box truck. Good riddance to that rolling piece of shit, too.

I attempt to block out thoughts of Danny while placing the call to Sharon. I'm only moderately successful, but her sunny attitude, even temperament, and ever-positive outlook make it bearable. As expected, the call doesn't last long, and Sharon cheerfully reports all is quiet on the home front. Check that box. Now to call Pammy.

I go to my 'recent calls' menu to locate her contact information and initiate the call. "Hey, how are you?" She asks cheerily, answering on the first ring.

"I'm okay. How are you?" I respond apprehensively.

"Really good!" She replies. "I've missed you at church! I'd love to get together sometime soon. I haven't seen you in so long!"

This is totally strange ... *I've missed you at church* ... her behavior right now isn't what I expected or experienced. If she's reaching out to me, there's a problem, but she's acting cryptic as well as upbeat. I decide to match her ambiguity and alter my tone to more closely match hers until I figure out what the deal is. "Absolutely! So, when do you want to connect?"

"What's good for you? Any time for tomorrow?"

"Yeah, I think so. Around noon. Does that work?"

"Definitely. See you at the chapel!" She ends the call.

Chapel? What chapel? We've met in two places: the strip club and outside the bookstore at Providence College.

I dial Enzo.

"Hey." He answers.

"Hey, Enzo. We might have an issue." I don't wait for him to acknowledge or respond; I have limited time before Alison returns. "I just got off the phone with Pammy, the dancer from the club – you know, the one that told me about Jimmy not having a heart attack?"

"Yeah, I know."

"She reached out to me earlier today to call her." I pause to organize my thoughts so I don't blabber on haphazardly.

Enzo interjects calmly. "And what did she have to say?"

"Not a lot she wanted to disclose over the phone. She was cryptic and wouldn't go into any detail, presumably because she doesn't feel safe." I pause again to allow him to respond. He doesn't. "Anyway, she wants me to come down and meet her in person."

"What did you tell her?"

"Honestly, I have no desire to go back, but I said I would. Don't really have a choice as I see it."

"Probably a good decision." He agrees. "I'd like to be there with you."

"I'm happy you said that. I was going to ask if you would. Can you go tomorrow?"

"Definitely." He confirms. "I was planning to head back, anyway. I have business to handle in the afternoon."

"With Frankie?"

He attempts to placate me. "Yes, but remember, it's only for a short period. I've got to keep him thinking I'm playing along."

I change the subject. "Is there a chapel at the Foxy Lady?"

"Come again?"

I exhale a frustrated breath. "A chapel. Is there a chapel at the Foxy Lady, or a room called the chapel there? Pammy wants to meet at 'the chapel.' "

"Not to my knowledge," He considers. "But because she's listening in on conversations at the club, I doubt she'd want to meet there. It doesn't mean there isn't, though."

I spot Alison leaving the department store, making a beeline to the Jeep. "Okay. I need to go. I'll call you later to firm up plans." I disconnect as Alison arrives.

"Who was that?" She asks while plopping into her seat and closing the door.

"Enzo."

"Again? What did he want? Everything okay?"

"It's all good. He asked if I'd go with him to Rhode Island tomorrow."

"For what?" She's on guard, and I can't blame her.

"He says he has business and he'd like me nearby for window dressing … to make everything look good."

"That means he's meeting with those guys. Is it safe?" She asks doubtfully.

"I think so. I don't anticipate any major concerns." As long as Enzo takes care of Frankie, that is.

"Then I'm going with you."

My first instinct is to protest, but given a moment to think about it, I'd rather have her near me than isolated up here. "No problem. We'll make it a fun trip!"

I can't believe that actually came out of my mouth, but it's too late to reel it back in.

She looks at me stone-faced. "Really?"

35

"Can you explain why Jon needs to go with you today?" Alison innocently asks Enzo from the back seat of his Caddy as we drive from Maine to Rhode Island. We got an early start this morning to ensure we save ample time to figure out which chapel Pammy has in mind for our noon meeting.

"A good-faith gesture. It will build confidence and trust in me and in Jon. If he doesn't come, that will more than likely generate suspicion."

I don't know why, but it's slightly unnerving to hear them talk about me as though I'm not riding shotgun with them in the same vehicle. Hello, I'm right here. At any rate, Alison's unspoken message, or possibly her plea, suggests she believes we're in danger, and Enzo can sense this.

"Don't worry. We'll be very safe." He comforts. "We're meeting in broad daylight in a local Providence laundromat."

A laundromat. We've come full circle. That must be where their crew keeps its headquarters. I remember when I was a kid, Mom used to visit Enzo at a laundromat in Maine. I wonder if they replicate that all over New England.

I enter into the conversation. "What about Alison? I don't want her coming with us. Where will she go?"

"With Bung." Enzo replies while glancing at Alison in his rear-view mirror for her reaction. "I have him meeting up with us to keep an eye on her."

I'm good with that. I pivot around and check in on her as well, attempting to gauge her comfort level. She nods in acceptance.

"Okay, I think we have a lay of the land here." I contend. What I don't have, however, is a lay of the land for where to meet Pammy.

§

We catch up with Bung at the Providence Place shopping mall nestled squarely in the heart of the city, adjacent to the financial district. The mall, with the majestic State House resplendent in its backdrop, provides a nice public space where Alison can do some shopping if she likes, and I won't have to worry about her safety. We spot Bung idling inside the parking garage in his white Econoline van. When he notices us, he shuts it down and exits the driver's side, sporting a wide, teeth-exposing grin. No easy reveal given the magnitude of his beard. As we approach, I see he's using elastics to hold its pointy shape, making his appearance even more intimidating. He could fit in nicely as a character in *Game of Thrones*.

"Hey, Bung. It's good to see you, buddy. Thanks for being here with Alison."

"Yeah. Hey, Jon. Hi, Alison!" He responds equally as warmly. "So, we're hanging out here today?"

Enzo responds. "You and Alison, yes. Probably not a great idea to leave the mall."

"I think so, too." I agree.

"Cool." He says, then addresses Alison. "You ready to shop?"

I laugh quietly at his question. This not-so-gentle giant asks Alison if she wants to shop. It makes for an interesting scene. In response, she turns to me for a hug and whispers in my ear. "Be safe. If you see it going sideways, get the hell out of there."

"Straight away." I promise.

Alison offers her arm to Bung, interlinking hers with his. "Let's shop 'til we drop!"

Bung stays with Alison and Enzo and I pull out, headed for the west side of Providence, the locale of the college and strip club. In the Cadillac, Enzo gets right to business. "Have you figured out the chapel thing yet? It's coming up on noon."

"Not yet. We've only met in two places, though. The strip club and the college. You said you didn't know of a chapel at the Foxy Lady, right?" As I say this, I casually remove my nine-millimeter pistol from my jacket pocket and place it on the bench seat between Enzo and me. It has the intended effect. He looks at the firearm intently and then to me, but says nothing. I follow this up with removing magazine after magazine; fully-loaded clips from my pockets and setting them down as well. He knows I have firearms, but I've never been so brazen about showing them off. Until now. "You know Uncle Danny taught me firearm safety. I've spent a lot of time shooting with him over the years."

Enzo turns his attention back to the road. "Right. Anyway, the chapel. I think it would have to be in one place or the other. Providence College is a religious-based school. It would make sense for her to meet over there again."

"That's right!" I blurt out in an 'aha!' moment. "I'll do a search on their website and see what comes up."

I key in 'providence college chapel' into my phone's internet browser and come up with immediate hits. "St. Dominic's Chapel. It's right on campus. Has to be it."

"I think you're right."

Within five minutes of leaving the mall, we arrive at the rotary security gate of the college. The campus buzzes with students finishing up the semester and preparing for summer break. It's a warm day – co-eds meander throughout the grounds, some playing frisbee or tossing a football, while others lay out and soak up the warm late-Spring sunshine. We park the car, check the campus signboard for directions to the chapel, then begin the walk over.

"Do you think the DEA dicks followed us back here?" I ask.

"It's possible, maybe even likely, but I didn't see them. I don't have any trackers on my car, either. I've been checking and rechecking."

I bet you have. We complete the remainder of the trip in silence, arriving at the chapel by way of a well-maintained, red brick walkway leading to a circular driveway out front. It's small, as chapels usually are, with a traditional bump-out entryway leading into a hexagonal rotunda. When I enter, I feel a calmness wash over me I can't easily explain.

Pammy sits in the middle of the center pew facing the altar with no one else in sight.

"Hi, Pammy." I softly call out, slightly startling her.

"You figured it out." She replies while swiveling around in the pew. "I tried to be discreet. I was worried someone could find out I was talking to you."

She notices Enzo and shivers. I realize Pammy's afraid of him.

"It's okay." I comfort her as we approach. "He's no one for you to be afraid of."

She turns back to the altar as I take a seat next to her. Enzo sits to my left, so I'm sandwiched as a buffer between them. Pammy doesn't make eye contact with me.

"Don't go meet them today." She warns, placing her hand onto my thigh. "It's a set-up. They're going to somehow have you take drugs away and when you leave, you'll be arrested. They're setting you up to take a fall for them. I heard that guy Pete say it."

"Pete O'Shea? Who do they have to take us down?" Enzo delicately asks.

"I don't know. I don't get a lot of time to listen. I pick up things when I'm around." She stares at the floor, continually flicking each of the fingers on her hands with her thumbs in a nervous twitch. "I can't let them know I'm eavesdropping."

"Smart." Enzo compliments. "Thanks Pammy, for what you've done for us." He reaches into his pocket and pulls out a knot of cash and hands it to her.

She looks up at him. "Oh my God. You don't need to do that!"

"Please, take it. And thank you again."

She starts to tear up. "Thank you so much."

"Thank you." I offer while Enzo gets up and walks back to the entrance. "You need to be careful. Do you understand?"

She looks at me, nose red and eyes watery, and nods knowingly. "Will you stay with me?" She invites sadly, her hand still resting on my thigh.

This poor girl's hugely distraught. I don't want her to feel manipulated in her fragile emotional state, and at the same time, I'm nervous she'll walk away and stop helping us if she feels rejected. I gently lift her hand and wrap it warmly within both of mine. "Pammy, I can't do that." I faintly shake my head, then squeeze her hand in a signal it's time for me to go.

"Please." She whispers desperately.

I exhale audibly. "I'm truly sorry. Thank you, again."

I do feel sorry for her, that's not a lie, but not because I want to stay. I feel empathy for the pain and anguish she's dealing with, whatever the reason. I suspect it's familial. It almost always is.

I quickly turn and leave the chapel, meeting up with Enzo out front just as he disconnects his phone call. He reached out to Frankie and canceled the afternoon meeting, making up some lame excuse. Frankie's pissed, as expected, which in my mind confirms Pammy's forewarning.

"She's a brave girl." Enzo says.

"I agree. I just hope she doesn't go off the emotional deep end. We're fortunate she's on our side." I hesitate. "This changes everything. You know you can't engage with Frankie anymore, right?"

He pauses for a moment. "If what she contends is accurate."

I'm surprised at his response. "Why wouldn't it be? She knew we had a meeting today with Frankie and you had a supply pickup."

"I'm not saying she's wrong. I'll do some detective work on my end to make sure. Jon, I'm grateful, don't misread me, and she's probably right, but I need to make sure I have the whole picture. Remember when she contacted you and said she heard I took out Jimmy? Sometimes things aren't exactly as they seem."

I consider his viewpoint. He's not wrong. We really don't know Pammy all that well and it's good to be thorough. "You're right."

"Thanks. For now, we'll keep a safe distance from Frankie until I know better what the deal is."

§

When we get back to the mall, Enzo and I separate. He breaks away with Bung to handle their matters, and I wander off with Alison to fill her in on our meeting.

"You guys are back fast. I didn't expect you so soon. I barely got any shopping time in." She jokes.

"I know, we finished up quickly." She can sense I'm not upbeat about how it went.

"Okay." She says cautiously, drawing out the word. "What happened? Is everything alright?"

"Tough question. So far, everything's okay."

I rewind back in time and tell Alison about my initial encounter with Pammy at the Foxy Lady. Not the stripper she initially thought of with the alcohol test tube shooters, but the Egyptian-themed woman.

"Yes. I remember her. She gave you the lap dance. Marion?"

"Not quite. Meridian, but close. Listen," I pause and take a deep breath. "She's been reaching out to me."

Alison's face instantly contorts to hold back from crying.

"No, no, no." I hastily interject. "It's not like that. She's overheard stuff."

I quickly relate to her my entire timeline of meeting Pammy as 'Jimmy's personal dancer,' her inadvertent discovery of my cell number and Enzo's purported involvement in Jimmy's death, and her contention Enzo and I will walk into a set-up if we meet with Frankie later today. I leave out the part of Pammy propositioning me to stay with her, though. During my account, Alison displays a host of emotions alternating from sadness to irritation to thankfulness for Pammy and her contribution to our safety.

"I hear what you're saying," Alison cautions after I finish my narrative. "But from here on, you need to be totally open with me if, or when, she reaches out again."

"Absolutely."

Enzo returns from Bung's van not long after we finish our conversation. "Ready to get back to Maine?"

"Yup." I confirm while looking for Bung. He's seated in his van and waving to us through his lowered window. We all wave back before piling into the Caddy and heading for home.

36

I'm psyched to finally be back in the office. The prospect of dealing with mundane paperwork presents a welcomed opportunity for some degree of normalcy today instead of my typical comings and goings of late, contending with local mafiosi, illegal drugs, and money laundering. I'll also have time to reconnect with Kelly; I haven't seen him since the going-away dinner.

Sadly, though not surprisingly, my outlook derails quickly. Instead of typical cheerfulness, I'm greeted by Sharon's worried face as I walk through the front door.

"Hey, Sharon. What's the matter? Are you … "

I'm unsuccessful in finishing my query before Agents Calhoun and Harmon rise from the waiting room chairs they occupied moments before my arrival.

"We thought we might bump into you at Frankie's yesterday." Special Agent Calhoun pseudo-threatens. "So, tell us, how does he do it? How does Antonetti get his poison to the street?"

"Sharon, could you give us a moment, please?" I politely request.

"Yes. Of course." She chirps nervously while bumbling to find her personal belongings. She manages to grab her purse and phone then hurriedly disappear out the front entrance door.

"I don't know what you're talking about. I'm not into drugs." I maintain after Sharon leaves.

"C'mon. Are we still doing this?" Agent Harmon sarcastically sneers.

I don't acknowledge his quasi-question. We plainly stare at one another in an obvious stalemate. After what I suspect is a DEA best practice for a psychologically strategic waiting period, Calhoun walks past me, purposefully bumping into my shoulder in the process. Harmon follows closely behind. Before exiting, Calhoun turns back to me. "See you around, Jon."

Son of a bitch. My first order of business – fire off a heated call to Enzo. I catch him in his car and begin my rant, starting with Calhoun and Harmon, then demanding he tell me where he is with Frankie.

"First thing's first." He interrupts. "Don't talk to me from inside. Go out to the street."

I always forget about the likelihood of listening devices. Some gangster I'd make. I step outside, then turn the corner and walk down the adjacent cobblestone street. "Why would they say they missed us yesterday at Frankie's? Were they the ones Pammy said would take us down? If so, why would they offer for us to work for them to capture Frankie if they were part of a set-up to have us take a fall?" I have tons of questions and no answers.

"Listen to me. They have nothing. Think about it – you haven't done a single thing wrong. I haven't either yet, at least with drugs, and they more than likely don't know about the darker side of my ATM business."

"Money laundering goes hand in hand with the drug trade." I counter.

"True, but it isn't their focus. They're DEA. Relax, you handled everything just right."

"What's your plan for getting out of this now? You can't accept anything from Frankie. These guys have you … us … handcuffed. Did you find out anything to corroborate Pammy's story?"

He only answers my second question. "No. Nothing to confirm what she says. But I also haven't found anything to refute it, either. It leads me to believe she's got it right."

My adrenaline starts flowing. "Then you definitely can't accept anything from Frankie. Your exit plan is exactly what you did yesterday. You called him from the chapel and told him you couldn't meet. That needs to stick for good. I'm withdrawing from the audit as well."

"Hang on. Let's really think about the domino effect from quitting the audit before you do it. That will piss Lorraine off, which I really don't care much about. It's her response that concerns me. She knows my money goes through Jimmy's ATMs. She's vindictive."

"She can't rat on you. She's been taking a fee from you for hiding it. We can throw it right back at her. And besides, she was married to Jimmy. Even if she didn't know what he was into, we can say she did."

"That's true." He says, then hesitates. "Wait a minute, you just made me think of something. Can you see who has bank accounts there? What if Frankie does his business with them, too? Christ, Jimmy ran his drug proceeds from Frankie's operation through the credit union," He's rambling through a stream of consciousness. "What if he was setting up Frankie to wash his money, too? Wouldn't that make sense?" Enzo gets uncharacteristically excited. "It makes sense. That's why Frankie wants the audit. He's running his money through the credit union. Jimmy probably set him up!"

I see Sharon walking up from the base of the street, wobbling on its uneven surface. I wave to her and smile as she gets closer, attempting to allay her apprehension. She enthusiastically waves back, and I give her a thumbs-up to convey everything's back to normal and it's safe to go back in the office. She brightens and picks up her pace as she cruises past me.

"Kelly can get access to a customer depositor list, I'm sure," I reason. "But Frankie won't use a real name; at least not his own."

"Yeah, probably not. It's worth exploring, though. Could be advantageous for keeping Lorraine in line if we need it."

"Be careful what you wish for." I warn. "It cuts both ways."

§

After I got off the phone with Enzo, I went back into the office and called Alison to keep her up to speed on today's dysfunction. If nothing else, I'm going to be over the top careful with keeping her well informed. My next call goes to Kelly to find out where he is and ask about the availability of a customer deposits list.

"Yo." He answers. "What's up?"

"Hey. Listen, I'm at the office and I need some info. Can you get a customer deposits listing?"

"Uh … I have a partial one. It's a listing of the top twenty-five accounts. It's in my workpapers in my office. Hold tight, I'm on my way in. We can go through them when I get there."

"Good timing." I explain to Kelly what 'good timing' means in terms of him not showing up when the DEA dicks were here. I also fill him in on my conversation with Enzo and why we're looking for the list.

"This is kinda cool." Kelly reacts animatedly. "I feel like a detective or spy or something trying to smoke out a mafia boss."

That makes exactly one of us who feels this way. I validate his viewpoint before hanging up. "Essentially, it is. See you when you get here."

Sharon softly knocks on my door after patiently waiting for me to finish my call. "Is everything okay?" She asks tentatively.

For a split second, I contemplate disclosing in general terms the challenges I'm having, but quickly decide against it. There's no un-ringing that bell. Why chance a negative reaction? Instead, I tell a half-truth. "Everything's fine. Just working through some personal issues with my stepfather. He always has a problem with someone or something." I say with mock exasperation as though Enzo's engaging in adolescent mischief. "Thank you for asking, though."

She morphs from apprehensiveness into her usual kindhearted and compassionate self. "Oh, Jon. I'm so sorry. Can I do anything?"

"No, I'm fine. It's all good." I smile confidently.

Kelly breezes through the front door, allowing for an opportune breakpoint from the conversation. "Hey, guys!"

"Good morning, Kelly!" Sharon chortles.

I follow Kelly as he cruises into his office. "Alright, let's take a look." He says as I shut his office door behind us.

He shuffles through a large, expandable file folder loaded with manila tab folders, then places it aside and shuffles through another. After removing an individual folder, he drops a stapled document onto the table for us to peruse. "Top twenty-five depositors by dollar amount."

I place the document between us. "The guy's name is Francesco Antonetti. Frankie Humps." I remind him as I trace my finger down the list.

We comb through the document several times, finding no Francesco Antonetti. "He's not using his real name, he doesn't leave a lot of cash in the bank, or both." Kelly opines.

"For sure. Honestly, I didn't expect our search to be productive, anyway. I only did it so we could maybe get some leverage over … hey, hang on a second …" I pause. "What do you make of this?" I ask while pointing to a name close to the top of the list.

Anthony, Frances – Average balance – $1,568,734.65

I look at Kelly. "Frances Anthony … any chance you can get a record of transactions from this account?"

"I don't know. It's not part of generally accepted audit procedures to go that deep into a specific depositor."

"Can you try?"

"Sure, I can try. We test information technology and info security internal controls. Maybe I could get into it that way."

I shrug my shoulders. "Can't hurt. Let's give it a shot."

37

It was fortunate Enzo stayed behind in Maine for the weekend after dropping us off last Thursday. I had him come over this morning and check Danny's Jeep for tracking devices before we headed back to Rhode Island. I'd be lying if I said I wasn't relieved he shadowed Kelly, Alison, and me in his Cadillac as Kelly and I visit Lorraine at the credit union and, in her mind, finish the audit. In reality, we're here to access the customer deposit accounts.

I think I can do this drive blindfolded now. Jump on the southbound highway and cruise through New Hampshire in a blink of an eye. Then, once in Massachusetts, coast along and branch off to Lynnfield, down through Lowell, and finally, curve off at exit twelve. From there, it's an easy, straight shot into Providence. Like shooting fish in a barrel.

My phone buzzes from its dashboard cradle. Enzo's calling, and I activate the speaker function for everyone to hear. "What up, LoZo?"

"Hey. I need to stop for gas. Pull into the Citgo on the next corner and then Alison can jump in with me while you two go to your meeting."

"Sure thing." I say before disconnecting.

We're only a mile or two from the credit union. I haven't discussed our plan of searching for Frankie's bank account info any further with Enzo, not for any real reason other than it was his idea in the first place. He knows full well we're going there to placate Lorraine but that we have an ulterior motive.

We pull into the Citgo station and Enzo bypasses us on his way to a gas pump. I turn to Alison after we come to a stop. "You alright?"

"Meh. I guess. How long will you be?"

"I'm hoping less than two hours." I drop the Jeep into park and look to Kelly for confirmation.

"That's probably right." He shrugs in agreement.

Alison sighs. "Ya, I'll be fine, though I have no idea what we'll do for the next two hours. Probably get lunch."

"Sounds like a plan. I love you." I say, giving her a kiss before she exits.

"Love you, too."

"Hey Enzo," I yell out from my open window. "Take good care of her!"

Enzo flashes me a thumbs-up as Kelly and I swing around to leave. "You ready to do this?" I ask, trying to psyche him up while he climbs from the back seat into the front.

It wasn't necessary. In true Kelly fashion, he fires back, "Damn straight I am!"

§

We enter the credit union and Kelly wastes no time in engaging with the administrative assistant at the front desk.

"Hello, Madelaine. It's good to see you. In the back conference room today?" He asks while pointing in the general direction of the operations center.

"Yes, sir." She replies cheerily. "And it's nice to see you both."

We engage in some mindless banter for a few moments, but my patience runs at an all-time low. I want to get in and get out quickly, so I redirect the conversation back to business. "Is Lorraine here today?" I casually ask.

"Let me confirm." Madelaine commandeers her mouse and begins a succession of clicks on her desktop computer. "Yes, she is. Would you like me to call her?"

I'd rather come in unannounced. "No, that's alright, but thank you. We'll check in with her at some point while we're here."

Madelaine rises from her chair and smooths out her skirt. "Perfect. I'll walk you through the security door."

As we head to the conference room, I mull over our plan to determine if Frankie holds accounts here and any possible connection to Jimmy. We need to establish some level of leverage over Lorraine, that's for certain, but it occurs to me we may be better off with the suspicious activity reports.

Madelaine peels off, allowing for Kelly and me to talk. "Do you remember when I told you about Lorraine intercepting SARs generated from Enzo's business? She told me the audit should go smoothly as long as she catches them, and we don't go looking for them. I've got to wonder if any reports from Jimmy were generated as well. On paper, it looks like the same business."

Kelly looks at me. "You want to get those SARs, too? As a control over Lorraine?"

"Yeah, if any exist. It can't hurt. She can get screwed simply by not submitting them, right? It doesn't look good if she diverts SARs from her now-deceased husband."

Kelly nods in response. "She sure would. Regulators would ride all over her and the credit union."

"Well, I know she collects Enzo's; let's see if we can check out if Jimmy has any. Do you know how to access them?"

He shrugs. "Nope. She wouldn't let me into that area. She gave me a few benign SARs, like the marijuana-related business reports, but other than that, it's been hands off."

"I'm not shocked. She doesn't want us snooping around. All the more reason we should look."

The financial controller greets us in the conference room, and we ask to be set up with access to the depositor listing for balance confirmation testing. She, in turn, connects us with the information security officer who grants us remote access to the system.

"Let me know if you need anything else." She offers and thankfully leaves us to our business.

"Oh man, my hands are sweating." Kelly mumbles as he scrolls through the top depositor list. "*Anthony, Frances*. Right here at the top. Let's see what you've got here, Mr. Anthony."

Kelly enters the transactional account record as I peer over his shoulder. It becomes apparent we got lucky that Frances Anthony didn't clear out his cash before the fiscal year ended. His activity shows frequent withdrawals down to zero. If he had, he wouldn't have shown up on our top depositor list.

"Systematic cash deposits and withdrawals." Kelly observes.

"Lots of them." I add. "Can we drill down deeper into the deposits and see where they come from?"

Kelly expands the depositor account detail. "Coin City I, LLC. Coin City II, LLC. Coin City III, LLC. Coin City IV, LLC. All business deposits."

"Holy moly. This looks more and more like it could be Frankie Humps. Francesco Antonetti." I contend. "Enzo and I were scheduled to meet with him at a local laundromat before we canceled. On top of it, Enzo used to work at a laundromat in Maine. Coin City? What business uses more coins than a laundromat? Look at these cash deposits. He's got to be generating SARs."

"Let's look. The information security officer can also grant us access to the BSA software."

Not long after we call him, Lorraine barrels into the conference room. It doesn't take a genius to see she's irate. "I just heard you guys were here. Why didn't you come see me?"

"Uh, we didn't want to disturb you." I splutter.

"You kidding me? Why do you want access to SARs? What's left on the audit?"

I look to Kelly.

"We have to test a sample of your submitted SARs for validity. No big deal." Kelly explains.

Lorraine swivels her head to me.

"Yes. That's it." I verbally buffer between Kelly and Lorraine. "Only to show the credit union followed all proper protocols with SARs submission. I'm overseeing this piece of the audit." I try to get across to Lorraine I'm supervising this process to steer Kelly away from anything prickly to her or me. I'm marginally successful.

Lorraine snorts. "Maybe I'll stick around and watch your auditing."

Damn. That's not what we want.

We gather around the desktop computer with Kelly jockeying the keyboard and situated between Lorraine and me. She describes the process of making sense of what we're seeing on the monitor.

"Okay," She begins. "See this one here? The computer tells me something ain't right with this guy. It looks like he's doing something funny with check deposits. Like maybe kiting or something. I don't need to figure that out, I just need to send the report in."

"How do you do that?" I ask.

"See this right here?" She points to a small box next to the customer name. "I just check this box and it submits it electronically where it needs to go."

I ponder this for a moment. "So, if it's unchecked, it didn't get submitted? Can we look at Enzo's account and see that?"

"Yeah. Scroll down to 'G.' "

Kelly follows her instruction and finds *Garibaldi, Enzo*. Sure enough, he's generated a fair number of reports all of which register unchecked.

"See? Nothing transmitted. No trace." She brags.

"Can we delete these?" I ask.

"After we close out the year, otherwise it will generate an unfiled report. So I need to wait for you guys first. That's why I want you to get a move on."

"I get it. Alright, let us get a testing sample printed out for our files and we'll call it done."

"Good." She replies sternly but doesn't move. She sits like a stone in her chair with arms crossed and a sour look on her face.

Kelly looks to me for guidance.

"Okay, let's separate this by frequency and we'll select a few from the top generators." I instruct.

"Why do that?" Lorraine blusters. "Just pick a couple randoms and call it good."

"I guess I could do that." I reply resignedly.

How the hell am I going to pull this off? Kelly's already sorted the records by frequency, and within the top five, I see *Anthony, Frances* and *O'Brien, James*. Jimmy's made the list.

Before I can formulate a plan, Madelaine pops her head into the conference room. "Hey," She calls out to Lorraine quietly but concernedly. "I've been looking for you. Andrew's trying to find you."

"Shitbird CEO." Lorraine mutters while heading to the door. "You two finish up. I want you done before I get back."

"Dang, we just got lucky." Kelly says after she leaves.

"Damn right. Let's go."

Kelly quickly drills into Frances Anthony's account and a boat-load of reports show up. "All of his cash deposits in excess of ten thousand dollars triggered a SAR."

"Are they transmitted?" I ask.

"Check it out. None of the insignias are checked." He points the mouse cursor over an unchecked box. "She said if it had been submitted, this box would be checked."

"Print them out. Every one of them." I direct. "Then go to James O'Brien."

Kelly batch prints all the SARs for Frances Anthony and I retrieve them from the printer and sweep them into my workpapers as he moves on to Jimmy.

"Jimmy's report profile looks just like Enzo's and none of them are filed!" Kelly stammers.

"Yes, it does. It certainly does." I repeat, surprised by our findings. "She knows what Jimmy was up to … or at least knows it wasn't legit. Print these and then check out Coin City."

We discover an additional cache of unsubmitted SARs generated from the Coin City businesses. That suggests Lorraine likely knows about Frances being Frankie, his involvement in something illegal, and Jimmy's connection, too. We compile all the unfiled reports on the group and hightail it out of the building. We'll use the SARs to threaten Lorraine if she attempts to stop us from walking away. And I'll be damned if I'm paying back the audit fee.

38

The four of us crowd around a living room table in a junior suite at the Omni hotel. Alison's consumed the better part of a bottle of wine while Kelly and I are well into a twelve-pack of PBR pounders. Enzo hasn't had anything to drink. We decided to stay in Rhode Island after leaving the credit union to do a deeper dive into our documentation in anticipation of our forthcoming calls to Lorraine and Frankie. Truth be told, I'm pretty amped up and really didn't feel like making the drive.

Enzo finishes sorting through the sheaf of papers Kelly placed in front of him and organizes them into a neat pile.

"You were onto something." I confirm. "When you asked if we could find the customer deposits list and if it would be helpful, it led us squarely to Frances Anthony, the Coin City businesses, and the suspicious activity reports you have in front of you. None of the SARs were filed for Anthony or Coin City. She has to know what's going on, and we have her by the balls."

Everyone looks at me.

"Yeah, I said 'balls.' Wouldn't surprise me if she had a pair."

"Frances Anthony is Frankie, no doubt, and he runs Coin City." Enzo asserts. "I set the companies up for him a long time ago to hold the laundromats. Now, you say these SARs will be enough to keep Lorraine in check?"

Kelly responds. "Yes. She and the credit union will be in deep shit if we submit these to the regulators. The Fed will crawl up their asses with a microscope."

"Okay, so we've got that nailed down." I contend.

"And me? Jimmy?" Enzo asks.

He doesn't need to elaborate on his question. We know exactly what he means. "Jimmy's dead, so nothing to worry about there and right now, you're good. She hasn't submitted any SARs for you or Jimmy – yet. But to be safe, sweep any cash you have out of there and close your account. She'll most certainly file yours in retaliation when the shit hits the fan."

Enzo flinches at my mention of Jimmy. "I've already taken all my money out and closed the account. Later today, I'll sweep all the cash from my ATMs. Most of them are empty, anyway. I could see this train wreck speeding down the track." He pauses. "Okay, so if we go through with it, the filings, how do we do it? Who do we submit them to?"

Kelly explains the process. "We need to replicate what Lorraine should have done with them to begin with. This will probably take down Equinox and definitely will take down Lorraine. I'll submit the SARs I recovered from the bank software to the Financial Crimes Enforcement Network, or FinCEN. When the agency sees the unfiled reports, they'll crawl all over the credit union. They'll go after the CEO for not overseeing the BSA function, and then Lorraine as the BSA officer, for a negligent compliance program."

"Wow." Alison responds. "Hopefully, it doesn't come to that. That'll be a lot of eyes on us as well."

"Wow is right." Kelly agrees. "I won't be shocked if the Office of the Comptroller or maybe the U.S. Department of Justice rolls in as well."

§

After we spend a little more time discussing strategy and consuming Pabst Blue Ribbon liquid courage, Enzo broaches the subject of making the calls. "You ready to call Lorraine? Probably should call her first. It's almost the end of the workday. I'll connect with Frankie after."

"Yep. I'm ready. But first, I need to take a leak."

"Of course, you do." Alison chides good-naturedly.

I do have to pee like a racehorse, that's no lie, but I also need a minute to myself to get psyched up for the call. About the length of my bathroom trip ought to do it.

"Hey," Alison calls out. "A little courtesy here? Can you close the door?"

"Sorry. Can't reach it now."

She's not impressed. After I finish my business, I stare into the mirror while washing my hands. "You ready?" I ask quietly.

"Here we go." I announce to everyone as I stride back into the living room. I reach for my phone and scroll through my contacts list for Equinox, then hit the 'call' function.

"Equinox Federal Credit Union. How may I direct your call?"

"Hello, Madelaine?"

"Yes, this is Madelaine. How may I direct your call?" She repeats.

"It's Jon Williams with J.K. Williams, P.A. I was trying to reach Lorraine O'Brien. Is she still in?"

"Hi, Jon. Let me check." She pauses. "Yes, she is. One moment, and I'll connect you."

I cover the phone with my hand. "She's still there."

Alison gives me a thumbs-up.

"This is Lorraine."

"Hello? Lorraine? It's Jon Williams. I'm calling on the audit."

"I hope you're calling to tell me you're all done. You guys beat feet outta here pretty fast today." She grumbles.

"Well, yes and no. We are finished with the audit, but not in the way you want us to be. We're pulling out of it."

"What??" She growls. "What are you talking about? Get your ass in gear and finish this. Now!" She demands.

"Lorraine, hear what I'm about to say." I advise calmly. "We are not completing this audit. We have no intention of issuing a report. We are walking away from you and Equinox immediately."

"You little prick! You are doing this audit! I'll make sure …"

I move the phone away from my ear so everyone can hear her rant. I can't make out much of it aside from a string of expletives until I put the phone on the speaker function.

"… and you don't know who the fuck you're dealing with! I'll send Enzo's reports in and fist fuck you and your firm into next week, you …"

"Hey!" I bark. It has the intended effect as Lorraine instantly falls silent. After a short pause, I opt to employ Enzo's strategy of becoming cold … calculated. "Listen very closely. I strongly suggest you reconsider your position. I have in my possession every unfiled SAR for

Jimmy, Frankie Humps – yes, you heard me right – Frankie Humps, and all of his Coin City entities."

She expels a barely-audible breath. "I don't know what you …"

"Save it. You know Jimmy was into dispensing more than just cash from his ATMs. I suspect you know what his product of choice was, but in case you didn't, he was running drugs from his ATMs as bulk drop depots for Frankie. I know you know who that is. Mr. Frances Anthony. The individual you neglected to submit SARs for. You know Jimmy was working for him and by action and attribution, you are too."

Enzo nods his approval at my handling of the exchange.

"Now, here's what's going to happen. I'm going to end this call. Then, I'll call your chief financial officer at the credit union and explain to him we are unable to complete the audit. You will go back to your job, play dumb, and be happy … or as happy as someone like you can be. Do you understand me?"

"They'll bring in new auditors. We'll all go down." She submits resignedly.

"Regrettably for you, I will not. My fingerprints, both literally and figuratively, are nowhere near your reports. As for Enzo? You will do your very best to protect him, or the SARs I hold will become public. If you're unsuccessful? Well, good luck with anyone finding him anyway."

"You son of a bitch."

"My mother has nothing to do with this."

I disconnect the phone, breathe a deep sigh, and look around the room. "That went well, I suppose."

Enzo speaks first. "I certainly think so. You handled her perfectly."

"Agreed." Kelly adds.

Alison gets up from the table, strides purposefully toward me, and whispers in my ear. "Damn, you did it to me again. That was so hot the way you handled that."

She emphasizes her point by burying her tongue deep in my ear before disengaging. That doesn't really work for me, but I appreciate the effort.

Enzo removes a throwaway flip phone from his jacket pocket. "Alright, it's my turn to follow up with Frankie. If he has a connection to Lorraine as we believe, she'll reach out to him quickly. I would."

I'm feeling relieved and excited at the same time. I can't decide what I want to do first – open another beer or go pee again. I'm out from Equinox and Enzo's almost done with Frankie. If Frankie doesn't listen to reason, maybe we send the DEA his way. Enzo will need to weigh in on that.

"Frankie. Enzo."

He's opted to keep his phone off speaker, so we hear only one side of the conversation.

"I'm done." He pauses and listens to Frankie's response.

"No. I'm done. Find somebody else." He pauses again. "That's unfortunate, but that would be unwise. We have your bank information. Check with your person at the credit union. This can accelerate quickly beyond your local people."

Enzo disconnects the line and cracks his phone in half, permanently disabling it. We all sit staring at him expectantly. Finally, I can't take it anymore. "Well??"

"Well, what? That's that. It's done."

I look at Alison and Kelly then back to Enzo. "That was quick. What did he say?"

"Not much to talk about, really. Just what you'd expect. 'You'll pay for this … you crossed the wrong guy …' Crap like that. It's over.

Let's move on. He knows we have leverage over him. After he talks to Lorraine, he'll know to what extent."

If there's one thing I've learned in my time with Enzo – nothing's over. Today though, is a good development and a step in the right direction. With any luck, Lorraine will fade away and Frankie will keep his powder dry.

"Do you think we should send the DEA his way? Calhoun asked me how Frankie gets his poison onto the street. Should we meet with them and fill them in?"

Enzo contemplates my proposition. "Let's sit tight and see how this unfolds."

39

I cast an eye over the surrounding landscape to discover a shimmering lake set in the background of an overgrown field. The grassy expanse radiates with a certain familiarity and serenity. "Any idea where we are?" I ask.

Dad considers my question. "I'm not entirely sure … maybe the ball field where we had one of our season-ending little league celebrations?"

"Yes. That's exactly where we are." I confirm.

"I remember." Mom adds pensively. "I sprained my ankle here running to first base during a parent-versus-child softball game."

We stand in a dried-up dirt parking lot bordered by a discolored and decaying two-rail wood fence. Dust plumes puff from under our feet as we begin to walk toward the raggedy ball field. Mom and Dad look exactly as they did when I encountered them at the high school football field a while back. I think they're wearing the same clothes, too.

"I know why you're here." I say.

Neither responds. They simply gaze at me expectantly.

"I'm not out of this. I know that." I corkscrew my sneaker into the ground like an eight-year-old pretending to squash an imaginary bug because he's ashamed he's done something wrong. "You're here to warn me to be careful."

Mom answers me as Dad happily stands by her side. "Yes. Just as you say."

"Right, but this is a good first step. A move in the right direction." I contend.

"You don't have to convince us of anything, Jon. We agree with you, and we're on your side." Dad reassures me.

"Of course you are. Thanks."

"But you'll need to keep the lines of communication open with Enzo, now more than ever." Mom stresses. "As you know, there are two ways this may not be over. You have control over Lorraine. You don't have control over what happens with Frankie. You'll need to stay close to Enzo on that. He'll more than likely not offer up information to you. You'll need to press him on it."

"Good advice. You're absolutely right. You're always right." I say to both of them.

"Thank you, son." Dad chirps. "We're going to head out now. Be safe. We love you."

Mom gives me a warm hug, then withdraws. "Bye, honey. Love you."

"Love you both." I respond, before curiously watching them retreat toward the lake.

§

Holy hangover, I feel like garbage this morning. The beers were agreeable going down last night, but now? Eh, not so much. I'm anxious to put Providence in the rearview mirror, head back to Maine, and spend the day getting some solid gym therapy, pronto. Clear the cobwebs.

"Good morning, baby." Alison purrs while sprawling out in bed like a kitten waiting to be stroked. "You were awesome last night. Very creative."

My memory's a bit foggy. "It's all about the partner, baby girl. You make everything better." I mean that, despite the fact I don't re-member anything extraordinary occurring after we went to bed. "What say we get ready to bolt out of here?"

"Definitely."

We have one of the two bedrooms in the suite, so privacy isn't an issue for us as we dress and pack up for checkout.

"How're you feeling this morning, Champ? You're going kind of slow." She teases.

I break from mashing my clothes into a travel duffel bag. "Copy that, my pre-wife. I've been cracking ass all morning."

"What does that mean? Farting?"

"Affirmative."

"Ugh."

"No worries. I'll take it with me."

I sling my bag over my shoulder and walk out of the bedroom. Enzo stands at the kitchen counter pouring coffee while Kelly remains dormant under a heap of blankets on the couch. He drew the short straw on sleeping accommodations.

"Ah, Enzo. You're my honest-to-goodness hero." I drop my bag and gaze upon the array of fresh doughnuts tantalizingly positioned on the countertop, absorbing the glorious visual.

"I thought you might appreciate it. Dig in, I want to get out of here reasonably soon." He says this noisily, presumably to roust Kelly from the couch.

"Same. I want to get home. Alison's almost ready. Yo, Kelly," I holler. "Get up. Doughnuts over here."

Alison comes out from the bedroom as Kelly rolls off the couch and trudges over to the bathroom. "Jon, you forgot your phone. It just vibrated. I think you got a message."

On her announcement, Enzo pauses to casually observe. Understandable given the circumstances.

"Thanks."

I unlock it and check my texts. I experience an all too familiar pit in my stomach upon seeing I've received a new message:

Alison sees the change in my facial expression. "What is it?"

"It's Pammy." I answer halfheartedly. "She asks if we're still in Rhode Island."

Alison doesn't outwardly react, but I know she must be aggravated.

"How would she know if we're in Rhode Island?" I wonder out loud.

"Because she's listening in on people at the strip club. She has information." Enzo answers.

"Should I tell her we've gone back?"

"More information is better than less. Find out what she wants." Enzo predictably instructs.

I show the text to everyone and look for advice and guidance.

"I just want to get out of here." Alison states flatly.

I'm of the same mind. "Me too, but we ought to find out what she knows first. I'll ask her if we can talk over the phone."

Again, I pass the text around to everyone, including Kelly. Before I can take the phone back, another text pops in for all to read:

"Oh, shit!" I snap just as Alison lets out a huge gasp.

"Okay," Enzo quickly intercedes. "I thought this may happen; half-expected it, actually. Let's not get overly excited about it."

"What?! Are you kidding?" I stammer.

"He's only doing this to intimidate us. I know his tactics. We'll get this all squared away. I'll call him and make sure he knows the bank stuff we have on him is on autopilot to the Feds if anything happens to us. I was going to do that anyway as a precaution, but now I'll accelerate it."

"Am I supposed to be comforted by that?" I grouse.

My phone vibrates with another message from Pammy texting an address for an out of the way Baptist church located in Coventry, and a directive to meet there at noon.

"She says she doesn't want to risk anyone finding us." I inform the group, reciting from yet another follow-up text.

Enzo starts dialing his phone.

"You're calling Frankie now?" I ask, questioning his timing.

"No. Bung. We need to go alone. I want Bung to stay with Alison and Kelly."

Alison buries her head into my chest. "Don't go."

"We need to know what she knows. This will be all, though." I whisper.

"Promise?" She looks up at me with her beautiful eyes.

"Promise."

I send a text back to Pammy:

40

This must be it. There's no signage out front but it's the only building, let alone a church, for miles in any direction. This is without any doubt a place time forgot. We sit tight in Enzo's running car facing the church, inspecting the area through an unusually dirty windshield. Grimy, white paint curls and flakes from the timeworn exterior, exposing unprotected, rotted wood underneath.

Enzo kills the engine and turns to me, placing his hands on his thighs. "Alright. Ready?"

I open the door. "Yes. She wasn't kidding when she wanted an out of the way meeting place. This isn't St. Dominic's chapel, that's for sure."

"She's a smart girl."

I inspect my surroundings as we walk toward the front entryway. Weeds sprout up through the fractured asphalt parking lot, signifying traffic has been sporadic, and more than likely, nonexistent for some time. An old, unkempt ball field with rusted chain-link fencing spans the entirety of the side and back sections of the property. Hard-packed, bare patches of ground appear on either side of the first and third base running paths. I imagine the bare spots developed over many years of kid's feet shuffling impatiently beneath benches that once existed, as they waited for their turn at bat or sat when they weren't playing in the field. I have a fleeting thought of my little league days with Dad coaching the team.

"No cars here." I observe, patting my jacket pocket ensuring my loaded pistol stays handy and at arm's reach. I know it's there, but the act of checking for it has become somewhat of a compulsion of mine.

"So noted." Enzo pauses to look around. "She could've parked somewhere nearby and walked over."

"That's good, right? She's covering her tracks? There's nobody else here?"

"Presumably."

Alrighty then. That's a response I don't find especially comforting. Enzo doesn't wait to engage in idle chit-chat over it. He bounds up the crumbling concrete stairs, landing at the front door sooner than I can set foot on a single step. Without warning, my arm sears in psychosomatic déjà vu pain as my mind reverts to the crematorium's rear loading dock when we went to meet Bernie. Enzo launched into me as a consequence of Agent Brown's point-blank gunfire unleashed onto both of us as we entered the building.

"Door's cracked open." Enzo calls back, then disappears into the church.

"Here we go." I mutter and follow him up the stairs.

This may have been a church once upon a time, but no longer. Aside from the steeple and stained glass, one wouldn't know this formerly served as a place of religious worship. No pews remain, nothing adorns walls – not even fixtures – and it's completely devoid of religious artifacts. No crosses, bibles, symbols, or emblems. No indication of former church leaders. Nothing.

"No one's here." I announce.

"She's down below. In the basement." Enzo says, holding up a handwritten note.

I take it from him and give it a once-over.

Jon – down in the basement. Better to talk. P.

"Where'd this come from?" I ask.

"It was on the floor where we came in. I don't like this, Jon. I don't like it at all."

"Me neither. Let's get out of here."

Enzo hesitates. "Yeah. Let me take a quick pass over the basement and we're out."

"Okay. Let's do it."

We walk across a faded carpet, threadbare and ripped, steeped in mold and mildew. When we get to the doorway, I follow behind Enzo, who begins his descent more carefully and purposefully than when he entered the building. Man, it's dark down here. Our eyes begin to adjust as we come down the staircase, aided by slivers of jagged light passing through openings in cracked stained-glass windows, scattering faint optic prisms over the dusty floor.

Pammy's here. She must not have heard us poking around upstairs. We spot her at the far end of the room, situated in front of what appears to be a workbench replete with a peg board panel mounted to the wall bearing tools of all manner and type. She sits on a stool, her back to us, craning her head forward as though she's inspecting a scientific slide through an unseen microscope. I lurch ahead toward her.

"Pammy?"

No response as I approach.

"Hey, we're ... whoa! Ahh, no! Goddamn it! Nooo!"

I peer into her face as Enzo attempts to pull me away and shield me from what's presented in front of us. "No!" I roar, forcefully twisting my shoulders, countering his effort to redirect me. "Ahh! Goddamn it!" I repeat in anguish. "Why?! Why do this?! What animals do this?!?"

Pammy's warped, shattered skull sets cradled between the extended serrated steel jaws of a bench vise bolted to the tabletop, her hair caked with blood and brain matter. One of her eyes has burst from its socket and lays against her cheek suspended from the optic nerve. The other eye remains intact, though dripping with bloody streaks triggering me to numbingly recall the weeping statue of the Virgin Mary. Every facial orifice trickles blood. All except her mouth.

I blindly paw behind me for the mounted, swing-arm wall lamp fastened to the pegboard and reposition the dim light beam for a closer inspection. "What the … do you see this?" I look back at Enzo horrified. "Hey, do you see this?!" I gasp.

With eyes closed, he nods silently.

"Oh, God! They've stapled her mouth shut!" I wildly sweep the light back and forth. "She has construction staples punched into her face! They're all over! Enzo … they tortured her! We need to take her out of here!"

Enzo doesn't attempt to stop me. I loosen the vise, then wrap my arms around her shoulders partly in preparation to move her but also to embrace this poor young girl. My God, she's just a kid. As soon as I clasp my hands together, I remove them just as quickly. "There's something around her." I snap uneasily, taking a step back. "There's something wrong."

Enzo cuts in front of me, body checking me out of the way and tears open her stained t-shirt, revealing a section of an explosive vest encasing her chest and back.

"Goooooo!!!" He roars, grabbing me by my shirt and pushing me ahead of him toward the basement steps. I need no further reinforcement, and I vault to the top of the landing with him hot on my tracks. We cross the length of the church at full tilt, exit the building, and race to the Cadillac. Enzo starts the car, cuts the steering wheel hard right and guns the engine, spinning out in the sandy, crumbling driveway. I'm thrown into him from the force of his intense acceleration followed instantly by experiencing the piercing, ear-ringing whine triggered by a thunderous explosion. A surge of concentrated, penetrating heat ripples through us as a ball of orange flame washes over the Cadillac and evaporates. Bits of burning wood and debris rain down on us as Enzo squeals his tires, peeling out and into the road.

§

I feel Enzo's stare bore into me. Though shivering badly, I manage to shake it off and look back at him. His face conveys fear and surprise, but he says nothing. We lock eyes for about fifteen seconds in an unspoken exchange of thought. *We're in grave danger. We need to take action now!*

"It was a set-up." Enzo's eyes return to the road. "She wanted to tell us what she knew about the hit ordered on us, but she was discovered. She didn't choose that church for our meeting place; it was chosen for her."

"She probably saved us." I posit heartbreakingly. "Pammy gave her life for ours."

"Yes. She did. Now we know what we're up against."

As my adrenaline pump diminishes, I'm able to reflect upon the aftermath of the experience. "What set off the bomb vest?"

"I don't know what tripped it. I just know we got lucky getting out of there before it went off. It could have been on a timer, or it could have been electrically or mechanically generated. I don't know. My best guess would be that we set off a trigger when we entered the basement which initiated a timer. We got plain old lucky in getting out."

We drive for the remainder of the trip back to the city mostly in silence. I have a million thoughts running through my head and I need to organize them.

"Frankie stapled her mouth closed for being a snitch, didn't he? He was sending us a message." Anger seeps into my consciousness intertwining with fear.

Enzo nods. "Yes, he did."

"He's coming after us, Enzo."

"Yes, he is. Undoubtedly, his plan was to deal with all of us at the church." He pauses. "It's time now. We need to disappear – all of us. That includes not only Alison, but your friends Darcy and Kelly, too, if they want to stay alive."

"Then what?"

Enzo looks at me grimly. "We plan. It's time for Frankie Humps to retire. For good."

41

I disconnect my call with Alison. I instilled the fear of God, or maybe the devil; I honestly don't know which, into her with a quick summary rundown of our experience at the church. I described to her our gruesome discovery of Pammy, but I didn't go into detail. No point to it. She's aware Pammy was viciously and heartlessly executed and expanding beyond that accomplishes nothing. Alison and Kelly have cranked it into high gear, organizing our belongings at the hotel and readying to leave as soon as we get there. I got reassurance from Bung he would stay with them until Enzo and I arrive.

"They're moving. They'll be ready to take off as soon as we get there, and Bung will stay with them until then." I advise. "What's your plan?"

He seems puzzled. "For what? We're going to pick them up and get the hell out of here."

"What about your stuff? Do we need to stop by your house or apartment or … wherever you stay?" It occurs to me I have no idea where he lives. Sometimes I wonder if I even know him at all.

Enzo dials his cellphone while he responds. "Oh. Don't worry about it. I have everything up there already."

Of course, you do. I don't have the energy to ask why, nor do I truthfully care; however, I would like to know where we're going. I suspect he has no interest in sharing it with me right now, but he did say 'up there.' He's busy yammering into his phone, relaying our story to Bung and explaining what we're intending to do. It sounds like Bung may have a different strategy for himself, though I can hear only Enzo's side of the conversation.

Following his phone call, we close the remaining distance to the hotel rapidly. I message Alison when we're five minutes out to wait with Kelly and Bung in Danny's Jeep inside the parking garage.

"Are you comfortable with driving your car?" I ask skeptically. "I don't think you should take it with you. You should probably ride with us."

He agrees. "We're on the same page. These guys know my car. I plan to leave it in the parking garage at the hotel and ride with you."

"Perfect. Good call."

Enzo forces a high-velocity corner turn into the hotel's rear accessway to the self-parking garage, producing a sustained, low-intensity squeal of his tires.

"Where …"

I've anticipated his question. "Third floor, middle rows. Can't miss it."

§

With very few vehicles on this parking level, Enzo has no trouble locating the Jeep and wastes little time in his approach. Alison and Kelly wait at the front passenger door with Bung standing just off to the side. She wears her hair pulled back into a ponytail, exposing the exhaustion in her face. I can tell from her posture she's fearful – she stands with a slight slouch and arms folded, not in anger, but in self-comfort and self-preservation.

Enzo comes to an abrupt stop in an adjacent space and shuts the car down. "I need to grab a couple bags from the trunk."

"Sure thing."

I exit the Cadillac and beeline it to Alison. "Hey. You ready?" I ask, opening my arms to offer her comfort.

She burrows her head into my chest, interchanging me for Bung as her protector. "Yes. I *really* want to go."

I open the passenger door, wait for her to climb in, then close it behind her, leaving me facing Bung. "I didn't talk with Enzo about it yet, but I get the sense you're not coming with us."

He yanks on his beard, re-styling the point and revealing a slight smile. "Yeah. No, I'm gonna go radio silent, but I'll do it around here. I got places to go."

"You sure?"

"Yeah. I'm sure. Take it easy, alright? Maybe we can catch up some time."

"Definitely. See you, buddy."

We exchange a bro handshake and an awkward half-hug, half-bumbling chest bump before quickly recoiling as though it may somehow compromise our masculinity if it lasts too long. I turn and walk to the driver's side door as Enzo slams the trunk lid closed on his Cadillac, emerging with two duffel bags in hand. He offers one of them to Bung, undoubtedly stuffed with cash that Bung readily accepts; however, Enzo doesn't release his grip right away. He begins talking to him, or rather, at him in a one-way conversation. I'd like to hear it, but Enzo positioned himself back-to and speaks so softly I can't make out what he's saying. Bung periodically nods in silent acknowledgement throughout the duration of Enzo's discourse. Shortly thereafter, Enzo releases the duffel bag and claps Bung on the shoulder in what I interpret as a display of appreciation and respect. He then turns away and hops into our back seat next to Kelly with his other duffel bag while Bung disappears deeper into the recesses of the parking garage. Enzo leans forward, poking his head between Alison and me. I half-expect him to snarl, *Heeeeeeeere's Johnny*, in the vein of Jack Nicholson in *The Shining*.

"Alright. Let's roll." He quietly instructs.

His request is somewhat of a letdown, but I happily comply.

§

Similar to the easygoing rides down, I've been pleasantly surprised with our recent trips home from Rhode Island and the modest driving time needed to clear the state and pass into Massachusetts. We cruise on Route 95 north and within twenty minutes, whiz past Gillette Stadium in Foxborough. Really, Providence isn't very far from Portland despite having two states nestled in between. I can make the trip in roughly the same time it takes to drive from our apartment further up state to Bangor.

"Hey," I glance at Enzo through the rearview mirror. "What's the order of operations? Can we go to our apartment first ... or at all ... or do we go straight to your place?"

"We can do both. We go to your apartment first and then we do not go back. When we go inside, we move quickly and silently. I doubt your apartment's been compromised, particularly with the additional security measures you put in place after it was ransacked last."

Alison expels a faint, pitiful whimper triggered by Enzo's frank and unpleasant reminder of Agent Brown breaking and entering into her apartment. They installed audio surveillance devices in addition to burying a large kitchen knife into a picture of her and her mother mounted on the bedroom wall.

"Then after going to your friends' places, we head to our location." He finishes.

"Where?" Alison asks while staring into her lap, which to some extent muffles her voice.

Enzo's mood turns solemn. "We're heading to Camp Ellis. Sabrina and I used to go there and sit on the breakwater eating clam cakes and watching the boats come in. It was our spot – soothing and serene. We didn't hold property at the time, we only visited, but I closed on a small place in the village for a retreat."

Or more likely a hideout.

"I brought everything I'll need the last time I came up as a precaution in the event we had something like this happen – when we went to DiMillo's with your other friends."

Right. Santa and Merri's going-away dinner. How could I forget our DEA chaperones?

"Honestly, it's not very far from your apartment."

Alison peers at me with sad eyes and I sense she's about to make a request. Interestingly, it isn't one I'm expecting. "Tell me more about Pammy."

"Ah. I don't want to talk about that. I don't want to think about it, either. It won't do you any good to have more details."

"No, that's not what I mean. I don't want to know more about what happened in the church." She shivers. "I want to know more about Pammy. Personally."

I don't think she's implying I engaged in any inappropriate behavior with her. In a sense, like me, Alison's now connected to her. "I don't have much to share beyond what you already know. She was our eyes and ears. She may have … no, scratch that … she did save our lives, Enzo and me. She gave hers for ours, whether she meant to or not."

Alison doesn't interject or interrupt. She only listens.

I address the broader group. "As I see it, Pammy seemed like a young woman trying to make a better life for herself without much support, not unlike you and me." I glance at Alison. "Yeah, she was a stripper. So what? I'm not judging her. Nobody else should, either."

My rant's somewhat prickly, but Alison knows it's not directed toward her. I'm more just railing at the world in general and the injustices good people like Pammy seem to perpetually run up against.

"That's all I have." I conclude sadly.

The Jeep goes quiet for a period; the only major sound coming from its outsized tires and their rhythmic vibration at high speed on the highway. I find it soothing. It helps facilitate my thinking in developing an action plan for when we arrive home.

"Hey!" I whip my head around to Alison and Kelly in a fleeting panic. "We need to connect with Darcy. It totally slipped my mind!"

"Yes, you do." Enzo agrees.

Kelly calmly responds. "It's okay. It didn't slip mine. I've been reaching out to her since late morning."

I exhale a deep breath. "Whew. That's a relief."

"You spoke to her?" Alison hesitates. "She hasn't responded to any of my messages. Text or voicemail."

"Not yet." Kelly admits. "I haven't been able to track her down, either."

"What do you mean? You don't know where she is?" I feel my anxiety rising again.

"Well … I know she was supposed to go out and do some errands and other stuff today and I haven't hooked up with her so far. I'm sure everything's fine."

It's obvious he doesn't believe his own contention that 'everything's fine.' I reposition my rearview mirror to establish a line of sight with Enzo and find him staring back at me intently. He subtly shakes his head side to side, conveying a resounding unspoken message:

We need to track her down. Now.

42

You've got to be kidding me. A three-hour ride home, and nothing from Darcy? No calls, not a single text … nothing. I'm trying to remain calm, but evidently, I'm failing. I pack clothes furiously while Alison silently collects her bathroom toiletries. Enzo investigates the apartment, sweeping his electromagnetic wand in search of listening devices.

"Simmer down, big boy. I'm uneasy too, but there's no problem until there's a problem." He counsels.

Standard Enzo-speak. I don't want to hear it.

"Anything from Darcy, yet?" I call out impatiently to Kelly.

He attempts to pacify me. "No. I'll let you know."

I suspect he wants to tell me to stop asking, but recognizes like Enzo, I'm on edge. Alison is as well, I'm sure.

I finish packing at the same time Enzo completes his reconnaissance and replaces his wand in the duffel bag.

"Brought your wand, huh?" I observe, although I knew he had it.

"Yes. I don't go anywhere without it, anymore."

"Probably a good idea."

"You're clear." He confirms. "I didn't get a hit. Not even a false red. It stayed green the entire time."

"That's a big relief." Alison says, breezing into the living room with her roller suitcase. "I'm ready."

Enzo looks at me.

"I'm all set. Let's do this. You ready?" I ask Kelly.

"Yep. We're only waiting on Darcy, now."

I pick up my bag and sling it over my shoulder. "Perfect. Let's go get your stuff and find her."

We bolt out of the apartment and take the stairway to the underground garage. Alison's Fiat sits next to Uncle Danny's Jeep in its assigned space. It doesn't get used all that much anymore, as evidenced by a fine layer of dust coating its surface. We load up our gear into the Jeep, hop in, and promptly cruise out of the building complex. I'm hyper-sensitive to activity swirling around me and I can't help but repeatedly scan my surroundings as we drive to Kelly's apartment. Enzo doesn't appear to be overly concerned, but it's tough to tell; he almost always keeps a cool exterior demeanor. I'm thinking through how we handle the search for Darcy, when Kelly's cellphone suddenly blasts an eighteen-wheeler, tractor-trailer air horn ringtone, startling me from my thoughts.

"Hello?" He answers through the phone's speaker function.

"Hey Kelly, it's me." Darcy replies.

Alison peers skyward, whispering, "Oh, Darcy. Thank God."

"Darcy! Where in the heck have you been?" I splutter. "We've been calling all over for you!"

"I see that from the seventeen thousand messages you've all left for me. I was at my mom's house. Really bad service over there and no Wi-Fi." She pauses. "I take it we have an issue?"

"We've got serious trouble." Alison confirms. "Look, we're on our way to Kelly's. We'll be by your place right after."

"Wait at Kelly's for me. I got your instruction and I'm packed already. I'll meet you over there."

Enzo wears a smug smile, and I don't want to give him the satisfaction of saying he was right, but he was right. And I couldn't be happier.

Kelly finishes up the call. "Great. See you there."

The mood for the remainder of the ride substantially improves as we banter about the logistics of our impending asylum at Camp Ellis. Apparently, it's a modest, two-bedroom beach house with a small study, where Enzo graciously offers to sleep, built near the head of the breakwater where the Saco River drains into the Atlantic Ocean. After picking up Darcy, we'll need to backtrack south about a half hour, maybe forty-five minutes from Portland to get there.

"How long will we stay in Camp Ellis?" Alison asks.

I look back at Enzo through the mirror in an indication he ought to handle this one.

"Until we're safe." He answers elusively, and I laugh to myself knowing his response will not placate her.

"And when is that?" She poses innocently.

His voice becomes harder edged. "Tough to say. Until Jon and I finish our work." His response ices out any further questioning Alison may have contemplated. She knows full well his inference, and it scares the daylights out of her.

I provide a breather and some levity to the conversation with an impromptu convenience store detour. I drop the Jeep into park and hop out. "Be right back. I need some provisions for our staycation."

I don't take long inside the store as my shopping list is super short – a thirty-pack of Pabst Blue Ribbon and a few bottles of Chardonnay. I'm in and out in under five minutes and we're back on our way.

"Next time give me a heads-up, will you?" Enzo requests stone-faced, suggesting to me he's been stewing over problems and concerns throughout the duration of our trip. He isn't pleased I deviated from his expectation.

"Sure. Sorry." I apologize.

Fortunately, we're barely a couple of miles from Kelly's apartment complex and the negative energy cast over the car doesn't last long. We pull into the parking lot and drive over to his building where surprisingly, Darcy's car already sits out front. Looks like my booze break allowed for her to beat us over here. I spot a suitcase and duffel bag on the curbing next to the car. Perfect – this will make for a speedy exit and an upbeat Enzo.

§

We ride to Camp Ellis predominantly in silence, the only sound coming from the radio set on low volume. The jam-packed Jeep carries five of us and baggage, and with plenty of time to plan at Enzo's house, it's not pressing to engage in conversation until we get there.

When we enter the Camp Ellis community, Enzo instructs me to drive its perimeter to assess the situation. This place appeals to me, holding a charm I can't easily describe. A quirky signboard denotes the entrance to the main access road, informing visitors of whale watching excursions, fishing charters, bait shops, and vacation rentals. It's not entirely a beach destination, per se, although that dynamic exists. It's better defined mainly as a working fishing village boasting a noteworthy rock breakwater where locals bring a pole and test their skill (or luck) at reeling in the big one. A municipal parking lot filled with work trucks overlays the point where river meets ocean. A public boat landing runs into the river on one side, with jet ski rentals and parasailing launching from the ocean side.

"Okay. Double back down this street right here," Enzo directs. "Then take your second left onto Hidden Dune. It's the last house on the right."

The roads are skim covered with fine beach sand spilled over from stone retaining walls positioned along the oceanfront. Many of the modest beach houses closest to the water sit elevated on substantial wood pilings for flood protection. Enzo's does not, however. I enter into his hard-packed dirt driveway layered with sand to find his place is less of a house and more of a cottage. It's far enough from the water so it doesn't need to be significantly elevated, but I can see through the latticework encircling the perimeter it's raised a foot or two off the ground.

"This reminds me a lot of your Uncle Danny's house." Alison reflects, reaching for my hand to offer support.

I laugh. "Agreed. I can imagine a giant, rusty anchor decorating the front yard."

"It's funny you say that." Enzo adds. "I thought the same thing when I first saw the house and decided to buy it. Maybe I'll pick one up somewhere around here."

Alison and I exit the front of the Jeep without difficulty while the others largely spill out of the back. After collecting our gear and provisions, we move inside to check out our home base for the foreseeable future.

Enzo heads over to a small room not much bigger than a decent-sized walk-in closet. "You guys take the bedrooms and I'll take the den." He calls back.

Fair enough. Alison and I drop our bags in the room closest to us and I leave to check out the other bedroom. It's a mirror image of ours – small and tidy.

"Will you guys be okay in here?" I ask Darcy and Kelly.

"Comfy cozy." Darcy responds dryly.

Kelly shrugs. "Good by me."

"Cool." I back out of the room and head to the kitchen lugging the beer and wine and run into Enzo coming out of the den.

"Get settled." He presses. "We've got some planning to do."

"Pitter patter," I acknowledge, cracking into the thirty pack for Kelly and me. "Let's get at her."

43

Kelly, Enzo, and I sit at a circular table taking up most of the dining space. We're spotlighted by a wide-rimmed, yellow-wired industrial pendant light that looks like it was manufactured in the seventies. Either it hangs too low from the ceiling, or we sit on chairs too high for the room. In either case, we need to slightly crouch underneath the light to see each other without obstruction.

"First off," Enzo begins, speaking directly to Kelly. "Are you sure you want to sit in on this? You'll become involved in something you may wish you hadn't."

"Realistically, I think it might be a little late to worry about that now." Kelly replies.

"Probably true." Enzo admits. "Fine. Let's get to it. I'll give you a lay of the land as I see it, and my assessment of how we proceed." He doesn't wait for acknowledgement before launching into a narrative of Frankie Humps' history and his present day-to-day living. "Frankie's old … in his eighties, now. When he was younger though, much younger, he was as fierce as they come. You know, there's an old truism about mafiosi – very few live to retire. Frankie's one of them. That's because he's smart." He stresses his point by tapping his index finger to the side of his head and making deliberate eye contact with each of us.

"When we were kids, Jimmy and me, we would go with his father on weekends to run errands. We didn't know where we were going or the people we met, until it came to Frankie. You knew there was something different about him. Anybody who was around Frankie was polite … respectful. Including us. Jimmy's dad made sure of that. Frankie was always nice to us; in retrospect, he was grooming. He was good at that. He knew what made people tick and he could capitalize on it." He pauses and breathes a deep sigh. "Then we got to high school … when Jimmy's dad was killed after the Superbowl."

Enzo becomes lost in his past, recounting from a bygone time playing out in his mind. I'm equally as interested in his childhood recollections as I am Frankie's story.

"After high school, Jimmy and I got more heavily involved with the organization. We mostly did smalltime stuff … running, collections, minor shakedowns. As time went on, and without really recognizing it, I ascended at a faster pace than Jimmy. He had the family connection, but I was smarter, and it translated to more responsibility. Frankie could see that. It allowed me to see more of the inner workings – and more particularly, the real Frankie. When I was in my early to mid-twenties, I came to a crossroads. Either I was all in, or I was out. Like I told you before," Enzo directs to me. "I went to community college and then worked some dead-end jobs before coming back into the fold – all in. I wish I'd made a different choice."

Enzo looks down at the table as he speaks, signifying the scenes play out in his mind as he recites them. He's unaware of his mannerisms during his recollection … the slight shake of his head when he's uncomfortable discussing an act of violence he committed, or gritting his teeth at an act of disrespect he had to deal with.

"Anyway, I progressed up through the ranks to where I got to prior to your mother and me reconnecting with you."

He stops to see if I want to interject. I don't.

"So, that brings us to today. Now, the question is, what do we do with him and how do we do it?"

"What do you think about blowing him up in the laundromat?" My suggestion triggers a kind of strange, out-of-body experience for me, like someone else said it. Then I think about what happened to Pammy, and Frankie's capacity for torture, and I'm okay again.

"I'd rather make him disappear as discreetly as possible. Explosives are complicated in occupied places, unlike the church we escaped from."

"I hear you. How you managed to wire the Harding-Williams building to blow, I'll never understand."

Kelly's head whips over to me. "What?!"

Enzo ignores his question. "That was a feat for sure, but we had key players inside to make it happen. We don't have that with Frankie. Also, everyone knows it's Frankie's place; an explosion would set off a firestorm I don't want to deal with. I'd rather have a quiet exit with no trace, if possible."

"A literal and figurative firestorm." I note. "Are you thinking a kidnap?"

"Yes. Exactly. We snatch him from somewhere and make him disappear."

"Do you have any watery grave sites in Providence, like in Portland?" I ask, going for a laugh.

Kelly stiffens while looking at me wide-eyed.

Enzo doesn't give me the reaction I'm looking for. "Not down there. I have something else in mind, though. Frankie spends his days at the laundromat – always has. I'm not sure where he goes otherwise. He used to have an apartment building and stayed in one of the units, but I suspect that place is long gone. We'll have to spend some time watching the laundromat to see where he goes. It would be good to intercept him along the way."

"Sounds like we have some investigating to do. Reminds me of camping outside the VA hospital when I had to sign for Uncle Danny." I reply sadly.

"That's right. We'll need to set up surveillance at the laundromat and see if we can track where he goes."

Kelly enters into the conversation. "Will that be a difficult proposition?"

"More than likely." Enzo responds. "He's always been a careful man … but we can be more careful."

"I can attest to that. You have an unbelievable level of patience when it comes to reconnaissance." I confirm, and he smiles slightly.

I toss down the rest of my beer. "Can we take a break? I need to hit the head."

Enzo raps his knuckles on the table in concurrence. "Sure thing. I've got to stretch my legs, anyway."

He rises quickly and promptly smacks his head into the rim of the pendant light. "Remind me to fix this damn thing." He grouses, rubbing his rapidly stiffening neck. He heads over to the refrigerator to get a drink, I scoot to the bathroom, and Kelly wanders over to see the girls.

After finishing my business, I go into the living room to check in with Alison, where I interrupt a fairly intense exchange. She's giving Kelly the two-minute, behind-the-scenes account of what transpired with our now-defunct CPA firm.

"This is mind blowing." Kelly sputters. "Enzo? Your mom? No one would believe this!"

"Tell me about it." I agree. "I'll fill you in on the details later. For now, let's finish up with Enzo."

I stop at the fridge for another beer before we pick up where we left off.

"Timing," Enzo begins. "It needs to be now. We want to get to Frankie before … well … we have to move fast. Logistically, Jon, you and I need to do the surveillance. The others can stay here, but if they're nervous or apprehensive, they can travel to Rhode Island with us and I'll have Bung meet us for support. Your choice." He directs this last part to Kelly.

Enzo looks back to me. "In the meantime, you may want to shut your office down for the foreseeable future. Tell your person out front to go on vacation or something."

"Good idea. I'll go see her tomorrow morning and we can leave right after. Also, we'll check in with the girls, but I'm certain Alison will want to go with me. Not sure about Darcy."

"Tough to tell." Kelly replies. "I think we're in unchartered waters."

Not for Alison and me, unfortunately.

44

Morning arrives exceedingly quickly, and as I expected, no way Alison wants to stay in Camp Ellis without me. After witnessing Alison's reaction, Darcy's of the same mind. So, the five of us once again will head to Rhode Island. Before we leave, however, Enzo insists on accompanying me to close up the office. He's concerned not only with my physical well-being – he also wants to run his detection wand throughout the office space. The earlier DEA visit concerns him as does the potential for Frankie's goons looming.

We eat a quick breakfast, and the others retreat to round up our belongings while Enzo and I head for the Jeep. As we draw near, I consider Alison's Fiat again. It occurs to me we should take her car today. No one in Rhode Island has ever seen the Fiat. It will give us some measure of camouflage rather than tooling around conspicuously in Danny's Jeep.

"Hey." I stop and turn to Enzo. "Think about Alison's car. Nobody's seen it. Why don't we take it? We can drive to Rhode Island in it and bring the Jeep, too. That way the others will have the Jeep in case of emergency, and we have the Fiat for our business. We can totally blend in."

"Outstanding idea. The vehicle situation crossed my mind and that we should find a new car when we get down there, but this solves it. Great work."

He knows exactly how to build up my self-esteem. I shoot back inside the house and dig out the keys to Alison's Tic-Tac twin-mobile, rapidly explain to her my 'outstanding idea,' then hustle back to the Jeep.

"Let's roll." I propose on the fly, hopping into the driver's seat.

Enzo gets into the passenger side. "Last time I was in the Fiat, I was nursing a bunch of broken ribs."

"I remember. All too well."

§

We cruise into Portland on this warm, sunny morning, finding a rare, on-street parking spot in front of my building. "Check it out," I boast while backing in. "This hardly ever happens."

Enzo's not as impressed. "Must be our lucky day."

He grabs his duffel bag, and we head up the steps leading to the front vestibule. As we enter the office, I plan to match Sharon's enthusiasm with my morning greeting like she always does for me. I yank the entry door open and quickly pop my head in. "Good morning, Sharon!" I croon.

No answer.

"Hellooooo." I call out in a sing-song voice, entering the waiting area.

Nothing.

"Hmm. The door's unlocked. She must be around."

"Maybe she went to get a coffee." Enzo posits.

"Could be," I agree. "But we have a Keurig."

I head off toward the kitchen while Enzo removes his detection wand from his duffel bag. As I round the corner, I see Sharon face down on the threshold of the doorway into the kitchen, still clutching a manila file folder.

"Sharon!" I holler.

I quickly flip her over and check for a pulse. Where in the hell can I see if she has a pulse? People on television make it look so easy.

"Sharon, can you hear me …?" I gently rock her, searching for any sign of life.

Enzo breezes around the corner as I begin CPR … or my version of CPR. "I'll call 9-1-1." He snaps, then disappears.

"Shit! C'mon, Sharon. C'mon!" I plead, cycling through chest compressions and rescue breaths.

I continue administering CPR, with no response, for the better part of fifteen minutes until paramedics arrive and take over. Enzo and I retreat to a conference room and wait for police to arrive.

"Is she gone?" Enzo calmly asks.

Although I'm pretty shaken up, I match his calm tone with my response. "I don't think she's alive anymore." As I verbalize my doubt, tears begin streaming down my face. "I need to call Alison."

As I make the call, Enzo leaves the room, presumably to check in with medical personnel. "Hey," I say when Alison answers, my voice cracking. "I think Sharon might have died."

"What? What happened?!"

"I don't really know. She was face down on the floor when we got here. Paramedics are here; ambulance, too."

"Was she …?" Alison trails off on her question.

"It doesn't look like anything happened. She was lying on the floor. There's nothing out of place."

"I'll be right there."

She forgets she doesn't have access to a vehicle. "No, it's okay. Please stay there. Too many people here. I'll keep you updated."

"Alright."

Before I disconnect the call with Alison, Enzo reappears in the doorway, slowly shaking his head.

"Ohhh! Alison, she didn't make it! Sharon passed away."

"Oh, no. I'm so sorry."

"I have to go. I'll call you soon."

Enzo waits for me to hang up before talking. "She's passed. The coroner's on the way. I'm sorry."

"What did the paramedics say? Anything?"

"Not much except that she's been gone for a while, well before we got here, and they didn't see any signs of foul play. Obviously, we'll have to see the medical examiner's report. How old was she?"

My head is spinning. I can't believe Sharon's dead. "Uh. I think sixty-three … maybe sixty-four. I'd have to check the payroll records."

"Well, she was no spring chicken." Enzo points out.

"No, I guess not, but she was in good health – "

"That you knew of." He finishes.

§

The coroner removed Sharon's body, medical personnel packed up and left, and the police completed their forensic and interviewing requirements, leaving Enzo and me alone in the building.

"Do you think …?" I ask hesitantly.

Enzo doesn't answer right away. "I really don't know. It doesn't seem likely, though. Why would anyone harm her?"

"Jimmy didn't look like foul play, either." I remind him.

"I know," He bristles. "That's what worries me. We need to go, but I want to finish scanning the office before we get out of here."

Enzo retreats with his detection wand and I trudge numbingly over to Sharon's desk, unsure of what to do next. Should I call her husband? Will the police do that? I notice a family photo set next to her inbox. She poses with her husband and teenage daughter in some far away tropical paradise. It must be an older picture. Sharon looks to be at least fifteen years younger, and her daughter's now married with kids.

I flop down onto her chair, dispirited, and feel something poke into my butt. I reach underneath and retrieve a coin. It's not real money. It's larger and thicker than a quarter, gold in color, with a city skyline on the front and a large washing machine on the back.

Acid rises up from my stomach, burning into my chest. Son of a bitch. Coin City.

Enzo, visibly excited, glides into the front waiting area and over to the desk.

"Hey." I snap, holding up the coin for him to see.

He puts his index finger to his lips, signifying for me to be quiet. "Looks like you ought to reach out to her husband, now." Enzo suggests. "I'm so sorry for your loss. Are you ready to lock up and go?"

"I guess."

I rise from the chair and begin shutting lights off. We move to the door and I lock up behind us as we exit. Enzo's not saying anything until we get in the car and moving.

"Okay. Go ahead." He instructs.

"You go first. You have me spooked."

He doesn't protest. "I found a listening device in almost every room in the office. That's why I didn't want you to say anything when I came out."

"You're kidding."

"I wish I were. You haven't spent much time in the office lately, have you?"

"No. Hardly any."

"Good." He says, zipping up his duffel bag. "The bugging probably didn't net them any usable info."

"Who's 'them'? Frankie?"

"I was thinking it's probably DEA."

"I wouldn't be so sure." I flip the coin to him. "He left a calling card."

Enzo glowers at it, turns it over, then squeezes it tightly into his balled fist.

"He killed Sharon." I maintain. "As a message to me. Just like he did Jimmy. I don't know how he does it, but he doesn't leave a trace."

Enzo nods, scanning the traffic around us. "Poison, most likely. Tetrahydrozoline."

"Tetra-what?"

"Tetrahydrozoline." He repeats. "The primary ingredient in eye drops. You know, Visine? It's fatal in high enough doses."

I'm unconvinced. "She was poisoned through her eyes?"

"No. Tetrahydrozoline can be fatal when ingested orally – if the concentration is high enough. It was likely placed in her coffee or some other drink."

I stare at him, shaking my head in disbelief. "Man, how do you know all this?"

He ignores my question. "Let's pick up Alison's car. I want to get back to the house and go."

45

Sharon. Pammy. Two innocent, caring souls. I'm as focused as I've ever been. I have my nine-millimeter in one pocket, and I stashed Uncle Danny's Ruger in the other. I'm fully strapped and ready to engage. Alison and I, along with Darcy and Kelly, ride down in the Fiat while Enzo leads in the Jeep. It's tight quarters for the four of us, but my greatest bucket of responsibility is keeping Alison out of harm's way, and her Fiat's the safer bet. Enzo says we're heading to a safe house he uses when he's in Rhode Island. That answers my long-standing question as to where he stays when he's there.

The drive down doesn't go as smoothly as it recently has. It's a tedious trip today, undoubtedly because of what we've suffered through with Sharon and Pammy and the unpleasant task Enzo and I face.

After entering into Rhode Island, we continue nonstop through Providence without so much as flickering a brake light, heading southeast toward the coast. Within thirty minutes or so, we find ourselves in a low-population, densely-forested town in the middle of nowhere. Enzo winds our way through the back country where sunlight glints intermittently through a thick foliage canopy overlaying the road.

Eventually, he slows down and ultimately comes to a stop, lowering his window and pointing his finger signifying we're to turn here. There's no house visible from the road. We pull into the tree-lined dirt driveway and wind our way through thickly-wooded property to find a sizeable building set on a thinly-cleared plot of land. It appears less of a residence and more like a small commercial inn or a bed and breakfast. It features a haunting, faded light-blue exterior framed with darker blue trim, shutters, and ornamental window finials.

"Man, right out of a Stephen King movie." Kelly quips.

"I'd say." Darcy agrees. "Let's hope there's no pet cemetery on the property."

"I'd rather deal with that." I half-joke.

We choose to leave our baggage in the Jeep as we wait for Enzo to introduce us to our host – an elderly woman standing on the front stoop waiting in anticipation. Enzo leads the way, giving her a warm embrace as the rest of us tentatively approach.

"Abigail, let me introduce you. This is Jon; Sabrina's son, his fiancée Alison, and their friends, Kelly and Darcy."

"Hello, everyone." She offers kindly in a sweet, grandmotherly voice. "Welcome."

She can't be five feet tall. She wears her silver hair pulled back tightly in a bun, and a food-stained white kitchen apron stretched tightly over her portly body. She looks to be the epitome of a classic grandma. We offer our greetings and awkwardly wait for an invitation inside.

"Oh, where are my manners? Please, go get your bags and bring them on in. I have rooms for all of you."

As we walk back to the cars, I whisper to Enzo. "Not what I was expecting."

"What'd you think? I stay in a brothel?"

"Well, no, but …"

"C'mon." He laughs. "Let's get your stuff and go in."

It doesn't take us but a moment to grab a bag and walk back to Abigail, who now stands in the front foyer. "Follow me, everyone. I'll show you upstairs."

She turns and starts up a grand staircase leading to a railed landing abutting a long hallway. It doesn't appear the house has been updated since the forties, both structurally and in décor. Antique parlor furniture decorates the great room and ornate, tarnished wall sconces dimly light the interior. Old cast iron radiators, the type that rhythmically tick when hot water flows through, are situated sporadically throughout the house.

Then, there are the paintings. Mostly eerie, somber portraits of nineteenth-century affluent people whose eyes inescapably follow you around the room as you move. We pass closed bedroom doors flanking either side as we move down the hallway. I half-expect to see the *Scooby Doo* gang crisscross the hall, scurrying from room to room trying to solve another ghoulish mystery.

Abigail abruptly stops. "Okay, you two can be here," She offers to Alison and me. "And how about you two next door?" She proposes to Kelly and Darcy. "Let me know if you need anything. I'm always happy to help."

"What about you?" I ask Enzo.

"I have my own room. How about we get settled, then you and I leave in thirty minutes?" He suggests.

"Sounds good."

Alison enters our room and I fall in behind her. Predictably, it's modeled like the rest of the house. A faded, flowery duvet overlays the undersized bed supported by a wrought iron frame and headboard. Billowy discolored curtains, once white, drape from wooden rods over old metal frame casement windows.

"This is the house that time forgot." I joke, dropping my bag on a red-velvet upholstered armchair. "Is this the Queen of England's Coronation Chair?"

"Seriously. I don't want to be here any longer than we need to." She plops down on the bed, generating a harsh squeal of metal on metal. "Oh boy, I know what we're not doing on this bed tonight."

I let out a small laugh. "Right. Enzo and I will be out for a long time tonight, most likely, anyway."

She looks at me with her irresistible eyes. "Will you go over the plan with me?"

"Absolutely. We're going to the laundromat where Frankie has his headquarters. Enzo says he goes there every day for whatever people do at eighty-plus years old. He has a driver bringing him back and forth from where he lives, which by the way, Enzo doesn't know where that is. He thinks tonight's for watching and tomorrow's for action."

Alison's unsettled and who could blame her? I'm agitated, too. The difference is, hers is more of a sadness and mine consists of straight-up anger. Frankie's got to go and I'm glad to be a part of it.

"Will you keep me updated? All day?" She asks adorably.

I lean down and kiss her forehead, placing my hands gently on her cheeks. "Of course, baby. All the time."

46

"You're shotgun. I got the wheel." Enzo instructs unthreateningly. "This is my turf."

I'm more than happy to let him drive. He knows the roads, the routes, the plan, and I can ride hands-free for easy access to my firearms. I toss him Alison's cluttered keychain.

He catches the ball of mess mid-air, hefting its bulk. "Jesus."

"I know. Typical Alison keychain." I laugh.

"Right. Andiamo."

We jump in the Fiat, spin out in the loose dirt, and begin retracing our route back to the capitol city.

"So, how do you know Abigail?" I ask, catching a slight smile emerge on his face.

"Oh, Abigail …" He begins after a moment's pause. "Abigail has seen it all. She must be in her late seventies by now. Her father and his father before him were bootleggers. Whiskey mainly. They distilled on this very same property since before the Civil War. Abigail grew up around it. She's seen all types pass through here and continues her family's legacy of providing safe haven for … well, certain types of people, let's say."

"She seems so unassuming."

"I wouldn't recommend crossing her. She has more weaponry and know-how stashed in that house than you'd ever believe. She had a husband once. He was a deadbeat and thought he could run all over her. He disappeared one day." Enzo laughs. "She never told me outright, but I think he's still somewhere on the property."

"How'd you meet her?"

"Through people I've come across. Nothing too exciting. Your mother got along with her really well."

"I could see that." I say, then switch up the subject. "Alright, we get to the laundromat and park somewhere no one will notice us and basically stake out the place, right?"

"Basically."

"If Frankie leaves, we follow him. What if he's only going out for a short trip and then back to the laundromat?"

"We still follow him. See where he goes. It might be an interception point, either then or later on."

"Okay. What if he doesn't leave all day and then goes straight home? How do we intercept him if we don't know if it's his final destination until we get there?"

"I see where you're going with this. People could spot us from his house and see what's going on. If it's late in the day, he'll more than likely be going home. As you know, we may have to burn this afternoon simply to see his total route and then try again tomorrow. Hopefully, that doesn't happen, but there's a good chance it could."

No sense in me bellyaching about the possibility. There's nothing Enzo can do about it, and safety is our number one priority.

When we get to Providence, we make our way over to the Federal Hill section of the city. Restaurants and shops line the street that cuts through the center of the neighborhood. It's really a cool setup. Lots of activity going on, lots of people. Enzo says back in the day, you didn't come through Federal Hill unless you were known. You might find yourself in a heap of trouble, otherwise. He maneuvers through the streets, eventually stopping in a crumbling parking lot adjacent to an obviously abandoned warehouse or storage facility. Connected to the empty building? Frankie's laundromat.

"Good positioning." I compliment. "Perfect sight line and inconspicuous."

"Thanks. I thought so, too. It's a solid vantage point and makes for a quick exit if necessary."

"What now?" I ask, as if I didn't already know the answer.

Enzo looks at me wearing a smirk on his face. "Funny. We wait. The good thing is, it's getting late in the afternoon. Old men don't like staying out late."

"What if he already left?" I point out.

"Don't even say that."

I pull out my phone and start playing internet poker to pass the time. Enzo does nothing but focus on the laundromat. I suppose he makes for a more proficient mobster than I do. I'm half-crazy after a half hour. I'll be full-crazy after a full hour.

Another thirty minutes of zero activity passes, and I need to relieve myself. "I gotta go pee. I'm going behind that dumpster over there."

I walk behind the nearby dumpster, unzip, and get down to business. I have an unobstructed view of the laundromat, and as I'm passing time, a dude opens the front door and peers sideways in either direction while holding a cellphone to his ear. It's Pete O'Shea. I bolt upright and lean forward for a sharper view. I press hard to finish peeing, uncomfort-ably pinch it off early, then hastily tuck myself in and charge back to the Fiat. A custom black Mercedes SL-550 with blacked-out windows glides around the corner and rolls up to the front. A hefty, stylishly-dressed man exits the car, quickly scans the area, and disappears inside. I feel my body tense up and I have to consciously remind myself to breathe.

Enzo transforms into a laser-focused machine. "This is it. His driver."

He starts the car and shifts into drive in anticipation of cruising out. Within minutes, the front door opens and two men appear. I instinc-tively pat down my firearms, ensuring they're in my pocket and readily accessible. The driver exits first, providing arm support for his boss, Mr. Francesco Antonetti. It's a strange feeling for me to see him in real-time. He looks frail … weak.

He helps Frankie into the passenger seat, then swings around to the driver's side. He takes another long look around before entering the car and shutting the door. After they take off, Enzo allows a three or four second differential before pulling out and tailing them. My heart races, but I show no outward sign of how jacked up I am.

Surprisingly, they lead us out of the city and into a very unex-ceptional neighboring town. As we cross a bridge, I read a sign welcom-ing us to the Seekonk River Basin. An archaic dam, appearing to be on its last legs, spews yellowish water from rusted slats stretching the wide span of the river. I expected Frankie Humps to live in a lap of luxury, but it doesn't appear so.

"Doesn't this guy have tons of money?" I ask.

Enzo nods.

"Why does he live around here? What the heck does he do with all of it?"

"These houses may look ordinary, but inside I bet his is a pal-ace. And very secure." He pauses. "Jon, I'm afraid we're not going to be able to do anything tonight. We're getting close to his home."

"That's alright. I didn't expect to, anyway."

The Mercedes travels a few more blocks before turning onto a side road and then into the driveway of a modest, single-story ranch. We stop a half block away and observe. Frankie exits the vehicle alone and trudges to the front door.

My heart skips a beat. "Look. The driver's not getting out. He didn't shut the car off, either."

"He's only stopping to visit. He doesn't live there!" Enzo realizes excitedly. "Hang on!"

His directive startles me, and I tense up as he shifts into reverse and accelerates to the intersection behind us. He swings the Fiat around and backtracks a quarter mile down the neighborhood's main access road bordered by a swath of vacant land running its length, separating the road from the river. He turns down a side street and drives about fifteen yards, then swings the car around to face back to the main road we came in on. I desperately want to ask him what the heck we're doing, but I see he's completely single-minded and absorbed in thought.

A moment later, I catch a glimpse of the Mercedes cruising up the main road, traveling perpendicular to us. With no warning, Enzo guns the engine and shifts the car into gear. "Roll down your window!" He commands. "Brace yourself!"

I quickly lower my window. Enzo accelerates toward the Mercedes just as it reaches our intersection.

"What are you doing?! Crashing into him?!" I shout.

Enzo rams Alison's Fiat into the driver's side door of Frankie's sedan, crumpling the side panel into the poor bastard sitting behind the wheel. Our airbags deploy, momentarily pinning us to our seatbacks before deflating.

"Check your door! Move!" Enzo barks.

I unbuckle my belt and reach for the handle. With great effort it moves a crack, forcing me to shoulder ram it open, generating a groan of crunching metal. After I climb out, I look back at Enzo as he's crawling out through his window. The front of the Fiat looks like a clothes iron set to its steam function. Smoke spills from the mashed-in engine compartment and glass shards litter the roadway.

"Holy shit! Alison's car!" I sputter.

"Pull Frankie out!" Enzo yells. "Stuff him in the back!"

I grip my loaded Glock and race over to the passenger side door and yank it open. Frankie's disoriented but conscious. "I can't feel my legs." He moans. "My legs."

I push his deflated airbag aside, unfasten his seatbelt, and forcefully haul him out, where he promptly spills onto the road. As I drag him to the back seat, Enzo dives into the spot I just vacated and attends to the unconscious driver. I manage to stuff Frankie inside and close the door. Enzo rolls the driver out, depositing him on the vacant land.

"Let's get at it!" Enzo yells. "You drive. I'm in back with him." He gestures to Frankie.

"What about the Fiat?"

"Leave it. We'll have Alison call it in as stolen. It'll fit the profile, especially if anyone saw Frankie's car was involved in the accident. Now, let's move!"

I hop in and slam the Mercedes into gear and take off.

"No need to go fast. We don't want to draw attention once we get out of here." Enzo counsels.

Rational thinking returns, spurring panic and fear. "Where am I going? What are we doing with him?"

"Head to the Omni. We'll dump this car and pick up my Cadillac."

"What the fuck are you gonna do with me?" Frankie interrupts, snarling in his old man voice and attempting to sound tough. I hear the fear, though. Up close, he looks even older and more feeble.

"I'm going to end your miserable life." Enzo advises matter-of-factly while unzipping his duffel bag. I hadn't seen him retrieve it from the Fiat – he must've grabbed it when I was tending to Frankie.

"You're gonna die, Garibaldi. You'll never make it outta here. You neither, Jonny." He directs to me.

'Jonny.' It sounds strange to hear someone call me 'Jonny.' Especially in a Rhode Island accent.

Enzo pays him no mind. He removes a massive syringe, a cough syrup-sized bottle of clear liquid, and a plastic cup not unlike one used when submitting a urine sample. He pours the clear liquid into the cup, removes the cap from the syringe, and draws a full dose through the needle. He turns the syringe upside down and flicks the side like you see in medical dramas on television.

"Half of this is for Jimmy and the other half for Jimmy's dad." Enzo says, inserting the needle into Frankie's jugular and injecting him with what appears to be enough tranquilizer to kill a grizzly bear. Just as Frankie's eyes begin to roll back in his head, he whispers, "I didn't kill Jimmy ... I swear ..."

Frankie goes limp and Enzo withdraws the syringe, caps it, and deposits it into his duffel bag.

"Did you hear him?" I ask. "He says he didn't kill Jimmy."

Enzo zips up his bag. "Don't believe him. He'd say anything to save his life."

"I get that, but he never said he didn't kill Jimmy's dad."

Enzo doesn't acknowledge. Instead, he focuses on what looms ahead for the evening. We utilize back roads as much as possible as we drive to the hotel, trying to deflect attention away from a vehicle so unmistakably involved in a collision. The setting sun makes driving a challenge, but luckily as darkness looms, we'll be camouflaged in no time.

"What happens when we get to the hotel?" I ask.

"We go to the self-park and stuff him in the trunk of the Caddy. Then, we wait for a late-night disposition."

"Where?"

"You'll see."

47

It's closing in on midnight, and Enzo adeptly navigates his Cadillac through downtown Providence, driving on a combination of primary access roads, side streets, and little-more-than back alleys. He glides around the city with familiarity, guided by experience and lighting from abundant streetlamps and exterior buildings.

"Can you share with me where we're going now?" I ask guardedly. Enzo's been exceptionally reserved for the duration of the ride. It's unnerving.

He audibly exhales a deep breath while once more glancing into his rearview mirror. "Sorry. I'm still trying to lower my heart rate. Providence Place mall."

Undoubtedly, we're not going to the mall itself. I remain silent, letting him gather his thoughts to continue without me prompting him.

"We're going to dump him in the underground tunnels where he ordered a lot of his disposals. I can't resist the irony, plus it's an ideal spot. No one will ever find a body there."

"What are the underground tunnels?"

"It's where cable and telephone companies bury their wires under the city. With all the advances in fiber optics and 5G broadband, nobody really goes into them anymore. There's a well-hidden access point by the mall. They're deep, dark, and mostly inaccessible."

"Mostly?"

He looks at me with a crooked smile. "Yeah. Mostly. When you pop the manhole cover and look down, you see a platform about twenty feet deep. Guys climb down there and work on the cable wires from the platform. But there's another section below the platform. It goes down about another ten feet or so. It collects all the rainwater, washouts from the road, oil from cars, and everything else coming off the roads. Over the platform," He gestures with two fingers imitating a man running and jumping off a cliff and falling to his death. "That's where we dump him."

After another few minutes, Enzo backs into a gravel road access point located beneath a series of highway overpasses far enough so we're hidden within thick underbrush. We hop out of the car and I look around. I can see lighted signs for the mall's North and South parking garages roughly a couple hundred yards from us.

Enzo strides purposefully toward the back of the car. "Let's get this done."

I'm all for that. Enzo bypasses the trunk, where Frankie meets with his maker, and stops at a grungy, spiderweb-fissured concrete pad some ten feet behind the car. I follow him over. Weeds protrude from its cracked surface, and I think back to the dog I saw at the jetport when Alison and I picked up Santa and Merri. In my mind, I imagine Alison counseling me – *pee on the weed, Jon, just pee on the weed.*

Enzo bends over and examines a manhole cover with a company insignia imprinted on its face, searching for something. He runs his fingers slowly and deliberately over its surface until he finds what he's looking for.

"What is it?" I ask.

Enzo stands up and walks back to the car, opening the door to the back seat. "I was looking for the jack insert on the lid. They're custom built so only a specific jack can fit in and open them. Luckily," He says while walking back and holding up a pry bar with an oddly-shaped tip. "I have one. And don't ask."

"Roger that." I'm less interested in where he got the jack and more curious if he's personally dumped anyone down the pipe. I won't ask that either, I guess.

"Here, give it a shot." He says, offering me the jack. "The cover weighs two hundred … maybe close to three hundred pounds."

I take the jack and insert it into the slot. It doesn't budge. I put everything I have into it. Nothing. I look at Enzo and shrug my shoulders.

"C'mon. You need to put those girly-man muscles to work!" He teases. "Here. Give it to me."

He makes a big production of pretending to stretch out, wildly windmilling his arms to warm up before carefully reinserting the jack. He steadies himself and leans back, using his bodyweight as an anchor. I'm positioned to help grasp the cover and deadlift it from the opposite side in the event he manages to create a gap.

"Ready?" He asks but doesn't wait for my response. He levers downward, working it loose with no trouble, creating an opening so I can lift the cover up and out easily.

"Funny guy, eh? What was the trick?"

"When you're as good as me …" He begins, struggling not to laugh. "No, it's all technique. There's an inner rim on the cover, eight or so inches below the opening for the jack hook. You have to catch that to lift it, or it's nearly impossible to open."

"Cute. Okay, what's next?"

Enzo removes a flashlight from his coat. "Let me see what we have here."

He shines the light into the concrete cylinder, sweeping it from side to side, then examining top to bottom. He has a troubled look on his face.

"What do you see?" I ask.

"I'm not sure. Something's on the platform blocking the opening to the bottom level. I haven't seen that before. Normally, the platform would be clear." He continues to shine the light. "If that wasn't there, we could aim Frankie to pass right by the platform and hit the bottom, but that won't work now. We need to move it."

A moment of panic flashes through me. "What if we can't?"

"We'll have to go someplace else. Which I don't want to do. I want to get rid of him."

"You and me both."

"Jon, if I go down, I might not be able to move whatever's down there. If I can move it, you'll need to pass Frankie down to me."

I get his unspoken, intended message. "I'll climb down and see if I can get rid of it. Then you can drop Frankie past the platform, so he falls all the way to the bottom. You know how to position him better than I would, anyway."

"Good call. That's what I was thinking, too. I'm also too damn old to be climbing down there."

"Right." I chuckle, stepping up to the cylinder edge while Enzo hands me the flashlight. I flip it around and peer down. "I see it. It looks big."

"Try and move it. If it's too heavy, come back up and we're out of here."

"Got it." I place the light into my pocket, swing onto my stomach, locate the steel rungs cemented into the wall with my feet, and begin the descent. "Hey, yo. It smells down here." I gag. "Aw, man," My voice begins to echo. "It's bad."

"Yeah, it's bad, I know. Hold your breath." He laughs. "Like I said, you're getting a whiff of everything that washes off the road. Garbage, oil, gas, you name it. That's the other reason I didn't want to go in."

That's lovely. I drop the twenty-foot depth in no time and stand on the grated platform, about five feet from the unidentified blockage. I remove the flashlight from my pocket and turn it on.

"What is it?" Enzo asks.

"It's a whole lot of wet cardboard, it looks like." I say as I cautiously approach.

I lift the disintegrating lid and peer in. A pack of king-size sewer rats explodes from the opening, causing me to jar backwards. "Ah! Goddamn it!" I flail my arms ineffectively in a lame, karate chop attempt to deflect them away. The rats spill over and scatter, dropping over the side of the platform to the substructure below. I can hear them splash as they hit.

"Jon!" Enzo calls out.

My hands involuntarily shake, zig-zagging the flashlight beam. "I'm good. I'm okay. Just some rats. They're gone."

I hadn't let go of the lid when I jolted backward, resulting in me shredding the front and most of one side from the decaying box. As the trembling in my hands subsides, I reposition the light back to the container and reacclimate my vision.

"Shit!" I bark, rearing backward again. A rat-chewed corpse faces me – no eyelids, no eyes, and barely half of a nose. It's Fat Mikey. I remember his long, stringy hair. It's unquestionably Fat Mikey.

"Hey! Talk to me!" Enzo demands nervously.

"Fat Mikey's in the box. Rats have been working him over, but I can tell it's him." I bluster, then kick the box, causing a few leftover, stray rats to skitter away. It moves a few inches. "Go get Frankie." I say, looking up at Enzo. "I'll have this guy out in thirty seconds."

Enzo disappears from the concrete opening and I set back to the task at hand. I kick the box again, moving it further to the edge, but it's clear to me he won't simply drop over the side. The opening's barely two feet wide – I'll have to stuff him through. I don't touch any part of him with my hands; I use only my feet – moving him to the edge, pulling the box down around him, and positioning his body over the opening. I'm able to ram the cardboard through easily; it essentially disintegrates with very little effort. Fat Mikey … not so much. I stomp on him repeatedly, alternating each attempt with reflexive retching. I feel his body squish with every try. It takes me approximately a dozen or so tries to get him sufficiently forced through the gap, and on the final push, Fat Mikey pops through and vanishes. I count nearly three full seconds before I hear him hit. Unlike the rats, Fat Mikey produces less of a *splash*, and more of a *SPLOOSH!*

"You all set?" Enzo calls down.

"I'm good. I'm ready."

"Climb back up."

"No. You need to drop him first. It's only a couple of feet wide from the platform to the edge. He's going to need some help. That's why Fat Mikey got stuck."

"Oh. Okay. Hang on." Enzo momentarily disappears from view and reappears almost as quickly. "Alright, move over to the far end of the platform. He's coming!" He grunts as he maneuvers the body and I see a dark silhouette materialize and fill the opening, blocking out what little background light existed. As he releases his grasp on Frankie, I hear him softly talk to his dead childhood friend. "This is for you, Jimmy."

Just before Frankie hits, I feel a rush of displaced air, followed by the distinct crack of bones breaking. I spring into action and kick him over to the edge. He's smaller and lighter than Fat Mikey and I have him rapidly into position for the final push.

"Sharon … Pammy, I'm so sorry. This is for you both." I stomp on Frankie Humps' ashen, dead face and send him down for a long visit with Fat Mikey and whoever the hell else rots down there.

"I'm pretty sure I know what happened." Enzo says as I emerge from the opening.

"To Fat Mikey?"

"No. I think we both know what happened to him. To the tunnel. They must've expanded the platforms some time ago. They reach farther over, so it's shrunk the gap down to the bottom level." Enzo surmises.

"Good to know." I reply sarcastically. "Can we get out of here? I need a shower."

"Yeah, you do."

48

Enzo wastes no time putting the car into gear and beating feet out of here. I thump my head into the headrest in exhaustion, anxious to get back to Maine. If I weren't so drained, I'd suggest we travel now and take advantage of the early hour darkness and lack of traffic.

"I guess I should call Alison and explain about her car. Tell her to report it stolen, too, like you said." I say glumly.

"Why don't you wait until we see them so we can download the whole story? Text her it all worked out perfectly; she'll be able to relax, and you can fill her in when we get there."

"Good idea. How long before we get back? Thirty minutes?"

"More like forty-five. We have to make a stop along the way."

I deliberately turn my head and glower at him.

"What?" He deflects. "Relax. It's nothing."

I don't have the energy or desire to protest. I take out my phone and craft a text to Alison letting her know all is good and we're on our way back. Clearly, she's been waiting on an update because she responds immediately and with great relief.

"All set." I report. "She's good."

Enzo nods his approval. "Perfect."

I close my eyes and attempt to rest, but my mind amps up as my body relaxes. I think about Sharon and her husband and what he must be going through, as well as her daughter and grandchildren. I also contemplate Pammy's family – if she has any. No one will know what happened to her. To them, she will have simply vanished. Same as Frankie.

I'm jostled awake by a slowing of the vehicle and gentle pull of a slight turn. We've exited the highway.

I scan the area. "Where are we? Did I fall asleep?"

"Yes, you did. Not for very long, though. We're at T.F. Green Airport. This is our stop."

"For what? We're not flying anywhere."

"No shit." He looks at me like I'm a dope. "Hang on a minute. You'll see."

Enzo pulls into the long-term parking garage and winds his way up the corkscrew ramp to the third level. He parks the Cadillac in a center row and shuts it down. He reaches back for his duffel bag and opens his door. "Let's go. We're doing a dump-and-run with the Caddy."

I can only assume that means he has another car here. He leads me across two rows of vehicles until we stand facing our newest ride: a shiny, black Mercedes SUV.

"Is this the same one?" I ask, smiling at the memory.

"Sure is."

"Well, I'll be …"

I open the door, climb in, and promptly recline in its luxurious seats. I activate the heated massage and relax for the ride back, recalling the first time I rode in this car. I sat in the back seat with Alison, contemplating my mom's profile and how young she looked as she sat in this very seat. She wore her hair in a high ponytail making her appear much younger than her fifty years. Man, I really miss her.

"LoZo, I love this ride. Glad you still have it. What are we looking at? Fifteen … maybe twenty minutes to get back?"

"Probably twenty. I thought hard about off-loading the car, but I couldn't part with it. Too many memories."

"I hear you." I respond somberly, then switch the subject. "Was Frankie's driver dead when you dragged him out?"

"Not when I pulled him out. I could hear him groan. Maybe he died later, I don't know." He speculates.

"You remember the guy poking his head out of the laundromat door? He was on a cellphone." I don't pause for his response. "That was Pete O'Shea. He's the guy Bung knew from high school that got up in my face at WaterFire. They called him Piece O'Shit. We wondered if he was working for Frankie."

"Looks like you got your answer."

"Yeah. Too bad it wasn't him behind the wheel with Frankie."

After a stretch of riding through back country roads, we finally pull up to Abigail's driveway. It's more difficult to see down the narrow dirt driveway under cover of darkness than when we first arrived, though Enzo manages well. When our headlights wash over the house, the front door swings open and Alison and Abigail rush out to greet us.

"Oh baby, I'm so glad you're back!" Alison gushes, throwing her arms around me. "I've been worried sick. Thank the … hey, where's my car? Who's is this?" She adopts a defensive stance while pointing to the Mercedes.

I struggle to make eye contact. "Well, I was getting to that … we had a little accident."

"Jon! Where's my Fiat?!"

I catch Enzo grinning from out of the corner of my eye, clearly amused at my uncomfortable interrogation. "We kind of left it behind." I stammer while staring down at my feet.

Alison's eyes widen. "You what?!"

"Can we go inside and I'll fill you in on everything? Please?"

She spins, arms folded, and marches into the house.

I glare at Enzo. "Thanks for the help, compadre."

"Anytime, buddy." He laughs.

After we get inside, we gather in the great room – minus Darcy and Kelly who opted for bed – and discuss the events of the evening. We touch upon the major points: waiting at the laundromat, the driver arriving, following Frankie to the house, and ultimately, destroying the Fiat. Enzo handles much of the narrative; he has a knack for painting the picture without revealing the most unpleasant portions of what happened. For instance, when explaining the cause of the Fiat's demise, he portrays it as having 'been involved in an accident.' Technically it was, but from purposefully ramrodding it into Frankie's car. Minor details.

"So, where is it?" Alison fumes.

"We had to leave it. It was dead and we had to get out of there." I sheepishly answer.

She begins to piece together the gravity of the position we were in and her tone softens considerably. "How were you able to leave? Did you steal their car?"

I don't respond but continue to maintain eye contact.

Enzo mercifully intervenes. "I told Jon to forget about your car and to report it as stolen. You'll get the insurance proceeds, and for your trouble, I'd like to subsidize the amount you receive so you can get any vehicle you want."

"Oh. Okay." She replies demurely, our earlier 'transgressions' quickly forgotten.

"Yeah, I thought I heard a party going on down there." A booming voice interrupts from the upstairs landing.

I look up to find Bung leaning over the railing peering down on us. "What? Are you kidding me?"

"Oh, right, Bung lives here. I neglected to tell you." Enzo says jokingly.

"That's right. We visited with him most of the evening." Alison adds.

I guess that's what Bung had in mind when he said, 'I got places to go' after we left him at the Omni's parking garage. Either Enzo introduced him to Abigail, or the reverse.

Abigail brings refreshments to the great room – warm cider and cinnamon. It tastes absolutely wonderful. Bung joins us while Enzo and I report to the group we were exceptionally successful tonight. Following a few cursory, general questions, we move off the subject and chat casually while finishing our drinks before going to bed.

"Bung, how'd you end up here?" I ask.

Bung smiles widely. "Yeah, well, see this lovely lady here you all know as Abigail? I call her grandma. She raised me."

"Oh, Tommy, you're such a good boy." Abigail praises.

True to form, Bung fashions his beard to a point, outwardly loving and protective of his grandmother.

"Tommy was kind enough to introduce me to Abigail." Enzo explains respectfully.

Abigail smiles warmly. "You're always welcome in my home, Enzo."

I drain my cider, and its intoxicating warmth coupled with my exhaustion pushes me into a pre-sleep coma. I rise from my chair and offer a hand to Alison. "Everyone, it's been fun, but I need to crash."

"Baby, haven't you crashed enough today?" Alison teases, and the group erupts in laughter. It's nice to see Enzo laughing the loudest.

"Nice. Let's go, funny bunny." I sweep her up in my arms, toss her over my shoulder, and head up the staircase.

"Bye, everyone!" She giggles, waving to the group as I haul her to our room.

I dump her on the bed, generating a shrill metal screech. "Don't even think about it! It's way too loud!" She mildly protests while unfastening my jeans. "But I have a good substitute. Here, lay down on your back …"

49

A number of days has passed since we got back from our Rhode Island undertaking. The dust has settled somewhat, though life hasn't returned completely to normal. Our office remains shuttered and I'm not sure I want to reopen it – certainly not in the near term. Enzo decided to come back to Maine and spend some time alone in his Camp Ellis beach house. Thankfully, he made his first order of business searching our apartment for listening devices, of which he found none.

I spoke with Sharon's husband. The medical examiner ruled her cause of death an acute myocardial infarction. A heart attack. He doesn't understand the how's or the why's – she was in great health and had no family history of heart disease. In a futile attempt to console him, I said there're some things in life we weren't meant to understand. I don't understand this one either, but for an entirely different reason than him. He thinks it's bad luck. I know it's murder.

Alison followed through on reporting her vehicle as stolen, and it seems to have worked out well. I have no idea what she's getting for a replacement; she wants it to be a surprise. I won't be in the dark for long

– she's out right now picking it up. Who knows? Maybe she'll roll with the newer model Fiat again.

I plan to spend my morning and early afternoon at the gym. It's Arm Day today. Possibly my favorite workout. I'm psyched up to clear my head and sweat it out on this warm, late-Spring morning. I stow the rooftop panels on Danny's Jeep in the back and crank up the music. As I drive off, my head bounces to the driving beat of *YYZ* from Rush as I air drum on the steering wheel. Rest in peace, Neil Peart, you were one of the best.

Whenever I approach the gym's parking lot entrance, I always quickly scan it checking to see how many cars are here. Saturday mornings nearing summertime routinely attract the less-dedicated fitness enthusiasts. They're of the mind they can work off years of sedentary living and carve out a slamming beach body over the next six weeks for a dramatic unveiling at the annual Fourth of July picnic. The only other time these individuals make it in is during the two weeks following their New Year's resolutions. Neither attempts ever stick. This morning, the beach-body hopefuls pack the lot.

I fortuitously snare a spot up front, glide into the check-in area, and inspect the floor to see what my people-watching supply looks like for the day. I see a couple of Creepers right off. Plenty of Hardos dot the weightlifting floor, too. And although I can't see them, I hear Grunters howling in unison, harmonizing like an ugly, caveman *a capella* group. As I warm up and stretch, I take note of the Makeup Mirror Workout girls flaunting their stuff, strutting by the floor-to-ceiling mirrors spanning the length of the building. If I'm honest, without Alison in my life, I might be a trace more interested in this gym patron demographic.

I see One Upper on my way over to the dumbbell racks. Looks like he's working shoulders today. Bummer. Though I was irritated with his uninvited competition at first, he motivates me to work harder and get the extra repetitions.

I grab my phone to crank up the music and see I got a text from Alison:

I respond back to her equally as excited. She'll want me to see it, so I suggest she drive over to the gym to kill two birds with one stone. I can work out and she can show off her car to everyone here. Honestly, I am curious as to what she bought. She's been tight-lipped since picking it out and Enzo hasn't spilled the beans, either. In the meantime, I'll need to accelerate my weightlifting routine to finish before she gets here.

Biceps and triceps. Two components of the California Workout triad, with chest being the third. Many dudes here subscribe to that mediocre training program. The California Workout trains the 'show off' muscles of arms and chest and ignores other perceived 'less interesting to female' body parts such as legs or shoulders. You can easily spot the CW guys because they exhibit well-developed upper bodies connected to spindly legs and calves, reminiscent of a flamingo. I'm not a fan.

Luckily, working arms moves quicker than bigger, denser body parts like legs and back, so I can hit it hard, but also fast. I blast through my program and text her when I'm fifteen minutes away from finishing. She gets right back to me, responding she's on the way.

I wrap up before she gets here, then head over to the smoothie bar to order a protein recovery drink and pass the time before she arrives. I notice Alison way before she makes it to the building, her hair perfect and outfit on point. She struts her fine self through the entrance door, still sporting her sunglasses while I wait for my smoothie.

"I'm over here." I wave to her.

"Hey, luvah!" She bubbles. "Wait 'til you see my new ride!"

I'm super excited for her. "I can hardly wait!"

I pay for my drink, grab my gym bag, and we head out the door to the parking lot. I look around trying to spot it, but I don't see anything new. "Where is it?"

"I'm out back. I don't want anyone near it."

We cut through a few rows of cars to the back edge of the lot. Set apart from all other cars and parked at a slightly obnoxious angle to block anyone from coming near it, sits a brand-new, brilliant-white Mercedes G-Wagon. That ain't no Fiat.

"Holy shit! Alison, this vehicle costs a hundred grand!"

"Ya, well, I'm worth it!" She breathes in mock arrogance, then whispers, "It was a hundred twenty."

I walk its perimeter, admiring the exceptional lines and superb craftmanship. "Wow. Incredible. This ride produces six hundred horsepower."

"Ya, whatever. I like the way it looks."

"Mmm. Same here. How did Enzo respond when you told him about it?" What I'm really asking is if he balked at the cost.

"Nothing. He only warned me I would be very much noticed in this car and if I would be okay with that."

Leave it to Enzo for thinking about practicality. "Can I get inside?"

"Of course. It's unlocked."

Alison fires up the engine and boosts the Burmester sound system. "What do you think?" She yells over the booming output.

"What's not to like? This is awesome."

"Totally! I love it!" She squeals, then shuts the car down.

She's pumped, and with good reason, but as much as I'd like to tool around in it with her right now, I'm super hungry.

"What do you say we chase down some lunch? I could use a Treacherous Triple right about now." I propose.

"Absolutely. My treat!"

Her excitement's short-lived, however. Before I can get out and walk back to the Jeep, a large SUV squeezes in uncomfortably close to my door, preventing me from exiting. The darkly-tinted window lowers gradually, overdramatically revealing Special Agent Calhoun and Agent Harmon.

"Woo-hoo. Look at that new whip … must have cost you a fortune. Accounting biz must be doing really well." Calhoun needles derisively. "But wait … I see your firm's closed. How can you afford that?"

Agent Harmon leans forward from the passenger seat, poking his pointy nose around Calhoun's body for a better view.

"What do you want?" I grouse.

"What's the tone for? You might want to be a little more agreeable around us, Jon." He suggests. "We haven't been able to locate Mr. Garibaldi. Know where he is?"

"Nope. I don't keep tabs on him."

"Right. Well, maybe you could help us out anyway. Could you tell us where Francesco Antonetti is?" Calhoun requests.

My body tenses. I hadn't given these guys a second thought after dealing with Frankie. Of course, they'll be on the lookout for him.

Calhoun continues. "He's a reasonably predictable guy, and we haven't seen him in some time. Leads us to believe there might be something more to it. Wouldn't know anything about it, would you?"

"Not a thing. If I had anything to share, I absolutely would share it." I offer earnestly but dishonestly.

Calhoun turns heated. "It's time to cut the bullshit! We know Antonetti wanted Garibaldi to run the bulk drug distribution and Garibaldi turned him down. Antonetti must be pissed off, and either it escalated to Garibaldi taking matters into his own hands or Antonetti disappeared. Maybe it's both. Now, I'm not sure how you fit into all of this, but I know you do. If you don't cooperate, and quickly, I'll drag your ass so far down, you'll have to look up to see hell. You got that?"

"Yes, sir." My voice quakes, and not because I'm acting. "I really don't know what's going on. I don't want any trouble."

He exhales a deep sigh. "Look, you seem like a decent kid. I've done your background – you were a good student, clean record, no problems I could find. Why do you want to be tied into these guys?"

Alison reaches for my hand as I respond quietly and truthfully. "I ask myself the same question."

Before driving off, Calhoun concludes our impromptu meeting with a thinly-veiled threat couched as a warning. "This isn't going to end well, Jon … and there'll be nothing I can do to stop it."

50

The Treacherous Triple burger isn't nearly as satisfying following our encounter with the DEA guys. Obviously, they keep a close watch on the higher-ups controlling the drug trade in Providence. Enzo's on their radar screen, and by association, so are we. I can't determine if they've factored our accounting firm into their equation, but I can't rule it out. Alison's new car doesn't help the situation, either. Calhoun's quick to point out the questionable action of buying such an expensive vehicle at the same time we shut our accounting firm down. That being said, I don't see how they could make the connection between the credit union and Frankie's operation unless they've connected the dots with Jimmy and Lorraine. What about the destroyed Fiat we left behind? Do they know about it, and can they link it to Frankie's disappearance? There are so many wildcards at play.

"So, what do we do about those guys?" Alison asks worriedly.

"Calhoun and Harmon? Nothing, really. Look, Frankie's gone, and Enzo never worked for him – at least not on the drug operation." I reason. "We're not doing anything with Enzo, and we pulled out of the audit. I don't see how this goes any further."

She sighs resignedly. "I guess that makes sense."

I'm not sure I'd buy what I'm trying to sell, but honestly, I think it's counterproductive to hash out prospective courses of action with her. And forget about the potential outcomes and consequences. "After lunch, I'll connect with Enzo and get his take on it."

We spend the rest of our lunch date talking about trivial matters, attempting to avoid discussing our sticky situation and also to sidetrack our anxiety. We're only marginally successful.

Alison abruptly pushes her plate forward a few inches in a signal she's done eating. "I had a long conversation with Darcy earlier."

"How'd that go?"

"I guess she and Kelly are getting pretty serious. Darcy's really into him. I'm actually surprised because when we first reconnected, she always talked about what jerks men are, how she'll never marry again … stuff like that."

I reach for her unfinished plate. "Good for them. You know, it doesn't surprise me. We've all had some pretty intense experiences recently. People often connect when emotions run high."

"Hmm. I never thought of it that way. You may be right; we're a good example of that. Has Kelly said anything to you about Darcy?"

"Nope."

She waits a moment to see if I'll elaborate. I don't. I'm content to finish her Simple Single and half-eaten onion rings.

"Oh, I forgot. Guys don't talk about their emotions. You're all so tough." She teases lightheartedly.

I see now she was expecting more. "He says he likes her a lot." I fib.

That placates her, but just barely. I think my response was fair, though Kelly and I truthfully haven't spoken a single word about it.

"I'm stuffed." I announce, patting my stomach in an attempt to derail a would-be runaway train conversation. "Let's square up with our server and test out your new Bluetooth and call Enzo."

§

"Hey, Alison." Enzo answers.

"LoZo. It's Jon. I'm on Alison's cell. We're in her brand-new, Enzo-sponsored G-Wagon."

"How do you like it? I may get one for myself."

I measure my response. "I have mixed feelings."

"What do you mean?"

"I love the ride, but I'm worried about the impression."

"Yeah, it's flashy, but so what?"

I spend the next ten minutes explaining to Enzo the substance of our unexpected meeting with Calhoun and Harmon, and he sees what I'm talking about.

"I get it." He agrees. "I was hesitant, too, but I thought the DEA mess would blow over ... I still do. Just lay low and let some time pass. Any case the DEA may have had died alongside Frankie."

"I agree, but his comment about the firm closing up and asking about Frankie and where he is has me spooked. What if they can link it all together?"

"Keep your nose clean and admit to nothing. They have nothing, otherwise they'd officially present you with a warrant, or had you arrested, or something like that. It's all been informal."

"True, and on the flip side, it doesn't appear DEA knows about your beach house. That's a bonus."

"Good to hear. I'd like to keep it that way. Not so good to hear they're looking for me, but I'm in the same situation as you. I never did any running for Frankie. If they link my ATM business to Jimmy though, I may have a problem."

"So, where do we go from here?"

"Nowhere. Don't come over here just in case they have a tail on you. Go about your business as usual. The gym, grocery store, A's, and wherever else you go." He advises. "If you need me, call on this number, but do it outside or somewhere in a public area. If you need to go to your office, don't talk about anything and don't mess with the bugs. We don't know who put them there. If it was DEA, we don't want them to know we found them. Sound good?"

"Yeah. I think I got it."

"Okay. Talk soon." Predictably, Enzo hangs up without waiting for a reply.

"We have bugs in our office?" Alison asks.

I nod. "We're not sure who put them there. Enzo scoped it out with his detection wand the morning we found Sharon. DEA could have bugged it when they were waiting for me or it could be Frankie's guys. We're not sure. I don't plan to do anything in that office again, so I don't care."

"I can't deal with this anymore." She murmurs under her breath.

I try to console her, recognizing I won't succeed. My words will ring hollow. "Totally understandable. I'm really sorry."

She shifts the car into gear then reaches for my hand. "I know something that'll make us feel better. Let's take this baby out for a nice, long ride."

51

The G-Wagon makes Enzo's Mercedes SUV seem like a minivan. We spent about two hours tooling around southern Maine before coming back to pick up the Jeep and heading for home. I advocated for 'christening' the G-Wagon while we were on tour, and I was swiftly rebuffed. I think the term Alison used was 'request denied.'

It's approaching late afternoon, and Alison's relaxingly curled up on the couch scrolling through her phone. My Bulldog Brewing lunch worked its way through my system, exiling me to the bathroom to play internet poker on my phone. I pause the game when I'm interrupted by an incoming call with a blocked number.

"No, thank you." I grunt. "I've had more than enough of these calls from Pammy."

"Who are you talking to?" Alison calls out.

"How could you possibly hear me? No one. I'm getting a call from a blocked number."

"You never shut the bathroom door, that's how. Who is it?"

As I see it, I have two ways to answer this question. One, I could be uncomplicated and repeat, 'I'm not sure. It's from a blocked number.' Or two, I could test the limits of her patience and say, 'Hold on, let me channel my telepathic powers to reveal the unknown caller's identity.'

"I'm not sure. It's from a blocked number."

"Probably a spam call. Let it go to voicemail."

Possibly, but Alison wasn't subjected to the string of blocked-number calls from Pammy, so she doesn't experience the visceral reaction of seeing it light up on the screen like I do. "Yeah. I will."

After a minute or thereabouts, the call registers as delivered to my voicemail and I quickly check it. "This message is for Jon Williams. I'm Agent Dan Kramer, Federal Bureau of Investigation. I'd like to ask you some questions regarding the audit you performed, and subsequently withdrew from, for Equinox Federal Credit Union. Kindly return my call at area code four-zero-one, two-two-two, two-seven, five-seven. Thank you."

"Oh, shit." I groan.

Alison's interest perks up. "Who was it?"

I exit the bathroom and plop down with her on the couch. "The FBI." I say dejectedly.

She bombards me with questions. "Are you for real? Is it legit? What do they want?"

I shake my head. "I don't know. They want to ask me questions about our audit with Equinox and why we withdrew. I don't know if it's legit, but he gave me a number to call back."

"Should you call Enzo?"

"Absolutely, but I'll call this guy back first. Enzo will want to know what he wants."

Alison adjusts her position on the couch to sitting upright. "Will you put it on speaker so I can hear?"

"Yes." I reply while dialing the number.

"Kramer." A gruff voice answers.

I utilize my best professional 'accountant' voice and demeanor. "Good afternoon, my name is Jon Williams returning your call regarding Equinox Federal Credit Union."

"Mr. Williams. Thanks for calling back so quickly. This is Dan Kramer. We're investigating a matter concerning Equinox Federal Credit Union. We understand your firm was engaged to perform an independent financial audit and subsequently withdrew from the engagement prior to issuing an audit opinion. We'd like to ask you some questions regarding your audit experience and reasons for your withdrawal."

It sounds like he's reading from a script. "Can we do this telephonically?" I propose.

"I'm afraid we typically don't work that way. We'd like to conduct the interview on site, at the credit union with management present."

"Why do I need to come down? I simply didn't want to perform the engagement. If this is about the audit fee ..."

"I appreciate your position, Mr. Williams. No, this is not about your audit fee. Let me expand upon our purpose and objective. We were contacted by the Financial Crimes Enforcement Network concerning irregularities occurring within the credit union's safety and security compliance program, of which I am sure you are familiar with. In fact, I suspect you may have discovered some of these irregularities yourself. This may have factored into your decision to withdraw from the engagement."

I look at Alison, and she's shaking her head. "Respectfully, I'd prefer not to." I reply.

"That's your prerogative Mr. Williams, however, I have a duty to disclose to you we will show up on your doorstep with a subpoena in the event you decline. We can do this voluntarily in a collegial manner, or we can go through official channels and force you to come down."

"Am I in trouble here? Do I need to show up with a lawyer?"

"Why would you believe you need a lawyer? It's not a crime to withdraw from an audit. Do you have reason to be concerned?"

Answering my question with a question. So frustrating … and tactically smart. "No, sir. I have no reason for concern."

"Well, we'd like to conduct the interview as soon as practicable. Does tomorrow work for you?" He doesn't wait for my reply before supplementing his question. "We'll need you, your associate … let's see … a Mr. Kelly Cookson … and the review partner listed on the engagement, Alison Brigham."

I need to buy some time to discuss with Enzo. "Let me check my commitments for tomorrow and get right back to you."

"Thank you."

"He wants everyone." Alison laments after I disconnect the call.

"I'm afraid so."

We sit in silence for a time, letting the conversation with Agent Kramer digest. It becomes clear we'll have to go.

I exhale a deep sigh. "I'll call Enzo. He'll tell us to go down and meet with them, there's nothing for us to worry about, they don't have anything, and blah, blah, blah …"

Alison raises a solid point. "You asked if you should bring a lawyer. What do you think?"

"I think I sound like a broken record, but let's check with Enzo."

I dial his cell and leave it on speaker before Alison asks me to. "Hey, Jon." He answers.

"Hey, Enzo. We have a problem."

"I can tell. Usually you call me 'LoZo' when there's no problem. What's up?"

I relay the gist of our exchange with Agent Kramer along with the FBI's request, and as predicted, Enzo responds with self-confidence and aplomb.

"Well, it's not ideal, but I think you need to go down and meet with them. Someone gave them some information. Probably that Financial Crimes outfit you talked about."

"Exactly." I confirm. "Financial Crimes Enforcement Network or FinCEN. Kramer said FinCEN contacted the FBI about 'irregularities,' which likely means they got hold of the withheld suspicious activity reports. The same reports we printed out as ammunition to stop Lorraine from blowing everybody up." The call goes silent for an extended period. "Hey. Did I lose you?"

"No. I'm here. Just thinking. Have you tried calling Lorraine?" He suggests. "Maybe she can give you a sense of what we're up against. If she's pissed or doesn't take your call, you know something's up. She could be a good source of information."

"True. I expect her to be her normal irritable self, but even so, that will be telling. I'll call her now."

"Alright. Let me know."

I hang up with Enzo and scroll through my contacts listing for Equinox. "Man, I so don't want to call her."

"I don't blame you. Hopefully, she's still in. It's late in the day; they'll be closed soon."

I check the time on my phone while calling the number – almost ten minutes to four. "You're right. I need to hustle."

"Make sure I can hear the call." Alison requests.

I give her a thumbs-up as the call connects on speaker. "Good afternoon, Equinox Federal Credit Union, how may I direct your call?"

"Hello, Madelaine? This is Jon Williams calling from J.K. Williams. How are you today?"

"I'm fine, Jon. How are you?" She responds pleasantly.

"Excellent, thanks. I'm trying to connect with Lorraine. I hope she hasn't left for the day."

"Ah … well … Lorraine no longer works here."

"Really?" I respond with surprise and look at Alison. "Did she take another job … or …?" I leave the question hanging open, hoping she'll fill in the rest, but she doesn't bite.

"I'm sorry, Jon, but I can't disclose information regarding current or former employees. You understand."

"Yes, of course. You just caught me off guard is all."

"That's understandable. Is there anyone else you'd like to speak with?"

"Uh, yes, could you connect me with the CFO?"

Alison projects a puzzled look and I respond by holding up my index finger in a signal for her to wait a minute.

"Very good. One moment please, and I'll transfer you."

As the call leaves Madelaine, I disconnect. Alison waits for my explanation as to why I asked for the transfer. "I didn't want the administrator to think I was calling strictly for Lorraine. It might look personal if I stopped with her instead of trying to reach someone else."

"Got it." She bobs her head. "So, that's a dead end."

"It appears so. Really strange. I wonder if she got exposed and canned or if she took off because she's afraid of getting busted."

Alison doesn't really care. "Who knows?"

She's right. There's no way to know, at least not now, anyway. Maybe we'll put the pieces together in our FBI interview. I guess I should call Kelly and get him up to speed. He's on the government's guest list as well.

It's early evening before I get off the phone with him. He's such an easy dude to talk to. He's fine with going down for the interview, his contention being that our hands are clean. We've done nothing wrong – he's followed all Generally Accepted Accounting Principles, or GAAP, and utilized established and accepted audit practices with firm-prepared workpapers backing it up. He'll present our documentation with confidence, demonstrating the veracity and legitimacy of our audit. If the FBI contends there was a deliberate attempt to circumvent the BSA process by the credit union and its staff, we can agree with them it was our concern as well and we were in the process of reviewing our responsibilities for disclosure and action under GAAP regulation. In the course of reviewing our circumstances, we realized we needed to withdraw from the engagement immediately, and before we had an opportunity to reach out to appropriate law enforcement, the FBI contacted us first.

After conveying the proposed action plan to Enzo, Kelly shoots up even higher on Enzo's respect list. "He's good, Jon. Honestly, let him do the talking in the interview. Sit back and enjoy the ride. This will be over before you know it. If the FBI says case closed, then it's case closed. For us, anyway."

Kelly's self-assurance and Enzo's endorsement boosts my and Alison's confidence as well. With the approach to the meeting settled, we only need to plan for the ride, which doesn't take much. We're going down and back in the same day and taking Danny's Jeep. The last thing we need is for the FBI to watch us rolling up in the G-Wagon. Enzo will follow us in his SUV and lay low in the credit union parking lot to observe.

"Game plan in place, then." I declare after Alison sanctions the approach. "Want to get takeout and watch a movie or something?"

"I have a better idea. Let's get takeout, watch a movie, and then something …"

52

I called Kramer first thing this morning and told him we'd be arriving by noon. He seemed appreciative and set a meeting time for twelve-thirty to give us a chance to 'grab a bite.' Enzo met us at a highway Park 'n Ride on our way south and fell into line for what's hopefully our last trip to Rhode Island for the foreseeable future. Too bad we couldn't all ride down in Alison's new car. It would make for an extraordinary – and extraordinarily short trip. Even so, with good company and spirited conversation, it passes by quickly.

A few minutes after entering Providence, Enzo calls us from his car. "Hey, I'm going to stop at the Citgo on the corner – the same one I did the other time we came down. I'll gas up, then drive over and wait in the parking lot until you're finished. If you have any issues, call me right away. Tell them you need to use the bathroom or something, which isn't a stretch for you, Jon, and Kelly, just do your thing. If it turns hostile – leave. If they don't let you, then it's time to shut up and lawyer up. You'll have to use some solid judgement if you see it going sideways. You okay with that?"

"We're good with that." I respond. I didn't think the comment about needing the bathroom was necessary, but whatever.

"Alright. Talk soon."

We peel off and complete the short ride to Equinox while Enzo makes his refueling stop. As I pull in, I notice there aren't many cars in the lot. I choose to park in an area furthest away from the building for ease of exit and lower visibility.

I shut the Jeep off and address my trip mates. "How're we doing? Feeling okay?"

"This sucks." Alison gripes, cracking a small smile.

I chuckle in response as Kelly chimes in. "Yup, but it's all good. We have nothing to worry about."

I love his self-confidence. "Perfect. Let's get this done."

Unexpectedly, I catch sight of a silver SUV in my rearview mirror slowly rolling up behind us and boxing us in. I turn around for a closer look and see a 'Rhode Island State Police' insignia emblazoned on the passenger door.

"What the heck?" I grouse as Alison and Kelly turn for a look as well. An imposing, uniformed state trooper exits the vehicle and approaches, lightly tapping his night stick on my window in an indication he would like me to lower it. I glance at Alison and shrug, conveying an unspoken message of *what now?*

I lower my window and purposefully say nothing. He'll expect me to say something along the lines of, 'Can I help you?' or 'Is there a problem, Officer?' or something like that, but I'm not going to. He has no reason to detain me. I'm correct in my assessment because we stare at each other for a moment in awkward silence.

"Sir, I'd like to ask you a few questions." He states authoritatively.

I'm agreeable. "Alright."

"You have Maine license plates on your vehicle."

He looks at me expectantly. Again, I don't respond.

He leans in for a closer inspection of the Jeep's occupants. "You can't hear me?" He asks, his tone harsh.

"You said you had a few questions. I didn't hear any questions." I counter calmly and Alison cracks me on the leg. "Look, why are you questioning me? What's the issue?"

"Sir, the issue is, I see an unfamiliar, out-of-state vehicle parked on the outer edge of the parking lot of a Rhode Island financial institution while there are plenty of open spaces much closer to the building."

Fair point. We may appear suspicious. "I see what you mean. Sorry about that. I'm Jon Williams. My accounting firm audits the credit union and I have a twelve-thirty meeting inside."

"Well, let's hope you're not late to your meeting, Jon Williams. License and registration, please."

"Really?" I sigh reluctantly. "I need to reach into my pocket for my license and the glove box for the registration."

I pull my license from my wallet and hand it to him. He gives it a once-over and snaps a picture of it from a tiny body camera attached to his uniform. Interesting.

I reach across Alison, open the glove box, and at the exact moment I appreciate what's about to happen and it's too late to stop, panic washes through me. My Glock nine-millimeter pistol painfully falls out and to the floor with a thud followed by a dozen-plus stray bullets tinkling off of it and scattering.

"Pull back right now!" He commands.

I sit bolt upright and freeze.

"Do you have a State of Rhode Island concealed carry permit?" He asks, already knowing the answer.

I hang my head dejectedly. "No sir. But I have one for Maine."

"Unfortunately, Rhode Island does not offer reciprocity. Everyone, exit the vehicle immediately."

We do as we're instructed, and the trooper leads us to his police cruiser, placing the three of us in the back seat.

"Is this necessary?" Alison asks.

"It is until I run the identities of all of you to ensure there are no outstanding warrants for your arrest."

"What will happen in the event there are none?" I ask.

He inputs our information into a laptop computer. "More than likely you'll be issued a summons to appear in court and be subjected to a fine. Also, your firearm will be confiscated. At least for now."

That's not so bad. I can deal with that. "Would it be possible to make a call? I'd like to inform the people I'm scheduled to meet with I need to reschedule." I contemplate disclosing I'm meeting with the FBI thinking it might get us out of this, but I worry it could backfire and cause more harm than good.

He continues typing. "Go ahead."

I hit redial on Agent Kramer's number.

"Kramer." He answers on the first ring.

"Uh, hello, Agent Kramer," I begin sheepishly. "I have a slight problem. I've been detained by state police and it appears I'll be tied up for an undetermined amount of time."

"Undetermined, like an hour, or undetermined, like all day?"

"Probably somewhere in between, I'm guessing."

He takes a deep breath. "Alright. Why don't we reschedule. Call me when you've cleaned up your issue, and we'll set up a new time."

"That sounds great. Thank you so much. I'll be back to you as soon as I have this cleared up." I disconnect and update Alison and Kelly. "Kramer says we can reschedule. That's a relief."

"That's fortunate." The trooper interjects. "What's not fortunate is the outstanding arrest warrant for you I discovered, Mr. Williams."

"That can't be! I've never been in trouble for anything!" I vehemently protest.

"Not for me to determine." He says while shifting the SUV into gear. "You can sort it out at the police barracks."

§

I lock up Danny's Jeep using my key fob as we drive by. Enzo should pull in at any moment, thinking we're inside. I need to text him we're not here and to find us at the state police barracks. Not sure where that is yet, but hopefully I'll know soon.

We remain silent in the back seat and I'm thankful for that. Not that we have any secrets I'm concerned might spill; I just don't like police listening to our conversation. A light rain gently falls as I stare out the window, lamenting our predicament while watching houses and businesses as we pass by. The route he's taken cuts through Federal Hill and I imagine having lunch in one of the many superlative restaurants lining the street that without a doubt won't happen today.

Oddly enough, our route will take us past Frankie's laundromat. We stop at a red light a block or so away from his business and I catch sight of the dimly lit neon-yellow sign. I'll bet whoever's in there wonders where Frankie's hiding.

When the light turns green, the trooper accelerates, but not very much. In fact, when he gets to the laundromat, he slows to a crawl before turning into the adjoining warehouse parking lot.

I'm instantly panicked. "Hey, what's happening here? Why are we stopping?"

He ignores my question and enters into the warehouse through the loading dock located on the side of the building. An overhead door closes behind the SUV, leaving us in complete darkness. Alison keys in on my uneasiness and I feel her stiffen next to me.

Abruptly, the door to my side of the cruiser swings wide open. "Get out." A male voice commands.

An arm reaches out, dragging me from the seat and spilling me onto the cold, concrete floor. I hear Alison and Kelly fall down after me as something hard presses painfully into my back. I think it may be someone's knee, holding me stationary while my wrists are tightly bound from behind. After a moment, we're lifted to our feet and escorted to another section of the building where we're pushed up against a wall.

"Alison! Kelly!" I whisper.

"Yeah." Kelly whispers back.

"I'm right here!" Alison breathes. "What's happening?!"

"Shut up!" An unseen man barks.

I smell dirt. Not like gardening soil, but dusty, fine dirt similar to what collects on an unswept garage floor. Unexpectedly, numerous portable floodlights positioned at various angles simultaneously flash to life, effectively going from blinding us with darkness to blinding us with light. My eyes take thirty seconds or so to acclimate, and when my vision sharpens, I see we're in a dingy warehouse space crowded with row after row of industrial racking. They're crammed tightly with cardboard boxes measuring twenty to thirty feet high. Alison stands a few feet away from me with Kelly next to her, our hands bound with zip ties. There's no one around, but clearly, we're not alone. I swivel my head around frantically, looking for an escape route.

"You won't find a way outta here. Don't bother." A man snarls, his shoes clicking on the concrete as he appears from the backdrop of the intense lighting. It's Pete O'Shea. He's twirling a martial arts Bo staff.

"Sit down." He snaps, cracking my knee with the wooden rod.

"Fuck!" I grimace and comply.

Neither Alison nor Kelly require any further enticement. They drop before any physical inducement is needed. Oh man, we're in trouble. The state trooper works for Frankie and his guys. Enzo said Frankie owns anyone who matters in Providence. How the heck did the trooper find us at the credit union? How the heck will Enzo find us? Before I can begin to formulate a plan, my thought process is disrupted by a menacing command.

"Not you."

I don't see the person behind the order. I don't need to. It's Lorraine. What the hell? We dodge Frankie and it's Lorraine who brings us here?

Her girth wobbles toward us from the shadows of a racking corridor as she points a pistol at Kelly. "Get up."

Kelly awkwardly rolls over onto his knees and begins rising to his feet, leaving Alison and me sitting up against the wall, our hands still uncomfortably zip-tied behind our backs.

"You fucked me over." She growls through clenched, crooked teeth. "Took all those SARs with you. I don't take kindly to that."

Before Kelly completely stands up and turns around to face her, Lorraine presses the pistol to the back of his head.

I begin to yell. "Nooooo! Wait!!"

Prior to the words leaving my mouth, Lorraine pulls the trigger, terminating Kelly's life in a bath of carnage, spraying his brains against the wall with no mercy or emotion. He falls lifelessly to the floor.

I scream in anguish. Alison wails in pain.

Lorraine turns to us. "I never liked him, and I don't need him. You two," She alternates leveling the pistol between Alison and me. "I need. For now, anyways."

"Please," I beg. "I'll do anything you want. We never did anything to harm you or the credit union. We only walked away!" I plead.

"I know you will. Don't worry, you'll get your chance. Pete," She directs to O'Shea. "Take all of their phones and go ahead and clean this mess up. Chuck him in the box crusher."

53

I hear O'Shea drag Kelly's feet along the floor. I can't see either of them, though. I'm swirling through a black and white spiral tunnel hole. Wait … I'm stationary. The vortex swallows me, deeper into its void and ultimately dumps me into a dark room. A dim lightbulb dangles from a thin wire, casting shadowy light and revealing two dark figures.

"Jon! There's no time left to waste!" Dad fearfully presses as he strides toward me. "This is your most important bucket! This is what it comes down to!" He's not smiling like he normally does. Mom, either. She's right on his heels, equally panicked.

"Hey! There's no more time!" She implores, slapping my face. "Snap out of it!"

My eyes blink open to find Lorraine crouched down in front of me. She slaps my face again. "Snap out of it!"

"Uh, no … God." The reality and gravity of the situation boomerangs back into me. "Let me …"

"Shut up." She commands, struggling to stand up while rubbing her knees, wincing in obvious pain. She waddles over to a table set some ten yards away where O'Shea stands, his back to us, and begins a conversation we can't hear.

I check on Alison. She sits beside me, motionless, looking at me with her stunning eyes. There's nothing behind them. She must be … has to be in shock. She's been chained to the wall, as have I, and I don't even remember it happening.

"Where's Enzo?" Lorraine poses calmly. "He came down with you. Separately, but I expected him to go to Equinox with you."

My brain spins. How does she know that? How do I respond?

"Forget trying to make up a story. The truth will do. I'll get it, anyways."

"I'm not sure. I guess he'd be in the parking lot waiting for us to come out from our meeting with the FBI." I'm hoping if I disclose we were scheduled to meet with the FBI, it may frighten her some.

O'Shea laughs and looks at Lorraine.

"Want to know why he's laughing?" She asks bitingly, watching O'Shea as he approaches.

He can't wait to tell us. "There's no FBI, dummy. We faked the calls. The FBI and credit union don't know you're here."

Lorraine elaborates further. "I had my state trooper waiting at the Rhode Island border for you guys to come in. He saw you in the Jeep and Enzo in his black truck. Why didn't he go with you?" She snarls.

Holy shit. We've been played, and played hard.

"He had to get gas." I mumble.

"Oh, for Christ's sake." She complains.

I've got to do something, anything, to try and get us out of this. "Can we work something out?" I pause in case she explodes on me, but she doesn't. "We didn't do anything to get you in trouble. Really. That's the God's honest truth. I'll give you the audit money back. It's no problem. Really."

She ignores my plea. "Do you know where Frankie is?"

Shit. She's asking us about Frankie, just like the DEA. This isn't about the credit union. This is all about the drug operation. She definitely plays a role. "No. I didn't want anything to do with any of that stuff."

"You lie! I know you came down for a meeting with Enzo and Frankie at least once!"

She's right. Enzo and I killed him that day. "Yeah, but that was about me pulling out of the audit I thought. I didn't do anything with the distribution operation. I only knew he wanted Enzo to step in for Jimmy."

"I wanted Enzo to step in for Jimmy." She clarifies, collapsing onto a stool at the table and resting her hand on her forehead. She seems in distress.

I have a blank stare on my face. No doubt, both of them know I have no idea what she's talking about.

O'Shea watches Lorraine while casually twirling his Bo staff. She nods to him, granting him permission to take over. I tense up as he reaches me, expecting him to strike. He doesn't – at least not yet.

"Listen up good." He growls. "I work for Lorraine. Everybody works for Lorraine. You think Frankie Humps can do all this." He waves his arm as if showing me the empire I believe Frankie built. "He can't. Frankie's too old now. Lorraine controls it all. Everything!"

Lorraine gingerly stands up. "You guys fucked me over and you don't even know it. The Coin City companies come back to me. Everything comes back to me. I had to uproot and disappear."

I don't know what to do or how to respond. I struggle to process it.

"You think you're so smart," She sneers. "Figuring out the hit put on you. Who do you think ordered it? You only got lucky that whore from the strip club warned you."

"I was at the meetings at the club and kept Lorraine informed. I saw that bitch watching us and listening in." O'Shea adds.

Lorraine undoubtedly killed Pammy. She killed Kelly. No doubt she killed Sharon, too, while looking for me. Pure evil stands before my eyes. She'll kill us next, once she has what she wants.

She divulges another shocking secret. "Jimmy was so into that whore, why do you think I killed him?"

Frankie was telling the truth after all. He didn't kill Jimmy. His own wife did. Hope for a positive outcome rapidly fades and I grasp for anything that may help us. "I'm so sorry I don't know where Frankie is. I know he probably holds a special place in your heart. A mentor can be very …"

She leans in close to me, gritting her teeth. "You think he's my mentor? He's not my mentor, shitbird. He's … my … *FATHER!* Now, let me ask you one last time. ***WHERE'S MY FUCKIN' FATHER?!***"

I'm dumbstruck. Lorraine is Frankie's daughter. Jimmy married Frankie Humps' daughter! Enzo can't possibly know this. He would have approached Frankie differently, if at all, and it would have been too dangerous to keep from me. I slowly shake my head indicating I don't know. To tell her the truth would be suicide.

Lorraine directs her attention to Alison. "C'mon, pretty. We're gonna play a little game called, *Let's Make Jon Talk.*"

"No, no, no, no, no! Please, find Enzo! Please, please, I'll help in any way I can!" I beg.

She ignores me. O'Shea snatches Alison up by her hair causing her to scream in fear and pain. O'Shea unlocks the chains, and they flank either side of her, steering her back to the table. I writhe on the floor in agony, unable to intervene.

"Lorraine! Lorraine! Look at me!" I screech.

Lorraine turns to me and wobbles over determinedly. She awkwardly bends over and positions herself nose to nose. She places her pistol onto the center of my forehead and spews venom.

"Shut your pathetic shitbird piehole or I'll end you right here. You hear me?" Her double chin vibrates violently, spittle flying into my face. "Now, where was I?"

She returns to the table, where O'Shea stands clenching Alison. He steps to the side, revealing a newly-attached bench vise. Oh, God no! He set up a bench vise!

"Did you get to see the whore before you left the church? She found her way into a vise just like this one." Lorraine sweeps her arm to the side as though showing off a game show prize. "It made for an awful mess. Unfortunately, I didn't bring my staple gun today."

My body goes numb. I'm paralyzed from terror and torment.

"Now, I'm gonna shove her head in the vise like I did with stripper girl, and slowly tighten it until you tell me where my father's at."

"Jon! Help me!" Alison cries out. "Help me! I love you!"

"Shut up!" Lorraine hammers her in the back of the skull with the butt of her pistol and Alison falls limp in O'Shea's arms. He drops her onto the stool directly in front of the vise, resting her up against the table.

I'm dying. I know I'm dying. Alison looks almost exactly like Pammy did when I saw her from behind in the church basement. I can scarcely process what unfolds in front of me.

"My phone. Please." I gurgle. "My phone …"

Lorraine and O'Shea stop and gawk at each other for a few seconds. "Put her head in and tighten it enough to hold her steady, then go get his cell." She orders, then glares at me. "You got one shot. One shot to get Enzo here or she's gonna die exactly like the whore … and you're next."

§

A moment of reprieve. One shot. God help me.

O'Shea returns holding three phones. "Which one's yours?"

"Middle one." I wheeze.

He drops the other two into his pocket. "What's the passcode to get in?" He demands.

"Nine, twelve, two, two." Our future wedding day.

"You got a text from him. He wants to know how much longer. That means he's waiting for them." O'Shea directs to Lorraine.

"You call him." She barks at me. "I'll get the Statie back over there to pick him up and bring him here." She says to O'Shea.

He redials by activating Enzo's last incoming call notification and puts it on speaker. Enzo answers on the first ring. "Hey. Everything okay?"

"Listen to me very closely." I instruct. "We're being held at the laundromat. Lorraine – "

"Gimme that." Lorraine cuts in, yanking the phone away. She still has her own phone to her ear. "Listen carefully, Garibaldi. There's a state trooper pulling up to you right now. Look up. See him?"

Enzo responds without emotion. "Yes."

"Get into his cruiser and don't try to fight him. He's gonna bring you here. Give him your phone right away. If you fight him, Jon dies. His girlfriend, too. The other guy? He's already dead. Got it?"

"Yes."

Lorraine disconnects and chucks my phone into the darkness of a racking corridor. "There. They'll be here in five minutes."

I alternate between watching for signs of distress in Alison and searching for a way out of here. Even if I could fashion an escape plan, I don't see how I could follow through with it. I can't get loose from the chains and I don't have my pistol. I can only pray Enzo has a way out. Alison sits on the stool, her head wedged in the vise and hands still bound behind her back. She isn't moving. I'm not certain she's conscious. Man, what I wouldn't do to see Uncle Danny blast in right now and square off with Piece O'Shit, O'Shea. He'd waste him in a second. If I escaped, I'd waste him in a second. Any hesitation I may have had in ending some-one's time on this earth has long since disappeared. I'd put a bullet into both of their skulls, then spit in their dead faces.

I'm brought back into the present by a sliver of light cutting into the loading bay and hearing the overhead door rattle open. They're here. O'Shea leaves to escort them over, and Lorraine waits expectantly with her pistol plainly visible for obedience. The door ratchets closed again followed by footsteps. Enzo comes into view, hands zip-tied behind his back, with O'Shea ushering him into our section of the building. Enzo doesn't say a word. I know he's assessing and calculating everything and everyone around him. You wouldn't see it from looking at him, though. He shows no outward signs of analyzing the situation.

"Sit down." O'Shea commands, and Enzo complies. O'Shea at-taches the chains formerly used to shackle Alison to the wall onto Enzo's legs and then retreats.

"Here's his phone." O'Shea offers it to Lorraine.

"Thanks. Gimme your stick." She directs. O'Shea hands it over and Lorraine trudges slowly over to us. "Enzo, I don't want to make this long. I'm tired. Where's Frankie?"

He's understandably confused. He wouldn't make the business connection between Lorraine and Frankie until now or envision the fam-ily relationship. "Frankie? I don't know. I didn't know he was missing."

Lorraine rears back and wallops me with the Bo staff. I let out a muffled grunt. I will not give her the satisfaction of hearing me cry out.

She shakes her head. "Jon says he doesn't know, either. I don't believe you guys. Pete, take off his shirt." She instructs, motioning toward me.

O'Shea complies, ripping my shirt from my body, causing me to flip onto my side. She cracks me again with the staff, and a line of deep red blood appears along my arm and midsection.

"Now, where's my father?"

Enzo's eyes widen. "Your what?"

Lorraine hauls off on me a third time. "My father. Frankie's my father." She says coolly. "Honestly, I'm surprised Jimmy kept it a secret from you all of these years. Probably the only secret that shitbird kept."

"Lorraine," He appeals. "I don't know where Frankie … uh … your father is. Truly. We don't want anything to do with his operation. We only wanted to go away."

I hear the distress in his voice. Strangely, I'm no longer scared. Have I resigned myself to my fate? I don't know. Maybe the mind shuts down fear in a self-preservation tactic.

"Liar!" She whirls around and moves behind Alison, pulling the stool out from under her and whipping the backside of her legs. *"And it's my operation!"*

Alison's conscious. She cries out in pain, her body twitching as she falls into a prolonged moan. She's hunched over, head trapped in the vise, stomping her feet in place attempting to alleviate the pain. Oh, baby, I'm so sorry. I struggle against my zip ties and chains, to no use. Enzo doesn't respond to Lorraine's declaration it's her operation. He can only hang his head.

His silence infuriates her. "Alright, let's try some more pressure on the vise. Maybe that will trigger your memory!"

"No!!" I yell before trailing off. "Please, don't …"

Lorraine ignores my plea. She tightens the vise another quarter turn and Alison screams in agony, her legs flailing behind her. Lorraine backs off the pressure and turns to Enzo. "Ready, yet?"

He screeches in anger and fear. "Goddamn it! I'm the only one who's involved in this!" He explodes. *"I KILLED HIM!!"*

Lorraine freezes, her mouth slung wide open. Slowly and methodically she approaches him, forcing the gun into his mouth. He stares her down with a look of hatred and bloodlust, lips wrapped around the barrel, never breaking eye contact with her.

She smoothly racks the firearm's slide. "Die …"

54

My mind drifts. Do I look away? Should I watch? Does it really matter? No, it doesn't. I'm as good as dead, anyway. Maybe I'll close my eyes and never …

I'm jolted back to the present by a concealed door somewhere in the intake bay forcefully beaten open and slamming loudly against the wall. Daylight cuts into the room and two people burst through the doorway.

"Don't move a Goddamned muscle!" Special Agent C.J. Calhoun barks, his DEA service weapon drawn, alternating his aim between O'Shea and Lorraine. "Not a single twitch. Ron, process them." He instructs.

Ah, thank God! Calhoun and Harmon! I've never been so happy to see anyone from law enforcement in my life. "Please," I beg. "Alison. She's in the vise behind you. Please, get her out!"

Calhoun keeps his firearm steadfastly trained on Lorraine and O'Shea. "Hold tight. I will in just one second."

Sweet Jesus! These bastards are going down! I can't wait to … uh … what? "Oh, shit!" I roar.

Agent Harmon coolly raises his firearm, placing it against Calhoun's temple and squeezing the trigger. Calhoun's head jerks sideways as a plume of blood, bone, and brain explodes from the exit wound of his shattered skull. His lifeless body collapses to the ground in a heap, mere feet from us. I numbingly contemplate how long it will take for the blood oozing from his head to reach me.

"That's how you kill a motherfucker!" O'Shea giddily shouts.

Harmon throws him a dirty look, then approaches Lorraine. She intentionally offers her cheek, inviting a kiss, to which he gladly obliges. "Thank you, Ronnie." She coos affectionately.

"You're welcome, Rainy." He replies, equally adoringly.

"Now, where were we at? Oh, right. Time to take out the trash. That means you guys." She needlessly clarifies.

Alison whimpers in response.

Harmon wipes his firearm clean with a white handkerchief. "I never liked that asshole."

"Yeah, me neither." O'Shea agrees.

Harmon throws him another nasty look. "Shut up. I was talking about you. Piece O'Shit."

"I said don't call me that!" He threatens.

Harmon's patience wears thin. "What are you gonna do about it, you piece of shit, weak, mother …"

"Okay guys, that's enough." Lorraine mediates. "Let's take care of business and get out of here."

Enzo and I observe the exchange. There isn't much else we can do. Harmon and O'Shea obey her like scolded puppies, sneering at each other but remaining silent. Calhoun's mostly bled out on the floor at the hands of his traitor partner. I abstractedly watch his flow of blood divert away from us over what must be an uneven floor.

"Pete, why don't you prove you're not a piece of shit to Ronnie by stepping in where I left off and blow Enzo's brains out through his mouth?"

"He won't do it. He's a pussy. Can I get you a sippy cup? Maybe a binky?" Harmon taunts.

I hear it in his voice now. It was Harmon pretending to be FBI Agent Dan Kramer. Bastard.

"Oh, yeah? I'll show you." O'Shea blusters like a second grader dared to eat a worm on the school playground at recess.

Lorraine hands over her pistol. He makes a big production of attempting to look like a master marksman by twirling it on his finger in the trigger guard. After a few revolutions, he loses his grip and the pistol falls to the concrete floor with an embarrassingly loud 'clank.'

Harmon laughs and Lorraine shakes her head at his stupidity.

O'Shea timidly reaches for the pistol and drops to his knees in front of Enzo. "Open your mouth!" He demands.

Enzo doesn't comply.

"I said open your mouth!" He attempts to wiggle the gun barrel through Enzo's clenched teeth. "How about I smash through them?"

Enzo shrugs his shoulders, brazenly signaling he doesn't care. O'Shea looks up at Lorraine, bewildered.

"Oh, for Christ's sake, Pete." She grasps Harmon's firearm and points it at Alison's head. "Enzo, open your mouth, please."

Enzo opens his mouth and O'Shea inserts the barrel nearly half-way in. As hope for a positive ending evaporates, my fear morphs into fury.

"Hey, O'Shea." I growl. He hesitates, then glares at me. "You really are a piece of shit."

"I told you." Harmon laughs, thoroughly pissing him off.

"Fuck you, Williams." He counters. "You're next."

O'Shea refocuses on Enzo and re-racks the slide. Without warning, a muzzle flash from the doorway lights up a silhouetted figure and at the same time, a bullet rips completely through O'Shea's neck. Blood spurts from the exit wound in jets, spraying me as he collapses into my lap. Harmon springs into action, grabbing his weapon from Lorraine and returning fire while attempting to shield her. I vaguely think about how ineffective that is; she's twice as wide as him. The two swiftly disappear, retreating into the recesses of the dark racking corridor. Drenched in his blood, I wriggle enough to maneuver O'Shea off me and kick-thrust him over near Calhoun. I struggle to see what's happening around me – I'm blinded by blood and a lack of light.

I hear a door open and a shaft of light streams in from the back of the warehouse where Lorraine and Harmon disappeared to. Moments later, it slams shut with a 'crack' and everything reverts to darkness and silence. I was unable to see who shot O'Shea.

Enzo furiously tries to retrieve the pistol O'Shea dropped when he collapsed, but it slid just out of his reach. "We need this." He grits his teeth in determination, stretching his legs as far as the chain will allow. "We're not out of this. Whoever shot O'Shea might not be our friend."

"You got this. Reach! A little further!" I encourage.

"Uhhh." He strains, squirming and twisting. "Son of a bitch!"

"Shit! Somebody's still there!" I hiss in a low whisper. "I can't see who it is!"

Enzo looks up to where the broad figure looms in the doorway, still shrouded in darkness, then slowly enters the room and stops. We're frozen in fear and uncertainty until the black form expels a watery cough and emerges into view.

"Bung!" Enzo calls out. "Over here!"

Sluggishly, Bung stumbles forward, eventually dropping to his knees. His mouth hangs open, his eyes heavy-lidded. He's hurt, and hurt badly.

"Bung! C'mon, buddy. Focus on me. You can do it!" Enzo encourages.

With maximum effort, Bung shuffles on his knees before ultimately sinking to his hands and elbows and dragging himself. He collapses only feet from us and mere inches from the pistol.

Enzo guides him. "Reach out and push it a couple more inches. That's all I need."

Bung doesn't look up. He starts to move his arm, and from underneath his body, pushes his own pistol toward Enzo in one final burst of what remains of his energy and mobility before falling unconscious. Enzo drags the gun over with his feet and drives it under his leg. He flips onto his back and feels around with his zip-tied hands for it.

"I hear someone else!" I whisper frantically.

Enzo pauses to look, then frenziedly goes back to feeling for the gun.

The shadowy figure comes into a silhouetted view and soundlessly glides through the doorway.

"Left!" I breathe. "Go left! Three or four inches! You're almost there!"

He locates the pistol and grabs it with both of his bound hands. He's on his knees, his back to the unknown person, blindly aiming for a target he can't see.

The person stops. "Tommy? Enzo?"

"Abigail?" Enzo calls out. "We're here! Quickly! It's okay, no one else is here!"

Abigail hurries over and Enzo gives swift instruction. "I have a knife; right side, front pocket."

She removes a pocketknife and slices Enzo loose.

"The guy right there." He points to O'Shea. "There's a key in his pocket for the chains." He leans over and slices through my zip ties.

It takes her longer to locate the key than it did the pocketknife, but eventually she finds it and unlocks Enzo. She immediately tends to Bung, while Enzo races to Alison and loosens the vise. He slices her zip ties and carries her to me. After removing my chains, he joins Abigail in attending to Bung.

"What can you see? Is he breathing? Pulse?" Enzo asks rapid-fire.

"I'm not sure. I think so. He's been shot in his lower back. Right here where the blood comes out."

"Here, let me in." He begins a diagnostic on Bung. "I definitely feel his breath and he has a pulse. Let's get his shirt coat pressed into the bullet hole."

As Enzo and Abigail work on Bung, I care for Alison.

"Hey," I caress her face. "Are you with me?"

Her closed eyelids flutter and she shivers uncontrollably. "I'm here. I want to go." She whimpers.

No truer words were ever said.

"We need to get him out of here and to the hospital." Enzo directs. "Alison, you should go, too."

"I don't want to." She protests.

I can't blame her, really.

Enzo doesn't waste time arguing and hurriedly rises to his feet. "Abigail, how did you get here?"

"Tommy and I came together. He said he was going to check on you and I didn't want him going alone. I knew something was wrong, so I insisted he bring me. I was outside waiting in his van when I saw two people come out from the back of the building very fast and take off. I waited for a while and when I didn't see Tommy, I came in to check on him."

"Will you go get the van and drive it in here? I'll open the overhead door so you can get in."

Abigail retreats and Enzo gives me instruction. "Jon. Grab an arm and leg and let's get him over to the door."

I do as I'm told, and Enzo and I have him moved in no time. He activates the button to raise the door, revealing Abigail sitting in the van, ready to pull in. Enzo yanks a side door open and with some effort, he and I have Bung up and splayed out on a bench seat. We all hop inside – Enzo driving with Abigail up front, Bung in the middle row, and Alison and I in the third row.

"Abigail, I want you to call Rhode Island Hospital and tell them you're coming into the ED with your grandson and he's been shot. We have to go right by the credit union; the three of us will hop out and go back to your house. When you get to the hospital, medical staff will attend to him right away. They'll ask you a bunch of questions – just say you don't know anything yet. He stumbled home like this, passed out behind the wheel, and you brought him straight here. Okay?"

Abigail nods. "Yes. I can do that."

Enzo regards her lovingly and squeezes her hand. "That's good. We'll be up as soon as we clean up to check on him and get you. Okay?"

"Okay."

55

I still smell his blood. I've scrubbed my face a dozen times and even so, I smell it. It may be psychosomatic, though. Maybe the traumatic impact of what I experienced results in my brain mistakenly inform- ing my nose of its presence. Or maybe it's the other way around, I don't know.

We didn't anticipate staying in Rhode Island overnight or need- ing a change of clothes. I had no choice but to dump mine into the great room fireplace and set them ablaze. I subsequently rummaged through Bung's room and found a reasonably fitting flannel shirt and jeans. I'm hopeful he won't mind. Alison showered and redressed, and aside from a monster headache, appears relatively unharmed. Physically, anyway. She sits pensively on the edge of the bed in our room, staring at the floor, waiting for me to finish dressing before we go downstairs.

"Kelly." She whispers.

"God, I know." I croak.

She looks up at me. "Jon, we have to go get him."

"I don't know how." I murmur, my voice breaking down. "We can't ever go back."

We leave the room and walk down the hall, pausing at the landing. Enzo's downstairs looking up at us, probably trying to get a read on our affect and attitude.

"How are you two?" He asks as we come down the staircase.

"I'm okay." I reply.

"I'm not," Alison speaks softly. "But I will be."

"We need to somehow get Kelly." I want to get this on the table straight away.

"I completely agree with you and I'm truly sorry. I'll call police and have him retrieved. There's no chance of going back – no doubt we'd be arrested on the spot. The state trooper will more than likely watch for us." He doesn't wait for our reaction. "Where exactly is he?"

I feel the anguish in his voice. "Lorraine told O'Shea to put him in a box crusher. In the warehouse section. You'll call anonymously?"

"Yes. I have a burner phone I can use. I'm guessing Kelly has ID on him? They'll get him back to Maine."

"Oh, God. Darcy." Alison realizes. "I didn't even think about Darcy."

"Let's work on getting him back and we can deal with her later. One step at a time." Enzo counsels, removing a one-use flip phone from his pocket. It reminds me our cellphones are still in the warehouse. "I think nine-one-one is a good option. I don't want to call Providence police directly. I want a record of the call."

"They could trace our location." I speculate.

"Not with this number. Plus, I'll trash the phone when I'm done. It won't take long to relay the information." He punches in the number and places the phone to his ear. Unfortunately, we'll only hear his side of the conversation.

"Yes. I'd like to report a body." He hesitates, then his eyebrows rise high on his forehead as he rolls his eyes. "Deceased, yes." He waits another moment. "I'd rather not. I'll remain anonymous, thank you. He's located at the Coin City laundromat. There's a box crusher in the warehouse; you'll find him in it. You may find others as well."

Enzo listens for an extended period then lets out a deep breath. "I see. Thank you. No, I'm sorry, I can't do that."

He disconnects the call and cracks the phone in half.

Alison and I stare at him. "Well?" I press.

"They torched the building. The dispatcher told me firefighters are on scene. It's fully engulfed in flames."

I'm incredulous. "How? There's no way they went back there, did they?"

"No. I'm sure they had it set up to burn to the ground. It's clear they expected us to die there and then they'd destroy all the evidence, and possibly collect insurance money, too. They would only need an associate – probably the state cop – to go by and set it off."

"So, now what? We need to find them. They're going to come looking for us." I reason. "The question is, how?"

"Abigail says they left in a big black SUV. That's the DEA's car." Alison interjects. "Can we call the DMV or something? Find out where they live?"

"She's right. We've seen them in it a bunch of times." I confirm. "It's a DEA vehicle. Won't there be a tracker on it? Can we locate it?"

"Possibly. Let's see if we can find out. I still have Brown's credentials – I may be able to get into a tracker database. It's a longshot, but the FBI doesn't know he's dead. They think he disappeared and maybe they didn't deactivate his credentials yet. If I can get in, I could look for the location of the SUV. I used to keep an eye on Brown and Reyes, so they had my backup if they ever got into a sticky situation. That's kind of how Bung found me." He digresses. "We keep track of each other on the 'find my friends' function on our phones. I told him to watch out for me today, and if he saw me leave the credit union before I checked in with him, I was in trouble and he ought to come."

"How does an FBI database help us? These guys are DEA." I question.

"The tracking website – and its database, is a redirect from the FBI's website administered by a third-party contractor. When you enter the site, it asks you which agency you want to access – DEA, FBI, ATF, and a couple others; CIA, I think."

I'm anxious to get at it. "Alright, let's find it."

Enzo agrees. "Let's go after Abigail first and then we'll see if we can get into the site. My laptop's in the car."

Alison changes the conversation flow, trying to process what's happened. "Abigail said this morning she insisted Bung let her go with him to wait for you. Why would she do that? Why wasn't she upset with you Bung got shot while helping you? I'd be pissed."

"Because I got her and Bung out of a very dangerous situation. I saved Bung's life; hers too, and now we're family."

That has me curious. "What happened?"

"Not now. Let's focus on Lorraine."

I have a fleeting thought about Lorraine and Harmon's syrupy pet names for each other. Ronnie and Rainy. "They're a couple. Unbelievable."

Enzo nods his head. "Agreed."

§

Rain falls steadily as dusk approaches. Abigail exits the hospital's entry vestibule and walks over to our SUV parked curbside. "He's alive. He's in a medically-induced coma, but he's stable." She explains, rubbing her hands together fretfully while Enzo holds the front passenger door to his Mercedes open for her. "The doctors aren't certain how his body will respond. He was injured very close to his spinal cord and the swelling eventually squeezed so hard, he couldn't walk. We need to wait for the swelling to go down to see how his body reacts."

She's super talkative, so we mostly listen. "I did what you told me to do," She continues. "Not telling them anything except for saying he showed up at home like this. They told me he was lucky to drive all the way back before he lost use of his legs. Poor dear."

"Do you want us to take you home?" Enzo asks her as we exit the valet vehicle lane. "We have some business to attend to after."

Unexpectedly, her worried demeanor transforms into blistering anger. "Does it include going after these bastards?"

"Yes, as a matter of fact, it does." Enzo confirms.

"Then I'm staying with you."

Enzo expels a truncated laugh. "I expected as much. Okay, let's get down to business. As a quick recap for you, Abigail, we need to track down a DEA vehicle one of the responsible parties, who happens to be the daughter of Rhode Island's largest crime boss, rides in with her boyfriend. He's a DEA agent named Ron Harmon. He shot your grandson."

"How do you find them?" She asks.

"One of my former associates, Scott Brown, was an FBI agent. In the course of our partnership, I had cause to know where he and his partner were at any given time. They have tracking devices installed on their vehicles and Agent Brown gave me access to the tracking system so I could keep an eye on them. We're hoping Agent Brown, who incidentally is no longer with us, still has valid credentials."

Abigail nods her head. "I understand."

Enzo abruptly turns into a nearby fast-food restaurant parking lot. "Jon, hand me my laptop, will you? It's in the back in a black canvas bag. Should be right behind you."

I unbuckle my seatbelt and reach around, pawing into the cargo area for a computer bag. I quickly find it and hand it over. Enzo removes the laptop from the bag and fires it up as I look over his shoulder from the backseat. He connects to the restaurant's public Wi-Fi, then activates a direct link to a website that looks nothing like a secure government site. It appears more of a business transportation website.

"This doesn't look official." I note.

"As I said, it's not the governmental site."

Enzo inputs Brown's log-in credentials, which the site accepts as valid, but sequentially asks for multi-factor authorization in the form of an agent registration number.

Enzo thinks out loud. "Well, we got into the first layer. Now I need the number it's looking for. Where would I find that?"

"I might know." I offer. "It's on their ID badges. I saw numbers, lengthy numbers, when Calhoun and Harmon showed me their IDs. Any chance you have Brown's badge?"

He cracks a small smile. "No, but I have the next best thing. I have a photo of it saved to my laptop."

Enzo administers a series of keystrokes and retrieves Brown's photo identification. He does a cut-and-paste, then inputs the number and … we're in! Holy! Now the question is, can we search for a DEA vehicle or are we limited to FBI?

"Okay. The guy with Lorraine, you said his name is Ron Harmon." Enzo articulates as he begins the search. "I don't see anything for a Ron Harmon, or Ronald Harmon. Not good. We may be limited."

"Check for C.J. Calhoun. He's his partner and the Special Agent in charge. Well, he was in charge."

Enzo keys in the name and looks perplexed. "I see a Clyde Calhoun. Same guy?"

"Yes! His name's Clyde. He goes by C.J."

"The DEA guys were Ronnie and Clyde?" He shakes his head. "You can't make this shit up."

"I know, right?" I agree. "Worse than Rainy and Ronnie."

He administers another series of keystrokes. "Alright, hang on. Let's see what we have here."

Our internet path redirects us to another section of the website, then promptly displays a message across the screen:

<u>You do not have permission to view this form</u>

Enzo retraces his steps from the log-in page, and ultimately, we get the same message. However, this time we're jettisoned from the website. I don't hold out much hope as he re-enters and attempts a third time. Predictably, we're not successful, and to add more salt to the wound, we receive notification Brown's credentials are now invalid and we're declared locked out of the system.

I'm not shocked, but still disappointed. "Dead end."

"It looks like it." Enzo agrees, closing his laptop. "But I have an idea. We're out here, anyway. I want to check something out."

56

It's early evening and Enzo cautiously guides us through Providence amid a torrent of rain. Today's earlier drizzle progressed into a driving rainstorm causing headlights from oncoming cars to cast a blinding glare as they cut through the darkness. Windshield wipers slap violently against the glass at top speed and still they can't keep up with the volume of water.

I want to know where we're going and I'm far beyond the point of being too intimidated to ask. "So where are we heading? What's the situation?"

Enzo has no problem divulging his plan. "Yes, sorry. I've been silent. I tend to do that when I'm processing."

"Don't I know it."

He doesn't acknowledge my reply. "Do you remember when I told you Frankie had an apartment building and he used to live in one of the units?"

I see where he's going with this. "Yes, I do!"

"I thought we could swing over and see what's what. It's a shot in the dark, but worth a try."

"Totally." I agree. "It's a shot in the pouring rain dark, but definitely worth a try."

The nasty weather makes for slow going. Enzo says we're driving to College Hill on the affluent east side where former mayor Buddy Cianci once lived and Brown University and the Rhode Island School of Design are located. After we finally enter into the neighborhood, I come alive in my seat, attentive to the surroundings.

Enzo wasn't kidding when he said this neighborhood's affluent. Many of the historic homes located on tree-lined streets feature names of influential people and the years in which the structures were built prominently displayed on front yards and façades. Churches of varying architectural style dot virtually every street corner. Well, like the Puritan John Owen once said, *'be killing sin, or it will be killing you.'* I'm in complete agreement with him.

"Here it is." Enzo points. "Right there."

We slowly drive past a brick-faced, multi-story building, taking a hard look for cars and activity, but nothing stands out. No black DEA SUV, no visible lights, no movement. We double back and perform the same exercise with no different result.

"Let's set up here at the corner for a while and wait." Enzo suggests, shutting the vehicle down at the street's entrance.

No need for any of us to respond. I reach into my jacket pocket and remove my pistol, placing it in my lap. I follow up with loaded clips and loose rounds. Alison glances at them and pays it no mind. She's either become used to it, or hardened by our experiences. Maybe both. We engage in small talk but sit mostly in silence for nearly an hour. The rain never lets up and we see nothing to indicate they are, or ever were here.

"We're wasting our time." Enzo grouses. "Let's go."

"I'm sorry, dear." Abigail consoles.

Enzo fires up the Mercedes, drops it into gear, and slowly drifts off. We make our way out of College Hill, backtracking to the highway and heading for Abigail's home. I stare out my back window through the driving rain. It reminds me of watching where we went earlier in the day from the back seat of the state police cruiser. Who could have possibly predicted how the remainder of the day would unfold? I re-live the warehouse experience and shudder at how close Alison, Enzo, and I came to not making it out alive. And Kelly …

We pass a sign indicating we've entered the Seekonk River Watershed … The Seekonk River Watershed …

"Hey!" I abruptly holler, jumping everyone in their seats. "Oh, sorry." I apologize. "LoZo, we just passed a sign that read, 'Entering the Seekonk River Watershed.' "

He watches me in the rearview mirror, waiting for me to elaborate.

"Go back to when we trailed Frankie from the laundromat. We passed over a river and the sign said Seekonk River Basin, remember?"

"I remember the river; I don't remember the sign."

"Doesn't matter." I shake my head impatiently. "What matters is Frankie wasn't on his way home – he was on his way to see someone."

"Lorraine!" Enzo exclaims. "Brilliant!"

"Who else could it be?!" I speculate. "She might live there!"

Enzo accelerates toward our new destination.

§

"Look, there it is." I point out triumphantly. "The sign for the Seekonk River Basin."

"So, this is where you took down Frankie. Rhode Island's biggest crime boss." Alison snorts, unimpressed with the neighborhood.

"Former." Enzo amends.

At night, one wouldn't know that as we cross the bridge, below us sits a decrepit dam spewing yellowish, ugly water. I suspect the huge volume of rain has caused the river to surge considerably and the water flow to violently rush.

Enzo stops the Mercedes at the end of the bridge and examines the area. I see the empty lot where we dumped Frankie's driver. I wonder if he's alive. After a few minutes, Enzo turns the steering wheel and advances slowly down the street running parallel along the river. The same street we were on when we crashed into Frankie. Our slow roll reminds me of a wildcat stalking its prey, acutely aware of the surroundings. As we approach the intersection where we turn to have the house come into view, I feel every muscle in my body tense up. I focus intently as our line of sight opens and the house becomes visible.

In the driveway, sits a black Ford Expedition.

I slap Enzo on his shoulder. "It's them! It's them! This is where Lorraine lives!"

"Yes … yes." He placates me like a parent speaking to an over-excited child. "Strange. This isn't where she lived with Jimmy."

"Well, then it's Harmon's house, right?"

"That's probably the case." He agrees.

I tap him anxiously on his shoulder. "Hey, hey, hey! Back up a little. Someone's coming out the front door!"

Enzo inches the SUV backward, affording us an obstructed, yet functional view, while lessening our chance of discovery.

"It looks like they're bringing suitcases out." Abigail says.

I reach for my pistol. "I'm ready!"

Enzo stares at me like I have three heads. "We can't take them out in the driveway. Look around. There're houses all along the street."

He forgot to call me a dummy. "Okay. What, then?"

Enzo slowly backs out until we reach the intersection. "When you find something that works, stick with it."

He spins the SUV around and backtracks to the side road where we waited for Frankie to drive up in his sedan. This time though, he parks the Mercedes on the other side of the intersection, so any impact we generate will be to the passenger side of the Expedition.

"You're going to crash into them? Again?" I question.

His lips purse and he slowly nods his head, staring unblinkingly through his side window.

I look at Alison. "Buckle up honey, and Abigail, you may want to switch seats with me ..."

We lie in wait for fifteen minutes or so, before we see a glare of headlights from the end of the road illuminate the intersection.

"Be ready." Enzo warns.

The vehicle takes the corner headed our way, and before we're blinded by its lights, I see it's the black Expedition. "It's them!" I bark.

"Yes ... it ... is." Enzo replies calculatingly. "We'll hold tight another thirty seconds or so, and then ..."

The Expedition stops. Forty yards or so away from us, the Expedition stops.

"Did they see us?" I wonder out loud.

Enzo's hesitant. "I don't know."

We maintain this posture for about a minute or so, until we're suddenly bathed in the Expedition's high beams.

"Jon, have your Glock ready, and ladies, get down!" Enzo commands.

I extend my arms, pistol solidly in my grip, resting my forearms on the Captain's armchair for support and accuracy. Lorraine and Harmon gun the engine and wildly accelerate in an apparent attempt to race past us. Thirty yards, twenty … when they get within ten yards, muzzle flashes ignite and bullets whiz into our vehicle's body and front window as we return fire through Enzo's open window. The Expedition flies past us, our headlights illuminating its passenger side. I catch a brief glimpse of Lorraine's demon head framed by the open window, her fat face contorted in pure rage, shrieking as she empties her pistol before disappearing from view.

Enzo throws the car into gear, spinning out in pursuit. "Is everyone okay? Quickly. Answer!" He demands.

We issue a chorus of positive responses as Alison and Abigail sit back up in their seats and I reload my firearm.

"Can you see out the windshield?" I ask doubtfully. Spiderweb cracks rip through the glass, and with the pouring rain, my vision's completely distorted.

"Good enough." He answers bluntly.

"How long should we pursue?" I follow his lead and keep my dialogue brief as well.

"Depends. The bridge is the practical way out of here, but they went straight. They're probably trying to lose us on the side roads. What I'm worried about is if they'll be able to buy time for help to come."

Enzo crisscrosses rural town roads, some populated and others not, with no success until we find ourselves a few blocks up from where this all began.

"Behind us! Look!" Alison screeches, peering through the rear window.

We all spin around to see Lorraine and Harmon racing toward us.

"They're going to ram us? I don't believe it!" I sputter.

Enzo shakes his head. "No! They can't get out!" He pulls a U-turn and guns the engine. "They're making a break for it back over the bridge!"

Both SUVs speed headlong toward one another in a mobster's version of a game of Chicken.

I can scarcely contain myself. "They'll make the bridge before us!"

"Not if I can help it!" Enzo roars.

Alison reaches for my hand, squeezing tightly. As Lorraine and Harmon breach the entrance to the bridge, they pull hard left, fishtailing the Expedition on the wet roadway. Enzo pulls hard right onto the bridge right behind them, hot on their heels.

"Hang on!" He shouts, barely maintaining control of the Mercedes rounding the corner.

The Expedition overcompensates for its fishtail, skidding in the opposite direction and Enzo anticipates it. Before they can adjust, he inserts his front bumper into their correction space, thrusting them further into an uncontrolled spin. The Expedition continues wildly out of control, punching through the guardrail before coming to a smoke-filled rest wedged with the hood tilted upward toward us and the tailgate sagging precariously above the river.

"Let's go!" I howl, removing my seatbelt and securing my firearm.

"Wait!" Enzo orders, swinging his arm back in a gesture for me to halt. "Hang on one minute."

He repositions his Mercedes so we directly face the Expedition, its ass end hanging over the side of the bridge. Our headlights illuminate the interior, and although we have limited vision, we see Harmon, apparently unconscious, slumped behind the wheel. Lorraine, very much conscious, screams what appears to be expletive after expletive at us. Enzo inches the Mercedes ahead until his front bumper touches theirs. He depresses the accelerator, spinning his wheels and grinding the Expedition the final distance over the edge. Lorraine violently flips us off with both hands, and we're close enough to read her lips and interpret her parting words as she falls backward and into the river:

Fuck Youuuuu, Shitbirds!!!!!

I hop out and run to the railing while Enzo moves the Mercedes to another, less visible spot. Rain pounds gloriously down upon me as I watch the Expedition's hood, with Lorraine and Harmon trapped inside, go under and completely submerge. I stand there and watch for over five minutes for any sign of life. Enzo eventually joins me and we both stare silently. After a time, he puts his arm around me. He's done this before. It's his nonverbal way of telling me it's time to go with a gentle guiding hand. I don't protest, and together we walk back to the Mercedes.

57

Nothing compares to a Maine summer day. We're not quite there yet as the calendar goes, but you wouldn't know it from the thermometer. The sun feels so good, so warm, as Alison and I walk along the dirt driveway leading up to Uncle Danny's vacant parcel. We worked out this morning and she had the awesome idea to walk the property afterward, planning for our new home construction. It's time for us to leave the apartment complex. Too much negative history there.

We left the G-Wagon behind and drove in Uncle Danny's Jeep. I wanted to ride in it with the roof panels off and soak up a little sun, but now I feel nostalgic reuniting it with his property. Sounds silly, I know.

"So many memories come rushing back to me when I'm here." I reflect.

Alison smiles at me. "I bet. I can picture a teenage Jon, pimples dotting his face, doing his thing when his Uncle's away."

"I may have done a few things back then, but I never abused it. I was too scared of him." I chuckle. "Honestly, I was thinking about more recent memories, like you and our first night together." I stop to give her a warm embrace. "Our first *real* night together … one without vomit."

"Hey!" She lightly cuffs the back of my head before breaking away, feigning anger. "You're lucky I even came back to your apartment that night."

"Don't I know it!"

Alison abruptly reaches into her back pocket and pulls out her new cellphone. "Oh, here we go. Darcy's texting me. She wants to know where we are. She wants to meet."

"Can we go to Bulldog? Maybe have her meet us there?" I suggest.

"Ya. That sounds good. I think we're going to need some drinks for this one."

"I think you're right."

§

"You're not going to believe this. Look at this." Darcy throws a handwritten letter onto the table and plops down angrily in the booth.

She looks raggedy, like the day I first met her. She sports a loose t-shirt that does nothing to enhance her figure, ratty gym shorts exposing her scraggly legs, and a well-worn Red Sox baseball hat. It might be the outfit she had on the day I met her. Alison and I brace for the uncomfortable exchange we're about to have, and the one we've been sidestepping since we've been back from Rhode Island.

"Can you believe this?" She scowls. "Who even writes letters anymore?"

I gingerly pick up the letter and Alison and I read it together:

Dear Darcy,

I don't know what to say, really, so I'll just say it. I'm leaving Maine. I'm sorry to hurt you. I truly am. You were the best thing that's ever happened to me. I can't deal with the mess at the firm – that's way too complicated for me, and honestly, I never liked auditing, either. I moved all my stuff and I'm headed down south to stay with my brother. I was going to do that anyway before Jon asked me to work with him and before I met you. Please don't think bad of me. I will always love you.

Kelly

I set the letter on the table. "I don't know what to say."

Alison reaches out for her hands to offer comfort and support, but Darcy wants none of it. She's madder than a wet hen. "I'm surprised he didn't DM me, too. Did you know he left?! He bailed! I hate men!"

"We knew he wanted out of accounting. He said he was sick of what we got wrapped up in and he was done with the work, but we didn't know he planned to move." Alison explains.

"I've so had it with men and relationships." Darcy blubbers, her voice cracking as she begins to cry. "I'm so done. I knew this would end badly. It always does. I've tried to text him and call to talk, but he doesn't respond or answer his phone. It's like he vanished."

Alison gets up and sits alongside Darcy, offering a hug to which she accepts. Alison tries her best to put a positive spin on a terrible situation. "I'm so sorry, honey. He must be battling his own demons."

The ringtone on my newly-purchased cellphone goes off. I look at the screen and see it's Enzo. I've only connected with him once since we've been back. Although he's nearby at his beach house in Camp Ellis, we thought it best to take a break from one another for a while. We both needed it.

"LoZo. What's going on, my man?"

"Hey, Jon. Not much. Just hanging down at the docks. Making some new friends. I really connect with the old salts and the commercial fishermen here."

"I bet. They're tough guys, just like you. Everything okay?"

"Yeah, it's all good. Listen, what are you guys doing this afternoon?"

"Hang on. I'll check."

I put the phone on mute and turn to Alison. "He wants to know what we're doing this afternoon." I whisper, though I'm not sure why. I have him on mute.

"Oh, jeez. What now?"

"I don't know. He didn't say. Want me to make something up?"

"No. That's okay. Find out what he wants."

I take the phone off mute. "We have nothing going on. What's up?"

"Today is my and Sabrina's wedding anniversary." He pauses. "I thought it might be a good day to spread her ashes off the breakwater down here. I wanted to see if you two could be here."

His invitation is so kindhearted, so genuine, I need to catch my breath before I can respond. Even then, I'm choked up. "We wouldn't miss it. We'll be down soon."

Alison sees the dramatic change in my demeanor. She fully understands why after I explain to her how the conversation progressed.

"Darcy, would you like to come with us?" Alison offers.

"No. Thanks." She rises from her seat. "You two go. I want to be alone, anyway. Jon, I'm sorry about your mother."

§

Enzo meets us outside at the end of his driveway. He's carrying the same satchel he had when he met us at A's some time ago. No doubt, it holds an ornate, monogrammed oak box containing Mom's ashes.

"Hey guys, thanks for coming down. Ready to walk over?" He asks cheerfully while patting the satchel.

"Sure thing." I reply. "Thanks for calling us."

Alison gives him a warm hug. "Happy anniversary, Enzo. We miss her so much."

"Yeah. Me, too." He says softly.

We meander through his neighborhood on roads coated with a fine layer of beach sand on our way to the jetty. People riding bikes and scooters zigzag about unobtrusively, adding to the anticipation of an upcoming summer of fun.

"We saw Darcy earlier today." Alison says to Enzo.

He stops and turns to her. "And?"

"I guess it went as well as could be expected. Thanks again for the idea, and also for writing the letter."

He nods and begins walking again. "You're welcome. I bet that wasn't easy. I'm sorry you had to go through it."

"I felt terrible for her." I add.

"Time will help to heal." Enzo counsels. "Or so I hear. At least I hope so. And speaking of healing, Bung's out of the hospital and in a rehab facility. I've spoken to him and he sounds good. Very upbeat. Abigail says he has a challenging road ahead of him, but with hard work, he ought to be back on his feet again."

That lifts my spirits. "Great news. Really great news. Bung's a special guy."

"Yes, he is." Enzo agrees. "Just like you."

We reach the sweeping shoreline on this spectacularly beautiful mid-afternoon. Sunlight reflects off the water, creating countless shimmers in the backdrop of the man-made stone breakwater. We begin walking along the flat-topped rock until we reach a point where we can spread her ashes without difficulty. Enzo removes the oak box from the satchel and places the empty leather bag at his feet. He runs his fingers over the box as though absorbing and embracing every ounce of Mom's vibrant spirit. Eventually, he opens it, revealing a sealed plastic bag filled with ashes. Mom's ashes.

"Take turns?" Enzo chokes out the question as he reaches for a handful of ash and releases it into the water.

My turn next. It's not until I spread the ash, I realize I have tears streaming down my face.

"Rest easy, Sabrina." Alison says softly as she scoops a handful and lets it sift through her fingers and into the water.

We follow this approach until the bag's empty and needs to be flipped over to shake loose the last tiny remnants trapped in its creases. When it's all gone, Enzo places the bag back into the oak box and slips the box into his satchel. No one says a word. We're content simply to be in each other's company.

We stare out over the water for a long time, feeling Mom's presence, before finally, I put my arm around Enzo, conveying to him with a gentle guiding hand it's time to go.

ACKNOWLEDGEMENTS

I wrote the lion's share of this book throughout the devastating global Coronavirus pandemic. Everyone was affected to some measure – life changed as we knew it. Face masks became commonplace, and remote work and schooling morphed into the 'new normal' as the world distanced from one another.

Yet within tragedies, heroes arise. Frontline clinical caregivers, essential workers, and scientists working on a vaccine mobilized with striking and focused effort. For that I am enormously thankful, chiefly because this pesky bug found its way into my personal realm. I suffered through the COVID-19 illness at the end of 2020, as did members of my family. I don't recommend the experience.

As with most things in life, one cannot do everything singlehandedly. We need help along the way, ranging from substantial physical or emotional support, to maybe simply an occasional check in. My children motivate me incredibly, and without them, this book doesn't happen. Ian and Sydney are young adults now, making their own way, but I will forever be grateful for their inspiration. You'll always be my *IanSydious*.

I'd like to express gratitude for those who helped me with technical banking specifics, provided unprejudiced reactions to storylines, joined in the proofing and editing process, or simply allowed me to bounce ideas off of them.

My son, Ian, provided me with excellent commentary, exposing me as a never-before-captured-but-often-claimed-to-have-been-seen-over-the-years-excessive Hyphenator. The book may be a page or two lighter after removing a great many of them.

A sincere thank you to insurance executive Nicole Stevens, not only for providing advice on the technical aspects of banking risk management, but also for her impressions as an independent reader.

Big appreciation to my edit and proofing partner extraordinaire, Aaron Baltes, Esq. I appreciate the camaraderie of enjoying a few Kölschs from various watering holes while hashing out the particulars of single and double quote usage under British and American English.

I've known Pete O'Rourke since I was five years old. He's living proof a brother isn't always by blood. Thanks for sharing your knowledge and experience with the underground cable and telephone wiring passageways. Your secrets are safe with me.

Thanks to Lisa Openshaw, CPA, an audit partner in public practice concentrating on financial institutions for sharing her experience in bank auditing. Also, to my banking colleagues, much gratitude Julie Brooks and Maria Poulin for allowing me a look under the hood into your daily work lives.

To my fitness brethren, a big thank you for the entertaining (and accurate) book material and motivation on the gym floor. I have nothing but respect for my fellow muscleheads.

And as always, thanks to you dear Reader. I genuinely hope you enjoyed *The Dispensary*. After all, what good's a dispensary without someone to dispense to?

JERE G. MICHELSON

A CPA by training, Jere spent his early years in public accounting, specializing in corporate taxation. He shifted to the non-profit sector years ago, first as Chief Financial Officer of a prominent Maine private foundation, then adding the title of President to his résumé. He is past-Chairman of Maine Medical Center and serves on its parent health system board. He also serves on a bank board as well as multiple for-profit entity boards. Jere is very grateful for his appointment by Sen. Susan Collins of Maine to serve on the first district's United States Military Academy Nomination Committee.

www.ingramcontent.com/pod-product-compliance
Lightning Source LLC
Chambersburg PA
CBHW021723110726
47902CB00005B/1318